EXECUTIVE
Samurai

BY JOHN DUR

1/25/14

Produced by:

FriesenPress
Suite 300 – 852 Fort Street
Victoria, BC, Canada V8W 1H8

www.friesenpress.com

Distributed to the trade by The Ingram Book Company

Table of Contents

Acknowledgements

I could not have completed this without the help, support and encouragement of many. When I started this project back in 2007 I had the good fortune of discovering a web-site, 'The Next Big Writer'. Through this site for aspiring authors I received invaluable help from many members. Everything from basic grammar to clarity of key character profiles, to adjustments in sub-plots to numerous other aspects writing.

The number of contributors from members of 'The Next Big Writer' is too many to list individually. However, there were two that were persistent reviewers that ultimately made the completion of this work possible. The first is 'Archie Hooton', alias 'Sonny' who has coached me in every aspect of writing this since I posted my first chapter. 'Sonny's' ability to balance encouragement with constructive criticism was unique and exemplary. James Hawkins of Hawaii was a loyal, consistent supporter who was always available for questions concerning his comments.

Three friends of mine were of enormous encouragement to me. First, Tom Evangelista, a close friend and colleague of mine from Stanhome Inc., who has supported me through many drafts of this novel, David Clarke, an attorney and friend of forty five years and Will Shane, a recent friend and a colleague from Diramed LLC.

My eldest daughter, Jessica Dur Taylor, a writer herself, completed the final edit. Thanks pumpkin!

And finally I would like to recognize my team at FriesenPress publishing, especially my account manager, Kathie Allen.

Introduction

This work is a novel. All of the characters are fictional and a product of the author's imagination. Any resemblance between any of the characters and persons who actually worked for similar companies in the positions described herein is purely coincidental. The companies included in this novel do not exist.

This novel is primarily set in the U.S. and Japan during the mid – 1970s. It is written for Western audiences and therefore some of the subtle, unique Japanese nuances are left out.

The mid-1970s in Japan were an economically dynamic time. The reconstruction following WWII was complete and the Japanese economy was rapidly growing, despite the pause caused by the 1973 oil shock. The Japanese economy would go on to become the second largest in the world by the late 1980s.

In 1970, Japan had slightly less than half the population of the U.S. The country is roughly the size of the state of California, however only 15% of the land is arable, and less than 10% of that is devoted to urban population. The country is dependent upon imports for most of its natural resources.

The Japanese language is very polite and largely indirect. This is both a by-product of the homogeneity of the people and also the extremely crowded conditions in which the majority of the population live. (Imagine putting nearly half the population of the U.S. in southern Louisiana). "Pushers" are literally employed to cram people into subways and trains during the morning and evening commuting hours.

After the war and during reconstruction, Japan erected numerous barriers to prevent penetration of its domestic markets by foreign companies. The U.S. government was aware of this, and indeed supported it, to help Japan regain its economic stability. Also, U.S. diplomatic missions were instructed to help Japanese companies gain access to export markets. Japan was, and arguably still is, a major strategic military priority for the U.S. following WWII. Japanese trading companies were the center of the "Zaibatsu": the enormous, highly diversified, industrial giants that controlled the Japanese pre-war economy. They established offices in all major countries of the world. One of the primary objectives was to study foreign markets for export opportunities for their customers, the large Japanese industrial companies, and to participate in international companies' entrance into, and development of, the Japanese market.

After the war, Douglas MacArthur carefully directed a new Constitution, which excluded a military and supposedly broke up the Japanese Zaibatsu. During that time, Japan was in full reconstruction with dedicated United States support—political, economic, and military. Capital investment was exploding and exports were a primary focus. The trading companies, which were the control units of the former Zaibatsu, were front and center in the reconstruction effort. The Westernization of Japan, which had begun with the late Emperor Meiji, was in full swing.

By 1958, Japan had largely rebuilt its infrastructure and had begun to focus on its international image. Key in this regard was winning the host country status for the 1964 Olympics and the related infrastructure development. Additionally, the United States diplomatic missions had been charged with helping Japanese industry acquire foreign technology and investment and aiding the country in securing exports for its products.

Because it enjoyed one of the best-educated labor forces, with literacy rates in the 98th percentile, it was becoming one of the most productive countries in the world. But most important to its economic success was something that could not be understood by the West, and therefore not duplicated: the power of consensus and group effort. In Japan, one's identity was defined by one's group affiliation. Of great importance was one's affiliation to one's employer. It was through this affiliation that social status was determined. It was even more important than one's affiliation to one's family. Because the group was more important than the individual, the performance of the individual was maximized naturally by group pressure to perform. In fact, in the West one worked to live, while in Japan, one lived to work. (Although this has evolved in recent years, as the country has become more affluent and westernized).

The homogeneity of the culture provided a unique opportunity for the Japanese government, labor and business, to cooperate for the good of Japan. Most of the key government bureaucrats and the captains of industry all graduated from one of the top five universities in the country and were peers and often classmates. Through this cooperation, "Japan Inc." was gradually created.

It is important for the reader to keep in mind that the time frame is the mid-1970s. There were no fax machines or cell phones. The telex, a combination of a sort of slow electric typewriter and a telegraph, was used for written international communication. There were no laptops or PCs of any kind. Most large companies had mainframe computers and specialists were required to operate them. The 747SP had just come out in 1976, which allowed the first non-stop service between New York and Tokyo in just over 14.5 hours.

In the mid – 1970s, strategic planning was taking corporate America by storm. Almost all Fortune 500 companies brought in strategic planning experts. Consulting companies like the Boston Consulting Group, McKinsey, and Arthur D. Little were becoming very popular sources for hiring strategic planning experts by corporate America.

Glossary

Many Japanese females are given names that end in *ko:* Yuko, Sachiko, Tomiko, Kyoko, Hiroko. In this work, any Japanese first name that ends in *ko* is female.

Respect is an essential part of Japanese society. The term *San* is the equivalent of the English Mr., Mrs., or Miss. It is used for both males and females. The term *kun* is used among children, or when a superior is talking to a subordinate. It clearly demonstrates a difference in level within an organization. A subordinate would never consider using *kun* with a superior.

One always refers to oneself by one's last name and never applies *San*, unless the relationship is intimate, in which case referring to oneself by one's first name is acceptable. Titles in Japanese business are critical, and are always used by subordinates when addressing or referring to superiors. Not following this custom is considered unacceptable. Even between different companies, titles will be used as a sign of respect.

- Chairman of the Board = *Kaicho,* normally not the CEO

- President = *Shacho,* normally CEO

- Vice President = *Fuku Shacho,* a relatively underused title to show superiority to the Managing Director but inferiority to the President

- Senior Managing Director = *Senmu,* very powerful and often the COO

- Junior Managing Director = *Jomu,* below a *Senmu* but above a *Hon-Bucho*
- Senior Division Manager = *Hon-Bucho,* generally responsible for more than one department
- Division Manager = *Bucho,* responsible for more than one department
- Section Chief = *Kacho,* responsible for one section within a department
- *Sakura* = cherry blossom
- *Desu* = The verb *is*
- *Gomenasai* = I'm sorry
- *Ohayogozaimasu* = Good morning
- *Wakarimashita* = Understood?
- *Hai* = Yes
- *Hanko* = A stamp used in lieu of a signature, for official documents
- *Moshi moshi* = Hello on the telephone
- *Nemawashi* = A process used in Japanese companies to obtain consensus. Ideas are proposed to employees who are invited to comment on them. The objective is to create a consensus of support within the organization to maximize execution. The process begins with a "tadakidai" which refers to a wooden platform used to beat rice cakes into sweets.
- *Kumicho* = head of Yakuza

Japanese organized crime is referred to as *Yakuza.* It is organized on a regional basis and has a well-deserved reputation for violence.

The Characters

Main Japanese characters:

Kenji Kato – The Managing Director *Senmu* of TFC Japan
Ozawa San-Hon-Bucho – The Senior Division Manager *Hon Bucho* of Mitsugawa Trading
Inoue San-Senmu – The Senior Managing Director *Senmu* of Sawamura Trading
Fumiko or Fumichan – The accounting clerk at TFC Japan who seduces Bill Sanford
Saji San – Head of the Osaka Yakuza and part of the espionage chain

Minor Japanese characters:

Joji Sakurai – President *Shacho* of TFC Japan
Nakamura kun – Kenji's secretary
Koji San – Kenji's Operations Director at TFC Japan
Ishikawa San – TFC Japan's CFO

Major U.S. characters:

Bill Sanford – The main character of the novel

Sharon Moran – Bill Sanford's lover and the Manager of EDP, TFC Int'l

Ray Easton – The Chairman of TFC Japan and Regional VP Japan, TFC Int'l

Dave Liberwitz – VP Strategic Planning

Mr. Willis – CEO, TFC Corporation

Ashley – VP Strategic Planning, Aunt Sally Mae's Southern Fried Chicken U.S.

Gene Friedman – CFO, TFC Corporation

J.J. – President and CEO, Aunt Sally Mae's Southern Fried Chicken U.S.

Minor U.S. characters:

Ralph Ovunc – CFO, TFC Int'l

Susan Sanford – Bill Sanford's wife

Adam Rosenberg – President, TFC Domestic

Jim Meyer – President, TFC Int'l

Junior – General Consul, Aunt Salley Mae's Southern Fried Chicken U.S.

Sam Liberwitz – Bill Sanford's attorney and Dave Liberwitz's first cousin

Carmen – Dave and Bill's secretary

Bing – The travel agent for TFC Int'l

Prologue

Tokyo, Japan June 1975

Knocking lightly on his boss's bedroom door, sweating slightly, the thug said:

"Master Saji Kumicho, please forgive me but this is the third time this morning that Takahashi Senmu of Nishimura Fishing Company has called. He says it is absolutely essential that he speak to you this morning concerning an opportunity that is worth thirty million, but requires immediate attention."

The thug was a new member of the Osaka Yakuza and had only met its leader Saji Kumicho once, but he had heard numerous stories about other new inductees who had very short careers after upsetting Saji Kumicho. There were many theories about what had happened to them, but the only thing that was certain was that they had disappeared, never to be seen again. The thug took a deep breath waiting for Saji Kumicho's answer as beads of sweat appeared on his forehead

"All right, come in," Saji said in a sleepy, annoyed voice. "You're sure this Takahashi said the opportunity was worth thirty million yen to him?" Saji added, as he sat up in bed, pushing the naked blond lying next to him off his chest. Thirty million was quite a lot, five million higher than his most expensive offering, a revenge-based execution, with torture, and guaranteed disappearance.

"Tell him to call back in twenty minutes," Saji said waving his hand for the thug to leave. Turning to the blond he added, "Be available for the rest of the week, and bathe next time before getting into bed!"

They are young and beautiful, these foreign
wannabe models, but they do smell.

★★★

The clerk in the Human Resources department of the Nishimura Fishing Company, hurried toward Ginza subway station, concerned about being late for his second off-site meeting with his boss. As the subway doors closed, he looked at his watch. He was breathing hard and dripping with sweat.

Damn it, he thought, *now it will be at least four minutes until the next train comes.* He was terrified of angering his boss. He recalled their first off-site meeting and cringed at the memory. *Ah, but tonight will be very different. The five million yen bonus-- hell, I'll be set for at least twelve months. I might even resign after tonight.* The thought of the promised bonus relaxed him and replaced his memories of the first disastrous meeting.

Earlier that day, his boss had received a call confirming a nation-wide recall of the company's biggest competitor's canned tuna. The evening news reported that an obscure bacterium had contaminated the company's canned tuna. Laughing out loud at the news report, Takahashi had thought, *Ah, what a splendid day this has been! And tonight will be even better.*

The companies had been archrivals for eight generations. In the present generation, the hatred had escalated, after the President of Yamaguchi married Takahashi's daughter without consent. The couple's thirty-four-year age difference only compounded the resentment.

The clerk had been discovered as a mole for Takahashi's major competitor eight weeks earlier. For the past two months, he had continued to supply the hated competitor with his company's formulas. He had been terrified when he was caught copying the formulas, but to his complete surprise, Takahashi had simply given him an address and told him to meet him there that night after work. When he'd arrived, his boss was already there, accompanied

xii — Executive Samurai

by two thugs and a short, middle-aged man, who he later discovered was the head of the Osaka Yakuza .

He cringed as he recalled the details of that first meeting and his panicked thoughts upon seeing the thugs. Both were missing the little finger of their right hand.

Oh shit, he'd thought, *these guys must be Yakuza! At a minimum, they'll cut off a finger and, at worse, kill me!* With tears streaming down his face and urine streaming down his leg, he had confessed all.

"Calm down and tell me exactly what happened, and leave out no detail," Takahashi had whispered.

"At the end of the New Year's holiday, a friend of my mother's asked me to have lunch with the President of Yamaguchi."

The two thugs had stood looking at the clerk's growing urination stain with broad smiles on their faces.

"Go on, you son of a whore! We don't have all night to watch you cry and piss yourself," Saji Kumicho had yelled, as he removed a short Samurai sword from its scabbard, the ten-inch blade glistening. Saji was well built with broad shoulders and unusually large arms. His crew cut and thick neck made him look like a military prison guard.

The clerk remembered falling to his knees and bowing his head to the ground, the ultimate sign of respect.

Thankfully, Takahashi had intervened, putting his hand on the Yakuza leader's broad shoulder and saying, "Saji Kumicho, let him continue before we decide what to do with him."

With his head still on the ground the clerk had said, "Senmu, thank you so much!" Lifting his head but staying on his knees, he continued, "I had lunch with Yamaguchi's President on the fourth of January at a small Tonkatsu restaurant in Azabu Juban." Looking down he continued in a small voice. "He offered me one million yen for every recipe I could provide. I have given him eighteen so far." Reaching into his coat pocket he withdrew a piece of paper without looking at his boss. "This is a list of them all. I swear. If you spare me, I'll do anything you ask!"

"Watch him, and keep him thinking carefully about his reward," Saji told the two thugs as he walked off with Takahashi, laughing.

Returning five minutes later, Saji had said, "Okay, against my advice you're going to be given a chance to make amends for your disloyalty." To lend emphasis, Saji ran his thumb down the edge of his sword and watched it bleed. Licking the blood, he continued, but this time with a smile. "You'll continue to provide information to Yamaguchi's President only now it will be supplied to you by Takahashi Senmu. Do you understand?"

"Yes, yes of course!" The clerk said, bowing repeatedly. He remained on his knees, with his head down, until Takahashi and the Yakuza group left.

To his surprise, the next morning, Takahashi told him he could keep his job and continue to collect his fees from Yamaguchi Fishing. Takahashi had then handed him an envelope and said, "Make sure he gets this today. You will notice that I've included a two-million-yen bonus. Make damn sure you remain loyal." Takahashi dismissed him with a wave of his hand.

Since being caught, things were going great for the clerk, at least financially. His income had doubled, as he was still collecting his salary, the bribes from Yamaguchi Fishing for the stolen information, and nice bonuses from Takahashi Senmu after each successful delivery of a now doctored formula.

★★★

The president of Yamaguchi Fishing was sitting in his office reviewing the sales performance for the last quarter. He was very pleased with the forty percent increase in sales he had achieved since he acquired his mole.

"President, there is a call from the Ministry of Health, are you available?" his secretary said, interrupting his train of thought.

"Did he say what he wanted?

"No, should I ask?"

"No, just put the call through."

"Shacho, I hope you will forgive this intrusion, but I am Harada Bucho of the Ministry of Health. I'm calling to inform you that your company's canned tuna has been found to have unacceptably high bacteria levels, and the Ministry is implementing a nation-wide recall, effective immediately."

Nearly dropping the phone, he yelled, "This is impossible! You can't do this! It'll ruin my company."

Takahashi had seen to it that the false information he was feeding through his clerk included a bit too much, in fact, four times the normal quantity, of a protein that was required to maintain flavor. This protein had stimulated excessive bacteria growth after the tuna was canned.

Later that afternoon, after confirmation of the recall, Takahashi called Saji Kumicho.

"Saji San, the meeting has been set for eleven this evening. I assume your people will be there?" he asked excitedly. *Ha, Takahashi thought, as he rubbed his hands together, I finally got that bastard! His company will never recover from this recall. And by midnight tonight the only link back to me will be gone.*

"Of course," Saji said in a business manner, "and I know your tribute will be transferred to my bank account tomorrow." He hung up without further discussion.

At exactly 10:55 p.m., the clerk loosened his tie and wiped his face with his already damp handkerchief. *Thank God I got here first.*

The street dead-ended into the back of a new building project. He wondered why such an unusual meeting place had been chosen. There was plenty of heavy construction equipment but no people, which was unusual for Tokyo. All he could think of was the five-million-yen bonus Takahashi had promised. *Hell, with this I'll have twenty million saved that Mother doesn't even know about. I think I'll go to Taipei next month on one of those sex weekends my brother-in-law is always bragging about. Ah, life can be good!*

He noticed a car parked under a burned-out streetlight, an unremarkable Toyoda Sedan. *Hmm, that's not Takahashi's Mercedes.* He heard a car door close behind him. A short, stocky man, holding what looked like a baseball bat, exited another nondescript Toyoda Sedan. He hadn't noticed the cars before, as they were concealed in the shadows. He recognized the two brutal-looking thugs approaching quickly from the first car. Saji San wasn't with them.

"Good evening, gentlemen," He said, as he bowed respectfully. "Where are Takahashi Senmu and Saji Kumicho? Am I early?"

He had forgotten about the short, stocky man approaching from the rear, and as he turned, the baseball bat, which had a steel head, smashed into his skull, splitting it like a watermelon and killing him instantly.

"Take the body to the disposal site at Kofu," the man with the bat said, as he wiped blood and brain matter from his shirt, "and don't speed or drink anything until you dump him. Our police contact at central traffic says there are three speed traps on the Chuo Expressway before you reach the Kofu exit."

★★★

The club had a twenty-foot brass railed mahogany bar and five tables surrounded by sofas. There were only two customers at the bar, and both appeared to be drunk junior managers complaining about their boss. Only one of the five tables was occupied. An elderly gray haired man, surrounded by three young hostesses (two Japanese and one foreigner), was enjoying a bottle of XO cognac while the hostesses laughed and fawned over him, hoping for a big tip. When the short, stocky man arrived at the bar, one of the Japanese hostesses got up to greet him and offer him a table with her company. Shaking his head, he grunted *No* and ordered a Dantori Reserve (the local premium whisky) with water and went to the public phone to call his boss, Saji San.

"Hello, Kumicho please forgive this intrusion. Our assignment has been successfully completed."

Pushing the foreign model out of bed, Saji sat up and said, "Good job, Yoji kun, where did you tell the boys to plant the tree?" After the short, stocky man told him, Saji continued, "Good choice, you've earned a bonus," Saji said hanging up. "Now go take a shower and come back to bed," he yelled at the blond.

That Yoji is one reliable soldier. But he probably has only a couple years left at best. To think he started for my father as my body guard. Hell saved my life more than once. Saji thought back to day after a high school volley ball final on a Saturday afternoon. In the excitement of the victory Saji had become separated from Yoji. This presented an opportunity that rival, minor Yakuza groups looked for to kidnap and then extort the major Yakuza players for concessions and financial favors. Two thugs grabbed Saji from behind and pulled him to the ground, covering his face in an either soaked towel making him unconscious. Once outside, a car with three other thugs was waiting. As they attempted to load him into the car Yoji appeared out of nowhere and charged the group of four thugs. He was shot three times but continued until he freed Saji and killed the other thugs. When Saji woke up he was in the hospital in the same room as Yoji who said feebly, bowing from his bed,

"Forgive me master, I should never have let you out of my sight."

When the line went dead, and the short, stocky man hurried back to his seat, where he found his drink, but not the hostess. After he gulped it down, he lifted his empty glass and barked at the bartender, "Another Dantori Reserve with water, and be quick about it."

This damn heat! I'm getting too old for this, he thought, *especially in the summer. Besides, I can't stand these uppity Tokyo people acting like they're special and pretending they don't understand my Osaka slang.* He wiped his forehead with his handkerchief, appreciating the air conditioning.

Chapter 1

"That fucking Ray Easton! The cheating son-of-a-bitch!" Gene Friedman yelled, slamming his fist on the table. His imposing six-foot-five frame and bushy gray eyebrows made him look like a former professional football player, not the Chief Financial Officer of a Fortune 500 company.

Gene ran his hand through his hair and added, "Well that settles it, Bill, I want you in Tokyo next week to do a complete audit of the new store-build program. Who the fuck does Easton think he is? Opening twelve new stores without one completed, never mind approved, request for Capital," Gene said, pacing. "I'll bet you that asshole is on our Joint Venture Partner's payroll somehow. I'm sick and tired of hearing, 'But this is Japan and Mitsugawa Trading approved it.' No." He shook his head and pointed his finger. "He's not going to get away with this bullshit any longer. I've had it!"

Red faced, Gene picked up his briefcase and stormed out of Ralph's office.

Ralph Ovunc, Vice President of Finance for Tennessee Fried Chicken International, was the physical antithesis of Gene. At five-foot-three and one hundred ninety-five pounds, and sporting a double chin, Ralph looked like Humpty Dumpty. Born in Turkey of affluent Jewish parents and educated in France, Germany, and Brazil, Ralph was fluent in five languages, although when he got excited his English took on a distinctly German accent. Technically, Ralph's boss was Jim Meyer, President of Tennessee Fried Chicken

International, although Gene Friedman as Chief Financial Officer of corporate was also a boss.

"What was that all about?" Bill asked, shaking his head and causing his long blond hair to fall over his bright blue eyes. At six one and one hundred seventy-five pounds, with a distinctive baby face, he looked like a college student. "Hell, I just got back from Germany last week and Susan's counting on me to take Sarah so she can take a long weekend in Maine with 'friends.'"

"Come on, Bill, you heard Gene," Ralph said, scratching his balding head and leaning forward. "He's absolutely determined to get Easton."

"Ralph, this can't be just about TFC Japan building a few stores without approval," Bill said, shifting in his seat and tossing his head. "I've never seen him so agitated. Come on, what's really going on?"

Ralph got up and closed the office door. "Listen! What I'm going to tell you doesn't leave this room—understood?" Ralph whispered, shaking his finger.

Bill nodded, and Ralph sat down again. "The Domestic Group is way off budget. They say it's only a temporary problem but Gene isn't buying it."

"That's it?" Bill asked, raising his eyebrows.

"Well, not all of it." Ralph took a deep breath. "You may have heard the rumors that Willis is hiring a Corporate Vice President for Strategic Planning."

Bill nodded.

"Well, what you don't know is that the guy starts next Monday and reports directly to Willis, not to Gene. His name is Dave Liberwitz and Gene is fit to be tied."

★★★

Shit, I know she's going to think I'm trying to keep her from taking a weekend with that fucker from Texas that "Daddy Bucks" introduced her to. What a joke this trial separation is! Bill thought as he dialed Susan's number.

"Hi Susan, listen I'm—"

"God damn it, Bill! Where in the hell are you? It's seven thirty and you were supposed to pick Sarah up a half hour ago!"

"Susan, what the fuck is the matter with you? Gene Friedman was over here this afternoon raising hell about TFC Japan. In fact, he insisted that I go to Tokyo next week and do an audit. Whether you like it or not, he's the boss!"

"You son-of-a-bitch! You know I have plans! Ever since you got that miserable promotion to Manager of Capital *whatever* you're never able to keep your commitments."

Shit! Here we go again, he thought.

"Susan, can't we stop fighting over the same fucking old things? You've known from the get-go that my objective has always been to get an international controller's position. Hell, this job is only a steppingstone. You've obviously forgotten our endless discussions about how cool it would be to live in the various countries I grew up in. Besides, you forget that the forty percent more that I'm making since we moved to Hartford has allowed you to be a stay at home mom," Bill said, running his hand through his hair.

"That's bullshit! We were just kids at UCLA, and I certainly don't feel like that anymore. And, for your information, I didn't love LA either, but at least I had a network of friends, and Mom and Daddy loved to visit us there."

"Jesus, Susan, you were just down in Texas two weeks ago visiting your parents. Besides—"

The line went dead and Bill just looked at the phone.

★★★

As Bill was repacking his suitcase for the fourth time, his eight-year-old-daughter, Sarah, came bounding in. She had her father's blonde hair and her mother's brown eyes.

"Now, Daddy, don't forget to bring me lots of presents, okay? For sure I want a Japanese doll, but everything else is up to you," Sarah said, wagging her finger.

"Oh, really? Thanks for leaving me some leeway," Bill said, laughing, as he chased her around the room. "Hey, it's nine. What are you doing up? Come on, let's get you back in bed before Mrs. Kowalski sees you up and we both get in trouble," Bill said, turning his head side to side. "You have a big day tomorrow; you're going to Six Flags."

Suddenly looking very sad, with her lips quivering, Sarah said, "Daddy, why aren't you coming with us? Mommy says it's because you only care about your job."

Picking Sarah up and looking into her eyes, smiling, Bill said, "Hey, pumpkin, you know better than that. How much does Daddy love you?"

"The whole wide world and much, much more!" Sarah responded, smiling again.

"That a girl, now off to bed," he said as he kissed her, put her into bed, and pulled the covers up to her chin.

★★★

When Bill found his aisle seat in first class, he noticed an attractive blonde was in the window seat. She looked to be in her early twenties, and was dressed in a short, blue skirt and tight, v-neck yellow shirt, both of which accentuated her physical assets.

"Hi, I'm Bill Sanford," Bill said, smiling as he took his seat.

"I'm Lisa Thomas," the beautiful blonde replied, with a show-stopping, dazzling smile. "Is this your first trip to Japan?" she added excitedly.

"The first in fourteen years," Bill said, as his eyes inadvertently focused on Lisa's cleavage. "I lived in Osaka for three years growing up. My father was the U.S. Consul General there."

"Did you learn any Japanese?"

"Actually, I did. Dad put me in a Japanese grade school for three years. What about you?" Bill added, feeling older than his twenty-eight years.

"No, this is my very first trip anywhere out of the country. I'm from Maine and have never been out of New England," Lisa said, with that remarkable smile. "I got a modeling contract from the Raphael Modeling Agency in Tokyo. I can't wait to get there. The agency told me I could expect to make over fifteen-hundred dollars per job, and they already have four lined up: two beer commercials and one cosmetic commercial. It's all so exciting."

"Where will you be staying?" Bill asked.

"I'm not really sure. The agency said that I'd be staying with two or three other models at a sponsor's home. And they'll take care of all my expenses."

"What about translation?" Bill said, cocking his head. "You know, very few Japanese speak English—at least that most foreigners can understand," Bill added, as the stewardess paused at his seat.

"So what can I get you folks to drink?" she said with a smile.

"I'll have a glass of champagne, please," Lisa said, crossing her legs.

"And I'll have a Johnnie Walker Black and Seven," Bill added. The stewardess nodded and continued down the aisle.

"About translation, I think they said we'd have translators with us all the time," Lisa said, furrowing her eyebrows. "Could you teach me a few words to help me get around?"

"Sure. I'm a bit rusty, but I can certainly teach you some of the basics," Bill said. The stewardess returned with their drinks.

The non-stop from JFK to Tokyo's Haneda airport took just over fourteen and a half hours. Bill and Lisa talked and drank for most of the flight. They finally fell asleep three hours before landing. They both arrived exhausted and hung-over.

Since Bill and Susan had separated three months earlier, Bill found himself increasingly taking notice of attractive females. While the separation was supposed to be a trial, Bill was becoming less optimistic that they would reconcile. Despite the weekly sessions with the marriage counselor, Bill just couldn't bring himself to forgive Susan for her affair. He was convinced she was continuing to see her lover.

Chapter 2

Ray Easton looked younger than his forty-three years. His sandy hair was thinning and, at five-foot-five, he was on the short side. To add discomfort to his ego, his right leg was slightly shorter than his left; the difference caused an almost imperceptible limp. His height and limp were things that largely went unnoticed in Japan, and that was one of the reasons he decided to move there--that and the availability of young, attractive women. Ray had an impressive record of seducing foreign models coming to Tokyo. Typically, most of his conquests were young wannabe models sold on the Japanese male appetite for blonde, western women who dominated their liquor and beer commercials.

He had lived a fairly unremarkable life. Born in a small Midwestern town and raised by a divorcee, Ray never knew his father and was utterly spoiled by his mother who felt guilty over his father's departure. He was an outgoing, natural-born salesman with absolutely no scruples. He could and would lie spontaneously if it suited his objectives. He also had an uncanny ability to remember what lies he had told to what people.

Ray had been in the Korean War stationed as a noncommissioned officer on an army supply ship. Before being discharged in 1955, he had made friends with a Staff Sergeant, Joseph Durant, who worked in awards and decorations and was able to supply Ray with a military ID. The credentials provided Ray with access to military bases and commissaries, where he could purchase food, liquor, furniture and other products at less than 30 percent of the local Japanese retail price.

Over the years, Ray maintained contact with now Master Sergeant Joseph Durant, and obtained updated IDs periodically in exchange for stock tips, based on insider information, which always paid off. Sergeant Durant was pleased with the arrangement, given the low pay in the Army and the increasing demands of his two ex-wives and current string of girlfriends.

Ray had been the Chairman of Tennessee Fried Chicken Japan and Regional VP Pacific since the establishment of TFC Japan six years earlier. Following the war, he was one of the first salesmen with IBM, posted to Memphis where he had had the good fortune of running into some up-and-coming rising stars. Most noteworthy was Major Tom, founder and inventor of Tennesee Fried Chicken. Ray ran into Major Tom by chance in a TFC outlet. They struck up a long conversation and over time developed a friendship.

Among others was Jim Meyer, his boss, president of TFC International, a soft spoken and thoughtful man, who had served in the U.S. Navy during the Korean War. Jim had jet-black hair and stood a mere five-foot-seven and weighed in at just under one hundred forty pounds. He had an array of unusual scars on his hands and arms, as though he had fallen into a fire. Also, like so many of his peers, Jim was a bright rising star, but with no international experience; in fact, he got his first passport just two weeks after being appointed to head TFC International. Jim was a by-product of the strategic planning craze that swept U.S. Fortune 500 companies in the mid-seventies, focusing them on international opportunities.

Ray learned very early in life that leveraging others was the best way to achieve one's objectives with as little effort as possible. That made having fun and doing the absolute minimum amount of work Ray's overriding objectives in life.

★★★

Kenji Kato, Managing Director of TFC Japan, arrived at the Ile de France restaurant in Roppongi, a fashionable entertainment district in Tokyo. The restaurant was a small bistro with only six tables, and as one walked down the stairs it was like entering a family restaurant in Lyon. The white stucco walls set off the rich, warm, wood wainscoting and original French country art. There was an open barbeque with a leg of lamb roasting over it. Cured hams hung from the ceiling, and the smells emanating from the kitchen were a combination of garlic and roasting meat.

The owner and chef, Andre, who had studied under world famous chef Paul Bocuse, personally greeted Kenji and led him to the only corner table. Andre had fallen in love with a Japanese woman who was attending the same cooking school in the late 1950s and moved to Tokyo, where his restaurant became an immediate success.

Fumiko was already there, sipping a glass of champagne. She looked almost Eurasian. She had a remarkable figure for a Japanese woman, one that she proudly showed off through her choice of clothes. This evening, she was dressed in a short red skirt and a tight black blouse.

Fumiko worked in the accounting department of TFC Japan. Another of Ray's finds, she was good looking, fluent in English, and often an overnight guest at his house, which was why Ray had hired her in the first place.

"Good evening, Senmu, you're early," Fumiko said, bowing her head slightly as a sign of respect to the Managing Director who she didn't particularly care for. "Unfortunately, Easton Kaicho called twenty minutes ago to say he would be at least an hour late, but to wait for him because he had important details to go over concerning next week's home office audit."

"Did our illustrious Chairman say why he'd be so late?" Kenji asked, looking at his watch and frowning. Kenji was a workaholic, even by Japanese standards. He kept a bed in his office and used it at least three nights a week to avoid the hour-long commute by subway and train.

"No, but he was calling from the military commissary in Yokohama. I'm sure he's stocking up on liquor and food for the "Welcome to Japan Party" for the newly arrived models that's scheduled for Saturday night," she said, finishing her glass of champagne and motioning to the waiter for a refill. Kenji just rolled his eyes at the unacceptable behavior.

Fumiko was from a Samurai family but had proven to be a disappointment from an early age; her grades were only average, and she began drinking alcohol at thirteen. Her striking good looks brought a long line of boyfriends, and as a result, her father had banished her from his house when she was only seventeen.

"Oh, I guess I forgot about that party," Kenji said, motioning toward the waiter.

"Senmu, what can I get you to drink?" the waiter asked.

"Oh," Kenji said, somewhat distracted. "I'll have a Sapporo draft, and bring some assorted appetizers; whatever you think is best."

"Of course, right away, Senmu," the waiter said, bowing as he left.

Ray finally arrived two hours late swearing about how the "fucking traffic was ridiculous." The waiter appeared immediately with a double single-malt on the rocks and fresh appetizers.

"No problem," Kenji said looking at his watch. "So what's so urgent?"

"God damn it, that son-of-a-bitch Gene Friedman is determined to fuck things up for us. I don't know how bad our policy violations on the new store builds are, but the last thing we need right before the executive conference is a fucking audit. This presents a tremendous risk. We have to manage this situation or our great little gig is up!" Ray removed a telegram he had received that morning from Lindsay, Jim's secretary and one of his love interests. He handed it to Kenji, who read the missive aloud.

"Bill Sanford has been with the company for just over two years, and he's considered a young, up-and-coming financial manager by Jim and Human Resources. He is married with one young daughter, but is having marital problems and is currently separated from his wife; rumor has it she had an affair last year. His personal life seems to have deteriorated since his promotion to Manager Capital Expenditures six months ago." Kenji didn't read the last line, "Don't forget my pearl ring—Lindsay."

"Well fuck them. I don't see how anyone could be unhappy with our performance," Kenji said, his voice rising. "After all, every store we've opened in the last eighteen months has exceeded our projections by at least fifteen percent, and some up to forty percent; this while the fucking U.S. market is struggling. Besides, our local board of directors have approved all, well, almost all, of the new stores, and that's all the fucking joint venture agreement calls for!"

"Calm down, Kenji," Ray said, leaning over. "Believe me, those pricks can royally fuck up our sweet little deal here."

Relaxing a bit, Kenji asked, "Okay, how do you suggest we manage the situation?"

"Well, that's why we're having this dinner together, Old Dear," Ray said, smiling. He finished his single malt and raised his empty glass with two fingers extended, signaling the waiter to bring him another double.

"Fumichan, I've a very important assignment for you," Ray said with a smile. Kenji raised his eyebrows. "You have two roles to play. One is as the auditor's translator, since you're the only member of the accounting department who really speaks English. But you also need to put on your hostess hat."

"Hostess hat?" Fumiko asked, furrowing her eyebrows and cocking her head.

"Sorry, what I mean is you've got to try your best to seduce young Sanford," Ray said, leaning over, the smile gone. "As Lindsay's telegram indicates, Bill and his wife are separated. With a little luck, and a lot of your natural talent, Fumichan, we might be successful," Ray added. The smile returned to his face.

"Oh, now I understand," Fumiko said, nodding and smiling. After all, getting men into bed had always been her specialty.

Over dessert and cognac Ray said, "Fumichan, your first chance will be tomorrow night. As you know, I'm hosting a party for twelve new models at my house. I've invited Sanford, so why don't you come as well. Kenji, perhaps you can arrange to have lunch at the American Club buffet on Sunday with Sanford. That'll give you a chance to prime him before the audit begins."

★★★

The party for the newly arrived Raphael Agency models included the usual crowd of Tokyo's beautiful people. The senior expatriate contingent included Ray's cohorts from Cindy Bower's Cosmetics, International Foods, Sam's Cola, Morris Engineering, and Playbachelor Japan. Also present were the Japanese group of *gaijin* followers, whose businesses depended on foreign companies. The international advertising, auditing, and management consulting companies were all represented, and finally, there were the ever-present group of young Japanese women looking for foreign sugar daddies: singles preferred, but rich married men were also acceptable.

The party kicked off around eight, but things didn't really get moving until after eleven, when the models—all blonde, young, and exhausted--finally arrived.. Most were from small town USA with their first passports and dreams of stardom that would largely be replaced by nightmares. Among them was Lisa, whom Bill had sat next to on the plane.

It took the senior expatriates little time to sort through the models and select their targets. The *gaijin* followers largely spent their time networking with the expatriates, rather than pursuing models or young Japanese women who, themselves, were looking for new expatriate faces and the occasional regular visitor from headquarters.

Bill Sanford arrived at Ray's party late. His little nap had turned into six hours of solid sleep due to his jet lag and non-stop drinking and talking with Lisa.

Ray's house was actually two houses within a gated compound; both shared a quarter-acre yard and a well-maintained Japanese garden, complete with a *koi* pond that was fed by a small recycling waterfall. Numerous trees and flowers filled almost every available square foot of the yard. Amazingly, the compound was only a hundred yards from the main drag that ran through Roppongi, one of Tokyo's premier entertainment districts, only two blocks from Azabu Juban and five minutes from the Tokyo American Club. The house was a rarity in a city where the average family of four lived in a three-room, six hundred square-foot apartment in a high-rise complex.

"Hey Bill, you finally made it," Ray said as he opened the door. "I thought maybe you ran into something more interesting at the hotel and were going to stand me up."

"No, I just slept longer than I intended."

"Well, the bar is over there, but first let me introduce you to Fumiko San, who works in the accounting department. I'll see you later. Have fun."

Ray was off as quickly as he had arrived, in hot pursuit of Lisa. Bill recognized Lisa and thought, *My God, she's even more beautiful tonight in that halter top and those hot pants. Does Ray really think he can score with her?*

Fumiko was quite attractive and had a beautiful smile that lit up her whole face.

"So, Bill San, is this your first visit to Japan?" Fumiko asked, knowing better of course, in a tiny voice that was heavily accented.

"No, I lived in Osaka as a child. My father was the U.S. Consul General there."

"*Ja, anata wa nihongo hanashi masuka?*"

"*Sukoshi dake,*" Bill said, holding up his hand with a small space between his thumb and index finger. "I'm afraid I've forgotten most of my Japanese, and besides, your English is very good."

"You are very kind, Bill San," Fumiko said, lowering her eyes and smiling as she took a sip of her scotch and water. "It's so warm in here; shall we go into the garden? I could use a bit of fresh air and a cigarette."

"Sure, if you'd like."

When the Elvis hit "Love Me Tender" came on, Fumiko said enthusiastically, "This is one of my favorite songs, would you like to dance?" Before he could respond, she put her arms around Bill. As the song progressed, she began to run her hand through the hair on the back of his neck and steadily increased pressure on his groin. He responded with an erection and began to press back.

You can't do this, you fool! he silently shouted at himself.

"You know I'm married," Bill whispered.

Fumiko just laughed softly and kissed Bill's ear, gently inserting her hot tongue and whispering, "I just want to have a little fun tonight. Besides, aren't you separated?"

As the dance continued, Fumiko led Bill down a hallway and into a walk-in coat closet.

"Where are we going?"

"*Shush,*" *Fumiko said as she reached down and touched his penis lightly. She then very quickly loosened Bill's belt and had his pants down below his knees before he knew it. As he began to protest, Fumiko dropped to her knees and put Bill's entire penis into her mouth. With strong, long, flowing movements, she sucked Bill increasingly faster, until he could withhold no more. He shuddered as he came.*

"I hope you enjoyed that, Bill San," Fumiko said as she pulled up his pants and fastened his belt. "We should go back to the party and then you should go to bed soon since we have a big day Monday as you begin your audit. I've been assigned to help you, so why don't we meet for breakfast Monday morning at seven o'clock at your hotel. Oh, tomorrow there is a nice Sunday brunch at the American Club. I can pick you up at noon if you like."

Bill couldn't believe what had just happened, or how casual Fumiko seemed about the whole thing. He could only say, "Sure, tomorrow at noon sounds fine."

★★★

"Hello, Ray San," Fumiko said, looking at her watch. It was almost noon. "I hope I didn't wake you, but I'm getting ready to pick up Bill for brunch at the American Club, and I just wanted to let you know that I was successful last night, at least with oral sex. I will try again today and maybe succeed with everything." Fumiko sounded quite pleased with herself.

"Good for you, Fumi-chan, I knew you could do it!" Ray said enthusiastically, waking the young model sleeping next to him. "Keep it going if you can. Obviously the more involved Bill becomes with you the greater the influence we, or should I say you, will have."

"Ray San, please remember your promise to help find me another foreign sugar daddy. I cannot make next month's rent without a new one. Sam Sugarman has told me he is moving home next month and so his support will stop".

Ray thought for a moment and then said, "If you can keep Bill involved, I'll make next month's rent for you and find a replacement for Sam before August."

Fumiko was ecstatic. With July's rent solved and a replacement for Sam likely by August, she could afford to take that trip to Europe she had been dreaming of since last year. Philippe had promised her a place to stay on the Riviera if she just got there.

Well, she thought, *I had better get dressed in that new sexy thing Sam brought me from Paris last month. I want to make sure Bill has no second thoughts or gives in to guilt before I set the hook.*

★★★

"Hi, sweetheart, how's my little princess doing? Did you have fun at Six Flags with Mrs. Kowalski?"

"Yes, Daddy, have you been shopping for my Japanese doll?"

"Not yet, pumpkin, but don't worry. I'll bring you back lots of neat things. In fact, I bought you a *Yukata* today."

"What's a *Yukata*, Daddy?" Sarah asked excitedly.

"You'll see when I get home. Now go get Mrs. Kowalski."

"Okay, Daddy. I love you."

"Mrs. Kowalski, Daddy's on the phone and he says I don't have to eat my spinach," Sarah said, covering the phone's receiver.

"Good evening, Mr. Sanford. How are things in Japan?"

"Everything is fine here, how are things there?"

"Oh no worries, all is well. Although Mrs. Sanford called to say she won't be back until Thursday or Friday. I'm sure I can get my sister to cover my other commitments on Thursday, but Friday may prove difficult."

That bitch, Bill thought and caught himself before saying, *I'll bet Jimmy's talked her into staying longer since I'm not scheduled back until Saturday.*

"Well, Mrs. Kowalski, let me see what I can do about Friday, and I'll call you back by Wednesday."

"Very well, Sir, but don't worry, I'll take Sarah with me if need be."

"I'm sure that won't be necessary, but thanks for the offer. Good night--I mean, good morning."

He hung up. As he was walking to the bathroom, the phone rang.

"Hi, Bill San, I'm in the lobby," Fumiko said in her small voice.

CHAPTER 3

Kenji Kato was enjoying the brunch at the American Club. He was thirty-six, and at five-foot-ten was tall by Japanese standards. His crew cut and the air of decisiveness about him made him appear much like a military officer. The scar on the right side of his face, which turned red every time Kenji lost his temper (something that happened all too frequently), underscored the military look.

Ray had discovered him six years earlier when he was a salesman at a food distribution company and made him the first store manager for TFC Japan. Technically, Kenji worked for the company's President, Joji Sakurai, who was Mitsugawa's appointed representative to the joint venture. Joji, however, spent most of his time reading pornography, so Kenji ran the company as long as his actions favored Mitsugawa. This was easily accomplished, since Ray had absolutely no loyalty to TFC International and didn't care what Mitsugawa did, as long as they accepted him, which, of course, they were only too willing to do.

All parties were very satisfied and all were making good money, at the expense of TFC International.

Bill and Fumiko entered the main dining room of the Tokyo American Club at just after one o'clock in the afternoon, an hour before the brunch buffet ended. Immediately, he was very impressed, as the club occupied over two acres in the center of Tokyo and was, ironically, located right next to the embassy of the Soviet Union. In addition to its six-story main building, there was a four-story recreation building, and an Olympic-sized swimming pool between the two.

Kenji noticed Fumiko and the tall, fit man when they entered the dining room together. *Umm, so that is our major threat,* Kenji thought. *He looks too young to be much of a threat.*

Kenji waved them over. From the look on Fumiko's face, it was clear that she had succeeded in her part of the "winning over" process. He had decided earlier to employ, as his key tactic, asking for help in the upcoming strategic plan process; after all, playing stupid with regards to U.S. accounting principles would be easy.

Rising, Kenji smiled and said, "It's Bill isn't it? I'm Kenji Kato, Managing Director of TFC Japan." He motioned for Bill to sit down across from him before continuing with a wink. "How did you like Ray's party for the models? And did you have a good trip?"

"Yes I did, thank you, and yes, that was some collection Ray had," Bill said, smiling. "Why didn't I see you there?"

"Well, after you've been to a hundred of those parties, they lose their appeal," Kenji said, chuckling, as he motioned for the waiter.

The waiter arrived and Kenji said, "What can I get you to drink?"

"How about a Johnnie Black and Seven?"

"Done. Now tell me a bit about yourself," Kenji said as the waiter left.

"Well, let's see, I lived in Osaka for three years back in the early '60s, when my father was the U.S. Consul, and I attended Japanese grade school for two of those years. That was my father's idea. Too bad I've forgotten most of the Japanese I learned."

"Oh, I'm sure you'll remember more than you realize. Learning a foreign language as a child is much more effective than trying as an adult. Trust me, I know," Kenji said as he finished his beer.

Looking straight at Bill with his scar beginning to turn red, Kenji leaned forward and said, "Look, I'm glad you're here, because we need your help. It's very difficult for us to find accounting staff that understands U.S. financial techniques, but I'm sure Fumiko Chan can explain our more elementary financial analysis, which is all Mitsugawa requires of us."

"Kenji, you can count on me for whatever help I can give you in understanding U.S. financial analysis techniques, and, of course, the new corporate policy for requesting approval to build new stores which, incidentally, I wrote," Bill said with a smile.

Looking at his wristwatch, Kenji added, "Well, you better get over to the buffet table before it closes. Remember, you're in Japan now and everything is punctual.

Bill lay back in his hotel bed. Fumiko was in the shower. *There's no way Susan and I are getting back together. While I'm lying here waiting for Fumiko, she's with that Texas prick that her father introduced us to. This separation has been a joke from the get-go. She never broke it off, even after I caught them in Daddy's pool house.*

The memory of walking into the pool house at 2:00 a.m., jet lagged following a trip from Australia, and catching Susan and the prick in bed making love, was as vivid as though it was yesterday. *Harold P. Prather of Youngsville, Texas, millionaire and wildcat driller. The son-of-a-bitch has more money than God, but is still basically a redneck, still just a good ole boy roustabout. And to think Daddy Bucks actually thinks I'd consider a job at his high school chum's CPA firm. No fucking way! It's over.*

He continued an argument with himself over whether his marriage was salvageable or not. He kept replaying his wife's repeated demands for him to give up his budding international career and accept his father-in-law's offer.

As he dozed off, he felt Fumiko's naked body slide into bed next to him. She adeptly began to trace her tongue from his ear down his chest to his stomach and finally to his penis. Tonight she was much slower and deliberate than in the closet the night before. After what seemed like an eternity, she mounted him and proceeded to give him a sexual experience he had only imagined before. Sometime after midnight she slipped out, leaving a note. "Sleep well. I will see you in the lobby for breakfast at 7:00 a.m. tomorrow."

★★★

"*Moshi moshi*, Saji San, Ray Easton here. Have I got a deal for you," Ray said enthusiastically.

"Ah, my old American friend and Mr. TFC in Japan, Ray Easton," Saji San, head of the Osaka Mafia said in good English, but with a heavy accent. "So, what have you got for me this time, Ray San, and what is it going to cost me?" Saji added, chuckling.

"I've got the most beautiful blonde-haired, blue-eyed girl you've ever seen. If you can set up a few commercial shoots in Osaka, I can guarantee you won't be disappointed."

"Ray San, I have plenty of wannabe models already here in Osaka. Remember that is one of my family's business interests," Saji added, more seriously.

"Saji San, you know my taste in women. When I tell you this one is unbelievable, she really is!"

"Okay, so what is this going to cost me? It's not another DWI citation is it?"

"No it's much more challenging than that. We've got an auditor from TFC headquarters who could cause us some real problems. He's just a kid, twenty-seven I think, but he could really fuck things up for us."

"Umm, I'm going to have to think about this one for a while. Why don't you send the incredible blonde down, so I can have a look at her and then I can calculate what additional compensation will be necessary. This is no easy task, Ray San," Saji said thoughtfully. "Oh, and what is this girl's name?"

"Lisa Thomas, and if anyone is going to owe anything, it's going to be you who will owe me, and—" The line went dead.

I wonder what Saji will come up with this time? Whatever it is, I'm sure it'll be expensive, Ray thought. . Oh well, time to try and get Lisa in bed and give her the good news.

★★★

Although it was only two in the afternoon, Lisa was exhausted and famished. She hadn't gotten to sleep until three a.m. and was up at nine, unable to sleep any more due to the jet lag and the housekeeper, who insisted on vacuuming the upstairs.

As she walked down one of the alleyways off Ray's street, she heard an unusual calling sound. It grew louder as she continued down the alleyway. When she turned the corner, she saw a middle-aged man in a blue and white *yukata*, with a matching blue and white bandana around his head, pulling a cart and wailing, "*Yaki imo, hoka, hoka, o-imo.*" She later found out that he was saying, "Sweet potatoes, hot, hot, potatoes." The smell was delicious and she overcame her hesitancy at asking for one.

"One please, *i-chi ku-da-sai*," she said, raising one finger, hoping she had correctly remembered Bill's introduction to elementary Japanese, which had not included this phrase.

Smiling, the middle-aged man stopped his cart, opened the metal cover and, with his gloved hand, withdrew a piping hot sweet potato. Wrapping it in a piece of newspaper, he handed it to Lisa with a smile, and with a slight bow said *dozo*, or *please,* as Lisa remembered it.

Lisa pulled out a one –thousand yen bill and handed it to the merchant as she took a bite of the sweet potato. As she started to head off, the merchant said, "*chotto matte,*" and followed her, handing her seven hundred and fifty yen in change, including one five hundred yen bill, three one hundred yen bills, and a fifty yen coin. As Lisa tried to give him back the change, he just said *Aringato*, and bowing, went back to his cart and called the same, "*Yaki imo, hokka, hokka, o-imo,*" as he headed down the street.

Lisa finished her sweet potato, the best she had ever had.

She continued down the narrow street, and at every corner, there were mirrors that would show traffic what was coming perpendicularly to its direction. *What a good idea*, she thought, *why don't we use these, especially on narrow streets or country roads?*

As she turned around to head back to Ray's compound, she heard a high-pitched horn. *Now what?* she wondered. At the corner was another merchant with a noodle cart. Lisa's stomach growled noticeably as she approached. "*Ramen wa ikaga desuka?*" she said. It was another new phrase Bill hadn't covered.

The vendor, understanding the confusion on Lisa's face, simply took a bowl and filled it with steaming Chinese noodles. He then added strips of thinly sliced pork and seaweed and handed the bowl to Lisa.

"*Domo,*" she said, as she took the proffered chopsticks and immediately secured a generous helping of noodles and pork, only to have them slip through her chopsticks. Embarrassed, she handed the bowl back to the vendor. "I'm sorry, *Go-menna-sai,*" she said, blushing bright pink.

Still smiling the vendor said, "*Dai jobu,*" and handed her back her bowl and chopsticks. He then served himself and demonstrated the use of chopsticks. Lisa copied him and then ate the entire bowl, asking for a second helping when she finished.

The vendor was very pleased with the outcome. Lisa handed him the change she had received from the sweet potato merchant. Smiling, he took the five hundred yen bill and returned ninety yen in coins. "*Domo, domo,*" Lisa said, returning the empty bowl.

"*Ie, kochirakoso,*" he said, smiling and bowing slightly.

Feeling completely satisfied, Lisa returned to Ray's house and went straight to bed.

Chapter 4

Bill could not believe the state of affairs in the accounting department at TFC Japan. The department head, Mr. Ishikawa, was a fifty-something year-old transfer from Mitsugawa Trading with a background in purchasing and no accounting experience. His English was practically non-existent.

Gene Friedman had been spot on: Mitsugawa Trading and the TFC Japan board had approved thirty-two separate new store openings. However, only three of the requests had been sent to TFC International for approval and none had been approved. Meanwhile, thirty-six stores had been committed to, as evidenced by signed, long-term, rental contracts. Twenty-five of those were through Mitsugawa Realty and in five cases for properties it owned. Bill was overwhelmed by the magnitude of the problem.

At eight o'clock Kenji stuck his head in the visitor's office. "Hey, Bill, how about a break for dinner with Ray and me? We're going to a great little French bistro in Roppongi."

Bill was exhausted and looking forward to the end of the day, but said, "Sure, that sounds fine. Let me pack up my briefcase and I'll be with you in a moment."

After a couple of scotches and small talk about TFC International politics, Ray abruptly asked, "So how bad is it?"

"Too early to tell. How bad do you think it is?" Bill asked, looking first at Ray and then Kenji.

"Well I'm not sure," Kenji said, leaning over the table. "I'll tell you what I do know, though." His scar began to turn red. "Of the thirty plus stores we've opened this year, not one has failed." He downed his beer. "Have you ever compared the performance of Japan's new stores to other international markets, Bill?"

"Yeah, and even more importantly," Ray added, interrupting in a loud voice, "if you compare us to the U.S., you won't believe how good we are and how fucked up they are!" Finishing his single malt he motioned to the waiter to bring him another.

"No, I haven't made those comparisons," Bill said in a matter-of-fact manner. "However, I assure you I will."

"Bill, I'd like to make one other point," Kenji said. "I've reviewed the TFC policy on new store openings and there's a clear bias for purchase over long-term leases. However, in Japan, the only option for land is long-term lease. Outright purchases are unheard of. Remember, we're almost half the population of the U.S. confined to an arable land area the size of southern Connecticut."

He's got a point, Bill thought. I'll check this out with our local auditors. "So guys, the important question is, are you having fun?" Bill asked, as he took another bite of his *Cassoulet,* one of Andre's specialties.

At 10:30, after coffee and a fine old cognac, Ray suggested a trip to the Tokyo Playbachelor Club for a nightcap. Bill declined, citing jet lag and the need for an early start the next morning.

When he returned to his hotel, he found three messages: one from Gene Friedman, who was anxious for an update on his preliminary findings; one from Mrs. Kowalski, saying she had found someone to take over her baby sitting assignment on the weekend; and one from Fumiko, confirming the pick-up the next morning and leaving her telephone number, should he need anything before then. Bill was exhausted and rationalized that he would answer Gene's request first thing in the morning.

★★★

"So you've finally decided to join the living," Ray said as Lisa came down the stairs in a bathrobe with her hair wrapped in a towel. "Hell, I had a big night all planned for us," Ray added as he headed to the kitchen.

"Are you serious? I was so tired by five o'clock I went straight to bed and woke up only forty minutes ago. But thanks for the thought, anyway," she said as she poured herself a cup of coffee.

Opening a beer and sauntering over, Ray said, "Well sweet one, I've got some terrific news for you."

Maneuvering out of his grasp, Lisa sat down at the kitchen table and said, "Really, what might that be?"

"A good friend of mine, Saji San of Osaka, has got three jobs lined up for you, one tomorrow morning and one each on Tuesday and Wednesday."

"Wow! And so soon. What exactly are they and what do they pay?" she asked.

"I'm not sure, but I think one's a cosmetic magazine layout and the other two are liquor TV commercials."

"Really? Television commercials, that's great!" Lisa said, thinking of how this would help her portfolio immensely. "What does this Saji San do, anyway?" she added, raising her eyebrows slightly.

"He's into all sorts of different businesses. One of them happens to be a modeling agency specializing in...err...beautiful blonde-haired blue-eyed foreign bombshells...just like you," Ray said, finishing his beer and heading to the fridge for another. *Boy, is she going to be surprised when Saji sends her to the upscale Hostess Clubs to entertain the business elite.*

"Where will I stay while I'm in Osaka?" Lisa asked.

"Oh, Saji San has an enormous penthouse suite in the center of the entertainment district. He puts up all his foreign models there. You'll love it."

"Does he speak English?" Lisa asked, concerned.

"Yeah. He's almost fluent. Now go get packed. I've got you on the two o'clock bullet train, first-class seat, compliments of Saji San."

"How will I get to his place?"

"Don't worry, one of his people will meet your train carrying a sign with your name on it, hopefully in English," Ray said, laughing at his own joke.

"This is exciting!" Lisa hugged him and gave him a quick kiss. "Thanks so much, Ray!" she called over her shoulder as she turned to head up the stairs.

Ray waited a few minutes and then went into his downstairs office and turned on the hidden cameras that were located in the guest bath and bedroom. He was just in time to catch Lisa putting her panties on. *Yeah, she's a natural blonde. Saji is going to be pleased.*

★★★

Bill spent the rest of the week digging into the files surrounding TFC Japan's new stores. Almost every question he asked proved too difficult for the Chief Financial Officer, Mr. Ishikawa, who invariably assigned Fumiko the responsibility of getting the right answer. The "right answer" was one approved by Kenji after conferring with Mr. Ozawa of Mitsugawa Trading, the man ultimately responsible for Mitsugawa's interest in the joint venture. Ozawa Hon-Bucho was betting his career on TFC Japan's success; after all, he had used up almost all of his favors with fellow Mitsugawa board members to get the joint venture approved.

Bill had dinner with Ozawa San on his fourth night in Tokyo and was taken to a top sushi restaurant in Ginza, Tokyo's most prestigious commercial district. Bill was surprised to see the streets packed with people on a Wednesday night. The line for the Cinema, which was playing The Godfather II, stretched for three city blocks.

Seeing Bill's surprise, Ozawa said, "And that line is for a ten forty-five start time." Bill glanced at his watch; it was 8:15.

The discipline of these people, he thought. *Not a single person is trying to cut or save a spot in line.*

When they arrived at the restaurant, they were greeted with a chorus of "*Irashaimase*" from every employee wherever they happened to be. The owner, an older gentleman with silver hair and a black suit came to greet them. Bowing deeply he said, "Good evening Ozawa Hon-Bucho, you honor us with your presence." And turning to Bill and bowing slightly, he said in reasonable English, "Good evening and welcome." Leading the way through the standing-room-only restaurant, the owner said, "Ozawa Hon-Bucho, your private room is awaiting you. Geishas Yamamoto and Ishizaka are attending. Is that satisfactory?"

"Of course, Kamata Kun, please make sure my young American guest experiences the best. Perhaps have Yuko join the other geishas," he added, remembering what Ray had said earlier that day about Fumiko's limited success in seducing Bill.

As Kamata led them down a long narrow hall with polished maple floors, they passed a number of rooms with sliding bamboo doors. They could hear laughter and samisen music as waitresses dressed in traditional kimonos and wearing white tabbies on their feet hurried by with platters of sushi arranged to look like works of art.

At the end of the hall, they came to a somewhat larger room whose sliding bamboo doors were decorated with white rice paper adorned with mountain scenes that included a small village with women wearing large round black hats working the rice patties tiered up the side of the mountain.

Bill was astounded by the beauty and subtle colors of the mountain village scene. *My God, the detail is incredible,* he thought.

When the owner slid the door open, three geishas were already inside, sitting Japanese style on their calves and feet. All were dressed in ornate Kimonos of red, blue, and green, with their hair done up with colorful ornaments, and their faces covered with stark white powder.

All three bowed deeply and said, *Irashaimase*, then quickly rose to their feet and escorted Ozawa and Bill to a table in the center of the room. The floor was *tatami*, tightly woven rice straw, and the table was only fourteen inches high.

At first Bill was confused and thought, *God, I hope this doesn't mean I'm going to have to sit Japanese style all night, my legs won't take it.*

As though reading his mind, the youngest geisha lifted the apron that surrounded the table to reveal a three-foot deep well, while motioning to Bill. "*Dozo,*" she said smiling. The well and apron were historically used to heat the guest's legs in the winter, as rooms in Japanese homes were only heated with hibachis, large ceramic bowls filled with ash and burning charcoal.

The elder geisha put a bottle of Dantori Royal whiskey on the table with a silver bucket filled with ice that looked as though it had been sculptured, not cut. "So what do you think of my favorite sushi restaurant?" Ozawa asked.

"Well so far it seems like something out of an eighteenth-century Japanese novel," Bill replied, stretching his legs in the well beneath the table.

Ozawa simply sat Japanese style on a silk cushion and watched as the elder geisha asked Bill what he would like to drink.

"Dantori Royal on ice *kudasai*," Bill said, pointing to the squat bottle on the table. Bill didn't think it could be as good as Johnnie Walker Black, but since Ozawa was having it, he thought he would be polite. The elder geisha poured two tumblers of the whiskey over the cut ice. She added water to Ozawa's but just a splash to Bill's, as Bill raised his hand to stop her.

"According to the founder of Dantori, who, by the way, was a schoolmate of mine, a splash of water is required to release the oils that are imparted into the whisky from the barrels during the aging process," Ozawa said, smiling, while holding his glass up to look at the refractions the light made on the cut ice. Bill was amazed at how smooth and delicious the whisky was.

After the first platter of sushi arrived, Bill said, "Ozawa San, can you tell me why Mitsugawa does not consider long-term lease commitments the same as purchases of land in the investment evaluation process? As you may know, U.S. accounting requires this."

"That's a very good question, Bill San," Ozawa said, as he motioned the elder geisha to refill his guest's tumbler. "The answer is actually pretty straightforward." He watched the elder geisha pour more whisky, then picked up a raw piece of tuna belly and dipped it in soy sauce with wasabi. "Since our real estate prices are rising at over twenty percent per year, and we have the ability to sub-let, a long-term financial commitment does not really exist." Ozawa pointed to the middle of the table and, immediately, the young geisha came and removed a recessed metal cover and lit a gas burner. A large, round copper pot filled with water was placed on the gas burner.

Surprised to see the copper pot and a burner emerge from the center of the table, Bill was distracted. Turning his attention back to Ozawa's explanation, Bill had to admit that this was a reasonable position. Of course, he realized that Gene Friedman would not accept it.

Shit, this is potentially a no-win situation for me, he thought. *If I support the Japanese position, Gene will go ballistic. If I support the U.S. policy position, then TFC Japan will consider me an enemy. I'll check this issue out with the local CPA firm.*

After the water came to a boil, Bill was introduced to a Japanese favorite, *shabushabu*; paper-thin slices of Kobe beef and a variety of fresh vegetables were gradually placed in the boiling pot. The young geisha placed two small saucers in front of each of her guests, one ginger based, and the other soy sauce based. She then removed the beef from the pot and dipped it in the soy sauce saucer, then offered it to Bill.

The second eldest geisha, who had been bringing various platters of sushi and sashimi from the kitchen, removed a shamisen from a leather case and began to play the ancient, three-stringed instrument. When all the beef and vegetables had been consumed, the young geisha put a large bowl of soft noodles in the broth.

After tasting it, Bill thought, *Jesus, this is absolutely the best soup I've ever had.* "*Okawari kudasai,*" he said, smiling, as he passed his empty bowl over to the young geisha.

When Bill got back to his hotel, he found a card in the inside pocket of his suit. "I hope you enjoyed this evening. My phone number is 03-586-2465. I would like to show you Tokyo on your next trip to Japan. Yuko Sakumoto."

Well, at least it was the young one, he thought. *Hell, these guys will do anything to get me laid.*

★★★

General Manager Ozawa was in his early sixties, with a full head of silver hair and a trim, fit build. He spoke in a soft voice and had an excellent command of the English language which he acquired from thirty years traveling overseas and two stints living in Toronto and LA. Mr. Ozawa had had a respectable career with Mitsugawa, rising through the ranks to Hon Bucho, or General Manager, of the $2.5+ billion food division; however, descended from a long line of Samurai warriors, he was determined to end his career as Senmu, or Managing Director, of Mitsugawa Trading.

TFC Japan was Ozawa's baby. He correctly saw the tremendous shift towards western products following the 1964 Olympics, which had been held in Tokyo. Convincing his conservative colleagues had been an enormous challenge, aided by a serendipitous event at dinner one evening with the Managing Director of Nishi Poultry, one of the dozens of Mitsugawa-related companies. Nishi Poultry grew smaller-sized chickens that were uncompetitive with the larger imported chickens. TFC specifications called for smaller chickens, which would solve the problem.

Ozawa knew that to pull this joint venture off he would have to create scenarios with compelling opportunities for many different companies within the broadest definition of Mitsugawa affiliates, not just within the Trading Company. Specifically, Mitsugawa Realty and Mitsugawa Banking were key. He finally succeeded, and in 1969 he signed the joint venture agreement on behalf of Mitsugawa at TFC International's headquarters, then in Memphis Tennessee.

★★★

On his last day, Bill was rushed. He had agreed to meet Ray and Kenji at the American Club for a wrap-up meeting over lunch. While standing in the checkout line at the Okura hotel, Bill checked his watch and thought, *Shit, it's already 12:45. I told Ray I'd be there at 12:15 latest.*

When he finally did arrive, it was five minutes after one and Ray and Kenji were noticeably disturbed. With an annoyed look on his face, Ray waved him over to a table in the corner with no other parties within earshot.

"Hey, Old Dear, you're almost an hour late," Ray said with a frown.

"Sorry, guys, but checking out took forever."

Kenji was clearly agitated. "Alright. That's enough. Do you want a glass of this cabernet? It's really good stuff, especially with the steak sandwich we're having."

"Sure, that sounds fine."

Kenji motioned the waiter over and placed the order.

"So what's next?" Ray asked, leaning over and staring directly at Bill, eyes bloodshot from lack of sleep. "I hope you understand that Japan is different, and many of the bullshit U.S. policies just won't work here. And as you've found out, getting people who understand English and are familiar with U.S. financial principles and strategic planning techniques is almost impossible." Ray shook his head and finished his wine.

"Bill, as we discussed, also remember to compare our profit with other TFC units around the world. When you do, I'm sure you'll find we're stars, despite our leases," Kenji said, his scar turning red.

"Yes, I'll do that analysis, and if it's significant I'll—"

Looking at his watch, Ray interrupted, "—Listen Bill, Kenji and I have been discussing this whole fucking situation with Mr.

Ozawa, and we think we need a U.S. expatriate controller and CFO." He poured himself another glass of wine, just as the sommelier arrived, and he waved him away. After a healthy gulp, Ray Leaned forward and, looking directly at Bill, added, "You interested in the job?"

Bill was completely caught off guard; it was the last thing he expected. "Are you guys serious? I'm flattered, but I know my wife won't even consider it," Bill said, taking a drink of his wine. Leaning forward, Bill added, "Also guys, there is nothing in the budget to cover this kind of cost, never mind that the International Group is being squeezed to exceed its numbers this year to cover Domestic's growing shortfall. Ray, have you even discussed this with Jim and Ralph?"

"No, but I certainly plan to when I'm at the executive conference week after next. No fucking way we're going to be penalized because that cluster-fuckup Rosenberg is screwing up Domestic," Ray said, his face turning red. Several people at nearby tables turned, frowning at Ray's outburst.

Fumiko showed up and stood by the entrance, waiting to be signaled by Kenji, who motioned her to wait.

"Well, first things first, guys," Bill said. "I have to publish my audit report next week. I'll give you a heads up and make sure you get your copies first. In any case, you know headquarters isn't going to be happy about the policy violations; they're that extensive."

"Bill, will you at least include the analysis of our new store performance in comparison to other countries and our original projections?" Kenji asked again, his scar deepening its color.

"Yes, I will, and I'll also explain the local bias against capitalizing leases. I've heard that from Mr. Ozawa several times and, in fact, I've discussed it with the CPA partner at Simms and Durand who's responsible for your audit. Based on their experience with other clients, he confirms Mr. Ozawa's assertions."

"Bill," Ray said leaning forward and speaking in a low voice, "if you could postpone your report to the end of next week, I would really appreciate it."

"I'll see what I can do, but Friedman has already called for a preliminary. Ray, you know he's a stickler for policy and doesn't really trust International. He has Ralph constantly jumping through hoops trying to explain the exchange rate exposures and justify the spending for new company-owned stores. Hell, since

Domestic has virtually stopped building new company-owned stores and switched to a franchise strategy, International's spending most of the money on new stores."

"Friedman, that self important asshole," Ray said, louder than he intended; again, heads at surrounding tables turned. "I've told Jim he has to manage that son-of-a-bitch, or he's going to screw up International just as he has Domestic. Imagine, not building new company-owned stores just to save the company some cash. Franchisees will never be as committed to our business as we are, never mind that they're a bitch to manage. Shit, that's just common sense."

Bill took a deep breath. "Ray, what you don't understand is that interest costs are a much more important consideration in the States, where interest rates are over three times that of Japan. Why? I'm not sure I really know. But you better get used to it, because it's going to be a key part of the financial parameters in this first corporate-wide strategic plan starting this fall. Hell, Willis has just hired a Vice President for Strategic Planning from Washington Consulting and plans to introduce the process at the upcoming executive conference."

"What's this guy's name and who will he report to?" Kenji asked.

"The scuttlebutt is he'll report directly to Willis, and that has Gene threatening to quit," Ray said, waving for a waiter.

"Directly to the President and CEO? Isn't that unusual for that position?" Kenji asked, raising his eyebrows.

"Listen, this is fucking proof that this strategic planning is here to stay," Ray responded, pointing to his now empty glass and holding up two fingers, signifying to the waiter that he wanted to switch to double single-malt. "In fact, I'll bet you this will be the end of that *prima donna* prick Rosenberg."

Fumiko came over looking very nervous and said, "I'm sorry but it is 2:45 and the traffic to Haneda is always bad on Friday afternoons."

"Well, Old Dear, think about the CFO position and try to wait until the end of next week to issue your report," Ray said, as he stood to shake hands with Bill.

***

"Shit, Ray, wasn't that a bit premature? I mean offering him a job that doesn't even exist yet. Also, I know we've talked in passing to Ozawa San, but I seem to remember him saying only that he would think about it. Also, we can't afford another expat now." Kenji looked concerned and a little more than perturbed.

"Kenji, you run the company, I'll manage the home office politics. It's absolutely essential that we control Hartford or this gig is up. Remember, they're just a bunch of stupid *gaijin* who don't trust any foreigners; that's why they're going to approve this Controller CFO position and pay for it!" Ray said with a smug look. "And Ozawa San is going to agree, because I'm going to convince him that I can manage young Bill."

The waiter arrived with Ray's drink. After taking a large swallow, Ray continued, "Relax, trust me, Kenji. I may not know much about business, but I know tons about human nature. It's how I have accomplished so much while doing as little as possible."

Taking another large swallow, he added, "Can you come up with the ten thousand dollars for that condo development project in Hawaii? Kenji, this is going to be big; at least one if not two units each for ten thousand dollars. Hell, I'm investing fifty thousand dollars." Leaning forward, he added in a low voice, "But listen, I need to know by next Tuesday if you and Ozawa are in or not. The seed money has to be paid by next Friday. That should get us the planning board approval by next month."

Linking his fingers together and leaning forward, Kenji said, "Ray, are you sure this is going to work? Ten thousand dollars is a lot of money to me, and I will have to borrow at least four thousand."

"Trust me, and don't worry. In less than a year, you'll own one or two condos in Honolulu worth forty to a hundred grand. Didn't I promise you I would make you real money if you left your uncle and came with me?" Ray said, smiling, while finishing his single malt. "How about that insider tip this February? Hell, your four thousand got you twenty seven thousand, and it would've been closer to a hundred grand if you had come up with the fifteen thousand we initially talked about."

"Okay, I'll have the money by next Tuesday," Kenji said, smiling as he considered the riches he would accumulate through Ray's tips and "special" deals.

★★★

Fumiko was chatty on the way to the airport. She acted as though nothing had happened between them. "So, just let me know if there's anything you need to prepare your audit report next week. Remember, there is a thirteen-hour time difference this time of year. But call anytime, and I will go to the office and telex you the information. When do you think you will be coming back to help with the strategic plan? I heard Ray and Kenji discussing this with Ozawa San on Wednesday."

"Well, that'll be up to Gene and Ralph, I guess, although I think the process will kick off at the executive conference scheduled for week after next

When they got to the airport, Fumiko handed Bill an envelope addressed "Personal and Confidential" and a shopping bag.

"What's this?"

"Oh, just some mementos of Japan for your daughter. You've been so busy I knew you wouldn't have time to go shopping."

As Bill stood openmouthed, not knowing what to say, Fumiko kissed him and said, "*Sayonara*, Bill San, see you on your next trip." And then she smiled and walked away, swaying her hips, before Bill could say anything.

Two hours later, as the 747SP was taking off for its non-stop fourteen-hour flight to New York, Bill sat contemplating all that had happened in such a short week. After ordering a Johnnie Walker Black and Seven, he relaxed in his first class seat and opened the P&C envelope. Inside was one of Ray's business cards. "Buy Athena Mining below 50 cents on the pink sheets by next Thursday" was written on the back. Bill put the card in his wallet and wondered what Athena Mining was.

When the limo pulled into Bill's driveway, both Mrs. Kowalski and Sarah were standing outside waving Japanese flags.

"Oh Daddy, you remembered!" Sarah squealed with delight as she hugged her new Japanese doll.

★★★

The telephone rang at 9:50 in the morning, and Fumiko picked it up after the first ring, trying not to disturb Ray, who was snoring loudly. They hadn't gone to bed until two thirty. Ray had passed out drunk at a little after two, and it took Fumiko about half an hour to get him undressed and into bed.

"Hello," Fumiko said softly.

"Put Ray on! It's Saji from Osaka calling," came the terse response.

"Just a moment please."

Shaking Ray's shoulder while keeping the phone receiver covered, Fumiko said, "Wake up, Ray, its Saji San from Osaka."

"Shit, what time is it?" Ray said, rubbing his eyes. He had a horrible headache, and his mouth felt like he'd eaten sand. "Go get me a glass of tomato juice and vodka with a raw egg and a lot of Tabasco," he growled.

Taking the phone from Fumiko, Ray said, "Saji San, you're up early for a Saturday morning."

"Well, I'm off to Hawaii for a week, so I'm taking care of a few loose ends. Your request is one of them. The bottom line is I can arrange for customs to find a bag of marijuana in your auditor's luggage for two million yen, or arrange for a persuasive meeting with one of my men for three million yen. What's your pleasure?"

"Jesus, Saji San, I can't afford either of those options. I'm paying for this out of my own pocket. Can't you give me a better deal? After all, I sent Lisa down."

"Ray, I don't care where the money comes from, and as far as Lisa's concerned, I still haven't got her into bed yet. If anything, you owe me for the money she's costing me without the benefits. Call if and when you get the money." The line went dead.

Looking at the phone in his hand, Ray yelled, "Fumiko, where the fuck is my drink! And bring me four aspirin."

Chapter 5

Monday morning couldn't come fast enough. Suffering from a bad case of jet lag, Bill was up at 4:00 a.m. and decided to get an early start. When he arrived at the office at 4:45, Phil, the security guard, was surprised to see him.

"Good trip, Mr. Sanford?"

"Yeah, great, just incredibly busy. I feel like I've been gone two weeks; anything exciting happen while I was gone?"

"Well, we've got a new Vice President of Strategic Planning, fellow named Dave Liberwitz. A real hard charger, at least in terms of time he spends here; always in by 6:00 a.m. and never gone before 7:00 p.m. A bit of a strange fellow, though, never wears a suit, just a sports coat, slacks and a tie only half the time."

Hell, that schedule is going to raise the bar around here, Bill thought. .

At 7:30 the phone rang. It was Gene Friedman, just as Bill expected.

"Welcome back, Bill," Gene said, talking a bit faster than normal. "Listen, I need your audit report ASAP; the executive conference kicks off next Monday. When do you think you'll have it?"

"I should have something by the end of the week, if I don't get too many distractions."

"You won't! I'll call Ralph and make sure of it. Was I right, policy violations everywhere?"

"Yes, Gene. Your suspicions were correct. There's a whole boatload of policy violations. However, as Mr. Ozawa of Mitsugawa

Trading pointed out, technically the joint venture agreement requires only board approval from TFC Japan for new stores."

"To hell with that! That son-of-a-bitch Easton knows our corporate policies and just refuses to follow them! He's paid by us, not the fucking joint venture. Get me that report and don't sugarcoat anything, got it?"

"You'll have it by the end of the week," Bill said, as the line went dead. *Clearly he's on a warpath, and I'm right in the thick of things,* he thought. *Shit, how can I win in this shoot out?*

At 8:30, Ralph Ovunc, the International Group's Vice President for Finance and its CFO, stuck his head in. "So, did you behave yourself? I didn't the last time I was in Japan," Ralph said with a wink, sitting down across from Bill's desk.

"Ralph, no one's ever going to compete with you, not in any country," Bill said, standing up and putting his hands in his back pockets. "Seriously Ralph, how do you suggest I manage things?"

Pausing and putting his fingers together, Ralph said, "Look, you've already heard from Gene this morning, as have I. Gene wants your audit report yesterday. So, make it your only priority until it's done, and shoot me a copy before you send it over. I don't need to tell you to make it thorough."

"Got it. So tell me about the new VP of Strategic Planning, Dave something?"

"Yeah, Dave Liberwitz. He's from the Washington Consulting Group; a genius I hear, and as I told you he reports directly to Willis, not Gene."

"I bet that's got Gene's knickers in a twist. It certainly explains the cheery tone he had this morning."

"Listen, this strategic planning thing has Willis' total support, and he's determined to make it work. We'd better all get on board, and let me tell you, that's a direct quote from Jim. He said as much last week when he announced Dave's appointment!"

At 10:30, Jim Meyer, the President of International Group, stuck his head in. "Hi Bill, welcome home. Ray tells me you were a big help and seemed to understand some of the local peculiarities. Hell, he's already campaigning to have you come out to help with the strategic plan. I know you realize the politics involved with your audit report. Just be objective."

"Oh, I will, Jim. I've already heard from Gene and Ralph first thing this morning."

"Well, you know where I am if you need me," Jim said, tapping the doorframe as he departed.

After Bill had written up the details of his findings, he turned his attention to the task Kenji had asked him to address concerning comparative performance of the new TFC stores in Japan versus other markets. He chose Australia, the largest international market, the UK, a newer market, and of course, the U.S. Domestic, for the comparisons.

The results were nothing short of astounding. The sales averages for the stores opened over the past twelve months in Japan were eighteen percent better than Australia, twenty-four percent better than the UK, and forty-two percent better than the U.S. Store-level profits were almost as impressive, despite the high rents paid in Japan. Bill couldn't believe the results at first, so he double checked his data and expanded his audit to include Germany, Mexico, and Canada. The results were similar.

How can I include this analysis objectively in the audit report without Gene going ballistic?

***

When Bill arrived at the office Thursday morning, everyone seemed to be waiting for a copy of his audit report: Gene, Ralph, and, of course, Ray and Kenji. Jim's secretary had said that Jim and the new VP of Strategic Planning, Dave Liberwitz, wanted copies as well.

Bill handled both the shocking store performance comparisons and the capitalized leases as addendums to the audit report. His objective was to make it clear that Japan was legitimately different, and in doing so, he would endear himself to Ray, Kenji, and Ozawa San.

As the telex machine was busily sending Ray and Kenji their draft, Bill sat in Ralph's office, watching him as he concentrated on reviewing the document.

"Bill, are you sure of your store performance comparisons?" Ralph said, removing his glasses. "These are just remarkable, and it raises the question of why we weren't aware of this before, especially the international comparisons. Listen Bill, you were the auditor and this is your report, but do you really want to include the addendums and make so many references to them?",

"Ralph, I've put more time into this than any other audit report I've ever done, both here and in public practice. This report is objective, complete, and balanced," Bill said, his face turning a bit red.

"Okay, okay," Ralph said, raising his hands. "Send it, but be ready for the challenge of your young life, and remember I warned you!

★★★

Friday morning, Bill arrived at the office at 6:15. When he sat down at his desk, he found a note: "See me when you get a chance. Thanks, Dave Liberwitz." Bill looked at his watch and wondered when the note had been left. Just then, the phone rang. "Bill, Dave here, do you have a few minutes to spare? I've been through your audit report on TFC Japan and I have a few questions."

"Sure, I can come down now if you like. Where do they have you located? Okay, I'll be there in five minutes."

Dave had one of the corner offices, the only one with a view of the gardens. It was furnished in a business-like fashion. The focal point was an ebony standup desk in the corner, sort of like a large painting easel with drawers underneath. It faced the center of the room, which hosted a large coffee table made of chrome with a glass top. On either side were black ebony benches running the length of the table. Along the sidewalls were floor-to-ceiling ebony bookcases that were completely full of books and various files. In the other corner were two black-leather wingback chairs, with a small table between them. The chairs faced slightly towards each other and had a view of the gardens.

When Bill arrived, Dave was standing at his desk, deep in thought. He was a tall, lanky man with a very strong jaw and flaming red hair, with just a touch of gray around the temples. His tie was loose, his sleeves rolled up, and his sports coat lay across the back of one of the leather chairs.

"Oh, Bill is it? I'm Dave. Thanks for coming on such short notice," Dave said, as he came around from behind the easel to shake Bill's hand. He had a firm grip. "I've got a meeting at corporate in an hour and the addendums in your report will be front and center." Dave stared directly at Bill with unnaturally bright, green eyes. "This is the most succinct analysis of new store sales

I've ever seen." Dave waved Bill's report, which had clearly been marked up. He moved over to the coffee table and motioned for Bill to sit opposite him.

"How quickly could you expand your addendum on new store sales analysis to include all countries for the past three years, franchised versus company owned?"

"I don't honestly know. My desk is piled high," Bill said, shifting his weight on the bench. "At Gene's request, I've been working on nothing but the TFC Japan new store audit for the last three weeks. I'm therefore way behind on processing new store requests from around the world." Bill paused, waiting for some kind of a response that didn't come. "I guess it depends in part on how long it will take me to set up a program on the computer for the financial calculations. I'll see how busy the computer department is this morning."

Dave picked up the phone and raised his finger; a moment later, he began a message. "Ralph, this is Dave Liberwitz. I need Bill to do an urgent special assignment for me as part of the executive conference briefing next week. To complete it on time, he will need the computer department's time first thing this morning. Please arrange accordingly. Thanks, Dave."

"Bill, I would really appreciate it if you could get me something by Monday night. The executive conference kicks off at 8:00 a.m. on Tuesday, and I would like you to present this expanded new store sales analysis right after lunch at 1:00. I'll clear this with Ralph, Gene, and Jim. What do you say?"

Chapter 6

"Hello Saji kun, it's your old friend Inoue. When are you next coming to Tokyo?"

"Ah, Inoue San, to what do I owe the pleasure of a phone call from decorated war hero and Managing Director of Sawamura Trading?" Saji said with mock sincerity. "In any case, I'm coming in for a job next Tuesday. What did you have in mind?"

"I'd like to have dinner with you to discuss an idea I have where your various skills would be useful, and of course profitable."

"Of course, I'm always interested to hear your ideas, but I thought you avoided any of the activities my organization specializes in, especially since you've become so important," Saji said with a chuckle. "Where and when old friend?"

"Let's say next Monday evening, eight o'clock at the Happoen."

As Inoue put down the phone, he considered the risks of Saji's involvement. But he knew if he didn't get the inside information he needed, he'd never convince Aunt Sally Mae's Southern Fried Chicken to abandon discussions with Yotsui Trading and begin negotiating with Sawamura Trading. *Is this finally my chance to get even with that asshole Joji Sakurai?*

Ever since Inoue had discovered that Joji Sakurai was President of TFC Japan, representing Mitsugawa, Inoue had become obsessed with culminating a joint venture with Aunt Sally Mae's SFC, to seek his revenge on the man who destroyed his only opportunity for true love.

Growing up in Osaka on the same street, Inoue and Saji had been close friends. However, Saji's home was much larger and included an ever-present team of bodyguards; he was always accompanied by at least two. Most of his schoolmates shied away from Saji, as his father was known to be the fourth generation head of the Osaka's Yakuza. Inoue, however, had no problem with his friend's family business. After all, his ancestors had been Ronin Samurai who had worked for the highest bidder. Besides, Saji had always been loyal, and that was the most enduring trait to Inoue.

★★★

Ray walked into Bill's office at eleven thirty and asked, "So, did you buy any Athena Mining yesterday? It's up over two hundred fifty percent today. Time to sell."

"What are you doing here?" Bill stammered.

"The executive conference starts next Tuesday, so I thought I'd come early and see some of my favorite people, specifically the executive secretaries," Ray said with a wink. "Why don't we go over to Corporate for lunch? I'm starving."

On the drive over, Bill asked, "Say, did you and Kenji read the audit report? What did you guys think?

"Great stuff, Old Dear! The way you worked those references to the addendums was genius. Even Kenji was surprised at how much better the Japanese new stores had performed, over the U.S. in particular."

"Yeah, but you guys are still left with the policy violations, and I know Gene is determined to make a big deal of it."

The executive dining room was on the second floor and was surrounded on three sides by a large flower garden with a vast variety of roses of all different colors. The garden had been written up by Ladies Home Journal as the best rose garden in the Eastern United States. Major Tom's wife had been an avid gardener and had spent five years developing the garden.

On this day the executive dining room wasn't very crowded, so the wait in the buffet line was short. Ray loaded up with meat and potatoes, a salad, soup, a dessert, and a bottle of cabernet. Bill was so nervous he just got a tuna sandwich and a small Caesar salad.

When they were seated, Bill turned bright red and whispered, "Don't look now, but Gene is seated two tables over with Willis and Dave Liberwitz. Good God, I think Gene has seen us…he's waving his arm and pointing over here!" Bill was in a panic, his wine glass literally trembling. He just knew this was going to be the end of his promising career.

"Relax, Old Dear," Ray said, completely unperturbed. "You're going to die young if you continue to worry so much over things you can do nothing about. Gene's going to do what he's going to do, only now it will just happen sooner. Eat your lunch." Ray continued to eat his sizable lunch and polish off the cabernet while completely ignoring the group two tables over.

When the senior executives finished their lunch, Gene dragged Willis over to Ray and Bill's table. Not an easy task given that Willis, at six-foot-six and two hundred seventy pounds, was much larger than even Gene. Like Gene, Willis had played football throughout high school and college. Though now approaching his sixtieth birthday, Willis still worked out three times a week and it showed.

"This man has just returned from Tokyo and his audit report confirms that TFC Japan has completely disregarded our capital expenditure policies; twenty-six violations were noted. We can't tolerate this behavior any longer," Gene said with a loud voice, a red face, and a triumphant look.

Ray sat there placidly. Bill, however, thought his heart would surely stop. He could feel the sweat rolling down his face, soaking his shirt.

Willis ran his hand through his light brown hair, which was peppered with gray. He cleared his throat and with a stern look said, "Well, Ray, what do you have to say about this audit report?"

Ray looked up, and without a pause, said, "Well, if I've learned anything in my twenty years of corporate life it's that it's a whole lot easier to get forgiveness than it is to get approval."

Dave Liberwitz was the first to crack a smile and was quickly followed by Willis who couldn't help but laugh.

Gene looked as though he would burst and began to stutter, "This, this, just can't be...condoned. We have to take action..."

"Calm down, Gene, we'll meet with Jim, Ralph, and Ray during the conference and sort this out." Turning directly toward Bill, Willis added, "It's Bill, right? I was intrigued by your addendums and look forward to your presentation."

"Yeah, the numbers of the new store sales analysis in Japan are remarkable, especially compared with other countries," Dave added.

"Come on, Gene, we've got a lot to prepare for next week," Willis said, as he led him away from the table with his arm around his shoulder.

"See, Old Dear, don't sweat the small stuff, especially things you can't control," Ray said, looking quite pleased. "The addendums in your report did the trick. Kenji knew if he tried to make excuses, no one would listen, but in the context of an audit report, everyone would pay attention. He was right, and now you're in the limelight, Old Dear. So did you buy Athena Mining?"

★★★

The Happoen was one of Tokyo's most exclusive and authentic Japanese restaurants, complete with Japanese gardens, a carp-filled pond and a waterfall, and geishas for serving and casual entertainment.

Inoue was enjoying his second Wild Turkey and water when Saji showed up at the reserved private room. The geisha bowed deeply and asked Saji what he would like to drink.

"The same as my host," he responded, as he slid the rice paper door open, adorned with a night fishing scene with lanterns to attract fish and a full moon in the background. The fishermen were dressed in black leggings, a colorful *yukata* and broad rice straw hats. As required, Saji removed his shoes so as not to soil the beautiful *tatami*-floored room.

"So Inoue San, what is the interesting idea you have that might involve me? I've been trying to guess ever since I left Osaka this afternoon." The geisha poured him a healthy portion of Wild Turkey and water.

Finishing his drink and motioning to the geisha to pour another, Inoue took a deep breath. "Saji kun, do you remember after the war when I wrote to you and asked you to stand as my best man?"

"Of course, and I was honored to be asked," Saji said gently. He remembered a withdrawal of the wedding invitation had come the following week. The circumstances were never explained and Saji respected his friend too much to ask.

"When Keiko announced to her brother, Joji Sakurai, that she planned to marry me, he laughed." Uncharacteristically, Inoue took a handkerchief from his coat pocket and wiped his eyes as he removed a folded piece of wrinkled rice paper from his breast pocket, which he handed to Saji with a trembling hand.

Saji gently unfolded the ancient rice paper and read:

> *Inoue San, I love you more than life itself; never forget this. It is as perennial as the sakura. My brother has forbidden me from seeing you again. As I am Samurai, I must obey so as not to disgrace my ancestors. I know you understand this and will accept it, for you love me as I love you.*
>
> *Forever you will remain in my heart. The memories of our time together shall be my source of strength and happiness for the rest of my life. Be strong, my warrior, and become the great man I know you are.*
>
> *Respectfully with enduring love and devotion,*
>
> *Keiko Sakurai*

The note brought back memories from Saji's childhood days with his best friend. He recalled a spring evening so many years ago in Osaka when, after a high school baseball game, he was eating ramen at an outdoor noodle shop while waiting for Inoue. It was a Saturday, and the family had assigned only one bodyguard, as the other responsible for watching Saji was at a family funeral.

Two men dressed in non-descript suits had approached Saji; one had a club under his coat, which he used to dispatch Saji's bodyguard, the blow shattering his forearm. The second man grabbed Saji and dragged him towards the open back door of a waiting sedan, just as Inoue appeared, dressed in his baseball uniform. At five-foot-ten inches and one hundred ninety pounds he was enormous by Japanese standards.

"Hey Saji kun, where are you going? I thought we were supposed to have ramen," Inoue had said, perplexed.

Brandishing a Samurai sword, the kidnapper had snarled, "You'd better get out of here, kid, if you know what's good for you."

Without hesitating, Inoue swung his bat at the gangster. Not expecting this reaction from a high school student, the gangster veered, but Inoue's bat struck his right shoulder. With a resounding crack, the rotor cuff snapped and the gangster screamed.

Saji had broken free and was beginning to run when the second gangster swung a sword. Inoue stepped between the sword and Saji as he brought his bat across, like he was swinging for a home run. The bat struck home first and hit the gangster on the left side of his head, causing him to drop the sword, but not before it cut Inoue in the upper left thigh.

I wouldn't be here today if it wasn't for Inoue kun, Saji thought.

Carefully refolding the rice paper, Saji handed it back to Inoue and said, "*Naruhodo*, my friend."

Then he changed the subject. "So what's your idea, my friend, and how can I help?" Saji said softly, as he picked up a piece of raw tuna belly.

"I'm in discussions with an American fried chicken chain, but so is Yotsui Trading," Inoue said, as he motioned the geisha for another carafe of sake. "And I need to prove to the Americans that we're the superior partner. To accomplish this, I need inside information that'll show we're the more knowledgeable partner."

"Umm, this is an interesting challenge. Inoue San, how much of this is business and how much is personal revenge?"

"I will get revenge against Joji Sakurai, either through destroying him and his company or, well, that's a topic for us for another day," Inoue said, smiling.

"So, my friend, do I take it this insider information is necessary soon?" Saji asked as he motioned to the geisha, annoyed. His cup should have been filled as soon as it was empty.

"Absolutely! I'm coming into this late in the game, and I know Yotsui U.S. has been talking with them for several months."

"Can I ask what your budget is?" Saji said, sipping his refilled cup of sake.

"At least you waited until we finished eating before asking. Congratulations, Saji kun," Inoue said, laughing, throwing his head back and holding his stomach.

With a scowl on his face, a blushing Saji said to the geisha, "Get me some more sake, and be quick about it this time."

I'll have to call in a few favors from Sawamura Bank, Inoue thought. *Although Sawamura Realty should be supportive just on the merits. I'll begin the nemawashi next week at our corporate golf tournament,* he decided.

★★★

"Good morning, Aunt Sally Mae's Southern Fried Chicken, how can I help you?"

Inoue smiled as he remembered that familiar accent. "Yes, Mr. Johnson please. Mr. Inoue calling from Tokyo."

"Tokyo Japan?" the receptionist exclaimed. "What time is it for y'all?"

"It's ten p.m. Wednesday night," Inoue said patiently.

" No way! How can y'all be ahead of us?"

"Well, when I come to Mobile I'll explain it to you, now Mr. Johnson, please."

After a pause, he heard, "J.J. Johnson here, how can I help you?"

"Mr. Johnson, my name is Inoue Masahiro, managing director of Sawamura Trading. I was wondering if I could make an appointment to see you to discuss the possibility of a joint venture with your company for Japan."

I can actually understand this Jap, Mr. Johnson thought. *He really does speak English.* "I don't know, Mr. Inoue, we're already in discussions with Yotsui Trading U.S., and things are rapidly progressing."

"Mr. Johnson, we have a unique interest in the western quick service restaurant market sector. For reasons I will explain when I see you, we have detailed statistics on the market and are willing to make an aggressive investment to take significant shares away from Mitsugawa and TFC."

"Well, I can't make any commitments. How soon can you come to see us?"

"How about a week from this Thursday? I assure you it won't be a waste of your time."

Chapter 7

"Good morning, Phil, how goes it? Who's checked in so far today?" Bill asked the security guard at the office.

"Only Dave Liberwitz and Ralph Ovunc. Oh, and Sharon Moran from the computer department. I expect quite a few this weekend with the big conference kicking off on Tuesday."

"When did Ralph get in?"

"Early, about eight a.m., an hour after Mr. Liberwitz"

"Phil, can you give me a heads up if either Ray Easton or Kenji Kato shows up?"

"Sure, Mr. Sanford, still extension 245, right?"

When Bill got to his office he found notes from Dave Liberwitz and Sharon asking him to see them when he got in. He wandered down to Sharon's first.

"Hi, Sharon, how's it coming?"

"I'm almost finished," she answered with a smile filled with dimples. "But it's a good thing you didn't ask two hours ago."

Raising his eyebrows, and taking a seat across from Sharon, Bill asked, "Why's that?"

"Well, I was having problems getting data on U.S. stores. I asked corporate EDP for it yesterday morning, after we talked. In any case, Dave Liberwitz showed up and asked if I was having any problems, so I explained the situation. He picked up my phone, got an outside line, and called Gene's home at seven-thirty this morning, and demanded that Gene solve the problem immediately."

"What exactly did he say?" Bill leaned forward.

"Well, something along the lines of 'Gene, you get whoever is in charge of EDP at corporate in their office within thirty minutes or I'm going to call Willis at his house in the Hamptons!' I couldn't hear what Gene said, but Dave Liberwitz added 'Thirty minutes, Gene, no more,' and hung up. About twenty minutes later, I got a call from the Director of EDP at corporate, telling me he would have the data within forty-five minutes and was that okay." Sharon was satisfied; she was constantly fighting with corporate EDP for anything and everything she asked for.

"Wow! I wish I could have heard that exchange. This guy Liberwitz is something. I'll bet Gene has never received a call like that before," Bill said, laughing as he stood up. "I wonder if he would have really called Willis at home?"

Pausing at the door Bill added, "Well, let me get out of your hair. I'll be in my office when you're ready, just give me a shout. And Sharon, thanks again for all the help."

That Liberwitz has balls, Bill thought. *So my addendums got everyone's attention. I wonder if Ray and Kenji played me.*

On the way to Liberwitz's office, Bill bumped into a red-faced and quick-stepping Ralph.

"Where are you going?" Ralph shouted. "I've been looking all over for you. Gene is going absolutely ballistic over your presentation. He ordered me to work with you on it and make the presentation myself. So where do you think you're going now?"

"Gee, relax Ralph," Bill said, frowning. "I was just in with Sharon checking on the spreadsheet, and now I'm on my way to Dave's office. He left me a note to see him when I got in," Bill said defensively .

"Well, let's go see Liberwitz—together." Ralph marched off, leading the way.

When they arrived, Dave was busy writing at his easel, and when Ralph knocked, he looked up and said, "Good morning Bill, we've got a lot of work to do today and tomorrow. I hope your schedule is clear, as Mr. Willis has moved your presentation up to just after his introduction. Ralph, perhaps you could check with Sharon and see how she's coming along with the spreadsheets."

"Um, Dave, there's been a change," Ralph said slowly. "Gene has asked me to take over the comparative sales analysis project and presentation."

"Bill, will you excuse us?" Dave said. Come back in twenty minutes and we'll begin."

"Sit down, Ralph," Dave said, the color of his face matching his red hair.

Leaning forward, hesaid, "I don't give a shit what Gene told you. Sanford is doing the presentation. You tell Gene that if he doesn't like that he can call Willis. Further, you obviously forgot Jim's instructions that you take over Sanford's CAR responsibilities." Pausing and sitting up, Dave added, "Ralph, I'm here to tell you that the sales analysis project is going to last at least a week and I don't want you to interfere with Sanford. Do I make myself clear, or do you want to go see Jim now?".

As Ralph was debating what to say, Dave stood up and said, "Good. I thought you'd understand. My advice to you, Ralph, is to get on board with the new strategic planning culture. I guarantee it's here to stay. Now, if I were you, I'd go to work on my own presentation. Incidentally, I'll be happy to look it over if you like. Believe me, your numbers are going to look a whole lot better than Gene's presentation on the domestic business. International is clearly the rising star for the future, so don't forget this, Ralph, as you consider your priorities and, indeed, your loyalties." Dave returned to his easel, indicating the meeting was over.

Ralph got up with a dumbfounded look on his face and walked out the door without saying a word.

★★★

"So, here's the spreadsheet," Sharon said with a smile as she laid it on Bill's desk.

"Wow, this is super." He looked through the fourteen columns.

"Well, the real magic is in the manipulation. Follow me," she said, motioning. . She seated herself at the terminal of the computer in her office.

She typed quickly. Soon the screen showed the entire worksheet. "So, what would you like to change?"

Wrinkling his forehead, he asked, "What do you mean? What can I change?"

Chuckling, Sharon said, "Anything in the data base. For instance, if you want to compare California's new franchisee store sales to Australia and Japan's new company-owned stores, then…"

she typed on the keyboard, "…there you have it!" The screen displayed the new store sales data for the three countries.

"That's incredible! But no way am I going to be able to learn how to do that before the conference."

"Relax, I just wanted to demonstrate what the spreadsheet can do," she said, turning to face him. "Remember, I'm only a phone call away, and I can provide you with any permutations within minutes."

"Thanks again, Sharon, this is really something. Now I know why everyone calls you the *computer genie*," Bill chuckled.

"Well, call me if you have any questions. I'll be home all weekend, working in the garden."

Wow, Sharon is really something, Bill thought. *She's smart, talented, and gorgeous; someone's a lucky guy.*

★★★

The phone rang. It was the security officer. "Mr. Kenji Kato of TFC Japan has arrived and is on his way up to your office, Mr. Sanford."

"Thanks Phil," Bill replied. *Jesus, what poor timing, I've got to complete this presentation and meet with Dave in less than an hour and a half.*

"*Konnichiwa*, Bill San," Kenji said, as he stuck his head in the door. "You look very busy. Ray tells me you'll be making an important presentation at the executive conference. I just wanted to say *domo arigato* for your addendums. Listen, I'm staying at the Farmington Inn in room 212. Let's have dinner or drinks, if you can. Give me a call. I've got a lot to tell you."

"Dinner sounds fine, although I'm not sure what time it will be. I'll call you at six and give you a specific time if that works for you."

"Are you kidding? With my jet lag I won't really be hungry before eight," Kenji laughed, heading out the door.

★★★

The Corner House was a two story colonial built in the early 1800s for a local ship's captain. It had been converted to a Bed and Breakfast after the Civil War and became the Corner House in 1885 when the new owners from France arrived. The interior was adorned with original French art depicting country landscapes and hunting scenes. The furniture was all oak, stained in rich deep brown with a touch of mahogany, which contrasted perfectly with the stucco white walls. The original owner's grandchildren and great grandchild were the current managers and chefs. All had been trained in Lyon, France.

When Bill arrived at the Corner House at 8:30 p.m., Kenji was already there, enjoying a double martini with jalapenos. "Bill San, *kombanwa, o-genki desuka?* Did you finish your presentation?"

"Kenji San, *kombanwa, okagesama de owarimashita*," Bill responded, in relatively good and accurate Japanese.

"Bill, your Japanese is getting better."

"Well, I guess it's coming back somewhat. But my accent is Osaka slang, not *hyojungo*," Bill laughed.

Bill ordered a Johnnie Walker Black with Seven and Kenji ordered another double martini.

"Bill, before I left Japan," Kenji said, lowering his voice and looking around, "I met with Ozawa San and showed him your draft audit report, along with the addendums. Impressed, he asked that I convey his personal thanks to you. Have you given any more thought to Ray's suggestion that you come to Japan as CFO of TFC Japan? I know we'd work well together, and you could help Ray manage TFC International. You know Ray's not very good with numbers, unless of course they're his."

"Kenji, I'm truly flattered by your and Ray's interest in me, but there are two fundamental problems. First, Ray doesn't have any money in his budget for an expatriate position, and second, I'm certain my wife would never accept living in Japan, and while we're currently going through a trial separation until that's decided, one way or another, I can't relocate anywhere." The waiter came with their drinks.

"Also, Ralph has offered me a promotion to Director of Financial Planning, although based on what happened today, I'm not sure the offer is still on the table," Bill responded in a low voice. The Corner House was a favorite among TFC corporate employees.

As dinner progressed, Bill told Kenji about the lunch at Corporate, providing a blow-by-blow description. Kenji didn't seem at all surprised and said he was confident Ray would survive, especially as Bill included the addendums in his audit report. He thanked Bill again and said he considered Bill an *otomodachi* of TFC Japan.

They left the restaurant at 11:00, both having had too much to drink, and after sharing too many secrets.

Chapter 8

How will I convince the board to approve the joint venture project with Aunt Sally Mae's Southern Fried Chicken? Inoue wondered. *Getting Sawamura Bank on my side is critical, but Sawamura Realty should be easier to convince, simply on the merits and the greed of that old fart Nishimura.*

Like Ozawa of Mitsugawa Trading, Inoue had accurately predicted that Japan would become westernized following the 1964 Tokyo Olympics. However, he also realized the sensitivity of his major domestic customers, who feared that it would destroy their oligopolies. *They're right of course,* he thought, *but Westernization is inevitable, might as well benefit from it. Besides, most foreigners, especially those fucking Americans, are so self-centered and unfamiliar with the rest of the world, it will be years before they figure out our system.*

Like many of his fellow business leaders, Inoue secretly prayed for the day Japan would resume its rightful position as the undisputed leader of Asia. He had been a major in the elite 323rd infantry brigade that accomplished so much in Malaysia, and later defended Micronesia to the end, which happened when the U.S. invaded Saipan.

He was one of only twelve officers who were captured, while over six hundred members of his battalion committed suicide by jumping off the one-hundred-twenty-foot Banzai Cliff. Inoue often wondered if his capture had been inevitable or if he facilitated it to avoid suicide.

For the remaining eleven months of the war, Inoue spent his time as a translator, where his rudimentary command of English improved dramatically.

He smiled as he remembered the almost incomprehensible accent of U.S. Marine Captain Lee Davis, a great great grandson of Confederate President Jefferson Davis, who was from *Mo-bile*. *Capin Lee*, as he liked to be called, had been his boss and taught him the southern English used in the *Confederate States of America*.

It now seems as though this accent, which I'll never forget, might come in handy. How ironic. Inoue smiled at the thought.

The greatest benefit of a joint venture with Aunt Sally Mae's SFC, however, was a personal one. It would give him the opportunity to directly get back at his archenemy from Mitsugawa, Joji Sakurai, President of TFC Japan.

His eyes became moist, and his resolve to get even with Sakurai boiled inside him as he remembered the day he had invited Joji Sakurai to lunch to discuss his desire to marry his sister, Keiko. He could still see Sakurai's laughing face as he turned down the plea.

"You? You must be joking! You're Ronin, not true Samurai. Our family is descended from Daimiyo Sakurai, Lord of Yamanashi prefecture, who had hundreds of mercenaries like you working for him. And you want to marry one of his descendants? Don't be ridiculous!" Sakurai had yelled.

People at several surrounding tables had overheard the discussion and had also laughed. Inoue had never been more humiliated or embarrassed in his life.

Yes, I'll definitely ensure that this joint venture will proceed. TFC Japan is about to have some real competition. That son of a whore will suffer and be disgraced in his last corporate assignment!

★★★

"Hey Bill, how's the presentation coming along?" Sharon asked, sticking her head in the door on Sunday morning.

"Come in and have a seat. Things are going great, mostly because of your remarkable spreadsheets!" Bill said, giving her two thumbs up.

"I don't know about that," Sharon said, smiling and appreciating the compliment. "Have you got everything you need?" she added, raising her eyebrows.

"Absolutely, and I think I'm even beginning to learn how to manipulate the data."

"Well, I'm not surprised. I thought you'd get the hang of it quickly. Make a list of questions in any areas you're still having problems with, then stop by my office and I'll show you how to solve them. I'm around most of the morning, and after that I'm at home working in the garden again," Sharon said smiling, her dimples dominating her beautiful face.

As she got up to leave, she added, "Also, if you like, I'll be glad to listen to your presentation."

"You must have quite the garden, with all the time you spend in it," Bill laughed.

"Well, why don't you drop by this evening and see for yourself? I'll throw some burgers on the grill and you can impress me with your presentation."

"You've got a deal! I'll see you around seven."

★★★

The house was a classic off-white cape with dark green shutters that sat perfectly on a large lot. Enormous flowerbeds stretched in front of the entire house and held a variety of different flora and exotic plants. Bill was impressed.

When Bill arrived, he found Sharon in the backyard starting the grill. She was wearing cut-off jeans and a blue T-shirt, and while he tried to act casual, he was taken by Sharon's incredible figure and earthy beauty.

"Hey, so you found the house without any problems?"

"Your directions were perfect, and wow, what a garden. Where did you learn so much about plants?"

"Well, before I got hooked on computers, I wanted to be a botanist, but in spite of the degree, the only job I could find was at a nursery. After six months of living off spaghetti and hot dogs, I decided to go back to school. So, what's your poison?"

"If you have any scotch, I'll have a Johnnie Walker Black and Seven."

" I can do that! Pull up a lounger and I'll be back with your drink in a minute. Are you all set for Tuesday?" Sharon asked as she turned toward the house.

"Yeah, I think so. My biggest challenge is to cover all the material in twenty minutes, all twelve slides. By the way, it couldn't have been done without your help. Thanks again."

"Only too happy to help," Sharon said, as she handed Bill his drink. "It's great to have a project with real value and a customer who really appreciates what the computer can do."

"So I'm a customer?"

"You bet you are! But a nice one," Sharon said, laughing.

After two Johnnie Walker Black and Sevens, Bill began to relax.

"How many kids do you have?" she asked.

"Just one daughter, Sarah, who's eight."

After burgers, a spinach salad, and two bottles of wine, they went inside. The living room ran the depth of the house and had a field stone fireplace against a sidewall and a large picture window looking out at the flower garden on the front wall. It also had a cathedral ceiling with sky light windows. An overstuffed floral sofa faced the picture window while two recliners were in front of the fireplace.

After seating themselves on the sofa, Bill attempted to make his presentation. But after laughing uncontrollably on the first two slides, he stopped and said, "I can't do this now."

"Too much wine, I guess," Sharon said, laughing. "So tell me what's going on with corporate politics? Is Dave going to win and bury Gene in the process? Is strategic planning going to redefine our priorities and potentially our jobs? Oh tell me, Great Sage, you who have found an inside track to the Kingdom of Knowledge."

"Where do I begin? Yes, strategic planning is going to redefine our priorities and, indeed, our jobs. Yes, Dave is going to win, at least in the short term. I don't know if he'll bury Gene in the process, unless Gene gets in Dave's way, then, yes. Now, could I have another drink?"

"Sure, but before you get too drunk, tell me what politics I should play. Should I cultivate Dave or join Ralph in spying for Gene? Ralph was hinting he might need some help in tracking information."

"Too late, I'm already drunk. Seriously, though, you should play both sides for the time being, without over-committing to either. Things will be much clearer following the Executive Conference. There's likely to be a head-on confrontation between Dave and Gene next week. The comparative sales analysis presentation is clearly going to suggest that resources need to be re-allocated from Domestic to International and, obviously, Gene is going to resist that."

"Will you keep me posted? I really need this job."

About an hour later, Bill passed out on the sofa. It was 3:45 a.m. when he awoke and made his way to his car. He drove straight to the Farmington Inn and checked in at 4:15, leaving specific instructions to be awakened at 6:30. As he fell asleep, he thought of Sharon and how positive she was, the antithesis of Susan.

Chapter 9

Adam Rosenberg, one of the new leaders of the "me" generation, was born and raised on the West Coast. He was a small man at five-foot six-inches tall and one hundred thirty pounds. With his large ears and nose, he was not particularly attractive, but he was intelligent, just not as much as he thought; which he proved on a regular basis by underestimating his opponents. He'd run into Gene at American Labs where he had been a Division General Manager until an accusation of sexual harassment from a brand manager surfaced. He denied it, of course; however, the woman's husband had hired a private investigator that had sent convincing pictures to the American Lab's board. Gene had been assigned the task of negotiating Adam's quiet and amicable departure, which the board paid top dollar for.

Two years after joining TFC, Gene introduced Adam to Willis with a good deal of pre-selling. Willis was instantly impressed with Adam's intellect, but somewhat disturbed by his laid-back style and causal demeanor. In any case, Adam had been hired six years ago and was forever indebted to Gene.

"Hello, Adam, when are you and your team arriving?" Gene asked in an impatient tone.

"Hi, Gene, probably Sunday night, why do you ask?"

"I need to see a copy of your presentation. Dave Liberwitz is fostering a comparative new –store sales project, which Willis has completely bought into. And Adam, it's imperative that you have some answers ready for the relatively poor performance of new company-owned stores, especially in Region Three, and California in particular."

"Relax, Gene, what are you talking about? The agenda doesn't have a comparative sales analysis presentation by anyone. As far as California is concerned, as I explained at the quarterly review, it's just a short-term problem due to the growing Hispanic population's preference for spicy Mexican foods. Our new extra spicy original recipe should solve the new-store sales," Adam said in his normal relaxed tone.

"God Damn it, Adam! Listen! You've got to take this seriously! Time to get your team together and come up with some logical and convincing explanations, in presentation form, by Tuesday morning. Is that clear?"

"Yes, it's clear!"

Rosenberg was convinced that Willis would get over this strategic planning in short order. He attributed Gene's overreaction to his preoccupation with his wife's cancer.

★★★

"So when are you going to get me my insider information?" Inoue barked into the telephone receiver.

"Ah, good morning to you, too," Saji said, as he sat up in bed and rubbed his eyes. It was 6:15. "So how soon do you need the information and what in particular are you looking for?"

"I'm leaving for the States in ten days, so I need the information by then. Specifically, what I need is TFC Japan's new-store site plans and their most recent audited financial statements. Over time, I'd also like a copy of the joint venture agreement between TFC U.S. and Mitsugawa Trading," Inoue said calmly.

"You must be joking! I can't possibly establish a mole within TFC Japan in ten days—ten weeks would be more like it," Saji said defensively.

"Saji kun, I must have this information, at least the new store sites, in ten days. I know you are very resourceful when you put your mind to it. Besides—"

"—My friend, I can't possibly meet this deadline."

"As I was about to say, it would be worth twenty-five million yen to me, and that's just to start."

Twenty-five million yen was what Saji made on two eliminations of important targets, including torture and guaranteed disappearance. "Hmmm, you've raised the ante to the point that I'll make this my top priority. Can we agree on an effort fee of three million yen?" Saji asked gingerly.

"No, it's twenty-five million or nothing; however, if you can get it to me in nine days, there is a five –million yen bonus," Inoue said as he hung up the phone.

★★★

Bill arrived at the office with a head that ached from alcohol. It was already 9:30.. According to the operator at the Inn, he slept through wake-up calls at 6:30, 7:00, and 7:30, and now he was feeling anxious, due to his impending presentation and the lack of sleep.

As he was pouring over his presentation, Sharon stuck her head in the door. "So, how are you feeling this fine morning, champ?"

"Somewhere between dead and wishing I was."

"Well, I feel somewhat responsible, so why don't you stop by my office this afternoon around four and let me hear your presentation. I'll give you an honest critique. Don't laugh, but I was president of the speech club in college," Sharon said with a smile, her dimples dominating her face.

"That's a deal. I'll stop by around four, and listen, I appreciate the offer. In fact, I can use all the help I can get."

After his third dry run, Sharon took a deep breath and said, "You're getting better, Bill. However, you've got to relax and not refer to your notes as much. You know the material forward and backward, so don't try so hard to memorize specific words."

"Can you give me a specific example?" Bill asked, wrinkling his forehead.

"Sure, take the slide that compares U.S. franchisee stores growth versus International; it's the fourth or fifth slide I think."

"It's the sixth."

"See, that's how well you know the material. Now, without looking at the script, tell me what the key points are," she said, removing the papers from his hand.

"Simply stated, International franchisee sales growth is five times higher than the U.S., and Japan franchisee sales are up over

40 percent, and the U.S. Western Region, Domestic's largest, is actually down by five."

"See, that's exactly right. There's no need to say more or try to memorize detailed numbers while reading from your notes. Just relax and be yourself."

The fourth and final dry run went very well.

"Hey, what are your plans for dinner? I'd like to reciprocate for last night."

"What about your family?" Sharon asked, raising her eyebrows.

"Susan and I are separated, and next weekend is mine with Sarah."

"In that case, sure, what did you have in mind?"

★★★

Sharon arrived at Frankie's Italian Bistro ten minutes late, which had Bill wondering if she had changed her mind. He was nursing a Johnnie Walker Black and Seven when she arrived.

Dressed in a blue skirt and a red polo shirt, she was stunning. Her long blonde hair flowed over her shoulders, and her legs were long and tanned.

"Sorry I'm late, but I had trouble getting the car started. I guess I've got to break down and get a new battery," Sharon said, taking the chair opposite Bill.

After ordering a bottle of Chianti and a plate of antipasto, Bill said, "So when you're not working in your garden, what do you do for fun?"

"Well, my two loves are sailing and horseback riding."

"Really? I love to ride horses, too. How did you get into those two sports?"

"My dad was the captain of a destroyer during World War II, and from the time I could walk he took me sailing almost every weekend. During the winter, we switched from sailing to horseback riding. Dad was a real cowboy before the war," she said, taking a sip of her wine.

"What did your mom do when you guys were out sailing or riding?" Bill asked, chuckling.

"My mom died in childbirth."

Distressed, Bill leaned over and said, "My God, I'm sorry, I had no idea."

"How could you? Don't worry. I never knew her, although my father always sang her praises. I gather she was quite the woman and a wonderful gardener, as well."

"How about you? How did you get into horseback riding?" Sharon asked, as the waitress arrived.

"Excuse me," she said. "Have you decided yet?"

"I always have the lasagna, but the linguini with white clam sauce is also excellent," Bill offered.

"Lasagna is my favorite too as well, but I don't eat it very often. Got to watch the scale."

"In that case, we'll have two lasagnas please," Bill said, returning the menus to the waitress. "As far as watching the scale, you've got nothing to worry about."

Blushing slightly, Sharon asked, "Back to how you got into horse-back riding?"

"Well, after the war, my father joined the Foreign Service where he served for twenty years. When he retired, we moved to Kentucky, where he became a political science professor. Right behind our house was a farmer who raised Icelandic horses, and I would go over every day after school and help him with his farm chores. In exchange, he taught me how to ride, and when I was sixteen he gave me a mare."

It was 10:30 before they finished dinner and left.

What a bright woman! Bill thought. *She's quick, fun, and probably the most beautiful woman I've ever known. This may be going somewhere.*

★★★

"Good morning and welcome," Willis said, looking around the auditorium. "This conference is a critical turning point for our company. The world we live and compete in is rapidly changing, and the rate of change will only accelerate." He adjusted his glasses and continued. "I'm absolutely convinced that our way forward is through strategic planning.

"While it's recently become a popular concept, strategic planning has actually been around in one form or another since antiquity. Even Aristotle discussed the paramount importance of strategy. Today, however, strategic planning has become highly sophisticated and disciplined, involving many new analytical techniques and computer technology."

Willis paused to gauge the reaction of the audience. Only a few seemed to be paying attention; most seemed bored and several even seemed to be dozing, including Rosenberg, which infuriated Willis.

Willis introduced Dave, who was dressed casually, not looking at all like an investment banker. The audience provided only sporadic, polite applause.

Bill's presentation did get everyone's attention—especially those from the Domestic group. His comparison of Japan's new store growth of 41% versus the decline in California of 5.5% generated complete silence. Rosenberg just slumped in his seat.

During the break Willis walked up to Bill and putting his enormous right hand on his shoulder "That was a great presentation," Willis told Bill. "It was concisely delivered and nailed the key points. Well done. I expect good things from you."

As Dave walked up, Willis continued, "Why don't we have lunch together today? Isn't the lunch hour set aside for breakout meetings today?"

"Yes Sir, there's no formal lunch today. What did you have in mind?" Dave asked, raising his eyebrows.

Looking at his watch, Willis said, "Let's say twelve-thirty at the Corner House. You're invited too, Bill."

★★★

Lunch at the Corner House was surprisingly non-business related. Willis asked Bill about his background and seemed genuinely interested in his being raised overseas.

"So, which country did you like the best?" Willis asked.

"Well, I think I enjoyed Japan the most, then Holland."

"Why? They're so different."

"Well, the Japanese treated Americans with great respect, as the victors of the war. This was true even in the early sixties. I'll never forget when a neighborhood kid threw a rock at me and knocked me off my bike. I went home and told my mother and our gardener. That evening, the gardener showed up at the Consul General Residence with a policeman, the boy who threw the rock, and the boy's parents. They all apologized for the incident and begged my father's forgiveness. The policemen said the boy, who was twelve years old, would be arrested, arraigned, and punished.

The boy's father added that the boy's bicycle would be sold and he would be forced to quit the school's baseball team. My father and I were shocked. My father told the policemen that he did not want the boy to face any legal consequences."

"They sure have discipline, don't they?" Dave said. "It's precisely what's driving their current economic miracle. In fact, I'm willing to bet that Japan will become the second largest economy in the world by 1990."

"How did your father happen to be posted in Japan in the first place?" Willis asked.

"He was part of naval intelligence during the war. In fact, he was part of the team that broke the Japanese naval code."

"Really? That's what allowed the U.S. to be successful at the battle of Midway," Willis interjected.

"Well, after the war, Dad was part of MacArthur's staff. He tells the story of how a Japanese student broke into MacArthur's compound and took down the American flag and began to burn it before the Marine guards could get to him. The next morning, MacArthur received a visit from the Minister of Foreign Affairs who wanted to know whether he wanted the student hung or shot. Talk about discipline and respect."

"Wow, that's an amazing story," Willis said, as he finished his glass of wine.

"I was born and raised in Wisconsin, just outside of Green Bay," Willis said, signaling the waiter. "My father was an entrepreneur who owned a local construction company and believed that all of his six kids should learn to work, and work hard. It worked for me; I couldn't wait to go off to college.

"I was a sales manager at the Guttenberg wine and spirits company when the war broke out. I remember my three brothers and I enlisted in the Marines together on December 10, 1941. The line at the local recruiting station was long, and we waited six hours before we got to the front. We served in the Pacific and each of us took part in the invasions at Guadalcanal, Saipan, and finally Okinawa. My eldest brother, Stan, was killed on Saipan and younger brother, Phil, on Okinawa. My God, those Japs fought to the very end." Willis was obviously moved by the memories of his lost brothers.

When the waiter arrived, Willis ordered a martini straight up, something he rarely did at lunch.

"In any case, after the war I went to Dartmouth. They had a special endowment from a former Marine to provide graduate school for Marine non-com veterans, and as a Staff Sergeant, I qualified. Apparently, this benefactor was a Gunnery Sergeant in the Spanish American War and went on to become a Lt. Colonel in World War One, and then a real estate tycoon in Boston."

Willis took a sip of his martini and popped an olive in his mouth. "After grad school, I joined International Foods as Director of Sales for their mid-western region; then I went on to Canada as General Manager for four years. Canada Cheese Foods hired me away in 1954, as Vice President of Sales, and then Group Executive of their processed cheese division in 1959, where I stayed until 1966 when TFC's Chairmen and CEO, William Simmons, hired me as President and COO. When Simmons retired in 1971, I became CEO. Not very glamorous, but there you have it."

As Willis and Dave walked back to Dave's car, Willis said, "Well, that young man has enormous potential. How are we going to develop him and keep him interested? Should we be considering sending him to Tokyo as CFO?"

Chapter 10

The Osaka Bachelorboy Club was on the top floor of the Nomura Hotel. It provided a spectacular view of the city from almost any seat in the Club. An enormous teak bar was in the center of the Club for those customers who preferred to be unattended by hostesses. The hostesses included two foreigners and six Japanese, all in their twenties and wearing provocative clothing.

Weaving slightly, the short, overweight, sixty-something year-old General Manager of Tadashi Bank approached the Mama San of the Club. "Yuko Chan, I want to take that blonde foreign girl with me to Hong Kong," he said, smiling, as he pointed toward Lisa.

"Oh, Akiba Hon Bucho, I have the perfect escort for you," the Mama San said, laughing, as she led the tipsy customer to his waiting limo. "She's from Australia and is only eighteen—almost a virgin."

"No, I want Lisa! I'm leaving for Hong Kong at nine o'clock Friday morning. Have her at the airport by eight; my Sales Manager will be at the Japan Airline counter." Weaving further and shaking his finger, he added, "I'll make it worth your while, Yuko Chan. Don't let me down."

After he left, the Mama San headed over to the table where Lisa was hosting a group of young managers from Dantori whiskey. Lisa was serving a three hundred dollar bottle of cognac while trying to manage probing hands that were determined to slip up her short red dress. "Now behave, Masuzawa San," she said, removing the young salesman's hand from her lap.

Red-faced, the young salesman said in broken English, "'Bato I lobu you." He promptly returned his hand to Lisa's thigh and began to slip it up her skirt.

"Now, Masuzawa San, you know the rules," the Mama San said, smiling. "Besides, it's two a.m. and time to close," she added, putting the $1,100 tab in front of the senior member of the group.

Lisa had lost ten pounds since arriving at Saji's penthouse in Osaka, and her face showed the cumulative stress and fatigue. In the four weeks she had been held hostage by Saji, she had had only two modeling jobs, and both of those verged on pornographic. But with one of Saji's men constantly around her, she couldn't escape.

"Lisa, I have a wonderful opportunity for you," the Mama San said. "It involves traveling to Hong Kong with one of our most valued and generous customers, Akiba Hon Bucho," she added, smiling.

Lisa rolled her eyes as she considered how to get out of this trip with the roly-poly bank manager who always talked too loud and had horrible breath. "Don't you think Akiba Hon Bucho would be happier with Debbie? After all, she's younger and prettier than me," Lisa added hopefully.

"No, Akiba Hon Bucho insists on you. I offered him Susan but he said no. Besides, a couple of days in Hong Kong will be fun. I'm sure he'll give you plenty of money for shopping.

My God, what am I going to do! Lisa thought. *I've got to find a way to escape, and soon. I can't take much more of this!*

★★★

Dave spent the afternoon presenting the principles and processes involved in producing accurate strategic plans. He pointed out that while the principles themselves were relatively easy and straightforward, sticking to them was another matter altogether. He explained the steps in the *Logic Loop* and the critical importance of understanding the business' competitive environment and identifying and addressing the current *Key Drivers* deriving from that competitive environment.

★★★

The phone message light was on when Ray returned to his room, so he pushed the button to call the operator.

"Good afternoon, how can I help you?" the operator asked in a pleasant voice. Ray's interest increased at the sexy voice.

"Hello, Doll, my phone message light was on."

"Mr. Easton?" the operator said tentatively.

"In the flesh. So what's my message, Doll?"

"It's from a Mr. Saji of Osaka Japan and it reads: 'Ray San, please call me at 81-052-789-4450 as soon as you get this message. I have a time sensitive opportunity for you!'"

"Hmmm, could you place that call for me?" Ray asked.

"Of course, Mr. Easton, let me see if I can reach Mr. Saji and I'll call you back."

"Thanks Dear, I'll be waiting."

Ten minutes later, the phone rang. "Hello, Mr. Easton, I have Mr. Saji for you."

"Ah, Ray San, how would you like to make fifty thousand dollars?" Saji asked smoothly.

"Come on, Saji San, is this a joke? You're such a cheap—I mean frugal—guy. What do I have to do to earn fifty grand?"

"Simple. Get me a copy of TFC Japan's new store site selection file in the next three days," Saji said evenly.

"Why would you want that?"

"I'm afraid I can't share that with you," Saji said causally, "but I've already transferred the funds to a Swiss bank account in your name."

Ray realized that was equivalent to six months' salary—and it was tax-free. "Okay Saji San, let me see what I can do. Is this a one-time opportunity or a permanent relationship?"

Saji smiled to himself as he realized that someday Ray's greed was going to be his demise. "Ray San, let's see how you do with this assignment first. If all goes well, and on time, perhaps I'll have another project for you."

"How do I access my Swiss bank account?"

"When I receive the materials, I'll give you the account number and password," Saji said, and then hung up. Saji wondered whether fifty thousand was too much, given how easily Ray took the bait.

Ray, on the other hand, was ecstatic at his unexpected good fortune. He considered how these extra funds would allow him to double his stake in the Hawaiian condo deal. He also tried to figure out who would be interested enough to pay fifty thousand dollars.

"Hi, Doll, it's me again," Ray said. "I need to make another call to Japan," he said, pausing to look at his watch, "in about three hours. Are you still going to be on duty?"

"I'm sorry, Mr. Easton, but I'm off in ten minutes."

"Great, can I interest you in dinner? Then perhaps you could help; I'm no good at international calls."

Taken aback, the operator was apparently considering the situation. Finally, she said, "So what specifically did you have in mind, Mr. Easton?" Her voice sounded coy.

"Doll, call me Ray. Book a table for two at Mama Roselle's in my name for, say, seven-thirty. I'll meet you in the lobby in fifteen minutes."

"How will I know who you are?"

"I'm the good-looking one with a Navy blue sports coat and an apricot ascot. Besides, I know you're the gorgeous redhead with green eyes. See you in a few," Ray said. He hung up and headed to the shower.

★★★

The Wednesday morning sessions of the conference were a disaster. TFC Domestic was up first. Gene kicked things off with a financial review that confirmed the results included in the comparative sales analysis Bill had presented Tuesday.

"Actual year-to-date profit performance is even worse than anticipated," he said, pausing. "We're eighteen percent off budget and twelve below prior year."

Rosenberg got up next to present the marketing programs that were supposedly going to make the second half possible. Five minutes into his presentation, Willis stood up, red-faced, and shouted, "Adam, sit down and stop embarrassing yourself, and quit playing this audience for idiots!"

"But, Mr. Willis…" Rosenberg stammered.

"I said sit down, Adam," Willis said icily.

Rosenberg had a look of disbelief on his face as he returned to his seat.

Next up was Ralph with International's numbers, and they were nothing short of remarkable. Every international market was up over budget and double digits ahead of prior year.

Gene suspected Dave Liberwitz had a hand in Ralph's presentation, as it was far superior to anything else Ralph had ever presented before. It was concise, logical, and clear.

Jim Meyer followed with an overview of all the major international markets, and when he finished the Japanese overview, Willis stood up and said, "Now, that's what I call strategic success. Ray, Kenji, good for you both. That's a remarkable performance. Perhaps you guys would be willing to stop in Nashville on your way home and share some of your secrets with Domestic."

The Domestic team winced. Adam Rosenberg was beet red. He considered getting up and walking out.

★★★

After lunch, Bill went to his room to make arrangements to pick up Sarah. It was his weekend and he hadn't seen his daughter since returning from Japan. The phone rang and rang with no answer. That was unusual for the lunch hour, since "All My Children," Susan's favorite soap opera, was on. *Come on Susan, answer the fucking phone!*

Then he dialed Carmen's line in the hospitality suite.

"Hi, Carmen, Bill Sanford here. I was wondering if you could do me a favor and call my wife later this afternoon and let her know I'm not going to my daughter's ballet recital."

"No problem, Mr. Sanford. I'll be happy to deliver the message."

"Thanks, and please call me Bill."

"You're welcome, Mr. Sanford."

★★★

"Mr. Willis, could I grab a minute of your time?" Rosenberg asked outside of the conference room.

"Not now, Adam. I'll be down to Nashville next week and we'll have plenty of time to talk then."

"But, Mr. Willis—" Rosenberg started to plead.

"—Next week, Adam," Willis said, as he walked away.

Next it was Gene who accosted Willis. "Stuart (Gene was the only person in the company to address Willis as Stuart), I want to set up that meeting with Jim Meyer, Ralph, Easton, and Kenji Kato to discuss the new store policy violations. When will you be available?"

"Relax, Gene, Dave Liberwitz and I are planning an international tour next month, and I'll have a discussion with Ray in Tokyo," Willis said in an even tone. "I'll also meet with Ozawa of Mitsugawa and express my concern that our head office policies are not being followed.

"Although, as Sanford pointed out in his audit report, the joint venture agreement requires the approval of only the local board. In the meantime, write up a memo of reprimand, if you like, addressed to Easton and copy Jim Meyer, Ralph, Sanford, myself, and Dave Liberwitz."

"Why Liberwitz?" Gene snapped.

"Gene, I'm getting tired of your whining about Dave. I hand-selected him, and he's part of my succession plan. Take my advice and establish a productive and good relationship with him. Right now.

"Work with him, and you'll learn a ton in the process and secure your own future. Don't waste your time trying to defend Rosenberg; his performance is appalling. He's clearly demonstrating he's nothing more than a West Coast prima donna, and I'm damn tired of it! He better get onside now or he's out!" Willis said, his face turning red as he walked away.

Gene couldn't believe the exchange he'd just had with Willis. He wondered how things could have changed so fast and so drastically. In any case, he had to preserve his own position, and if that meant distancing himself from Adam and endearing himself to Liberwitz, so be it. With Meredith's illness not responding well to the chemo, he had to maintain the stability that TFC offered. Willis would be supportive if the worst came, and a new employer would definitely not.

Gene went off to find Liberwritz.

★★★

Bill stopped by the reception desk looking for Carmen. "Hi, were you able to get that message to my wife?" Bill asked lightly.

"I'm sorry, Mr. Sanford, I've tried all afternoon, but no answer."

"Well, I've got some time before dinner, so I'll just swing by the house. The phone is probably out of order," Bill said with a casualness he didn't feel.

He found the house locked with Susan's car in the garage. When he entered, not a single light was on. He went into the kitchen.

"Susan, where are you?" There was no answer, so he headed upstairs to the bedroom.

There was no sign of Susan or Sarah anywhere, and he began to panic. He noticed a partially open drawer, and when he looked, he discovered it was empty.

He quickly searched all the bedrooms and found that most of the clothes belonging to Sarah and Susan were missing.

"What the fuck!" he shouted.

When he went back downstairs, he found a note on the dining room table:

> *Bill, I've taken Sarah with me to my parents. I refuse to spend any more time in Connecticut, pretending that we might reconcile. If you want to continue the reconciliation process then you're going to have to come to Youngsville and take the job that Daddy's friend has for you. If you won't do this, then we're through!*
>
> *Susan*

Bill just stood there staring at the note, unable to believe what he was reading, and the more he thought about it, the madder he got. How could she possibly just leave and take Sarah with her without a word?

"God Damn it! This is the last straw. There is no fucking way things are going to work out. How do I get custody of Sarah!" he said out loud, shaking with anger.

★★★

When Bill returned to his room, there was a message to call Dave Liberwitz.

"Hello, Dave, Bill Sanford here. You called?" Bill said glumly.

"Yeah, I called, but what's the matter? You sound like you've been in a fight." Dave asked with concern.

"Well, it's a personal problem."

"Okay, but if you feel you want to talk, you know how to reach me."

After thinking about it for a second, Bill blurted out, "My wife took my daughter and left town, leaving me an *or else* note."

"Or else what?"

"Her father in Texas has a buddy at a CPA firm who will give me a job with partner potential within three years. Susan is very close to her family and desperately wants to move home."

"Well, how do you feel about it?"

"I've absolutely no interest in returning to public accounting," Bill said, louder than he intended. "Frankly, even if I did, I'd never consider living in the same state as her father, never mind the next town over. I've always been committed to an international career, and Susan knew that from day one. Hell, I was a foreign-service brat for the first fifteen years of my life."

"Well, I'm afraid you're in for a rough patch here for awhile," Dave offered. "I've been there myself, and I can tell you the good news is that it will eventually end. All but the children, that is. That's the really tough part.

"Listen, you can skip the social functions for the rest of the conference if you like. I'll clear it with Willis and Jim. And remember, I meant what I said. I'm available to talk anytime you want. Sometimes it helps to talk to someone who has been through it."

"Well, I really appreciate all of that, and I'll see how I feel, then make up my mind about the social events. Also, I'm sure I'll take you up on your offer to talk, once I've figured out what I'm going to do. By the way, do you know a good divorce attorney?"

Chapter 11

"Finally! Where the fuck have you been, I've been trying to get you for sixteen hours," Ray fumed, when Fumiko answered the phone.

"So sorry, Ray San, but Sam Sugarmen's going away party was last night, and—"

"Never mind about Sugarmen," Ray said, composing himself. "I need you to get to the office right away and make copies of the new store site selection file. Include only those stores considered in the past six months. Also, make sure no one else is at the office. Do you understand?"

Fumiko was confused, wondering why Ray wanted her to make copies of these files, thinking perhaps that he wanted her to translate them. "Ray, do you want me to translate the individual store site assessments? Also, what am I to do with these documents, and why do I have to wait until I'm sure the office is empty? Although I do have your key."

I better calm her down, and distract her. "Fumichan, how would you like to meet me in Hawaii Saturday? You could just bring the copied files with you. We'll stay at the Sheraton on Waikiki."

"Oh, Ray, are you serious! I would love to go to Hawaii on Saturday. Should I book the hotel, a suite?"

"Absolutely a suite, and since you'll arrive about four hours before me, go buy some nice sexy things, on my nickel of course,"

Ray said, looking at his watch. *Time to wrap this up and get ahold of Saji to set up a pickup time for day after tomorrow.*

"Oh, Ray, I'm so happy! I will show you how happy Saturday night," Fumiko squealed.

"I'm sure we'll have fun. Now don't forget, all new store site surveys over the past six months, as well as the summary report. Don't worry about translating them. And, Fumiko, be careful and say nothing to anyone about this—understand?"

"Of course—and thank you so much for this wonderful surprise!" Fumiko said excitedly.

★★★

Thursday was a long, tedious, and generally uninspiring day. It was filled with presentations from every corporate staff department, from human resources to marketing. Most of the senior group was absent. Rosenberg was there, however, looking frustrated and preoccupied. He still couldn't believe that Willis had been sold on strategic planning. The idea that there might be something in the competitive environment that could magically solve their problems seemed nonsense to Rosenberg.

After the coffee break at 10:30, the balance of the senior team arrived.

Up first was a forty-minute presentation by the Director of Market Research for the Domestic Group. "So, that is the top line of our recent U.S. Usage and Attitudes study. Are there any questions?"

Dave Liberwitz stood and asked, "Isn't that a significant increase in unaided awareness, and the *best value* rating for Aunt Sally Mae's Southern Fried Chicken, especially in the North East?"

"Well, yes, I guess that would be a fair characterization," the Market Research Director said, avoiding Rosenberg's stare.

"Come on now, don't be shy. What is the exact improvement in Aunt Sally Mae's ratings, and where's it coming from?"

"Well, let me see…ah yes, here it is. Aunt Sally Mae's unaided awareness increased from eleven percent to eighteen percent, and their *best value* rating increased from twenty-eight percent to forty-two percent. No, this can't be right," he said in a confused tone.

"Do you have the numbers for Southern California?" Dave Liberwitz continued.

"Well, let me see. Yes, here they are. In Southern California, the Aunt Sally Mae's numbers were not significantly changed," he responded, visibly relieved.

"How about Mexico Lindo?"

Rosenberg was shifting in his seat and looking very uncomfortable. *Where are all these questions coming from? Doesn't that prick realize we are in the fried chicken business!* he said to himself as he glanced over to look at Willis.

"Umm, we don't consider Mexico Lindo a direct competitor, so our information is limited. We only have it on a state-wide basis."

"That's okay; tell us what you've got on a state-wide basis then," Dave said in a relaxed tone.

"Let's see, here it is. Mexico Lindo's unaided awareness was—wait this has to be an error!"

"Go ahead. I'm sure it isn't," Dave said, smiling.

"Mexico Lindo's unaided awareness increased from twenty-two percent to thirty-seven percent last year, and *best value* rating increased from twenty-six percent to sixty-eight percent," the Marketing Research Director said, his shoulders slumping. When he looked over at his boss, Rosenberg just glared.

"And our numbers in the state of California did what?" Dave Liberwitz asked in an even tone.

"Our unaided awareness in California decreased from ninety-five percent to eighty-eight percent and our *best value* rating decreased from fifty-two percent to thirty-eight percent."

★★★

At the break, Bill returned to his room, where he had three messages. The first was from Dave Liberwitz asking him to meet him in his suite at three p.m.; the second was from Ralph, who asked him to call, and the third was from Sharon, inviting him to her house for dinner at seven p.m., if he didn't have other plans.

Bill decided to call Susan at her parent's house in Texas first. The phone rang six times before Susan's father answered. Bill almost hung up.

"Hello, Sam, is Susan there?" Bill asked, clearly annoyed.

"Bill, is that you?" Sam asked with a southern drawl.

"None other, Sam."

"Well listen, Son, I know y'all are having a few problems. But hell, you can solve all of this by coming on down to Youngsville and accepting that big job my ole buddy, Ron McDonald, has for you," Susan's father continued in his southern drawl.

Bill could not help laughing as the image of Ronald MacDonald popped into his mind. *Imagine me working for a clown in nowhere Texas,* he thought.

"What y'all laughing about?" Sam asked with obvious anger.

"Sorry, Sam, the image of Ronald MacDonald just popped into my head. In any case, is Susan there?"

"Yeah she's here all right, but she don't want to talk to you until y'all agree to come on down and meet with Ron," Sam said in a matter-of-fact manner.

"Son, you know Suzy just wants to come on home and be close to her people. After all, she's been away over six years. And let me tell you something about them Japs," Sam said in a lecturing tone. "I fought them sons-a-bitches all over the pacific in World War Two. You just can't trust them people. The last place you'd want to move is Japan," Sam added emphatically.

Bill could not believe what he had just heard. *How could anybody be so narrow-minded and bigoted in 1975? Sam is just one of those nouveau riche Texans who struck oil and had more money than he knew what to do with. It just proves money can't make a person something he is not.*

"Listen, Sam, under no circumstances am I moving to Texas to work for Ronald MacDonald or anyone else. Now, you can tell Susan for me she has exactly two days to come back to our house or I will sue for divorce!" Bill yelled. He hung up the phone before Sam could respond.

★★★

Bill arrived at Dave Liberwitz's suite right at three p.m. The suite was huge with a dining room table, a fully stocked wet bar, two large maroon leather recliners, and an overstuffed sofa. The walls were done in rust and yellow. There was a full kitchen and a balcony with a table and four chairs. Bill had been impressed with his own suite, but this was essentially a two-bedroom penthouse apartment.

"Hi, Bill, come on in," Dave Liberwitz said with a smile. He led Bill onto the balcony. "So, how are you doing?"

"Oh, I'm all right."

"How are things on the home front?"

"Well, I think I'm going to get divorced," Bill said in a matter-of-fact tone. "And you know, I feel okay about it. In fact, I feel relieved. My only concern is how I'm going to maintain a relationship with Sarah. I'm determined to at least try for joint custody, but I know Susan's father will have none of it."

"From my personal experience, the one thing I can recommend is to avoid becoming a Santa Clause Dad."

Raising his eyebrows, Bill asked, "What exactly do you mean?"

"Well, from my experience, it's necessary to have extended periods of time with your children if you want to have a meaningful impact on their lives without constantly trying to win their short-term favor," Dave said, leaning forward in his chair and putting his fingers together.

Bill had a concentrated look as he reflected on what Dave had just said.

Heading for the wet bar, Dave said, "What can I get you?"

"A Johnnie Black and Seven please."

"I see there's plenty left to teach you," Dave said, laughing. "First, Scotch is never served mixed with anything but water, and then only a splash," Dave added, handing Bill a glass of Johnnie Black with a splash of water.

After taking a sip, Bill crinkled his nose. "I'd get drunk too quickly on this."

After sitting down, Dave said, "Turning to business, I've a proposition for you. How would you like to be my Director of Strategic Planning? It's a grade eighteen position and, as such, comes with a grant of one thousand stock options and a fifteen percent target bonus in the Management Compensation Plan. The base salary is thirty-six thousand," Dave said, pausing to allow Bill to consider the offer. "Now, I know Ralph has offered you the Director of Financial Planning position. It's up to you to decide—either way I understand."

"I accept!" Bill almost yelled. "When do I start and what is the job description? By the way, you realize I know nothing about strategic planning?" Bill added.

"Relax! Strategic planning is basically common sense. I'll teach you everything you need to know," Dave said, smiling. "You start tomorrow; in fact, it will be announced at lunch. Now, read this over the weekend and develop a list of questions for Monday." Dave handed Bill a book, *Strategic Planning Made Simple*, by Steve Johnson and David B. Liberwitz.

Dave continued, "Welcome aboard! I promise you won't regret it. Now, here are a couple of business cards. This first one is for a Jonathan Frank, a very good psychologist in Hartford. He's great to talk to about marital problems, which he specializes in. The second one is for a good, reasonable divorce attorney in Avon, my first cousin, Sam Liberwitz. I have personally used them both, and they are great.

"Now go get some sleep if you can, and I'll see you tomorrow morning at nine a.m. for the International breakout sessions, beginning with Japan." Dave got up, signaling the meeting was over. It was exactly 3:20 p.m.

Bill called the front desk and asked for a call at 6:30 p.m. He then called Sharon and accepted her invitation to dinner, saying he would be there between 7:30 and 8:00, and he had a whole lot of news to tell her. Finally, he got undressed and got into bed for a long overdue sleep. He slept through the wakeup call at 6:30, but not Ralph's repeated knocking at 7:00.

"How could you accept Dave Liberwitz's offer without talking to me first!" Ralph exploded.

"Relax, Ralph. You know where this company is headed as well as I do. I'd be an idiot not to take the Director of Strategic Planning job. Besides, now you have a loyal friend on the inside of strategic planning," Bill said reassuringly. "Now, I've got an important meeting to get to, and I need a shower first, so I'll see you tomorrow at the regional breakout meetings," Bill said, as he closed the door and headed to the shower. He would not miss working for the ever-volatile Turk.

Ralph could not believe how quickly and dramatically things could change. He reflected on the fact that six months ago, no one outside of his department had ever heard of Bill Sanford and, today, he was the Director of Strategic Planning and was treating Ralph like a peer.

★★★

It was 8:10 when Bill arrived at Sharon's house. He'd stopped on the way to pick up some wine and flowers. He debated whether or not to bring flowers, but in the end picked up a dozen pink roses.

After all, I'm almost single and it actually feels pretty good.

"Hi, these are for you," Bill said, handing Sharon the flowers and the bottle of Dom Perignon.

"For me!" she said with mock surprise. "What's the occasion?"

"You're talking to the new Director of Strategic Planning," Bill said, beaming with pride.

"Congratulations!" Sharon said, as she kissed him. The first serious kiss she had given him.

When Bill entered, he found the formal dining room table set for two, with candles burning. Sharon was wearing a short red dress.

"I hope you like roast beef and Yorkshire pudding," she said with a smile.

★★★

"*Moshi moshi*, is Ozawa San there? Ray Easton calling from the United States."

"Oh Easton San, Ozawa San is in a board meeting. Can you call back in thirty minutes, or is there a message for him?" Hiroko, Mr. Ozawa's secretary, asked in good English with a small voice.

"Hiroko San, when are you going to let me take you out to dinner?"

"Oh, Easton San, you know I cannot go to dinner with you. I'm married and my husband is a sumo wrestler," Hiroko said, laughing. "Ah, Ozawa San just returned, please hold, Easton San." Hiroko's tone turned all business.

A few seconds later, Ozawa came on the line. "Hello, Ray, how is the conference going?"

"Ozawa San, we're stars! TFC Japan is leading the world in sales and the U.S. is in the tank. We've received no heat at all on the store-building program, thanks to Bill Sanford's addendums and his sales analysis presentation, although Willis is bound to say something directly to you next month when he comes to Tokyo to kick off the strategic planning process.

"Listen, Ozawa San, I'm about to head out for a dinner and I was wondering if the acquisition of the Canadian ball-bearing company was going to go forward?"

"Yes, I believe it will on Monday, although it will be an unfriendly offer of between C$12 and C$13.50 a share. Ultimately it should go for between C$15.00 and C$16.00.

Give me the dates of Mr. Willis' visit as soon as you have them, so I can mark them on my calendar. Oh, what about your plans to try and recruit support for getting Sanford San over to Japan as CFO for TFC Japan?" Ozawa added.

"I'm still working on that. Willis seemed receptive to the idea but wants Sanford to work on the new strategic plan first. He is absolutely determined to make strategic planning the catalyst of change, as he heads off for retirement. I'm sure he and Dave Liberwitz will try and pick your brain regarding Mitsugawa's own strategic plan," Ray said.

"Dave Liberwitz? How are you spelling that and who is he?" Ozawa asked.

"He is the head of strategic planning. He was scouted by Willis from Washington Consulting to manage the strategic planning process. Rumor has it he was promised he would be a key part of Willis' succession plans. Oh, and you know I can't spell."

"Dave Liberwitz, the name sounds familiar. I think he was working with International Foods on their re-negotiations with Yamato Foods, of their joint venture. A very bright and close-to-the-chest sort of guy if I remember correctly," Ozawa said reflectively.

"You're absolutely right. He gave a case study comparing International Foods' mistakes in Japan with Sam's Cola's highly successful strategies."

"Well, Ray San, let's have lunch when you and Kenji kun get back next week, and you both can tell me all about the conference and strategic planning."

When Ray got off the phone, he called his stockbroker in LA and told him to buy C$30,000 of Jacob's Industries when the Toronto Stock Exchange opened on Monday.

★★★

As Sharon served Bill his second plate of roast beef and Yorkshire pudding, Bill relayed every word Dave Liberwitz had said that afternoon.

"Grade eighteen, eh? That puts you in the senior ranks. Are you still going to be able to fraternize with us junior managers anymore?"

"Good question! We'll have to wait and see," Bill responded, laughing.

"Listen, not to bring up bad news, but rumor has it your wife has skipped town with your daughter," Sharon said gingerly, with a look of concern.

"Where'd you hear that?" Bill asked, raising his eyebrows.

"Well, let's see," Sharon said, tapping her temple with her finger. "I heard it from Ralph's secretary, who said she overheard Lindsay telling Ray Easton about it."

"Actually, it's not bad news at all. This will finally force me to take action and stop pretending things might get better. Hell, Susan has hated my career and living away from her family in Texas," Bill said, pausing to take a bite and looking into Sharon's beautiful blue eyes. "We've done nothing but fight over my job since we were in college. She knew from the get-go that I've been determined to capitalize on my international upbringing. But she's been nothing but unhappy. Taking Sarah to her parents in Texas without saying a word is the last straw, as far as I'm concerned. Hell, the affair she had last Thanksgiving should have been the last straw," Bill said, as he drained his Johnnie Walker Black on the rocks.

"Having been through this myself, I know you're in for a tough time, especially where Sarah is concerned. It's a horrible thing to say, but when it comes to divorce, the kids unfortunately become pawns in the game. Who's the lawyer Dave Liberwitz recommended?" Sharon asked, taking a sip of her wine.

She's absolutely right! There is no fucking way I'm going to win custody, and that means my little pumpkin is going to be living in Texas with Susan and that good ole boy lawyer Daddy Bucks set her up with. Bill's face turned bright red and his eyes began to water.

"Are you okay?" Sharon whispered, leaning over and taking Bill's hand in hers, as she wrinkled her brow.

"I guess I hadn't considered being separated from Sarah, until you just pointed out that kids are always pawns in divorce battles," Bill said, lowering his head as tears began to fall.

"Who says this has to be confrontational?" Sharon said, squeezing Bill's hand. "Given the affair your wife had and the repeated liaisons with her lover from Texas, she may well want this divorce more than you. Besides, nowadays joint custody is the preferred option in most states," Sharon said, flipping her hair.

"Maybe you're right," Bill said, wiping the tears from his face with a napkin. Blushing, he added, "I can't believe I broke down like this. You must think I'm—"

"I think you're a sensitive man and a caring father," Sharon said, looking directly into Bill's eyes. "In fact, for me those are your most attractive qualities," Sharon added, squeezing Bill's hand again.

"Now tell me who your lawyer is," Sharon said, smiling broadly with her dimples showing.

Regaining his composure, Bill said, "Let me see, I've got his card right here." Bill removed the card from his shirt pocket. "Sam Liberwitz. That's right, Dave's first cousin."

"Sam Liberwitz is sharp as a tack, but basically fair. He represented my ex in our divorce," Sharon said, laughing.

"What are the odds that I'd be here eating dinner and discussing my divorce with someone whose ex was represented by the first cousin of my new boss, and soon to be my attorney?"

After dinner, they retired to the den. Sharon poured them both a glass of cognac and sat right next to Bill on the sofa.

"Drink it slowly. You only get one glass tonight. I want to make sure you don't miss any more of my advances," Sharon said in a sexy voice.

They clinked their glasses and took a drink. Then they both put their glasses down and kissed, first very softly, then with more passion. After about ten minutes, Sharon got up and deliberately took Bill by the hand and led him into her bedroom. Bill started to say something, but Sharon just put her finger up to her lips and shushed him.

"Relax and enjoy," she said with a smile. She undressed him slowly, one button at a time. Then she took off her own dress and undid her bra. Her nipples were erect as she gently rubbed them against Bill's bare chest. Bill began to breathe hard. He thought he would burst and knew he couldn't hold off much longer.

"I'm, I'm going to come," he stammered.

"Yes you are, several times in fact," she whispered.

The next hour was the most memorable sex Bill had ever had. Sharon got up and went into the bathroom and took a long shower. When she returned to the bedroom, she found Bill sound asleep. She set the alarm for 6:30 a.m., turned off the light, and slipped into bed next to him, feeling completely satisfied.

Chapter 12

"Good morning. I see everyone must have had a good time last night," Dave said, as he looked around the room at the sleepy and hung-over faces. "People, we'll kick things off in Tokyo, then on to Sydney, London, Frankfort, ending in Toronto. The participants will be the Regional VPs, Country General Managers, and their direct reports. Corporate will be represented by Mr. Willis, Bill Sanford, and me; Group CEOs are intentionally excluded."

"Good idea, but why?" Ray asked. Laughter could be heard around the room.

"Because the purpose of this exercise is to see just how close the Regional Senior Management teams are to their local competition. Frankly, if you guys aren't closer to your markets than Corporate, we're all in trouble."

"That's easy," Ray said, "since Corporate knows fuck all." Laughter erupted around the room.

After the laughter died down, Dave added, "Now, it's my pleasure to announce that Bill Sanford is the newly appointed Director of Strategic Planning." There was a polite period of applause from the audience. Most did not know Bill before this conference. "Bill will be in touch with all the Regional VPs to schedule the details of the up-coming trip. In some cases, we'll want presentations from the local media and research companies, as well as any joint venture partners' senior executives. At all locations, we want to visit a random sample of new company and franchised stores, as well as stores of the top competitors."

The balance of the day was spent in individual Regional break-out meetings. It was clear that none of the Regions knew much about their competitive environment, with the exception of Kenji who had a pretty good handle on the competition.

Kenji was concerned that Aunt Sally Mae's Southern Fried Chicken was going to enter the market in a joint venture with Yotsui. He was certain this would put considerable pressure on site availability and rental prices. Ray had very little to add and seemed bored with the other Regions' reviews; this did not escape Dave's attention.

The domestic breakout meetings were a series of catastrophes. Willis was present in all of them, as were Dave, Gene, and Rosenberg. The Midwest and Southern Regions were the only ones beating prior year, and only the Southern Region was making budget.

The Southern Regional VP had been hired away from Aunt Sally Mae's Southern Fried Chicken two years before and the Midwest Regional VP had come from Mexico Lindo's eight years earlier. The other two Regional VPs were post-Rosenberg replacement hires with no prior fast-food experience. Gene gradually shifted from supporter to antagonist, as the day wore on and Willis' patience wore thin. Even the Regional VPs began to abandon Rosenberg.

At 3:00 p.m., a red-faced Willis stood up, and leaning against the podium while looking around the room, said, "In the Marine Corps we had a name for a situation like this; it was called a *cluster fuck-up* and today is the single best example I've seen since the battle of Corregidor in the Philippines.

"It's absolutely amazing that only one of four Regions is on budget, and no one seems to know why, except maybe the Director of Market Research. When I come to each of the Regional Offices in…" Willis paused.

"October fifteenth through twentieth, Mr. Willis," Dave Liberwitz said quietly.

"…in late October, I'd better have answers from every Region about their competitive environment. Also, I expect an updated estimate for the second half and how you expect to achieve it. This is outrageous!" Willis boomed, and then walked out.

Dave took over the podium. "Well, I guess we've a lot of work to do in the next six weeks to get ready for your first strategic planning meeting. I would suggest concentrating on your competitive environment and recasting your second-half forecasts. I'm sure Gene and his staff will be able to provide support on regional financials. You may also contact Bill Sanford for help on analyzing sales-analysis trends.

"Folks, this is a serious situation and needs to be addressed as your first priority. Bill will be contacting all the Regional VPs to coordinate the details of the upcoming strategic planning meetings, including agenda items that should be included, and those that should not.

★★★

"Adam, have you lost your mind?" Gene whispered in the hall. "You're going to get yourself fired, and for cause, which means you won't get a dime of severance."

"Fuck you, Gene!" Rosenberg exploded. "Where was your support in that witch hunt? You just jumped on the bandwagon, you prick," Rosenberg hissed, red faced.

"You idiot! Did you actually think you could come to this fucking meeting and spring a fifteen percent-plus shortfall of profits and say 'Don't worry, I'll make it up in the second half, and oh by the way, I don't have a clue what's causing the shortfall,'" Gene said mockingly. "You're right! I did jump on the bandwagon, and be warned, that is exactly where I'm going to stay, you self-centered son-of-a-bitch!" Gene said, loud enough to be heard by Dave Liberwitz, who just smiled as he walked by.

★★★

Fumiko and Ray were at the Sheraton on Waikiki. The suite Ray had booked was on the twenty-third floor with a panoramic view of Diamond Head. It had a curved balcony that was accessible from both the master bedroom and the living room. The bathroom had a shower and a Japanese hot tub.

After settling in to the suite they headed to the beach and ordered drinks under a private cabana. "Ray, what was that chore you had me do last week all about?" Fumiko asked. "I mean, it seemed so much like a spy movie."

Debating how to answer, Ray finished his Mai Tai and waved to the waiter for another one. "Fumichan, we have an opportunity to make a lot of money. You know that TFC corporate is going to try and force me out." Reaching over the table, Ray held Fumiko's hand and, looking directly into her eyes, added, "Fumichan, you know that if I go, so do you. Also, remember Kenji is very ambitious and would be only too happy to take over my position and fire you."

This struck a nerve with Fumiko; just last week she had overheard Kenji telling Ray that her salary was too high and causing problems among the other girls. "Ray, you know you can count on me. I'll do anything you ask, as long as you continue to take care of me," Fumiko said, smiling. "So, what are we going to do to make money? I feel like I'm in a James Bond movie," Fumiko added, wrinkling her nose.

The waiter arrived. "Mr. Easton, are you ready for your next round of drinks?"

"Sure, in a couple minutes," Ray said with a wink.

"Well, we are going to be spies," Ray said, chuckling, while squeezing Fumiko's hand. "I can't give you any specific names, but I have a friend who is working for someone else, who I don't know, who is willing to pay lots of money for confidential information from TFC Japan."

The waiter arrived with the drinks: another Mai Tai for Ray and a flute of champagne for Fumiko.

"To our new adventure," Ray said, raising his glass.

"How exciting," Fumiko said, as she sipped her champagne. She wrinkled her forehead and stared at the bottom of the flute. Suddenly she squealed. "Oh, Ray, they're beautiful!" Fumiko said, as she removed the two black pearl earrings from the flute with her spoon."

"Just like you, Fumichan," Ray said, smiling, as he handed Fumiko an envelope.

"What's this?"

"Well, it's a brokerage account with my stockbroker in Los Angles," Ray said, maintaining a straight face.

"You mean with Sherman Hosogawa, whom I get on the phone for you almost every morning?" Fumiko said, looking very confused.

"Yep, that's the one. Only this account is in your name and your first purchase of $5,000 is now worth $8,500," Ray said, grinning from ear to ear.

"Oh, Ray San, I can't believe this! I'm so happy."

Later that night, Ray said something he had never said before to any woman. "Fumichan, you were fantastic tonight, but you wore me out. I can't go again."

★★★

"Well, what can I do for you, Mr. Director of Strategic Planning?" Sharon said with a smile, as she walked into Bill's new office. It was right next door to Dave's office and was twice the size of Bill's old office. In fact, it was as big as Ralph's office. "Wow, quite the place; somebody really important must work here.

"What can I do to help? Ralph basically told me I'm seconded to you, as long as you need me during the strategic planning kickoff. Apparently, Gene told Ralph that he would send over someone from Corporate EDP to cover for me. So, I guess I'm all yours," Sharon said with that beautiful dimpled smile, winking.

"Great! We've got much to do in the next three weeks. Do you mind helping out with logistics and communication?" Bill asked.

"Seriously, Bill, I'll do anything I can to help you get this strategic planning kickoff successfully launched. Just tell me what you want me to do."

"Super! Task one is to create a matrix of all participants and locations. Human resources will provide all names and addresses of Regional VPs and their direct reports."

★★★

"Hey, Old Dear, you have only two-and-a-half hours to buy no more than one thousand shares of Jacob's Industries. It trades on the Toronto Stock Exchange under the ticker symbol JIA. Also, I can't seem to get a hold of Lindsay, so make sure she gets the same message within the next couple of hours. No more than one thousand shares, as well, and don't share this tip with anyone, okay?" Ray said.

"Ray, what are you talking about? I don't even have a brokerage account. More importantly, how risky is this stock and how long before it pays off? I don't have a lot of excess cash, especially with a divorce coming," Bill said.

"I realize your situation; that's precisely why I'm letting you in on this. The risk on this deal is zero. You will be able to flip this stock today with a fifty to sixty percent gain and one hundred-plus gain within a month. Now, get a pen and write this down: Sherman Hosogawa, 713-428-5581. Sherman works for Stern Investments and is my U.S. broker. I will call him when we get off the phone and ask him to open an account for you, and I will guarantee the cash on this transaction until you get your own funds wired. In the meantime, you get to your bank and have them wire transfer to your Stern Investments account the cash to cover your trade. This is a sure thing, but get busy, you now have about two hours and fifteen minutes before the announcement is made that's going to cause this stock to pop," Ray said and hung up.

Is this guy for real? How can he possibly know that a particular stock is going to pop on the basis of an announcement? Still, if he's right, it could be found money, which I could certainly use with the divorce coming, Bill thought. He then wandered down to Jim Meyer's office looking for Lindsay. He got there as Lindsay was coming out of Jim's office with her dictation pad.

"Oh, hi Bill, what can I do for you? Do you need to see Jim?"

"Hi Lindsay, I just got off the phone with Ray and I have an urgent message for you. Can you come down to my office for a minute?"

"Sure, I'll be right down."

Bill related the conversation he'd had with Ray, including the one thousand-share limit. "So, what do you think, Lindsay? Are you going to buy this stock?"

"Absolutely! I have never lost a penny on Ray's tips. In fact, my average return has been one hundred percent-plus and my lowest twenty-five percent."

When Lindsay left, Bill called Sharon and asked her to drop by for a second.

"What, more tasks? I'm just getting started on the ones you gave me forty-five minutes ago," Sharon said, laughing.

"Listen, I'm going to share something with you but you have to promise to keep it confidential—always," Bill whispered.

"Of course I will, Bill."

Bill then outlined what Ray had told him, and that Lindsay confirmed she had received several tips in the past and never lost a dime. He went on to say he could only afford to buy five hundred shares and did she want to pick up the other five hundred or a part of it. Sharon said she would love to get in on the deal, but she didn't have a brokerage account.

"No problem, I've just opened, I think, a Stern Investments account on the west coast. I'll go ahead and place the order for one thousand shares, and you arrange to have your bank wire the money for your share to my Stern Investments account."

"Thanks for letting me in on this, Bill. I can certainly use the extra money. Call me when you have an exact amount and a specific account number. I'll be setting things up with my bank in the meantime," Sharon said, as she walked out of Bill's office.

Bill called the number Ray had given him; Sherman Hosogawa was expecting his call. He got Bill's personal information and gave him the account number. "How soon do I have to get you the money?" Bill asked.

"No hurry, in the next two or three days will do. Mr. Easton has guaranteed the funds and that's good enough for me. Well, I better place that order, as we have only an hour or so before the announcement. Talk to you soon. Welcome aboard."

★★★

Walking quickly into Bill's office, Dave said, "I want you to take the U.S. and do a preliminary Environmental Analysis. Use the process steps covered in the Environmental Analysis chapter of the strategic planning book I gave you. Make up the data if it's not readily available. Have something available for tomorrow afternoon at three p.m. and we'll sit down with Mr. Willis and review it and compare it to my work at Mr. Burger."

Bill was overwhelmed. "But I don't even know where to begin."

"You'll do fine. Remember the principals you just outlined. And, Bill, you need to have more confidence in yourself. Believe me if we had any doubt as to whether you could do this job you wouldn't have it. Oh, I've told my cousin the lawyer to expect your call," Dave said as he walked out.

***

At 6:00 p.m., Sharon stuck her head in the door. "Hey, Mr. Director, are we millionaires yet?"

"You know, I don't have a clue," Bill said, looking up from the pile of paper on his desk. "Dave gave me an assignment to complete by three tomorrow afternoon, when we'll then sit down with Mr. Willis and review it. I've been flat out on this ever since."

"What is this critical assignment that has you so preoccupied? Is there anything I can do to help?" Sharon asked.

"Oh, it's just an Environmental Analysis for the U.S.," Bill said sarcastically.

"Well, why don't I head on home and make dinner for us? You stay here for another couple of hours, then come over for dinner, and whatever."

"Boy, I could certainly use some *whatever* tonight," Bill said, laughing, as Sharon headed out the door.

"See you around eight," Sharon called back.

***

At 7:00 p.m., it occurred to Bill that it was only four o'clock on the west coast, so he picked up the phone and dialed Sherman's number.

"Sherman Hosogawa, can I help you?" came the response.

"Hi Sherman, Bill Sanford here. I was wondering how Jacob's Industries did today after the announcement?" Bill asked nervously. *What if it tanked and I lost not only my money but Sharon's as well?*

"Great! Much better than we expected. Let's see, you got in at C$8.20 a share, so your thousand shares cost you about $8,500 US. The announcement was that Toyoda offered C$24.00 a share. The Jacob's Industry Board of Directors came back with an announcement that the C$24.00 was inadequate; that was at 2:30 p.m. EST. Then, believe it or not, both companies said they had reached an agreement on C$29.50 price per share and a friendly takeover," Sherman said.

"Are you serious! So what do we do now?" Bill asked.

"Well, you could put in a sell order and lock in your profit, or you could wait to see if some other company makes a counter offer."

"What do you recommend?" Bill asked.

"That depends on your tolerance for risk. The odds of another better offer coming out are relatively small, and the risk that the deal falls through due to regulatory approvals is possible, but remote."

"Okay, sell all one thousand shares tomorrow morning. I'll call later in the week to discuss what to do with the proceeds."

When Bill arrived at Sharon's, he found her in the kitchen. "Hey Good Looking, so what are you going to do with your fourteen grand share?"

"What did you just say?" Sharon said, spinning around.

"I said what are you going to do with your fourteen grand share?" Bill repeated, and then explained the details of his conversation with Sherman, ending with the sell order he had placed.

"My God, I can't believe it! That is almost an eleven thousand dollar gain in a day, what I normally earn in five months, and the timing couldn't be better," Sharon said, as she hugged Bill and added, "Boy, are you going to get some unforgettable *whatever* tonight."

Sharon had prepared a roast chicken with mashed potatoes and corn on the cob. All they could talk about was their good fortune and what they would do with it. They decided they would take $3,000 of the profit and treat themselves to a romantic vacation when the strategic planning kickoff was completed. The destinations ranged from scuba diving in Saipan to renting a sail boat in the Caribbean.

After dinner, they worked on Bill's Environmental Analysis. Sharon was a fast learner. By the end of the session, she was pointing out inconsistencies between some of the Key Drivers and the environmental assumptions. Bill was impressed and grateful. One of her most valuable observations was that you couldn't consider the U.S. one market or one environment—the regional differences were far too great. When they finished defining the regions it was 11:30.

Chapter 13

"Good evening, Inoue San, have you received the package I sent?" Saji said cheerfully, certain that Inoue had received it.

"Ah, Saji kun, good job. Everything is in order and received on time," Inoue said happily.

"In fact, ahead of schedule, qualifying for the bonus we discussed, right?" Saji asked.

"How can someone with as much money as you be such a miser? Of course you have earned your bonus; it will be paid tomorrow to your Swiss bank account," Inoue said, chuckling. "Now, when can I expect the audited financial statements?" Inoue added.

"Have you no patience my friend? I had to move heaven and earth to get you this first package on time. But now I have a reliable contact so I should be able to move more quickly, but with added expense. What is the value of the second delivery to you, and what is your target date?" Saji said, ignoring Inoue's previous reference.

"Saji kun, my target date will always be ASAP. The budget is twenty million yen," Inoue said evenly.

"Ah my friend, you are so difficult to please, but of course, I'll do my best. It's likely to cost thirty million yen, but I'll minimize costs as much as possible," Saji said with mock sincerity.

★★★

When Inoue arrived at Aunt Sally Mae's Southern Fried Chicken Headquarters Thursday morning, he was taken directly to the boardroom. The boardroom had oak wainscot with bright yellow walls above them. There were portraits of J.J. and his mother Aunt Sally Mae, and a picnic scene at a country church. The feeling was one of warmth and casualness.

When Inoue walked in, he was shocked to see his former captor, Capin Lee Davis.

Lee stood up. "*Ohayo Gozaimasu*, Inoue San," he said, bowing.

"*Ohayo Gozaimasu*, Davis Sensei," Inoue Senmu responded, bowing slightly lower in deference of his former captor. "I see you remember your Japanese, Davis Sensei," Inoue added with a smile.

"Not very much; however, your English has lost the special accent I worked so hard to teach you."

"Well, if I try, I think I might be able to talk like y'all," Inoue said, with an exaggerated, but near-perfect, southern drawl. Everyone in the room began to laugh.

"Inoue Senmu, that is just remarkable," Lee said.

Next, introductions were made around the room. In addition to Lee and J.J., Aunt Sally Mae's VP Strategic Planning, Ashley Beaumont was present.

Ashley was a classic Southern Belle with long black hair, startling blue eyes, and a perfect figure, which her clothes clearly accentuated. A small mole on her right cheek moved every time she smiled, which was often. Inoue was taken, for the first time in a long time.

She's probably the most beautiful woman I have ever seen, and no wedding ring. There must be a story there.

After twenty minutes or so of reminiscing, J.J. opened the meeting. "Mr. Inoue, thank you for coming to Mobile to meet with us. We have reviewed your draft Letter of Intent. To summarize, we believe there are four general areas of discussion to cover. First, timing is our number one consideration as we have progressed quite a bit in our discussions with Yotsui Trading; second, concerning management, we must have a CEO that we can communicate with and who understands our culture; third, investment levels and other financial considerations; and finally, royalties. People, do we have agreement on this?" J.J. asked. Heads nodded around the table.

J.J. continued, "If you don't mind I would like to begin with a little culture. At Aunt Sally Mae's Southern Fried Chicken, we believe in strategic planning. Ashley here was hired two years ago from The Washington Consulting Group, where she had been for five years, following her MBA and undergraduate degrees from Harvard. She was the catalyst for the creation of the International Group. The first step in any strategic plan is a complete understanding of the competitive environment. We know we cannot accomplish this in Japan without a strong local partner with this knowledge, who shares our zeal for strategic planning. Quite frankly that is one of our concerns with Yotsui Trading. Obviously, they understand Japan; however, they don't seem to understand the industry, and more importantly, the direct competition."

"I couldn't agree more," Inoue said. "If we could have a ten minute break, and assuming you agree, we could then begin our discussions with a short presentation on the market, which is the basis of our interest in this project.

"Absolutely! It's nine-thirty now. How about we reconvene at ten-fifteen?" J.J. asked.

"Perfect," Inoue responded.

When the Aunt Sally Mae's SFC group returned to the board-room, Inoue already had the overhead projector set up. When everyone was seated, Inoue stood and said, "Lady and gentle-men, my presentation will be in two parts. First, I will cover the country, the consumer, and the broad market. Then I will cover the direct competition."

After describing the country and the economy in detail, Inoue turned to the consumer and covered the diet and Westernization trends, which he asserted was affecting any number of consumer-oriented industries.

"Could we get a copy of your presentation?" Ashley asked, after Inoue finished his first presentation.

"Of course, and many more details, after we sign a Letter of Intent," Inoue said with a smile. "Now, let me turn my attention to competitors."

When everyone refocused their attention, Inoue continued. "As you know, there are two main and three secondary players in the Western Quick Service Restaurant Market in Japan. TFC Japan is the largest, with two hundred sixty-five stores; Mr. Burger is second with one hundred twenty-three stores, all franchised; Scalanni's

Pizza is next, with forty-five stores, and 6 & 13 has just started with twenty-four stores, although they have announced plans for fifty more this year. TFC Japan plans to build sixty-six more stores this year: twelve franchised and fifty-four company-owned."

"Excuse me," Lee interrupted. "How do you know that?"

"Japan is a very incestuous and homogenous culture, as you know, Davis Sensei. While the Zaibatsu are fierce competitors, they share many contacts and have overlapping relationships. It is through these that we collect the information," Inoue Senmu said.

"But can you be sure of the accuracy?" J. J. asked with some doubt.

"Absolutely!" Inoue responded.

When Inoue finished, J.J. said, "That was impressive. I am convinced that you indeed do know the competitive market. I just wish I knew how.

"Now if y'all are ready, let's break for lunch. I've made a reservation at my favorite southern restaurant, Granny Betty's Country Kitchen," J.J. said with an exaggerated drawl.

Granny Betty's Country Kitchen was the real thing. It was a restored, authentic plantation house that had been converted into a restaurant, complete with portraits of five generations of previous owners, including a Major General, Commanding Officer of the Alabama Volunteers, Horace Beauregard.

They were seated in a private dining room upstairs, overlooking the river and a spectacular garden, with hundreds of blooming magnolias. Granny Betty herself served them. It turned out she really was related to Lee, a second cousin once removed.

The food was traditional and included southern-fried chicken, mashed potatoes, collard greens, and corn on the cob. Endless hot biscuits with butter and honey were served. Iced tea was the norm, but beer was available. Nothing stronger though, as Granny Betty was a devout Baptist. The conversation over lunch was friendly and personal. Unlike Tokyo, there was no discussion about business.

"So Johnson Shacho, tell me about yourself." Inoue said.

"Well, let's see. I was born right here in Alabama on a farm about ten miles outside of Mobile. After World War Two, I stayed in the Marines until the Korean War ended and then took over the family farm. My Mama made some of the best southern-fried chicken I had ever tasted anywhere, so I decided to sell about a thousand acres of the farmland and start Aunt Sally Mae's Southern Fried Chicken, using Mama's recipe.

"The name Aunt Sally Mae's Southern Fried Chicken came from the fact that Mama would always make it for the annual picnic of the Westin Baptist Church, where her nephew was the pastor.

"Well, things were working so well by the early sixties that I sold the rest of the farm, some five thousand acres, and began to put my heart and soul behind Mama's fried chicken. In fact, it's so good, Granny Betty has asked me for the recipe any number of times."

Inoue thought, *Is he for real or is this just a disarming tactic for our afternoon negotiations?*

When they returned to the boardroom, J.J. opened the negotiations with the subject of timing. Inoue confirmed his previous estimate of one hundred twenty days, assuming Aunt Sally Mae's Southern Fried Chicken could respond quickly with its own legal processes.

"Can we assume that you have the go-ahead from your board to proceed with a deal?" J.J. asked politely.

"Yes, if we reach agreement on the three key areas, I will execute a Letter of Intent tomorrow," Inoue said.

The last topic was management of the joint venture. It was 6:30 p.m. by this time, and everyone was exhausted. The key points of difference were in the CFO and CEO positions. Aunt Sally Mae's Southern Fried Chicken wanted to appoint the CFO and have the joint venture pick up all costs, even if an expat was appointed. They agreed that the CEO be Japanese, but insisted on the right of veto. Inoue could not agree to an outright veto, explaining that in order to meet the aggressive, time-sensitive steps, continuity was essential.

"Can we continue this discussion tomorrow morning?" Inoue said in a tired voice.

"Of course," J.J. said. "Besides, I need a drink and some dinner after all this deep thinking. How does some of our fresh Gulf seafood sound to you, Inoue Senmu?"

"Johnson Shacho, I'm becoming worried about the rest of our negotiations, since you can obviously read my mind," Inoue said, laughing.

"It's settled then, seafood it is. My driver is downstairs and will drive you back to your hotel and wait for you while you freshen up," J.J. said.

***

The next morning, the debate over the CEO and CFO positions continued through the morning; everyone was becoming increasingly frustrated.

"Could we take a thirty-minute break here? I need to place a call to Tokyo," Inoue Senmu said.

"Of course; let's resume at nine-thirty," J.J. said.

It was a very productive afternoon for Inoue. His offer of accepting the joint venture CEO position in exchange for his veto over Aunt Sally Mae's Southern Fried Chicken CFO candidate worked like a charm. J.J. jumped at the deal. By mid-morning, the major issues had been worked out, and the meeting adjourned with an agreement to regroup at 3:30 p.m.

Inoue went off with Lee to work out the details of a Letter of Intent that the parties could execute in the afternoon.

Ashley spent the time preparing detailed estimates of various investment alternatives and discussing the joint venture with Allan Anderson, CPA's Mobile Office's Senior Partner. They worked on a critical path of actions that would have to be in place to get the joint venture up and running.

J.J. spent the time talking with his bankers.

The 3:30 p.m. meeting did not get started until 5:00. The details of the Letter of Intent took longer than expected. As the group reviewed the draft, a number of discussion points emerged.

Finally, at 10:45 p.m., all changes to the Letter of Intent had been made, and J.J. and Inoue signed the document. What started as a two-page, non-specific document ended up being twenty-six pages and highly detailed, thanks to Lee, who impressed Inoue with his quick, sharp mind, and Ashley, who had a unique ability to prioritize strategic issues.

Inoue had to call Tokyo and inform his peers he would be executing a much more comprehensive Letter of Intent. It took him two hours and much relationship equity to get a consensus. He shuddered at the thought of the "favors" his fellow directors would be asking for in exchange for their support.

After Inoue had left, J.J., Lee, and Ashley hung around for a post mortem. With a wistful look, J.J. said, "Yep, I'll never forget the stories I heard from the local women when we liberated Saipan. God I hate the Japs. My brother and two close high school chums I played football with were captured on Corregidor and were part of the Bataan Death March. My brother died on day seventeen, when he collapsed, and the guards wouldn't let my buddies pick him up. They both made it to the prison camp, but Jake was beaten by a guard for trying to pick up a crust of bread. He died three days later, in his bunk. Joe survived, although he was never the same."

"My God J.J., how do you even stand to be in their presence?" Ashley asked.

Raising his voice, J.J. said, " I promised Joe we would get even with the Japs, and I will! We're going to make a ton of money in that market and put TFC Japan out of business."

"Can you believe that arrogant son-of-a-bitch? Acting like the war never happened and he wasn't involved in the Bataan Death March that killed your brother, and ten thousand-plus others," Lee added, his face turning red and his giant hands trembling.

After regaining his composure, Lee said, "But one thing is for sure, Inoue wants this deal in the worst possible way."

"So you think there's more to Inoue's interest than just greed?" J.J. asked.

"I guarantee it. I worked with that fucker for eleven months and learned how to read him through my ole great, great grandson of Jeff Davis' routine. It always kept the Japs off guard," Lee said, laughing. "You're not too bad yourself, J.J., at playing the old southern plantation owner."

Chapter 14

Lisa had managed to avoid Saji's advances since Ray sent her to Osaka ten weeks earlier, with promises of numerous modeling assignments, only three of which materialized, and two of those almost pornographic. But something told her that tonight would be different. As it turned out, she was right.

"Lisa, come here," Saji slurred. "Tonight's your lucky night," he added, obviously drunk.

"But, but, I've got my period," Lisa said, her voice rising.

"I don't care—now get your ass over here immediately, you bitch!" Saji yelled, as he waved his hand, motioning Lisa to come toward him. "You've been here ten weeks and all you do is sulk and avoid me!" Saji added, finishing his Dantori whiskey.

Lisa began to cry as one of Saji's men took hold of her and physically forced her over to Saji's bed.

"Listen, we can do this easily, or my boys can make it even more fun for you. I don't care either way, because I get to go first!" Saji said, laughing.

★★★

"Mr. Sanford, Phil here, there is a Mr. Liberwitz here to see you."

A Mr. Liberwitz? Bill thought. *Who's that? Oh, that's right, Dave Liberwitz's cousin, the divorce lawyer.*

"Yeah, Phil, I'm expecting Mr. Liberwitz, I'll send Carmen down to get him."

"So, you must be Bill, Dave has had a lot of good things to say about you," Sam said, walking into Bill's office. Like his first cousin, Sam had striking red hair and bright green eyes. But, unlike Dave, he was short.

"Thanks for coming in. I'm really stretched at the moment. Have a seat," Bill said, motioning Sam to a chair. "Listen, Sam, I don't want to seem cheap, but what's this going to run me?"

"Relax, Bill, I'm here to help you. The cost will depend on how contentious things become. I assure you my fees will be reasonable. About half of what you would pay on the open market, and that's because of my cousin Dave. Now, the first question, are you absolutely sure this situation is not retrievable?"

"Yes, I'm sure it isn't."

Bill then spent the better part of the next hour explaining the details of the conflict, from Susan's affair to the demands of returning to Texas. Bill concluded with Susan's departure and his subsequent conversations with her father.

"Okay, I'll file for divorce on the basis of abandonment today. Give me her parents' address and she'll be served with papers tomorrow. Next question, and you should think about this one, do you want custody or joint custody of your daughter? From what you've said, your wife is likely to move in with her parents or at least be in the same town. That, of course, complicates joint custody."

After some reflection Bill answered, "I definitely want to maintain regular contact with Sarah and have a meaningful influence on her life. Personally, I'd like to have sole custody, but given my job's travel requirements, I suspect that is unrealistic. But joint custody is a minimum, with extended visitation in the summers. No way am I going to become a Santa Claus Dad."

"Next question, finances: how important is it to you to minimize your financial exposure versus how quickly you get divorced? Generally, if time is not of the essence, then you can minimize your financial exposure through a number of tactics."

"Well, I'm happy to provide for Sarah, but I'm not crazy about providing for Susan. After all, she left me," Bill said, leaning forward, as his face turned red.

"Listen, Bill, let me explain the law. While an over-simplification, whether it's Connecticut or Texas that has jurisdiction, child support to age eighteen is mandatory. The amount in both states is based on both parties' ability to pay. This includes earnings and other assets. Alimony is generally granted until the lower income earner gets remarried. Both states, however, grant an exception in the case of abandonment. This is why we sue for abandonment in the first place."

"What do you recommend?"

"Based on your description of the situation, I say we sue for divorce in Connecticut on the grounds of abandonment. Further, we seek sole custody on the basis of Susan's actions of taking Sarah out of state without your knowledge or consent. Given her parents' resources, I suspect they will try to negotiate a compromise."

"Okay, makes sense to me; let's do it," Bill said, leaning back in his chair and putting his hands behind his head.

"I'll keep you posted. By the way, don't speak directly to Susan, her parents, or their attorney. Refer all calls to me," Sam Liberwitz said, as he passed Bill a card with contact numbers.

★★★

"Oh, Mr. Director of Strategic Planning, what can I do for your Eminence that I'm not already doing?"

"Come on, cut it out!" Bill said, clearly annoyed.

"You come on. I was just kidding, you know that," Sharon said, raising her eyebrows.

"I'm sorry, I guess the time pressure is getting to me," Bill said, as went over and kissed her.

"Now, that's more like it," Sharon said with a smile, tossing her head. "But careful, stud, you don't want to start rumors around this place," she added, as she pulled back and pushed Bill away.

"Too late, the rumors are flying about this place," Bill said, smiling, as he returned to his desk. After sitting down and looking up with a smile, he added, "Guess who I just spent twenty minutes with?"

"Come on now, we don't have time to play twenty questions. I've got hotel and flight reservations to confirm, never mind producing detailed monthly databases for all the countries you're visiting on this trip," Sharon said, as she stood up and headed toward the door.

"I just met with Sam Liberwitz and kicked off the divorce process," Bill said, looking self-satisfied.

"That's great news. To be honest, I was concerned that you might have second thoughts. And where would that leave us?" Sharon said, frowning. "Well, I guess we won't have to worry about the rumors anymore," she added with a wink, as she headed out the door.

I'm one lucky guy, Bill thought.

Walking toward her office, Sharon wondered if she was falling in love with Bill.

★★★

Reading over the notes Sharon had left him, Bill paused when he read, "All the international regions are set, as are the Midwest, South, and East; only the West is still not responding, despite repeated telexes. I don't think they believe I have the authority to act on your behalf."

Bill's face turned bright red. "Carmen, get Stan Stevens on the phone for me right away," Bill yelled, louder than he intended.

"Right away, Mr. Sanford," came the nearly immediate response. Carmen was certain this was not going to be an enjoyable call for Stan Stevens.

Bill picked up the phone. "Stan..."

"I'm sorry, Mr. Sanford, his secretary says he's tied up in meetings with Mr. Rosenberg for the next two days."

"Carmen, pass me through to Steven's secretary, please," Bill said with a calm he didn't feel.

"Hello, this is Bill Sanford. I need to speak to Mr. Stevens, now," Bill said evenly.

After a moment's hesitation, the secretary said, "I'm sorry, Mr. Sanford, as I told your secretary, Mr. Stevens is tied up in meetings with Mr. Rosenberg for the next two days. Is there a message?"

"Yes there is. Tell Stan that he has exactly ten minutes to return my call, or the next call will be from Mr. Willis' office," Bill said, then hung up.

Six minutes later, Rosenberg came on the phone. "Who the fuck do you think you are threatening my people? We have pressing immediate issues to address, and we'll get around to the fucking strategic plan when we have time. Do you understand me, Sanford!" Rosenberg yelled.

"You've wasted six of the ten minutes I gave Stan. In another four, I'm going to Mr. Willis' office to report exactly what you just said. You seem to forget you were specifically excluded from this first round of the strategic planning process, apparently for very good and obvious reasons. And Adam, don't ever threaten me again. I will take it personally! And believe me, you don't want to be on the other end of that, especially a pansy wimp like you!" Bill said. He hung up before Rosenberg could answer. *Well, I've done it, now,* Bill thought, as he headed for Dave's office.

When Bill entered, he heard Dave say "...that is exactly what he's supposed to do. I suggest you have Stan place that call in the next two minutes, or I'll be going with Sanford to Willis' office. You just don't get it, Rosenberg, your days of getting away with brow-beating people are over. Two minutes only," he said as he hung up.

"So you and Adam have become even closer friends?" Dave said with a smile. "You're right, of course, in principle, but do not underestimate your opponents! Rosenberg is dangerous, as long as he remains. Remember—" Just then the phone rang.

"It's Stan, for you," Dave said with a smile.

★ ★ ★

When Bill returned to his office, Carmen said, "Mr. Sanford, there is a collect call for you from Osaka Japan, a Lisa Thomas. It's the third call in thirty minutes. Shall I accept the charges?" Carmen asked, wrinkling her brow.

Lisa, I don't know any Lisa in Osaka. Could it be that model I met on the flight to Tokyo?

"Sure, Carmen, accept the charges."

"Hello, Bill, I'm not sure you remember me but I sat next to you on a flight to Tokyo some weeks back," the trembling voice said.

"Yes, of course I remember, Lisa. What's up? You sound really upset," Bill said, putting his pen down and leaning forward.

"Well," Lisa sobbed, "I'm sorry to bother you but I'm in a horrible situation, and I don't know what to do. I couldn't think of who else to call."

"Now, Lisa, calm down and tell me what the problem is," Bill said evenly. *She sounds desperate,* he thought.

"Well, my host in Tokyo turned out to be a Ray Easton, who claimed to be Chairman of TFC Japan. I thought I remembered you saying you worked for TFC," Lisa said, blowing her nose. "In any case, all Ray did was try to get me into bed."

That son-of-a-bitch! Bill thought, his palms beginning to sweat.

"After my third day with him, he sent me to Osaka to work for a friend of his who owned a modeling business. He promised me I would be considered for TV commercials and magazine ads," Lisa added, beginning to cry again.

"Easy, Lisa, don't worry. I'll help you. Ray Easton actually is Chairman of TFC Japan," Bill said softly, as he got up and closed the door to his office, something he generally never did. "What happened next?" Bill asked.

"Well, as it turns out, I auditioned only once, for a liquor ad that bordered on porn. When I complained, Ray's friend, Saji San, sent me to work as a hostess in a hostess club. At first, it was just serving drinks and joking with the businessmen who were the clients. But then, the special customers began to fondle me. Finally, the Mama San said I had to go with a customer to his hotel. When I refused, she sent me home and called Saji San," Lisa said sobbing again.

What the fuck was Ray doing? That bastard has this girl in an impossible position. "Where are you now?" Bill asked in a caring tone.

"I'm at a public telephone two blocks from Saji San's penthouse. But if I don't get back soon I'm sure he'll send one of his men to get me," she said, bursting in to tears. "Bill, that son-of-a-bitch raped me last night—" The line went dead.

"Lisa, Lisa!" Bill shouted. *My God, what happened! Did one of Saji's men get to her? I've got to do something, but what?*

There was no response.

"Carmen, I've been cut off, see if you can get the international operator to get the call back."

Jesus, I hope she hasn't been caught by one of that gangster's men! Shit, what am I going to do?

★★★

"Hey, sweet one," Bill said as he arrived at Sharon's house.

"What's the matter?" Sharon asked, as she took hold of both of Bill's hands.

Bill explained the conversation he had had with Lisa.

Shocked, Sharon said, "Sweetheart, this is serious. Ray Easton is clearly a scoundrel and dangerous too, I bet. That Saji San sounds like a gangster. What are you going to do?" she asked, wide-eyed.

"You know, I don't know what I'm going to do. I know I've got to do something; I can't just leave that girl to fend for herself," Bill said, pinching the bridge of his nose.

"Sweetheart, you've got to be careful, whatever you do. You should consider sharing this information with Dave."

" I'll have to think about this a bit before I do anything."

★★★

The first stop on the regional strategic planning tour was Tokyo. Willis and Dave flew over on Japan Airlines via Hawaii, while Bill caught the Pan Am, 747sp non-stop out of JFK.

Bill was surprised to find that Dave had booked him in the first class dining room upstairs on his flight. The prime rib was perfect and the wine excellent. *This is the life. If only Sharon was with me,* Bill thought. They were getting very close; in fact, they rotated at each other's houses almost every night.

When he arrived at Haneda airport, Kenji was there to meet him. "Bill, welcome to Tokyo!" Kenji said smiling.

"What did I do to deserve this special pick up?" Bill asked, raising his right hand to his chest.

"Nothing, actually, Ray and I got here two hours ago to pick up Mr. Willis and Dave, but their flight was delayed, so Ray took them to the hotel twenty minutes ago. Hey, if you're feeling up to it, we've arranged a private room at the Seryna for dinner tonight at eight. Oh, and after that, Ray is having another party for the most recently arrived group of wannabe models."

Not wanting to run into Fumiko, Bill begged off Ray's party after dinner.

When Dave arrived at the party, Ray already had a young model on his arm. "Welcome, Dave. I want you to meet Ericka…"

"Kowalski," the tall blonde interjected.

"Yeah, Kowalski, from San Diego. Get yourself a drink and I'll introduce you around," Ray said, pointing to the bar, which was manned by a waiter in a white jacket.

Dave wandered over to the bar and ordered club soda with lime. Ray motioned him over and made a few introductions. "This is Koji Nakajima, President of Williams & Spencer Hirakikohoku. We'll be at Koji's shop tomorrow morning for a review of competitor advertising." Koji bowed slightly.

"This is Paul Manson, CEO of Sam's Cola Japan. Guys, this is Dave Liberwitz, our new guru of strategic planning." Koji and Paul smiled and shook hands with Dave.

"Paul, I think I met you in Atlanta three years ago when I was with Washington Consulting doing an international assignment," Dave said, wrinkling his brow.

"Yes, I remember now. You gave a presentation on establishing effective distribution expansion. The bottom line was that vending machines were an under-utilized tool that added significant impulse purchases.

"You'll be pleased to know that we went from just over one thousand units, which we owned directly, to over twenty-five thousand units that the bottlers own, and paid for. Your comments on capital maximization were not lost on our CFO. Ray, you're in for a real education in strategic thinking, by one of the best around," Paul said with respect, as he tipped his glass towards Dave. "Didn't we try to hire you?"

"Yeah, but your CFO took my capital maximization presentation to heart and the offer was a hundred grand short," Dave responded. They all laughed.

★★★

The dinner with Ozawa Hon-Bucho of Mitsugawa Trading was held in a private room of the Keyaki Grill, one of Tokyo's finest Western restaurants. Chefs from France, Italy and Spain were all on kitchen staff. Each day specials from each country were offered and at least one was season specific. It being late October, the French special this evening was *Caussolet*, slowly cooked white beans with duck and sausage, a favorite dish in Lyon. The French chef who prepared it had studied directly under Paul Bocuse.

Willis was in excellent form and demonstrated why he was CEO of such a large international company. After much small talk, extensive discussion of the competitive environment, leading to the identification of the Key Drivers, Wills said, "Ozawa Hon-Bucho, perhaps you could educate us on a technical point of difference between our countries? Specifically, why do you not consider long-term leases as a commitment of capital?"

"Because, as you can see, land is very scarce in Japan. Imagine putting half the population of the U.S. in an area the size of southern Connecticut, with two thirds of it used for agriculture. Therefore, as long as you have the right to sublet over the life of the lease, there is no risk, only upside, as rents continue to increase at double-digit rates."

Dave Liberwitz said, "If double-digit growth rates continue, then in twenty years, rents will be eight to ten times greater than they are today, and if current margins are held, our three-piece dinner, which now sells for about four dollars, versus two-fifty in the U.S., would be nearing forty dollars.

"I think part of the reason is the long-term interest rate differences between our countries. Today, in the U.S., the prime rate is about nine percent versus the two-point-five percent in Japan. This is primarily due to the sixteen percent personal savings rate in Japan versus the three-point-five percent rate in the U.S. Simply put, more low-cost cash is available."

Ozawa Hon-Bucho nodded. "Interesting points. I hadn't thought of rent rates eventually reaching unsustainable levels."

Willis then said, "Well, despite our differences in treating long-term leases, I assure you Ozawa San, TFC Corporate is committed to this market and developing new stores as quickly as prudent. I would, however, ask your support and understanding for our corporate policies concerning capital expenditures. As Bill's recent audit report has confirmed, over twenty stores have been committed to, without a request for approval."

"But as Bill San's audit report also pointed out," Ozawa interrupted, "in our joint venture agreement, only the approval of TFC Japan's board is required for capital commitments."

Willis was clearly annoyed at the interruption. "In any case, for us, twenty unapproved stores with twenty-year, long-term leases means a potential comment from our external auditors in their management letter, which becomes public, and therefore is a significant issue. Besides, since we own fifty percent of the shares, a board resolution cannot pass without our approval. Therefore, if Ray doesn't start following our policies, we'll have to replace him with someone who will," Willis said, smiling.

Everyone laughed politely. Ray, however, knew he wasn't kidding, and the look Kenji gave Ray indicated he had reached the same conclusion.

When dinner was over, Willis whispered to Ozawa, "Can we have a nightcap in private?"

"Certainly, one of my favorite hostess clubs is just around the corner," Ozawa whispered back. Willis and Ozawa said good-night to the rest of the attendees and went off to Ozawa San's hostess club.

When they were seated and the Hennessy XO had come, and the hostesses were dismissed, Willis said, "Ozawa San—"

"Please call me Tom," Ozawa interrupted.

"Okay, Tom, how do you feel about us sending over a CFO for TFC Japan?"

"Well, this is something I have discussed with Ray. I realize TFC Japan is weak in the financial area, especially as it relates to U.S. standards. However, most foreigners just cannot effectively adapt to Japan. So, the person selected would have to be special. Kenji seems to think your Bill Sanford might be appropriate."

"Well, we are considering just that," Willis responded. "How about costs? What should the joint venture be willing to pay for a CFO?"

"TFC Japan already has a Japanese CFO in Mr. Ishikawa."

Willis smiled. "Yes, I know. I met him today, originally from your purchasing department, right? Not exactly ideally qualified for the job, wouldn't you say? Also, your representative Joji Sakurai is a very pleasant fellow but not exactly a CEO. I was surprised to learn that he is being paid by our joint venture when we're absorbing all of Ray's salary, including his expatriate package. And believe me, Ray is even less of a Chairman than Joji Sakurai is a President."

"Let me think about this. What exactly are you proposing?" Ozawa asked.

"Simple, the joint venture picks up the expat CFO costs completely, and continues to pay for Joji Sakurai and Ishikawa San, or TFC Japan stops paying for both Joji Sakurai and Ishikawa San, and we pay directly for the foreign CFO. Your choice," Willis said. "Just let me know which you prefer before I leave day after tomorrow."

"You are a very tough negotiator, Willis Shacho," Ozawa answered.

"I learned it in the Marine Corps," Willis said, a smile returning to his face.

★ ★ ★

The rest of the trip, which Kenji had arranged, went without a hitch. It was clear he was in complete charge and control. It was equally clear that Ray and President Joji Sakurai, from Mitsugawa, were just there for home-office management and relations. In this regard, it was also obvious that Joji Sakurai was far more effective than Ray. In fact, during the dinner with Ozawa, it was plain to see that Ray's relationship with Ozawa was a bit too close.

During the wrap-up, it was agreed that Ray and Kenji would work on a draft of the strategic plan and get something in by October 15. They were to liaise with Bill on any help they needed.

Willis got his call from Ozawa about one hour before his departure for the airport. Ozawa reluctantly agreed to TFC Japan paying the full costs of the foreign CFO, as long as Mitsugawa was involved in the selection process.

Japan had certainly set a standard no other market could match. More specifically, Kenji Kato had set a standard no Regional VP could touch. He clearly knew his business and that of his competitors. Kenji lived his business.

On the flight down to Australia, Willis asked Dave and Bill, "Where do you think Kenji Kato's loyalties lie?"

"I'm not sure, but I'm sure it isn't to Ray or TFC corporate," Dave said.

"Um, Ozawa acts like Kenji is his boy, and Kenji is very respectful around him, but I think Kenji is ultimately only loyal to Kenji," Willis said.

The rest of the international trip underscored the problems in the business. To varying degrees, all the units were unaware of their competitors' businesses, and in some cases, indifferent to them. Germany and Canada were the worst offenders, Australia and the United Kingdom the best.

Chapter 15

TFC's Eastern Region's senior management team arrived at 8:30 a.m. The Regional Vice President, Charles Winchester, was one of Rosenberg's boys from American Labs who came over when Rosenberg "retired" his predecessor who had been one of the Major's early hires.

Debra Jones was the Operations Director and was also an early hire by the Major. In fact, she was the Major's first secretary.

When cash was tight, as it often was in the early days, she was paid partially in stock. Like all original employees, she became a millionaire when the company went public. Despite her wealth, Debra Jones stayed on after the company went public and worked her way up to Operations Director. She would often say, "TFC is in my blood!"

From the start of the meeting, it was obvious that Rosenberg had briefed his team to hold the party line, which was that the current downturn was just temporary and the strategies they had in place would resolve the problem by year's end.

After Charles' long-winded, but always articulate presentation, Willis just smiled and leaned forward to add, "I'm glad to hear that the forecast of the Eastern Region is secure, Charles. Can I therefore assume you are confident that a twelve-percent decline in the first half of the year can be reversed, and result in a six-percent full year gain?"

Without waiting for a response, he turned to Bill. "Given seasonality and August and September's performance, what kind of sales increase would be required to achieve a full-year increase of six percent?"

"About forty-six percent should do it, Mr. Willis."

"So, Charles," Willis continued. "Why don't you present those strategies? You did say strategies, didn't you? Things that are going to make that happen."

"Well, John here is going to present our third and fourth quarter marketing activities that we are confident will turn the business around," Charles said, relieved to pass off to anyone.

"John, before you get started, do you believe the marketing activities you are about to present will turn the business around in the fourth quarter?" Willis asked quietly.

"No, Sir, not a chance."

"Oh, why not?"

"In my opinion, we have fundamental problems that first have to be addressed."

"And those are?"

"Well, Sir, in my opinion, our biggest problem is that we don't have control over our franchisees."

Charles gave him a stern look.

Continuing, John said, "In the Eastern Region, franchisees account for over forty-five percent of our outlets, and less than fifty percent of those are in compliance with contractual advertising requirements. Further, those that are, generally do a poor job of implementing the promotional programs.

"Additionally, the results of our "mystery shopper" program confirm a full seventy percent of the franchisee store personnel are not aware of the details surrounding our promotions."

"John, don't exaggerate!" Charles said sternly. "You know we've made significant progress with our franchisees since Adam launched the TFC Family Team Initiative."

Dave stood up and interjected, "Is that one of the strategies that is going to turn the business around?"

"Well, yes it is," Charles answered defensively.

"What exactly are the details of this program?" Bill challenged Charles. "When I read the details that the franchisees got, it seemed to me that you're offering them profit incentives for opening more stores, even in areas that are apparently saturated. Did I get that wrong?"

"You certainly did!" Charles virtually yelled. "We're careful not to overbuild in any district. Of course, we offer incentives for developing new stores. That's how we build the business!"

"Hmm, it's interesting to note that in district three, which was a company-owned territory until 1973 with a total of seven stores, is today a franchised district, which now has fifteen stores. Five, however, are not profitable.

"I remember the capital appropriation request that was submitted for the sale of the seven company-owned stores in that same district. Didn't we take a fifteen-percent write-off on three of the stores? Let me see. I have it here…yes, 'The district is clearly overbuilt and,' well, I won't bore you with the rest of the details."

"Now wait a minute!" Charles exploded and turned red-faced. "What exactly are you insinuating?"

"I'm sorry, let me be absolutely clear," Bill said calmly. "I'm saying that you knew, or should have known, that the district was overbuilt when you sold the stores. And yet you more than doubled the saturation, causing the franchisee financial hardship.

"Your actions resulted in five of these stores becoming unprofitable, and you wonder why you don't have adequate influence over franchisees or why they're not following their contract?

"Finally, in that same district, Mr. Burger has only four stores, all company-owned, which is same number they had three years ago. How do you explain that difference? Now is that clear enough for you?"

For a moment, Charles froze.

Then he began looking around the room for support, but none was to be had. After a long pause, he said emotionally, "I don't care what Mr. Burger does! They're not in the chicken business; besides, they're not aggressive enough."

Willis got up and said, "Let's take a fifteen-minute break. Bill, could I have a word with you?"

Everyone left the room except Willis, Dave, and Bill.

"Jesus, Son, I would hate to get on your bad side," Willis laughed.

"That was great research, and being prepared with the capital appropriations request was a stroke of genius! I had forgotten all about that," Willis said, genuinely impressed.

"Yes, and the bit on Mr. Burger was priceless," Dave added.

"Well, thank you both for the compliments, but I feel a big *but* is coming."

"Ah, perceptive as well!" Willis answered.

"Listen, you're absolutely right about Charles, and exposing him is exactly what you're supposed to do. However, we don't want him to sabotage the operation while we figure out how to effectively replace him.

"In other words, be a bit more subtle. Make your points, but do it less aggressively, okay?"

"Yes Sir. I've got it."

***

It was an unusually quiet evening at the Ile de France, with only two other tables occupied. An assortment of meats was slowly grilling on the barbeque pit that was just off the entrance to the dining room. The evening's specials included fresh Dover sole with a lemon, butter and cream sauce, and a *cassoulet*. The suggested appetizer was sautéed *foie gras* served with a glass of sauterne dessert wine.

"So, Ray San, how are you progressing with the most recent information request?" Saji asked.

"Well, I think I can have the first part by the day- after tomorrow, but listen Saji San, it's worth a lot more than the fifty thousand you proposed. After all, you're talking about *the* joint venture agreement," Ray said as he took a large bite off his rack of lamb. He licked his fingers as he put the rib bone down.

Luckily I raised the price of the joint venture agreement to thirty million yen, Saji thought.

"Ray, a deal is a deal…"

As Ray began to protest, Saji raised his hand.

"However, since you have been so reliable, I'm willing to up the reward to sixty-five thousand, assuming you can deliver the package to me by tomorrow evening," Saji said with a smile, as he put a bite of sole in his mouth.

"Now that's more like it Saji San," Ray said, picking up another rib and motioning to the waiter for another double single-malt.

I wonder how many Americans are as barbaric as Easton, Saji wondered. *Look at the grease on his face; my dog eats more politely.*

The waiter arrived with Ray's single malt and, in Japanese, said to Saji, "President Saji, you have a phone call. It's an Inoue San, and he says it's urgent. What should I tell him?"

"Can I take the call in Andre's private office?" Saji asked, looking at his watch; it was 10:15.

The waiter nodded.

"Ray San, I have a call I have to take. Get me the package by four tomorrow afternoon, and I'll have your reward," Saji said, as he pushed back from the table.

"Ah Inoue San, your ears must have been burning. I was just securing the next item on your wish list for delivery the day after tomorrow."

"Saji kun, that's cutting it a bit close," Inoue said with urgency. I'm leaving day after tomorrow at seven in the evening."

"Relax, Old Friend, you'll have what you need in plenty of time."

★★★

"Hello, Mr. Sanford, sorry to bother you so late," Carmen said urgently, "but the woman from Japan called again and said it was urgent that she talk to you. She left a number where she will be in…forty-five minutes."

Looking at his watch, Bill saw it was eleven Pacific Standard Time. He rubbed his eyes. "Jeez, Carmen, it's two a.m. your time, did she say what the emergency was?"

"No, only that she had information that you should know about right away."

After Carmen gave him the number, he placed a person-to-person call.

"Hello, Lisa, is that you?" Bill asked when the operator put the call through.

"Yes, Bill, it's me. Now I only have a few minutes but I wanted to tell you that Saji received an envelope with Ray's return address on it last week."

"Well, what was in the envelope?" Bill asked, sitting up and grabbing a pen and pad.

"I don't know everything, but there was a thick document labeled 'new store sites.'"

"Are you sure!" Bill almost yelled.

"Yes, no question, as I said, it was in English. I've got to go!" Lisa said, hanging up.

Jesus, Ray is a fucking spy! The thought raced through Bill's mind. *What could be the connection between Ray and Saji? And what would a gangster want with new store site data? Kenji had said at the strategic planning conference that he was concerned Aunt Sally Mae's SFC might enter the market with Yostui Trading.*

★★★

The Western Region was something else.

The senior management team came to the meeting clearly defensive and disinterested in the subject.

The Regional Vice President, Stan, set the tone for the meeting when he suggested that other priorities would necessitate an end to the meeting by three-thirty in the afternoon and that they had not had time to arrange competitive store visits, as the nearest Aunt Sally Mae's Southern Fried Chicken was more than thirty minutes away.

Bill interrupted with the comment that they had passed a Mexico Lindo just two blocks from their location.

"As Adam explained at the executive conference, we do not consider Mexico Lindo a direct competitor," Stan said condescendingly.

"Why not?" Dave asked pleasantly. "It's the fastest growing fast food chain in the West."

"Because it doesn't sell fried chicken, and it's priced at a much lower price point," a clearly annoyed Stan answered. "Besides, there are no changes to our full-year forecast. We remain confident that—"

"Hang on," Bill interrupted, "do you mean that despite being down fourteen percent through the first half, and off sixteen and eighteen percent in August and September, your most recent forecast, which has you down less than two percent, is going to be achieved?

"You'd have to achieve a sales increase of nearly fifty-three percent in the fourth quarter to make that—"

"Would you be quiet and listen to our marketing programs before you judge our forecast," Stan yelled. "And who are you to question our forecast anyhow?"

Perhaps Willis was just tired, or in a bad mood, or forgot the advice he gave Bill at the end of the Eastern Regional meeting, or maybe it was a combination of the three, but whatever the reason, he stood up and his anger got the best of him.

"Stan, clean out your desk immediately. You're fired!"

The afternoon portion of the meeting ended at 7:45 p.m. and immediately afterwards, the group visited six other fast food outlets and two TFC stores.

When they finally finished their market tour and returned to the hotel, it was 11:15 and the restaurants were closed, so they all went up to Willis' suite and had room service.

★★★

"Hey guy, you certainly know how to keep a girl waiting." Sharon was smiling when Bill entered the suite. She was sitting up watching the *Tonight Show*, sipping a glass of white wine.

"So, how did things go today?" Sharon asked, turning the TV off.

"Never mind today. Last night I got a call from Lisa who told me she had seen an envelope from Ray addressed to the gangster, Saji San, who Ray set her up with," Bill said, as he took off his coat and tie and began undoing his shirt.

"Did she say what was in the envelope?" Sharon's interest was piqued, as she got out of bed and put on a hotel bathrobe.

"Only that she saw a folder labeled 'new store site evaluations' in English. Everything else was in Japanese."

Bill took his pants off and put on a hotel bathrobe as well.

"So what are you going to do with this information?" Sharon asked, as she began to massage Bill's shoulders.

"I don't know yet," Bill said, beginning to relax. "If it's true, then Ray is involved in industrial espionage, and that's serious."

★ ★ ★

"Time to get up, Sleepy Head."

Sharon kissed Bill to wake him up.

"What time is it?" Bill asked with a sleepy smile. "It seems like I just fell asleep ten minutes ago."

"Come on," she said. "Your surprise is waiting, and I don't want you to miss a minute of it!"

"Okay, time to tell me where we are going," Bill said, as he got out of bed and headed for the bathroom.

★ ★ ★

The Saint Francis was a fine old distinguished hotel, rich in tradition and heritage, if lacking somewhat in modern conveniences. It had been opened in 1904 and had survived the great earthquake of 1906. It was one of the few five star hotels in San Francisco.

As Bill showered, he heard Sharon telling him to hurry up and put on the new clothes she had laid out for him on the bed.

He smiled and thought, *Where has she been all my life?*

He shaved quickly, brushed his teeth, and dressed in the new clothes: an off-white pair of khakis, a light blue Polo shirt, a long-sleeved casual shirt, and a navy-blue parka. There was also a pair of Docksider shoes.

When they got downstairs, Dave was waiting in the lobby.

"You guys look ready, let's go."

"Where are we going?" Bill asked, surprised to see Dave.

"You will see soon enough," they both responded, laughing.

During the limo drive, Bill tried to imagine what Sharon and Dave had in mind, but he drew a blank until the limo pulled into a large marina.

A few minutes later, they were next to a twelve-meter sailing yacht. It looked enormous, with masts that seemed to reach up to the sky. The hull was jet black with white masts and trim. The decks were polished teak and all the metal was brass. Bill was impressed. *Wow, what a ship this is.*

A strong breeze was blowing, and the sky was a beautiful blue with a few drifting white clouds.

"Bill, you can stow the supplies below and put the food and white wine in the fridge," Dave said. "Sharon and I will prepare to get underway."

"Aye aye, Captain," Bill responded with a smile.

"No, I'm just the First Mate. Sharon's the Skipper."

While Bill was stowing the gear, Dave started the inboard motor and Sharon reviewed the charts.

"Prepare to cast off," Sharon said in a loud voice as she stood behind the wheel.

"Aye," Dave said, as he untied the mooring lines and shoved off. The wind picked up as the yacht moved into blue water, as did the waves in both size and intervals between the swells. The yacht cut through the increasing seas, albeit at a greater angle of heel.

Bill was genuinely impressed with Sharon and Dave's seamanship, and he thoroughly enjoyed the experience.

The sensation of the wind in his hair and the sun on his face was truly relaxing. All thoughts of business and the formidable tasks ahead were forgotten.

"Second Mate, take the wheel," Dave said in a crisp voice.

"Who me? You've got to be kidding!" Bill said, laughing. "I've never even steered a row boat!"

"How else are you going to learn?" Dave asked.

Bill came forward and took the wheel, and Dave said, "Look at the wind indicator and the telltales. Do you see the direction the wind is coming from? Turn towards the wind, and the yacht will begin to heel harder, turn away from the wind, and the yacht will begin to right itself. Now see for yourself, and turn the wheel into the wind."

As Bill did so, a bit too quickly, the yacht began to heel over dramatically. Bill panicked and cried out, "Now what do I do?"

"Steady now, it's almost impossible to capsize a sailing rig of this size, but it is very possible to cause an accidental jibe."

"That's when you inadvertently turn the stern through the wind. That can cause the boom to swing across the stern dramatically, taking anything and anyone in its way overboard."

Bill continued to experiment with the wheel and the direction of the wind while Sharon went below to prepare lunch.

"This is just incredible!" Bill said when Sharon came up on deck with his lunch.

"So, am I going to make a First Mate out of you?" she asked, smiling.

"First Mate, hell, I want to be a Captain."

"Not unless I'm the Admiral," Sharon laughed.

Sharon set the autopilot, while Dave let the mainsail out and hauled the spinnaker down a bit.

The yacht slowed perceptibly, and Sharon then served lunch on the chart table.

Lunch included both TFC and Aunt Sally Mae's SFC. Also, there was an array of French cheeses, including Camembert, Brie, Roblouchon and Roquefort, and two pates, one pork and the other rabbit, and logically, good French bread.

To drink, there were three bottles of wine, a 1970 George de la Tour Private Reserve Cabernet, a 1973 Sancerre, and a 1974 Pouilly Fuisse. A *tart aux pomme* was available for dessert.

"Where and how did you arrange this?" Bill asked, as he ate a piece of TFC.

"Well, while you guys were busy beating up the Western Regional team yesterday, I was out at the French market buying all these good treats. The chicken was delivered last night and reheated in the galley oven."

"And where did you learn so much about French delicacies?" Dave asked.

"When I was a little girl and my father was still in the Navy, we lived in Paris for eighteen months."

"What was your father doing in Paris?" Bill asked, raising his eyebrows. "There aren't any Naval installations nearby, are there?"

"He was the naval attaché to the U.S. Embassy."

"*Parlez-vous francais?*" Dave said with a reasonably good French accent.

"*Non, Monsieur. Je n'ai que très peu l'occasion de le parler maintenant.*"

"Your accent is near perfect," Dave said in a matter-of-fact tone.

"*Vous ets gentil,*" Sharon replied.

"Hey, enough of that," Bill said, laughing. "I can't understand a word."

After they finished the chicken, Dave said, "Aunt Sally Mae's product has a similar spice flavor, only slightly better for my taste. Also, I guess I just prefer crispy coating. Why are the pieces so much bigger?"

"Well, the larger pieces and crispy coating are part of their brand proposition. The rumor is that the mother of the founder taught the Major her secret recipe when they were courting. Only the Major got something a little wrong," Bill said smiling.

"How did they come up with the name Aunt Sally Mae's Southern Fried Chicken?"

"Well, the story goes, the mother used to make her fried chicken for the annual picnics at the local Baptist Church, where her nephew was the pastor, hence Aunt Sally Mae's Southern Fried Chicken."

"Very interesting, I'm surprised they haven't made more of the rumor concerning the teaching of the secret recipe to the Major," Dave said wrinkling his brow.

★ ★ ★

It was early evening by the time they tied up at their mooring. They were all exhausted, but in high spirits. Bill had thoroughly enjoyed his first sailing experience and decided he would sign up for a class.

Dave decided he would look into buying his own sailing rig, probably something in the twenty to twenty-five foot range, with a movable keel to start. Eventually, he knew he wanted at least a thirty-footer with a fixed keel. But all in good time, as he would first have to get his family interested.

Sharon never felt prouder or more fulfilled. Clearly she had been the Captain. Dave looked to her for guidance, and the love of her life had been completely dependent upon her.

More importantly, Bill had genuinely enjoyed the experience, which increased the odds that, someday, she might have her own sailing rig, something she'd dreamed of ever since she was a little girl, sailing with her father almost every weekend when the weather permitted.

Chapter 16

"*Moshi moshi*, Sachiko? Ozawa San would like to have a word with Kenji if he is available," Ozawa's secretary said politely.

"Of course, I'll put him on."

"Did you see Sawamura Trading and Aunt Sally Mae's Southern Fried Chicken International's announcement in Keizai Shimbum this morning?" Ozawa San asked Kenji when he got on the phone.

"Yes, in fact, I was just discussing this with Ray when you called," Kenji answered in a concerned tone.

Ray interrupted. "See if Ozawa San is available for lunch today, so we can discuss this before I call the U.S. tonight."

"Yes, I agree we should meet today to discuss the situation. I'll be at the American Club at one o'clock," Ozawa said, then hung up.

While driving to the American Club, Ray thought to himself, *So, Sawamura Trading must be Saji's client that's so interested in TFC. I wonder if Aunt Sally Mae's Southern Fried Chicken U.S. is involved. If so, there could be an opportunity to play both sides of this game. Hell, with the money I'd make, all tax-free, I could afford to tell TFC to go fuck themselves. Yep, this is exciting all right. But I'll have to play things very carefully going forward. Ozawa and Kenji are no fools.*

While Ray and Kenji were gone to lunch, Fumiko decided she would try to get a copy of the joint venture agreement; she had failed the night before because the operations department was pulling an all-nighter. Ray had promised her another $5,000 in her U.S. investment account if she could copy the document today.

When she returned from lunch, she went into Ray's office, having heard from her friend, Kenji's secretary, that Ray and Kenji were having lunch with Ozawa San. She began searching for the English copy of the joint venture agreement; as she suspected, Ray's file drawers were unlocked. She quickly took the agreement and headed to the copy machine.

As she was heading back to Ray's office, she saw Kenji returning from lunch earlier than expected. Fumiko froze with the agreement and the copy she had just made in her hands.

"Are you okay, Fumiko kun? You look like you have seen a ghost," Kenji said with concern.

"Umm, yes, I'm okay, I just have a little stomach flu. I'll be fine soon."

"Go home and go to bed, now. Fumiko kun, if you stay you will make everyone else sick. You should know better," Kenji said sternly.

"Yes Senmu. I will leave right away. You are right, of course. I am so sorry, please forgive me," she said as she hurried off to her desk. She packed her briefcase with both the original and the copy and left quickly.

Fumiko was distraught, convinced that Kenji would discover the missing joint venture agreement and figure out that she had taken it. She concluded she would have to warn Ray ASAP and went directly to his house to wait for him.

"Ray! We are going to be discovered, and I'm afraid it's today."

"Calm down, Fumichan, and tell me what you're talking about."

"Kenji saw me this afternoon. I had both the original and copied joint venture agreements under my arm. I was heading back to your office to return the original of the agreement. I told Kenji that I had stomach flu, and he sent me home. I've been calling you ever since!" Fumiko said, clearly excited.

"How do you know you were discovered if you left the office right away?"

Pausing for a moment with her finger on her chin, Fumiko said, "Well, I guess I don't know. But with the announcement that Sawamura and Aunt Sally Mae's Southern Fried Chicken have set up a joint venture in Japan, I'm sure the agreement will be reviewed soon."

"You're probably right," Ray said, tapping his fingers on his bar at home, pouring himself another single malt. "You have both copies with you, right?" Fumiko nodded. "Okay, give them both to me. I'll drop off the copy to our buyer and tomorrow I'll take the original in and give it to Kenji. I'll simply tell him I took it home because I wanted to look something up before calling Jim," Ray said, as he took a drink of single malt.

"Oh, you're a genius! Now I can relax," Fumiko said happily.

★★★

"Hello, Sherman, Bill Sanford here."

"Yes, Bill," the stockbroker said. "I've been trying to reach you for a week."

"I've been traveling," Bill said, "what's up?"

"What's up is you have turned your five-thousand-dollar investment in the Canadian brake pad company into forty-two thousand," Sherman said. "I was able to get you in at three-eight. When the announcement of the takeover broke, the stock went straight up to four dollars and then started pulling back. I tried to get you, but I couldn't reach you. So, when Ray called and told me to sell on the next morning, I sold yours as well. Good thing I did. Toyoda backed out of the deal due to some obscure Japanese regulation on the importation of brake pads that contain some substance not allowed in Japan. Today, the stock is back to one-quarter bid and three-eighths ask."

"Come on, Sherman, you can't be serious. I just can't believe this!"

"Well believe it," Sherman said, laughing. "Now, what do you want to do with the money?"

"How much is in the account?"

"Just under seventy thousand, eight hundred," Sherman answered. "Tell you what, why don't I put the bulk of it in short-term triple-A munis; there's a San Francisco school board issue that is currently yielding six-point-eight percent, tax free. Also, keep in mind that with these big gains, you are going to be in a higher tax bracket this year."

Chapter 17

"I don't know about this," Saji said, shaking his head, as he drained his cup of sake. "The Nakajima family is politically connected, and if the heir-apparent suddenly disappears, I'm sure the Patriarch of the family will use all his resources to discover what happened to his son," Saji added, rubbing his chin. "Besides, fifteen million yen is not enough for a disappearance of this complexity."

My father always said to be careful in the disappearance assignments you accept. The Nakajima family has more money than the Emperor. Maybe I should just tell the Patriarch about this deal, Saji chuckled to himself.

"Saji Kumicho, I will give you twenty, no, twenty-five million yen if you will do this favor for me," Hiro Ogawa, President of Ohashi Electric said, leaning over the table and looking right into Saji's eyes.

Twenty-five million, now this is getting interesting.

"Ogawa Shacho, why does this have to be a disappearance? It would be much easier if I just arranged for a tragic accident, and five million yen cheaper," Saji said, taking a bite of his raw fish after dipping it in soy sauce with wasabi.

Taking a deep breath, Ogawa said, "If he simply has an accident then my daughter will know that I arranged it. However, if he disappears, she will hold out hope for his return, and without a body, well, it's less likely she will accuse me of foul play."

Nodding, Saji said, "Yes, I think you're right. Disappearance is definitely the way to go; only it will be thirty million." Saji motioned the sushi bar master over. "I'll have a *negi hamachimaki* and another sake."

"Right away, Saji Kumicho," came the quick reply. This sushi restaurant was one of Saji's favorites in Osaka; in fact, his entire organization came frequently. The owner knew they were Yakuza, but Saji always paid his bills and provided the owner with protection for nothing. Just the previous year, the local bank was threatening to foreclose on the owner. After a visit by one of Saji's lieutenants, the bank decided not to foreclose and, indeed, extended the payment terms on the loan.

"Ogawa Shacho, how quickly do you need the disappearance to occur?" Saji said, sipping his sake.

"As soon as possible. The wedding is scheduled for a week from Saturday," Ogawa said, taking his handkerchief from his coat pocket to wipe the sweat from his face.

"Okay, the disappearance will take place next Monday or Tuesday. Fifteen million will be required up front and fifteen more when the job is done," Saji said, as the owner arrived with his order. "Oh, I assume you're not requiring any torture prior to disposal," Saji added, draining his sake cup and motioning the owner to bring another ceramic carafe.

Confused, Ogawa said, "Torture before, what do you mean?"

"Well, many of our clients are seeking revenge in addition to disappearance," Saji said, dipping his *negi hamachimaki* in the wasabi-laced soy. "I love wasabi," Saji added, smiling and shaking his head.

"No, no, I'm only interested in making him disappear. The thought of my daughter marrying into the Nakajima family is more than I can stand," Ogawa said, again wiping his face. "I'll have the fifteen million for you tomorrow morning before I head back to Tokyo. Thank you so much, Saji Kumicho, for taking care of this problem for me," Ogawa said. He stood up, bowed deeply, and left the restaurant.

I probably could have pushed him to thirty-five million. Oh well, thirty is still good for a night's work. I'll assign this one to Yoji kun. He is very careful and the Nakajima family will spare no expense in finding out who is responsible.

★★★

It was just after 1:00 a.m. on the following Tuesday, when an unusually tall young man with glasses rose to his feet, staggering, and in a slurred voice said, "A toast to our teammate, Hirohito Nakajima, who next Saturday will give up all women except one, my sister, at least until he's back from his honeymoon." The seven men sitting around the table erupted in laughter as they raised their glasses.

The next to try and stand, but failed, was the honoree of the bachelor party, Hirohito Nakajima himself. Sitting down again with some help, he raised his empty glass and said, "I'm drunk," and then collapsed.

Twenty minutes later, the best man loaded the groom into a taxi.

★★★

"Tsunamachi Park Mansion," he said, and then promptly fell asleep.

Saji's lieutenant, Yoji, the leader on this assignment, answered the buzzing walkie-talkie. "It's about time, hell it's almost two a.m.," Yoji yelled, looking at his watch and clicking the walkie-talkie to *receive*.

"So sorry, Yoji San, but the taxi just pulled into Tsunamachi Park Mansion twenty minutes ago. Kato and I are in the bathroom on Nakajima's floor."

"Have you checked the key to his door that I gave you?"

"Of course, Yoji San, both yesterday and today," came the whispered reply.

"How drunk was the target when he got home?"

"So drunk that his friend had to open the door and help him in. He must have undressed him as well, since he didn't come out of the room for twenty minutes," the gangster said.

"Okay, wait another ten minutes, then go in and give him the injection. Have Kato kun watch the halls, and remember, take a full set of clean business clothes with you, and dress the target in a *yukata*. I'm at the exit of the complex and will keep watch until you boys leave." *With the bonus on this one I should be able to retire in a year or two.*

★ ★ ★

The private helicopter was standing by at a small airfield thirty miles outside of Chiba, a new suburb of Tokyo. Yoji was sitting in the copilot's seat as the non-descript Toyoda Sedan pulled into the dark field with only parking lights on. It was 4:45 a.m., and Yoji was anxious and livid. Sunrise was at 5:58 a.m. on this Tuesday morning.

Getting out of the helicopter, Yoji rushed to the gangsters. "Matsuyama kun, tell me what happened right now," Yoji hissed as he put his face right up to the older gangster that had been with him for over ten years. Knowing Yoji's patience was wearing thin and his explosive reaction to failures, Matsuyama decided to break his pact with his younger partner.

Matsuyama remembered how eight years ago Yoji had cut off the left hand of a new recruit who challenged him and how he left the recruit tied to a pine tree in a lonely mountain park to bleed to death. Matsuyama could still recall the pleas for mercy from the young gangster as Yoji tied him to the tree and then tied a rope above the elbow of the severed hand.

"That should give you plenty of time to consider your mistake, and go to your death a wiser man. Unfortunately, you won't be able to use that wisdom," Yoji had laughed, holding his middle, as he'd tightened the tourniquet.

"Go on, tell me what happened tonight," Yoji said, looking directly into Matuyama's eyes.

"We were stopped for speeding on the Chuo Expressway. He was driving," Matsuyama said, pointing at the younger gagster. "The officer took quite some time to process the tickets, in part because his license was expired."

"Anything else?" Yoji asked conversationally.

"Well, the real reason we were held so long is he insisted we stop and get some ramen and beer. The officer smelled the beer on his breath and made him take a sobriety test. *Gomenasai*," Matsuyama added, bowing very low to Yoji.

Yoji began pacing and running his fingers through his hair.

Suddenly, he stopped and swung his left leg around in a perfect roundhouse kick, and struck the younger but much larger gangster in the side of his head. He quickly tied his hands together.

"Put that worthless piece of shit in the back of the helicopter with the target. Make sure you get the tickets the police issued out of the car, then drive the car over to the harbor and send it off the levy. We'll pick you up there."

"That asshole," Yoji cursed as he headed back to the helicopter, "now I'm going to have to arrange an accident for the cop. There goes my big bonus.

"Shit, Saji will make me pay for the car too. I guess I won't be able to retire next year!" Yoji said, entering the front of the helicopter as Matsuyama struggled to get the target and younger gangster in the back of the helicopter.

The sun was just beginning to rise; the colors began as purple and slowly turned to increasingly lighter shades of red, and finally yellow mixing with the red before ultimately replacing it. The helicopter pilot signaled Yoji that they had reached their destination, about fifty miles offshore.

"Look at that sunrise. Isn't it just beautiful?" Yoji said to the pilot. "It's my favorite sight, watching the sun rise over the ocean," he added.

Yoji then got out of his seat and went to the back of the helicopter and opened the back hatch. As the cool air rushed in, the younger gangster awoke and began to plead. "Oh, Yoji Bucho, please don't throw me in the ocean. I'll do anything you ask." Sobbing, he added, "I have ten million yen in a bank account which I'll give you. Please, please, don't kill me!"

"How do I know you're not lying?" Yoji asked, his interest piqued.

"Look in my wallet, it's in my coat pocket," the young gangster said hopefully.

"Hmmm, I see your bank card, but what is the pin number?" Yoji asked casually.

"It's 486-250. I promise you that's it and there is ten point seven million yen in the account."

"Okay, 486-250. It better be the right pin number, or I'll do far worse than throw you in the sea," Yoji said, poking his finger in the young gangster's chest.

With tears running down his face, the young gangster said, "Oh thank you, thank you, Yoji Bucho! You won't regret this."

"All right, enough of that. Take the target and dump him in the sea," Yoji said, as he untied the young gangster's hands.

"Of course, right away Yoji Bucho!"

The target was unconscious and difficult to move. The young gangster struggled but finally got the target to the open back hatch. With considerable effort, he pushed the target out. As he turned around, Yoji kicked him squarely in the chest, and he fell back screaming into the ocean.

Pin 486-250: well that'll take care of my missed bonus. Hell, I might be able to retire after all! "Pilot, let me buy you breakfast," Yoji said, returning to the co-pilot seat.

CHAPTER 18

"Hello Mr. Sanford, I have the travel agent Bing on the phone for you. Shall I put him through?" Carmen asked.

"Sure, thanks Carmen."

"Mr. Sanford, Bing here. I've got some exciting options for you," Bing said in an upbeat voice.

"Great, what do you have?"

"Well, how about a Sea Breeze, thirty-footer moored in St. John's, the U.S. Virgin Islands, available from November fifteenth to the twenty-second. I'm not sure about the First Mate, though," Bing said. "Or a twelve meter out of San Juan, a little older but with a great First Mate, a forty-something gal that works as a cook at the Hilton when she isn't out at sea. And finally, a twelve meter out of Normandy, two years old, and a male First Mate who is also the owner, and who claims to be a gourmet cook, certainly for Americans," Bing added in an exaggerated French accent.

Bill just laughed and said, "What about onboard accommodations?"

"All of them have at least two cabins, although the twelve meter in San Juan has the largest master suite and common living area, because it has only one other sleeping cabin. The other two yachts both have three sleeping cabins," Bing said.

"Now the big question: how much is this going to set me back?" Bill asked seriously.

"Well, including round-trip coach airfare for two, the total costs including everything but food and drinks range from thirty-three hundred for the yacht moored in St. John, thirty-six fifty for the yacht moored in San Juan, to forty-six hundred for the yacht moored in Normandy. By the way, did you find out what kind of license your captain has?"

"Yeah, she said she has her Masters Papers," Bill said. "I'll get more specific information, but this is supposed to be a surprise, so I didn't want to push for too much more detail."

"Oh, you won't need more specific information until a week or so before you leave, as long as her Masters Papers are up to date."

"Well, it sounds like San Juan is the best overall," Bill said. "But before we make a final decision, could you get me specific information on the three yachts, including pictures?"

"Absolutely, I have asked all three owners specifically for that information, including points of interest to sail to within the week," Bing said.

"Perfect! This should be a real hoot," Bill said laughing.

★★★

At exactly 11:00 a.m., Sam Liberwitz showed up for their appointment. "Good Morning, Sam, you're just as punctual as your cousin Dave," Bill said, as he stood up and shook hands with his new attorney.

"Well, it runs in the family. Our grandfather was an engineer on the Baltimore Central, which he said was never late on his watch."

Bill chuckled at the remark.

"So what have you decided?" Sam asked.

"I've decided to accept the offer, the total offer, including the twenty-five grand up front payment in lieu of periodic child support, and the visitation we outlined instead of joint custody."

"I think you are making the right choice. However, I'm a bit surprised that you can come up with the twenty-five thousand. None of my business, but what has changed since day before yesterday?"

"Well, I just found out that a stock tip I got from our Regional VP in Japan hit a ten-fold increase!" Bill said, as he leaned forward and grinned. "With that gain, which I share with my girlfriend Sharon, I can easily pay off the child support. This guy Easton is something. This is the second Canadian stock he has put us in, in less than two months, that has paid off."

"Canadian stocks that were presumably takeover targets, of what company, if you don't mind me asking?"

"Well, come to think of it, Toyoda was the acquiring company in both cases. Why do you ask?" Bill asked, raising his eyebrows.

"I'm not sure in this case, but I used to work at the Securities and Exchange Commission and this seems like a classical case of insider trading. Were you limited in the number of shares you could purchase? And were there only a few other people in the know that you knew of?"

"As a matter of fact, yes to both questions." Bill had a worried look on his face when he added, "I'm not in any trouble, am I?"

"Not at all, as long as you knew nothing about the circumstances in which this Easton got the insider information. Of course, assuming that's what it was."

Sam then went on to explain the divorce process from this point forward, including details on jurisdiction. Bill didn't really concentrate on the process details Sam was reviewing; all he could think about was whether or not Ray was really involved in some sort of insider trading.

"Do you have any questions, Bill? You look a bit distracted," Sam added.

"Well, your comments about insider trading got me thinking about Ray and his extraordinary relationship with Mitsugawa Trading. Just between us, Dave has his suspicions about Ray and his relationship with Mitsugawa Trading. As Japan's largest trading company, Mitsugawa is well connected to many Japanese industrial giants, and I suspect that includes Toyoda. I think I'll share this conversation with Dave."

"Good idea," Sam said, "if anyone knows about the convoluted relationships in Japan it's Dave. He has spent years dealing with clients involved in Japan. I'm sure he has shared his Sam's Cola versus International Foods in Japan study."

"Yeah, I've now heard it ten different times and can probably make the presentation myself."

"Well, back to our business. Since you agree with their offer, I'll formalize the agreement in writing and get you a final draft. You need to get me a certified check in the amount of twenty-five thousand, payable to the William Sanford escrow account. Finally, here is a list of items your wife requires that you ship to her, at your expense, as part of the divorce settlement," Sam said, handing the list over to Bill.

Bill reviewed the list carefully and then asked, "Is this it? What about her interest in the house and the various savings and checking accounts? Oh, and her car?" Bill was shocked.

"Nope, all you need to do is have all the items on that list packed and shipped to her, and she will release any and all rights and interests she has or may have had, in any and all property, personal and real," Sam said, in a matter-of-fact manner.

"Wow, she must be ready to settle down with that prick *Daddy* introduced us to last Thanksgiving; otherwise, they wouldn't be so generous."

"Hey, don't complain! You're the big winner here," Sam said.

"Yeah, you're absolutely right!" *I can't imagine how anyone could possibly love that bitch, never mind be around her insufferable father,* Bill thought.

Chapter 19

Haneda airport handled both international and domestic flights arriving in Tokyo. On the busiest days of the week, Monday and Friday, it was not unusual for ten flights per hour to arrive and be processed. A new airport for only international flights was planned, but since significant land had to be reclaimed from the Sea of Japan, it would be five years before it was finished.

When Ashley emerged from immigration, she scanned the mobs of people, looking for Inoue. She hadn't realized that while he stood out in a crowd back in Mobile Alabama, Aunt Sally Mae's Southern Fried Chicken headquarters, here he was just one of the mass of bodies mingling around.

Finally, she saw him and waved. But there were so many people it took her five minutes to make her way to him.

"Is this a holiday or something?" Ashley said, smiling. "There are so many people!"

"Not at all, in fact, since it's a Saturday, the crowds are actually rather thin."

The twenty-five mile trip to the Imperial Hotel took almost an hour and a half. Inoue commented that was about normal for a Saturday.

"So what does it take on a busy business day?" Ashley asked, smiling.

"On New Year's Eve it sometimes takes eighteen hours," Inoue said with a straight face.

"Tomorrow is Sunday, so I thought you might be interested in seeing my family's country place. It's a three-hour train ride, but it has been in my family for over four hundred years.

"The main house was built two hundred eighty years ago and sits on the shore of a beautiful lake. On a clear day, there is a remarkable view of Mount Fuji."

"I'd love to see it," Ashley said.

★ ★ ★

Due to her jet lag, Ashley had been up since 3:00 a.m. and it was nearly six before Inoue arrived. There was little traffic out at that time on a Sunday morning.

As they left the sprawl of Tokyo behind them, Ashley was surprised at the rugged beauty of the countryside. After two hours, they left the super highway, and as they progressed up the mountains, they traveled along back roads that were remarkably narrow and full of sharp turns.

Suddenly, they turned into an obscure driveway that was hidden from the road.

Ashley caught her breath and looked at the most beautiful Japanese garden she had ever seen. It looked like something out of a book.

The main attraction was a waterfall, emptying into a small, irregularly-shaped brook filled with enormous carp of various colors. Next to this was a small stone bench. Stark white pea gravel surrounded the brook and waterfall.

There were also four perfectly-shaped pine trees, each providing an element of shade to the bench at different times of the day, so that anyone who happened to be sitting on it was shaded from the sun the entire day.

Farther along, they came to an ancient entrance gate that was at least twenty feet high and twelve feet wide. It was deep red in color with gold and black trim. All along the perimeter was a ten-foot-high stone wall that was weathered to a dark gray.

Beyond the gate was another Japanese garden, leading up to what looked like a Buddhist temple. It was in fact the main house, as Ashley soon discovered.

A gardener greeted them; he was dressed in traditional garb that included black leggings, a waist-length cotton robe with mountain scenes on it, and straw slippers over black socks with only the big toe separated.

An older woman in a beautiful kimono met them at the entrance and bowed deeply as Inoue entered. "*Irashaimasei,* Inoue Sama," the housekeeper said.

"*Ohayo gozaimasu,* Yoko San," Inoue responded.

"Please take off your shoes and put these slippers on," Inoue said to Ashley, as he removed his own shoes.

The floors were solid wide pine, with the seams nearly invisible. They were so well polished they looked nearly like black mirrors. Inoue led Ashley through the house to the rear, which opened onto a beautiful patio.

Ashley gasped. Below them, in the distance, was an enormous lake, and above it was Mount Fuji, looking just like the postcards she had seen at the airport.

"My God, I don't think I've ever seen anything as beautiful as this scene."

"Well, you will see something much more beautiful in about seven hours when the sun sets," Inoue said matter-of-factly. "Fuji San will turn various shades of pink, red, and purple and reflect these colors on to the lake, which will subtly change the hues and reflect them up."

"I can't wait!"

The housemaid, Yoko San, called them for lunch at about 12:30. Lunch included an array of Japanese appetizers, such as tuna sushi roll, assorted sashimi, grilled chicken skewers with teriyaki sauce, shrimp and vegetable tempura, and assorted pickles. Finally, a large bowl of Chinese noodle soup with vegetables and shredded pork was served with hot sake.

They spent the afternoon walking the grounds of the estate and later exploring the village that was renowned for its local sake and lacquer bowls. Ashley bought several bowls, and they sampled the local sake, which Inoue said was excellent.

When dusk arrived, Ashley was on the patio as Inoue was preparing drinks at a beautiful teak bar. "This is the most spectacular sight I have ever seen! The reflection of the sunset off Mt. Fuji and then off Lake Hakkone is nothing short of amazing. It seems as though the entire spectrum of yellows, pinks, reds and purples are revealed in hues that could not be duplicated!"

They left Inoue's country estate at dark for what turned out to be an eight-hour drive back to the hotel because of traffic returning to Tokyo.

★★★

The next day Inoue and Ashley made the rounds. First they visited Adam & Young CPAs. The partner was an expat from North Dakota, just arrived, and the Japanese Manager was fluent in English but had just been hired and had no food experience. "So that is the firm you think J.J. wants to use?" Inoue asked.

Ashley was obviously a bit embarrassed and said, "Okay, be nice, I must admit that was a dismal experience." Next up was Aunt Sally Mae's U.S. ad agency's Japanese joint venture, Williams & Spencer Hirakikohoku, a premiere Joint venture of U.S. and Japanese advertising agencies. The agency's team was very buttoned up and professional.

Inoue was impressed with their presentation concerning the competitive review and consumer consumption trends. However, when they got to their recommendations, it was clear that they simply did a lift from the U.S. campaign and translated it into Japanese—and poor Japanese at that. Inoue's recommended ad agency, Yamamoto Senden, made their presentation the next morning. Ashley was astounded. It was the best agency presentation she had ever seen. Inoue's school chum, the Account Group Director Ohkawara San, was logical, thorough, and pleasant. The agency then reviewed advertising and promotions of TFC Japan's competitors, Mr. Burger, Scalanni Pizza, and Hokkaido Ramen over the past two years, Ashley was shocked; it looked nothing like the advertising campaigns running in the U.S. for TFC or Mr. Burger.

Inoue then explained the story of how the founder of Aunt Sally Mae's Southern Fried Chicken had taught Major Tom the secret recipe during a failed courting relationship, and how the Major never did get it quite right.

The Yamamoto Senden team was taking careful notes as Inoue relayed the story. When he finished, an older gentleman who hadn't said a word spoke up. "This story has the potential to leapfrog TFC in both authenticity and quality. I think it is possible to spread this story through image-leader publicity. The key will be timing. Not too soon, because TFC will react strongly and quickly if I know their Managing Director, Kenji Kato—he is ruthless."

Ohkawara San introduced the speaker as the Director of Publicity.

"How do you know the TFC Japan Managing Director?" Ashley asked.

"His Uncle and I grew up together in Osaka."

Inoue wrapped up the meeting by inviting Yamamoto Senden to participate in the agency pitch for the brand. Ashley thanked Ohkawara San for his presentation and told him it was the best she had ever experienced from an advertising agency.

The next morning, they caught an early flight to Sapporo, located on the northern island of Hokkaido. Ashley was surprised that they were able to put five hundred people on a 747. There was only one class and the upstairs was just more of the same coach seats.

When they arrived, the Sawamura Branch Manager for Hokkaido met them. He drove them to an expensive business district that had three large apartment complexes within a one-mile radius. The site was on the first floor of an office building with around twelve hundred square feet of usable space.

"Isn't this awfully small?" Ashley asked.

"Are you kidding?" Inoue said, laughing, "This is enormous by Japanese standards."

After driving around the neighborhood, they went to the realtor's office and Inoue signed the lease. When they had finished lunch at a Hokkaido Ramen shop, where they had *gyoza* (pork dumplings), two large bowls of noodles with tempura, and Sapporo beer to drink, they went to the airport to catch a flight to Fukuoka on the southern island of Kyushu, their second stop on the site-selection trip.

As in Sapporo, the local Sawamura Branch Manager met them at the airport.

The site location was different from Sapporo. It was a highly congested business district, but the real prize was a college just three hundred meters away and two apartment buildings within a half-mile radius.

The usable space was a little less at eleven hundred fifty square feet. Ashley was excited at the proximity to the college. She knew the college would be a great opportunity for cost-effective sampling among the target group.

After signing the lease at the realtor's office, they went to the Prince Hotel and checked in. Inoue told the Branch Manager that they would manage dinner on their own.

The next morning, they caught the 10:00 a.m. bullet train for Nagoya. Again, at the train station, they were met by the Sawamura Branch Manager and driven off to the site. This site was actually in a tourist area.

The Nagoya castle was less than two miles away. It attracted hundreds of thousands of visitors each year, mostly Japanese. The American consulate was only a mile and a half away, and there were two public high schools within half a mile.

At fourteen hundred square feet, this site was the largest. All agreed this was an ideal location.

Chapter 20

Bill walked into Dave's office. "Boss, do you have a minute?"

Dave was engrossed as he looked up from his easel. "Sure, have a seat and let me finish this thought."

"Can I get you a cup of coffee or a cold drink?" Carmen asked from the door.

"Thanks, a coffee would be great, black no sugar."

A couple of minutes later, Dave emerged from behind the easel and motioned Bill to one of the armed leather chairs next to the window overlooking the garden. This was the first time Bill had ever seen anyone in those chairs.

"So what's up? You look a bit nervous."

"Well, honestly I am; I've got two things to share with you in confidence."

"Bill, depending on what you tell me, I may have to share your information with others," Dave said. He leaned forward and put his fingertips together. "Now, tell me what's bothering you."

"Well, both issues involve Ray Easton," Bill said, taking a deep breath. "First, when I met with your cousin yesterday, he suggested I tell you about my good fortune in the stock market." Bill then revealed the stock tips he had received from Ray, pointing out he had not traded the first one.

When he outlined the incredible short-term gains, Dave raised his eyebrows and his expression turned serious. Bill left out the fact that Sharon had invested half the original capital.

"In any case, Sam thinks it might be insider trading."

"Well if it is, it's certainly serious. Insider trading is a class two felony. By the way, I wouldn't put it past Easton. Do you know if he has shared these tips with anyone else?"

"Yes, Lindsay, Jim's secretary, and Kenji. Dave, do you think I'm in trouble?"

"No, relax Bill, you're actually sweating," Dave said leaning forward. "As long as you didn't know it was insider information and you reported it when you discovered it might be, you'll be okay. However, if it turns out to be insider trading you'll be required to help the investigation." Bill winced as Dave continued.

"It's interesting that two of the tips were on small Canadian companies that were acquired, or at least received offers, from Toyoda. Mitsugawa has close connections with Toyoda. I'll find out how close. But I'll bet you if Easton is getting inside information it's coming from Ozawa."

"Are you sure I'll be okay if I cooperate?" Bill said, his face flushing. "I mean how do I report this to begin with?"

"You already have by telling me and Sam. Sam used to work for the Securities and Exchange Commission and has plenty of contacts left.

"Now, when you're in Tokyo this week, you've got to be careful not to let Easton know that we suspect insider trading. However, if you can, you should subtly see if you can get Kenji to talk about Ray's tips. Be casual, but drop the subject if Kenji seems at all reluctant to talk about it. Oh, and if Ray gives you any more tips, I would not act on them.

"Now, what's the second issue concerning our Artful Dodger?" Dave asked, crossing his legs.

"Well I'm not at all sure this information is correct," Bill said, leaning forward and interlocking his fingers. Bill then related everything Lisa had told him, including how he had met Lisa and indeed had seen her at Ray's party for the newly arrived models.

Uncrossing his legs and tapping his fingertips together, Dave sat without saying a word for several seconds.

"Okay, Bill, this second issue is industrial espionage. First things first, you need to go to Japan via Osaka and get Lisa out. Carmen will have Bing cut a one-way ticket. This host of hers sounds like he's Yakuza," Dave said. Pausing, he got up and went to his easel, where he picked up a pen and started writing.

Returning to his chair with pen and pad, Dave continued, "Next, you must not let on to anything when you're in Tokyo. Just watch for signs, in particular see if Ozawa acts strange.

"Also, we don't know if Kenji is involved in this espionage in any way. Somehow I doubt it, but we'll need to confirm this." Looking directly at Bill, Dave added, "Son, I'm sorry to put you in such a difficult position, but there is no alternative. You must be very careful and keep your wits about you. Remember, the objective is to investigate, without putting yourself at risk.

Dave rose from his chair, indicating an end to the meeting. "Bill, you've done the right thing sharing this information with me."

★★★

Standing at the stove in her bathrobe, with tears rolling down her face, Sharon said, "I don't want you to go! This is an unacceptable risk, and I can't believe you're willing to take it."

"Come on, sweetheart, I have to do this. I have a moral obligation; besides, the risk isn't as great as you think," Bill said, putting his hands on Sharon's shoulders.

"Bullshit! You yourself said you think this Saji character is Japanese Mafia," Sharon said, sobbing while shaking her shoulders free of Bill's hands.

"Look, my flight gets in at ten a.m. Osaka time," Bill said, turning Sharon around to face him. "I've arranged for a driver for the day. Lisa is going to meet me at the Osaka train station, which is just three blocks from Saji's penthouse. This is where she goes every day at eleven-thirty a.m. when Saji is sound asleep, and—"

"Yeah, and what if your flight is an hour late, or Saji is not asleep?" Sharon said, still sobbing. "Bill, I don't want you to go," she added, hugging him.

"Sweetheart, don't do this. I can't stand to see you cry," Bill said, squeezing her tightly. "I promise you, I'll be extremely careful," he said, pulling back and looking into Sharon's eyes. "Listen, if the flight's late, even by half an hour, or if Lisa is not at the appointed phone booth, I will go on directly to Tokyo."

"Promise?" Sharon asked, wiping her face with a dishcloth.

"I swear I'll do just that. Now, give me a smile and let me see those beautiful dimples of yours."

"Call me the minute after you put Lisa on her flight back to the U.S." Sharon said, putting her hands on Bill's shoulders.

"I hope this Lisa appreciates what you're doing. I know I'm not going to sleep a wink until I get your call!"

"Don't worry Sharon," Bill said as he got into the airport limo.

What if this Lisa appreciates what Bill has done too much? After all, she went to Japan to become a model and she lives in Maine. Oh, you're being silly, Sharon thought, *Bill is nothing like Jack. Stop torturing yourself!*

★★★

Bill was exhausted when the 747SP touched down at the Osaka International Airport at 9:45, fifteen minutes ahead of schedule. He hadn't slept a wink on the eleven-hour flight from LA.

All he could think of was how sad Sharon looked when the limo arrived at her house to pick him up for the two-hour ride to JFK. She waved goodbye from the driveway, but her tears had started again.

When Bill collected his bag it was 10:20 local time. *So far so good,* he thought looking at his watch.

When he exited the airport, he saw a non-descript black Toyoda Sedan; a driver with white gloves holding a sign that said "Pill Sand Fort" was standing next to it. Bill broke into a belly laugh. *Close enough!*

"*Osaka Eki made kudasai,*" Bill said, after he entered the back seat.

"*Okkyakusan, wa nihongo jouzu,*" the driver said, smiling at Bill in the rearview mirror. "But I also speak little bit English," he added, still smiling.

They arrived at the train station at 11:05. Bill remained in the back seat, remembering Sharon's concerns. *What if Lisa isn't here, or is followed, what'll I do?* he thought, as sweat began to bead on his forehead.

The driver turned around with a surprised look. "*Daijobudesuka.*"

"*Hai,* yes, I'm fine, just a little tired. I didn't sleep on the plane. Listen, I'm a bit early for meeting my pickup, so I'm going to go get a beer," Bill said, looking at his watch. "Be back in this spot at eleven-thirty sharp. *Wakataka?*"

"Yes, I understand, I'll be back at eleven-thirty," the driver said, smiling as he drove off.

Bill found an open seat at a small bar next to the bullet train platform. A bullet train bound for Tokyo was boarding for the three-hour journey.

"*Kato biru no chu bin kudasai* (Give me a large Kato beer please)," Bill said to the woman behind the bar.

"*Tabemonowa?* (And to eat?)," she said in a business-like tone.

"*Ja miso ramen* (Okay, a miso ramen)," Bill replied, looking at his watch; it was 11:12. The beads of sweat returned as Bill began to eat his noodles.

The beer certainly hit the spot, and he ordered a second one, hoping it would calm him further. As he was finishing his second beer, Lisa walked past him on her way to the public phone.

Almost choking, Bill yelled, "Lisa, Lisa over here." He stood and motioned her over.

Lisa turned and literally ran into Bill's arms.

"My God, it's you! You really did come," Lisa said, hugging Bill, as tears streamed down her face. "How can I ever repay you for this?" Lisa then kissed Bill passionately. "I'll think of something," she added, smiling.

Bill was surprised at Lisa's passionate kiss, and even more at his reaction. *What am I thinking? Sharon is my love yet the thought of Lisa's 'I'll think of something' is giving me a hard on—come on Bill!* Clearing his throat, Bill said, "I'm, I'm just glad you're okay." Looking around, he added, "You weren't followed? Was Saji asleep?"

"As far as I know, I've never been followed, and no one seems to look for me until around two p.m.," Lisa said, wiping her eyes. "Saji is on his way to Tokyo, I assume to see a client."

"What makes you say that?" Bill asked, raising his eyebrows.

"Because I heard him talking on the phone early this morning, and when he left he put the envelope with the new-store sites file in his briefcase, so I assume he's planning on seeing both Ray and his client," Lisa said, as she sat down in Bill's seat.

"You don't know who the client is, do you?" Bill asked, relaxed after Lisa's arrival and the two beers.

"No I don't. But I think it has something to do with Sawamura Trading, as I've heard Saji repeatedly refer to it in his telephone conversations with Ray.

"Hey, how about one of those beers for me?" Lisa said, smiling.

Looking at his watch, he said, "Okay, but just one. I've got you on a one-thirty flight to LA, connecting and getting you into Portland, Maine, at ten-thirty pm local time.

"I took the liberty of contacting your parents who are going to meet you at the airport," Bill said, smiling.

With the tears starting again, Lisa said, "God am I glad I met you on that flight over; it seems like years ago." Reaching out for his hand and squeezing, Lisa added, "Thank you so much, Bill. I hope you'll let me show you how much once we get back Stateside."

As Bill opened the back door to the limo for Lisa, she gasped, "Oh my God, that's one of Saji's men," pointing at a short, stocky, middle-aged man dressed in a dark blue suit, who was only ten feet away.

He had two big scars, one on his left cheek and another across his forehead, both purple.

Bill pushed Lisa into the back seat and jumped in himself, "*Hayaku! Hikojo made!*" Bill yelled to the driver.

"Don't worry, once we get to the airport, no one is going to try anything in a public place like that," Bill said, calmly looking directly at Lisa.

She began to cry and through her tears said, "Are you sure we're going to be okay?"

"Absolutely!" Bill said, putting his arm around her shoulder. Looking at his watch, he added, "You'll be home in seventeen hours, and this whole experience will be like a bad dream you've left behind!"

When Lisa and Bill arrived at Lisa's gate, the information board indicated the flight was delayed for two hours. Lisa couldn't believe her bad luck after all she had been through. As she started to sob, her shoulders shook and Bill put his arms around her.

"Lisa, don't cry, it's going to be alright, it's only a delay," Bill said as he stroked her silky blond hair.

"Are you sure?" Lisa said, lips trembling as she looked up at Bill.

"Yes, I'm sure," Bill whispered as he held her head in his hands and looked into her frightened eyes.

Lisa leaned forward and gave Bill another long and passionate kiss, to which Bill responded.

The scarred man did show up at the airport, but Bill was right, he tried nothing, although he did keep staring at Lisa from fifty feet away.

Finally Lisa's flight was called.

"Oh, thank God!" Lisa squealed. With tears in her eyes she hugged Bill and looking directly in his eyes said, "I can never thank you enough! Bill, I mean it! I'd love to see you again back in the States." Before Bill could say anything she raised her hand and said, "Bill, at least consider it."

She kissed Bill passionately again and hurried toward her gate. Bill waited until the plane backed away from the gate before going to the international pay phone. *What was I thinking, she's only a kid. Shit, what a stupid thing to do!*

★★★

It was just after 3:00 a.m. in Connecticut, but Sharon answered the phone on the first ring, "Bill? Is everything alright?" Sharon said, her voice cracking.

"*Moshi moshi, Moran San desuka,*" Bill said, with his best Japanese accent.

For a moment there was silence. "*Moshi moshi* yourself, you could never fool me. I don't care what language you use," Sharon said, laughing with relief.

★★★

When Bill arrived at the Haneda airport in Tokyo, Fumiko was there to meet him.

"Welcome back to Japan, Bill San. How are you? You must be tired after your overnight flight," Fumiko said pleasantly.

"Well, yes, I'm a little tired. What time am I scheduled to meet with Ray and Kenji?"

"We've already checked you into the Hotel Okura. Ray suggested that you get some sleep. I'll pick you up at noon and take you to the American Club to have lunch with Ray and Kenji San."

On the drive to the hotel, Fumiko said with a smile, "Bill San, congratulations on your divorce and your new girl friend."

After a moment she added, "Ray San tells me she is head of the computer department at headquarters, an important job."

"Well, yes, she has an important job," Bill said.

When Bill arrived at the American Club for lunch, he found Ray, Kenji, and Ozawa San deep in conversation.

When Ray noticed Bill, he motioned him over and said, "Did you get some sleep? I hope so, because we've got a lot to cover over the next couple of days.

"As you've heard, Aunt Sally Mae's Southern Fried Chicken has announced a joint venture with Sawamura Trading. Locally, we are absolutely determined to hit them head on and knock them out of the market before they get started.

"Further, I don't give a shit what Corporate thinks and I—"

Ozawa San, raising his hand, interrupted, "Ray, relax. Bill is not our enemy but our friend. Bill, in Japan Sawamura Trading is a very significant company—that's the bad news. However, there is some good news. I have schoolmates at Sawamura Trading and, according to them, this seems to be a project championed by the managing director, Inoue Senmu, for personal reasons. Apparently, he does not have broad-based support within the group. This means that if we ensure failure among their initial stores, there's a good chance this joint venture will simply disappear."

"Is it conceivable that a major company like Sawamura Trading would enter into a significant business transaction," Bill asked with a puzzled look, "like an international joint venture, simply because the Managing Director had personal reasons for it? I thought management in Japan was based on consensus."

"You're right, in principal. The Japanese management system is based on consensus. However, the Managing Director of any company has major 'favors' due him from his fellow Directors, which he can use at his discretion.

"Sawamura Trading had been a very traditional and conservative company until Inoue San became Managing Director. He has led Sawamura into much more aggressive business ventures. Like me, he believes that Japan will become much more westernized, and he is leading Sawamura in that direction," Ozawa patiently explained.

"Do you know what his personal reasons are?"

"There are a couple. First, Inoue San was a highly decorated officer during World War Two. After the war, he applied to Mitsugawa for a job. The senior team at Mitsugawa rejected him in favor of one of his subordinate officers due to family background.

"You see, Inoue San's family background was Ronin, the lowest class of Samurai, basically wandering mercenaries. The subordinate officer, who was not as highly decorated, but who came from a legitimate Samurai family background, was none other than me," Ozawa said with a smile.

"Additionally, Inoue Senmu later fell in love with a Keiko Sakurai. Her father had been killed in the war, so her eldest brother was head of the family. When he found out that Inoue San was seeing his sister, he forbade her from seeing him. Despite Inoue San's direct appeal, the eldest brother, Joji Sakurai, refused. Like a good Samurai, Keiko Sakurai complied and stopped seeing Inoue San. He has never recovered."

"Wait a second! Is this the same Joji Sakurai that is President of TFC Japan?" Bill asked with wide eyes.

"The very same," Ozawa San said with a smile, taking a sip of his wine.

"This certainly explains a lot," Bill said, nodding. "What a small world we live in."

★ ★ ★

When they returned to the TFC Japan offices, Kenji walked Bill through the "Stop Aunt Sally Mae's Southern Fried Chicken Now Plan." Basically, it called for opening outlets as close as possible to any and all of the new competitor's sites.

So far, only one site in Sapporo had been identified and TFC Japan was negotiating with the owner of a nearby tofu shop to rent his property for two years.

"Since the lease is short-term, we shouldn't have to capitalize it, right?" Ray asked.

"True, but you will still need a Capital Appropriation Request if the expenses exceed eighty grand, including the lease expense for two years. I imagine the equipment and remodeling will well exceed that."

"Not necessarily. We can reuse all the equipment at another store when Aunt Sally Mae closes its stores," Kenji offered.

"Yeah, I guess that's right."

Kenji explained the rest of the plan, which included massive price promotions at all 'flanker' stores. TFC Japan would offer two for one on all items, until the Aunt Sally Mae outlet closed.

"What is the cost of all this? Do you have any of this covered in the most recent forecast?"

"It doesn't fucking matter what the cost is, or what is covered in the most recent forecast!" Ray almost yelled. "I'm sick and tired of Hartford trying to micro-manage and second-guess us at every single turn. This, while they let that prima donna Rosenberg fuck up the U.S. by over-franchising already over-developed markets."

This guy deserves an Oscar for this performance, Bill thought as Ray continued railing against TFC Domestic and Rosenberg.

★★★

Bill spent the afternoon working on the estimates TFC Japan had prepared for the "Get Aunt Sally Mae's Now" promotion, which Bill renamed "Project Destroy." He went back to the hotel at 6:30 and called Dave at home; it was 6:00 a.m. in Hartford.

Dave answered on the first ring. "Good evening, Bill, so what have you learned?" Dave asked evenly.

"Quite a bit, actually," Bill said, and then explained what Ozawa had relayed concerning Inoue San and his vendetta against Joji Sakurai, President of TFC Japan, for preventing his union with the love of his life, and Ozawa himself, for being chosen ahead of Inoue San by Mitsugawa.

"Um, that would suggest that Inoue is certainly motivated to get Aunt Sally Mae going in Japan. Hell, not only would he get back at Joji Sakurai, but he would also hurt his former subordinate whom Mitsugawa snubbed him for," Dave said, pausing for a full minute.

"Incidentally, I got a call from Lisa's father yesterday, saying she had arrived safe and sound. He also said he definitely wants to meet you when you get back."

"Come on, Dave, it was no big deal. In fact, it was uneventful," Bill said, shifting in his chair.

"Have you picked up anything that would suggest that Ray is involved in industrial espionage? Ozawa's information certainly suggests that Inoue would do almost anything to get internal information," Dave said, looking at his watch.

"I'm afraid not—Ray is acting the Chairman role to the hilt. I'm sure both Ozawa and Kenji suspect nothing, although Kenji did ask about how much I'd made off of Ray's stock tips, suggesting that I could make tons more if I came to Japan as part of the team."

"Listen, I've got a meeting with Willis in thirty minutes. He'll be interested in TFC Japan's response to Aunt Sally Mae's launch. Give me a bottom line," Dave said, obviously anxious to get going.

"Well, the team here is absolutely determined to stop Aunt Sally Mae in its tracks. The project is called "Stop Aunt Sally Mae's," and all employees are aware of it. In fact, they're all wearing headbands that say "beat them now." The basic strategy is to build a 'flanker' store as close as possible to every Aunt Sally Mae store that opens. Then, and this is the expensive part, offer a two for one on every item, until the store closes. They estimate that it won't take more than two months for any given Aunt Sally Mae outlet to close. But it's only a guess, and at ten grand a week, this project can get expensive in a hurry."

"So, what are the specific numbers, how much of it is covered in the most recent forecast, and what is your recommendation?"

Bill hadn't expected that question, so he thought for a moment before responding. "I think we should approve three stores at no more than one hundred fifty thousand per store; then, I think we monitor the situation and approve additional stores on a case-by-case basis only. Part of the criteria for approving additional stores will be successful evidence of the project working, specifically, the Aunt Sally Mae stores actually closing within two months after our 'flanker' stores are opened."

"Makes sense to me. I'll inform Jim, Gene, and Ralph of what we're doing. You write up your plan as a proposal and have Kenji and Ray sign it, and you bring it back with you. Keep me posted, and don't take any unnecessary risks," Dave said as he hung up.

Chapter 21

The Italian restaurant, La Patata, was crowded for a weeknight. Bill was the first one to arrive and was seated at a large table at the rear of the restaurant, which offered some level of privacy.

The restaurant was small and considered one of the best Italian restaurants in Tokyo. Its owner, Giovanni Castillioni, had moved to Japan in the early '50s with his bride Yoko, whom he had met in Milan on her semester abroad in 1949.

Giovanni's father had been a master chef in Milan, where he was recognized as the best chef in the city. He taught his son well and it showed in the popularity of the restaurant.

Giovanni never provided a menu. This was one of the attractions; the same main courses were never offered on successive days.

After a couple of minutes, a large man in a white chef's outfit came over. "*Bienvenuto, et buona sera,*" he said, as he put a flute of sweet vermouth and a small plate of antipasto down. He moved on to the next table without saying another word, just wearing a large smile.

Five minutes later, Ray, Kenji, and Ozawa arrived and walked right over to the table. Clearly, they were regulars, as Giovanni returned immediately and welcomed them in Japanese.

Giovanni left after a few minutes of discussion with Ozawa. He returned with four different bowls of pasta, including fettuccine alfredo, Bill's favorite, spaghetti bolognese, spaghetti alla carbonara, and bowties with sweet sausage. A few minutes later, he came with an enormous platter of antipasto, salad caprese and two baskets of garlic bread. Another waiter arrived with wine glasses and served everyone a large glass of Chianti Classico.

"So, Bill San, what do you think of our "Stop Aunt Sally Mae Now" plan?" Ozawa asked.

"I personally think it has a good chance of working—especially if the Sawamura Trading Managing Director is short on board support. I estimate we'll lose between eight and ten thousand dollars per store, per week, and we'll spend one hundred twenty-five thousand dollars per 'flanker' store on set up, seventy-five thousand of which will be unrecoverable. Aunt Sally Mae's losses should be much larger. Probably between twenty and twenty-eight thousand per store, per week, and over two hundred grand on store set up costs."

Ozawa and Kenji were genuinely impressed with Bill's estimates.

Clearly agitated, Ray said, "Fuck the costs; we need to get moving on implementing this project right away. I'm not going to tolerate any interference from Hartford. They don't know their asses from their elbows."

"Do you think there'll be any problems with this project from Hartford?" Kenji calmly asked.

"Well, I've been in touch with Hartford tonight before dinner and should have an answer for you tomorrow morning. I think you'll be given approval for one 'flanker' store immediately and approval for two more when I get back and walk the proposal around early next week; additional 'flanker' stores will depend on the success of the first three."

"I guess we can live with that," Ozawa said, nodding. "I know you must have worked hard on our behalf to achieve this, Bill San, and I want you to know we appreciate it."

"Well, I still don't like the interference, but I do appreciate your help, Bill," Ray said distractedly. The cause of the distraction was a beautiful blonde who had just walked in with an equally good-looking brunette.

Ray excused himself and headed over to their table and promptly ordered a bottle of champagne. He was gone the rest of the evening. In fact, he didn't even stop to say good-bye. When he and the girls left the restaurant, after the champagne, Ozawa just laughed and said, "Ray really does have a one-track mind; actually two: one for women and one for money."

When they finished the pasta, Giovanni arrived with two platters. One was *osso bucco* and the other grilled shrimp with garlic sauce. Both dishes were absolutely delicious. It was after 11:00 when Kenji paid the bill and they left the restaurant. Ozawa invited Bill to his favorite hostess club for a nightcap.

★★★

When Ray returned home with his two new girl friends, he fumbled for his keys.

They were all drunk and the blonde was singing Elvis' "Suspicious Minds." She was actually a newly arrived singer and hostess at the Playbachelor Club.

When he finally opened the door and went into the living room, he found Fumiko on the couch in a negligee, smoking marijuana.

Turning red-faced, Ray yelled, "What the fuck are you doing here? And how did you get in?" he added in a slurred voice.

Fumiko wrinkled her forehead and said in a confused voice, "Ray, today is our two-month anniversary, and you said we would celebrate and spend the night together. I bought this negligee especially for—"

"What fucking anniversary are you talking about?" he exploded, as the blonde laughed and said, "You didn't tell us it would be three of us tonight, Wild Man." She swayed noticeably, rubbing Ray's chest.

"But, but, after the last delivery of the new-store sites for Tokyo, you said you loved me," Fumiko added, tears welling in her eyes.

"I must have been drunk then, too," Ray said, laughing and hugging the blonde. "Me loving you, you worthless whore. Now get the fuck out of here and don't ever let me find you here again, uninvited."

With tears streaming down her face, Fumiko got up and put on her overcoat. She picked up her clothes and put them in the Mitsukoshi Department Store shopping bag her negligee had come in.

"Go on, get the fuck out of here, you trashy bitch," Ray said, holding the door wide open.

Looking him straight in the eyes, Fumiko hissed, "I swear you'll regret this day more than any other in your life. I may be a whore, but I'm of Samurai ancestry, and I promise by all that is sacred in Bushido, you'll pay for this, as you can never imagine."

★★★

The next morning, when Kenji arrived at the office, he found what looked like a formal wedding invitation on his desk. It was only 8:30, so Kenji was almost the only one there.

That is, except for his Operations Director, Koji San, who was almost always in the office first thing in the morning, before he left for his store rounds, which lasted well into the night.

As Kenji was about to open the wedding invitation, the Operations Director stuck his head in and said, "Senmu, can I have a minute?"

"Of course, come in."

"Senmu, you know those great new-store sites we found in Nagoya and Fukuoka?"

"Sure, the ones in the business districts. If I remember correctly, the Nagoya location had apartment buildings nearby and was within walking distance of the Nagoya Castle, and the Fukuoka location had a university up the street. Why do you ask? Is there some problem? I thought we were closing on those leases."

"Well, I just found out that both sites have already been leased by Sawamura, I assume on behalf of Aunt Sally Mae Japan."

"So it begins!" Kenji said, with a determined look. "Koji San, you get on a plane today and fly out to both locations and find the best available nearby sites that you possibly can. Proximity is everything. The closer the better, and don't worry about cost. I want our 'flanker' stores open before Aunt Sally Mae's stores open. Understood?"

"*Hai*, Senmu, I understand completely! I will call you when I close the deals. Do you want me to run the contracts through accounting first?"

"No, call me directly."

Kenji immediately called Ozawa to share the news with him.

Kenji and Ray had lunch with Bill at the American Club for a wrap-up before Bill headed out to the airport.

"Bill, I'm counting on you to get those first three new stores approved the day you get back. My Operations Director is on his way to Fukuoka as we speak and I've given him approval to sign a lease for an acceptable site. He'll then go to Nagaoya and Sapporo and do the same." Kenji's scar was deep purple as he leaned forward. "Can I count on you?"

"I'll approve the first store now and push hard for the next two tomorrow." Bill glanced over at Ray before continuing. "Kenji, I know your passion for this company and respect you for it. You are critical to its future, more so than anyone. Therefore, be careful how you handle Hartford."

"Fuck Hartford! Those bastards aren't going to interfere with us." Ray downed his fourth double single malt, obviously feeling the effects.

That son-of-a-bitch is priceless. How he pulls it off I'll never know, Bill thought as he walked away.

★★★

When Kenji returned from lunch with Ray, he sat at his desk and saw the wedding invitation that had been there when he arrived that morning. He wondered who was getting married. He picked up the envelope and put it in his in-box.

Consumed with Aunt Sally Mae getting two of TFC Japan's sites, Kenji racked his brain trying to figure out how. *This cannot be a coincidence, and somehow they must be getting inside information—but through whom? The new-store sites analysis file is under lock and key. Only I, Joji Sakurai, and Ray have keys. Joji would never do this and Ray wouldn't know how, never mind that it would seem too much like work!*

Koji stuck his head in again, his briefcase and luggage in hand. "Senmu, more bad news. I just found out our new site in Sapporo, near the apartment buildings, has also been leased by Sawamura Realty."

"Damn it!" Kenji yelled, as he slammed his fist on his desk.
It was 8:00 p.m. when Kenji got up to leave the office. Glancing at his in-box, curiosity got the best of him, and he opened the wedding invitation.

Kenji Senmu,

I have disgraced myself, my family, TFC Japan and you, gomenasai. I know you cannot forgive me. I cannot forgive myself. When you read this note, I will have taken my life to repent for what I have done; my shame is unbearable. Ray is the spy in TFC Japan. With my help, he has been stealing new-store site data and selling it to a member of the Osaka Yakuza. Where it goes from there, I don't know. But I believe it ultimately gets to Sawamura and Aunt Sally Mae Japan. Ray pretended to love me. I was foolish enough to believe it, and so I helped, first by stealing keys, then copying materials. Recently we stole the English copy of the joint venture agreement between TFC International and Mitsugawa Trading from Ray's office. I'm not sure if Ray has had a chance to pass it along yet. I have no words to express my sorrow at this shameful action. As a Samurai I know what I must do for the honor of my ancestors.

Again, gomenasai.

Respectfully, Yamata Fumiko.

Kenji just stared at the note. He could not believe what he had just read. *Why would Ray do such a thing? He has more money than he could ever spend. Hell, he hasn't done an honest day's work since I got here. And getting involved with the Yakuza—he obviously doesn't know what he's in for. And Fumiko, how could she think that Ray ever loved any woman, especially her. He must have really upset her, though. That no good, selfish son-of-a-bitch!*

As he sat there, his anger grew so much he thought he would lose control.

No, you cannot lose control. Now is the time for clear thinking; you must get even, not mad, he told himself.

"Kasukawa kun, come in here for a minute."

"*Hai*, Senmu," his secretary said, as she walked in.

"Get me the telephone number of the police station nearest to Fumiko's apartment."

"Right away."

When the police sergeant answered, Kenji said, "*Moshi moshi*, I want to report a missing person; I'm afraid it might even be a suicide. My name is Kato, Kenji and I'm the Managing Director of TFC Japan. Last night, I received a call from one of our employees who sounded very upset over some conflict she was having with a friend.

"I didn't think too much about it at the time, but this morning, when she didn't show up for work and didn't answer her phone, I began to worry, so I'm calling in to report this," Kenji lied convincingly.

"What is the employee's name and address?" the sergeant asked.

"Yamata, Fumiko. Her address is Apartment 146, 3-15-4 Aoyama Dori, Minato-ku, Tokyo."

"Okay, we'll send someone to check things out and call you back. How long will you be at this number?"

"About another hour."

Kenji hoped the police would call back and report Fumiko just missing; but something told him they would find her dead. Now that he thought about it, Fumiko had changed recently: she seemed so happy, and her clothes had become even more fashionable and expensive.

He then remembered running into her in the hall and telling her to go home last week, because she looked so bad. *Was that when she stole the joint venture agreement?* he wondered.

As he waited for the police to call, he began to plan what he would do with Ray. His first thought was to turn him in. No, that was too risky. Kenji knew Ray would certainly rat on both Mitsugawa and him to TFC corporate on all the special arrangements TFC Japan had with Mitsugawa. Besides, it would only stop the flow of information from TFC Japan to Aunt Sally Mae Japan.

As he was thinking over his options, the perfect plan struck him like a lightning bolt.

Of course! I'll use Ray to feed Sawamura and Aunt Sally Mae Japan misinformation! I must be very careful, though, Inoue Senmu is no fool.

Yes, the Yakuza will eventually discover that Ray has been feeding them false information and take care of him in their unique way. No, this is not all bad news.

Kenji debated whether he would take Ozawa San into his confidence.

***

When the police arrived at Fumiko's apartment, the door was locked, so the sergeant knocked several times but got no response.

"Kageyama kun, go see if you can find the caretaker. If not, bring back the pry bar from the Koban," the sergeant said to his assistant. "And hurry. I've got tickets to the Tokyo Giants late game tonight. They're playing the Nagoya Dragons, and I don't want to miss any of it. I've got ten thousand yen on the Giants."

The officer returned with the caretaker, an older man in his sixties, who used a cane for support. As he tried to find the key to Fumiko's apartment, he asked, "Why are you looking for Yamata San? She's not in trouble, is she?"

He finally found the keys and opened the door to the four hundred-square-foot apartment.

There were only two rooms, a tiny kitchen with a bathroom attached and a general-purpose room, which served as living and dining during the day, and with a futon, a bedroom at night. There was a small desk and chair in the corner and a color TV on a four-foot-high bookshelf.

In the doorway separating the kitchen from the bathroom, Fumiko's lifeless body hung by a rope. Her face was blue and swollen, but she had an unexpectedly peaceful look.

She was dressed in a beautiful silk Kimono, white with blooming cherry blossoms. Her hair was done in the traditional style of a female Samurai.

Her body gently turned as the three witnesses stood and stared.

"She is at peace now," the caretaker said calmly. "I've only seen one other Samurai take his life," he added as he slowly turned and walked away.

"How did he know she was Samurai?" the younger office asked the sergeant, wrinkling his forehead.

"It's the kimono; it's probably worth over two million yen. What a waste!"

The younger officer wasn't sure if the sergeant was referring to the kimono or Fumiko.

The police couldn't find evidence of any wrongdoing, but neither did they find a suicide note.

★★★

At 9:00 p.m., the phone rang; it was the police.

"Kato Kenji San, *desuka*?" the sergeant said. "I'm afraid your suspicions were correct; we found Yamata San inside her apartment hanging from a doorway. So sorry to confirm this to you.

Lieutenant Ohashi would like to see you tomorrow morning at our offices. What time can you make it?"

"Of course, what time does Lieutenant Ohashi get in?"

"Any time after seven will be fine. Please call thirty minutes before you come, and I'm sure you won't be kept waiting too long."

***

"Senmu, you wanted to see me?" Ishikawa San, TFC Japan's Finance Director said, as he waited to be invited into Kenji's office.

"Come in and close the door," Kenji said.

"Is there something wrong?"

Kenji took a deep breath.

"Ishikawa kun, I have to take you into my confidence, but before I do, I need you to swear you will keep all of what I am going to tell you confidential for the rest of your life. Swear it on your ancestors' honor!"

Ishikawa San stood at attention. "Senmu, I swear on the honor of my ancestors, and my fellow comrades from the war, I will keep in total confidence what you are about to tell me. I will take this secret unto death."

"Okay, Ishikawa kun, I trust you completely."

Kenji handed him Fumiko's suicide note.

"She hanged herself last night; the police confirmed it minutes ago."

Ishikawa San was shocked. "Senmu, have you turned that gaijin son-of-a-bitch over to the police yet?" he hissed. "Prison is too good for that bastard!"

"No I haven't, not yet. Like you, my initial reaction was to tell the police immediately and give them Fumiko's note, so they could arrest Easton on a number of charges. However, I got to thinking. Ultimately, the information he's been stealing has definitely gotten into Sawamura and Aunt Sally Mae Japan's hands. See what I'm getting at?"

Ishikawa San's face lit up.

"Of course! We're going to use the son-of-a-whore to feed misinformation into Sawamura and Aunt Sally Mae Japan. Senmu, you're a genius!"

"We have a lot of work to do and very little time to do it. We don't know when the next drop is, but if Easton hasn't yet passed along the English version of our joint venture agreement, we have a golden opportunity to mislead Aunt Sally Mae Japan and create some real conflict between Sawamura Trading and Aunt Sally Mae U.S."

"Senmu, just tell me what you want me to do."

"First, come up with an excuse to get into Easton's office, then check his briefcase for the joint venture agreement and any new-store-site files.

"If you find any new-store-site files, replace the same number with the worst sites we have evaluated in Tokyo, after you've doctored them to show glowing reports. Any questions?"

"Just one, Senmu, if I find the English joint venture agreement, what do you want me to do with it?"

"Bring it to me immediately!"

Ishikawa San returned to Kenji's office in under fifteen minutes, out of breath.

"Senmu, we've hit pay dirt! I found the joint venture agreement and three new-store sites, two in Tokyo and one in Yokohama—all excellent sites. I'll go back to my office and pick the worst three Tokyo sites and substitute them."

Kenji picked up the phone and dialed his secretary's home number; it was 10:30 p.m. "Kasukawa kun, I need you to return to the office immediately. We've got some urgent work to accomplish before tomorrow morning."

"I'll be there right away, Senmu," came the reply.

She's the best secretary I've ever had and with sexual benefits as well. I'm going to have to give her a bonus.

Kenji and Kasukawa spent the next three hours retyping the joint venture agreement, changing all the terms to favor Mitsugawa. The actual royalty rate of three percent to TFC International was changed to one-and-a-half percent.

Several clauses were added, one suspending all royalties if losses were realized, a second guaranteeing local sourcing of all materials, and finally, Kenji's favorite one, giving Mitsugawa veto rights over the appointment of the Chairman and CFO positions, without a concurrent veto to TFC International over the President and Managing Director positions.

Based on what Ozawa had told him about Inoue Senmu, this last clause would surely cause him to try and renegotiate Sawamura's joint venture agreement.

Yes, Kenji thought. *This joint venture agreement was certain to cause a lot of turmoil.*

Kenji actually looked forward to the unfolding spy game. He relished the thought of supplying Aunt Sally Mae Japan with sites that looked good but were actually disasters.

★★★

At seven-thirty, Kenji showed up at the Aoyama police station to meet with Lieutenant Ohashi.

After serving O-cha (Chinese green tea) and complimenting Kenji on the quality of TFC, the Lieutenant said, "Thank you for coming in. I know you must be very busy, so I'll keep this short. What time, exactly, did Yamata San call you?"

"It was just after eleven p.m. I was working on a new store proposal."

"Was there anyone else in the office at the time who can confirm your presence?"

"I don't know. I don't think so, unless our Operations Director was still around; his name is Koji Oshita."

Kenji made a note to call Koji after this meeting and brief him on his need to confirmKenji's presence the previous evening.

"Did Fumiko Yamata San give you any indication of who this friend was who disturbed her so much? Did she indicate if the friend was male or female?"

"No, she didn't specify who the friend was, although I got the impression it was a female."

"Hmm, that's interesting. Her father told us she was having difficulty with a boyfriend that she wouldn't identify. Do you have any idea who that might be?"

Looking at his watch, Kenji said, "No, I'm afraid I don't, but if I think of anything I'll be sure to call you."

"Yes, well, thank you. That'll be all for today."

Lieutenant Ohashi thought there were some things about this case that just didn't add up.

★★★

"*Moshi moshi,* Koji kun?"

"Ah, Senmu *desuka?*"

"Koji kun, you're going to receive a call from a Lieutenant Ohashi of the Aoyama police station, asking you to confirm that I was in the office night-before-last at around eleven p.m. I need you to confirm it, understood?"

"Of course, Senmu, I was working on the Sapporo new store site problem.

"Very good, now tell me about the flanker store sites you found."

CHAPTER 22

When Bill arrived at baggage claim, Sharon was waiting with a big smile that highlighted those beautiful dimples on her face. "So did you miss me?" she asked.

"A little, I guess," Bill said, trying to look nonchalant.

"Me too," she responded as she turned and headed toward the exit.

"Hey, wait a second," Bill said a little louder than he intended.

She turned around with a smile and then kissed him. "You silly guy, you know I'm crazy about you."

He then handed her the shopping bag Kenji had given him.

"What's this?"

"I honestly don't know. It's something Kenji gave me to give to you."

On the drive home, Bill told Sharon about his trip. She was fascinated with the "flanker" store strategy and the whole "Stop Aunt Sally Mae Now" plan.

When Bill got to the insider trading by Ray with the help of Ozawa, Sharon became visibly concerned. He reassured her that Dave, and his cousin the lawyer, had told him they had nothing to worry about.

She was not convinced. "Well, we made plenty on the two tips we got, so let's not do any more."

With a smile on his face, he said, "You're absolutely right. Oh, that reminds me, I have to check on your third big surprise on Monday."

Dinner was just like Thanksgiving, including a roast turkey with all the trimmings. Sharon had made it before going to pick up Bill at the airport.

After dinner, she opened her present from Kenji. It was a small package with a card.

> Dear Sharon San,
>
> We hope you will come to Japan with Bill on his next trip and, of course, when he moves here to become our much-needed CFO.
>
> Cordially, Kenji Kato

In the package, she found a Pierre Cardin silk scarf.

Laughing, she said, "Wow, what a gift! Imagine what I'll get if we do move to Japan!"

That night, when they went to bed, Sharon wore a new pink teddy she had purchased as a homecoming surprise for Bill.

She was absolutely striking and gentle with him, as she slipped into bed next to him and began to lick his ear.

"Tonight I'm going to make you come twice," she whispered as she traced her tongue down his neck and chest and then began to suck his nipples, slowly at first and then gently biting them. From there, she traced her tongue down his stomach as her hand began to rub the inside of his thigh, moving lightly and slowly up to his testicles, which she then squeezed softly.

"Oh Sharon, I can't wait much longer," he groaned.

"Oh, yes you can, watch and see," she responded in that special husky voice of hers.

Ten minutes later, with a smile on her face she asked, "How was that?"

"I'm sure that was the best *whatever* ever!"

Propping himself up on his elbow Bill looked into Sharon's eyes. "I'm falling in love with you."

Sharon kissed Bill tenderly. "Me too."

The expression on Sharon's face told him she was serious.

She left the bedroom and returned with two snifters of Hennessey XO. Bill, however, was sound asleep, having succumbed to his jet lag. Sharon detected a smile of satisfaction on his face.

She thought, *Hey, I'm getting better and better; must be because I'm really in love for the first time.* Quite satisfied, she finished her cognac, cuddled next to him, and went straight to sleep.

★★★

Dave dialed Bill's number "Welcome back Bill!" he said energetically, when Bill came on the line. "Come on down; we've got a lot to cover, and Sam is here as well."

"I'll be right down, Boss."

Sam and Dave were seated across from each other over the black coffee table, talking intently when Bill walked in.

Sam stood up and handed over a thick manila envelope. "Good morning, Bill, here is your divorce. All finalized. You're now a free man."

"Wow! That was quick! This is fantastic news. I can't tell you how much I appreciate what you've accomplished, and all in less than three months."

"Bill, have a seat," Dave said casually. "Sam is here for another reason, as well." Bill looked puzzled.

"Yes, Bill, I contacted my school buddy at the SEC; I believe I told you about him at our last meeting. I informed him of Ray Easton's insider trading activities. He is very interested in talking to you, on a one –hundred –percent confidential basis, of course."

Looking somewhat alarmed, Bill said, "I thought we agreed I wouldn't have to testify."

"Relax, I assure you, you run absolutely no risk whatsoever, as long as you didn't pass the tips along to others," Sam said, leaning forward and looking directly at Bill.

"And you reported the income to the IRS. In fact, the SEC wants you to accept and execute one more tip. And, of course, share the specifics with them, again, on a hundred percent confidential basis.

"Further, the SEC will cover your losses if the tip doesn't pay off. By the way, they don't care if you keep the profits if the tip is successful, but they require you limit your investment to five thousand dollars."

Relaxing slightly, Bill asked, "So, I won't have to testify, right?"

"No, you won't. It turns out the San Francisco office has been following Easton for a number of years and was getting close to moving in on him anyhow. This last tip to you will just be the final nail.

"You know that what's been happening is wrong. Ray uses these tips to gain favors from all sorts of people. One example the SEC agent shared with me illustrates the extent of his dishonesty. It seems that while working with the IRS, they discovered a retired Master Sergeant Joseph Durant, who has since turned state's evidence.

"Apparently, Ray served on a supply ship during the Korean War with him. After the war, Durant was transferred to Awards and Decorations and somehow was able to get Ray a false military ID that listed Ray as a medically discharged Army 1st Lieutenant.

"The problem was that Durant became greedy and didn't report the income he made to the IRS, and when they caught up with him, he immediately revealed his dealings with Ray to avoid prosecution."

Bill took a deep breath. "Okay, if I don't have to testify and just set up one more tip, then I guess I'll cooperate; at least I'll meet with your SEC contact."

"That's absolutely the right decision," Dave said, smiling at Sam.

Sam added, "Well, we'll have to move quickly, since I know the SEC is planning on moving in when Easton's here for the strategic planning presentations week after next."

"Just by coincidence, Ray gave me a note last Friday when I left Tokyo. I'm supposed to buy Northwood Mines on Thursday and sell out on Friday."

After Sam left, Bill said, "Isn't this all going to be academic if Ray is involved in industrial espionage?"

"Not really. All of these charges are serious felonies," Dave said, tapping his fingertips together.

★★★

When Bill got home, he told Sharon about his meeting with cousins Liberwitz. While she was ecstatic with the news of the divorce, she was very concerned about him being part of the setup by the SEC.

"Sweetheart, aren't you concerned about what Ray may do to those who testify against him? He must have enormous resources if he's been trading tips like the ones he's given us—and in much bigger lots and over a much longer time. Also, how do you know the SEC will keep its part of the deal?"

"Babe, first, I don't have to testify at all. Second, I haven't agreed to anything more than meeting Sam Liberwitz's contact at the SEC. Believe me, I won't agree to anything without an ironclad guarantee. Now, I want you to relax and let's celebrate my divorce and our future."

Over dinner, Bill said, "About that third surprise, I want to play a little game with you."

"Oh, stop teasing me and just tell me what the surprise is!" she said, pouting.

"No, no that would take all the fun out of it. What I'm going to do is give you a hint a day."

"All right, but when I guess correctly, you have to tell me, okay?"

"All right, but only one hint a day and no further questions from you," Bill answered with a straight face.

"Okay, enough already, get on with the first hint."

"What is dependent on one of nature's greatest mysteries?"

She couldn't help but laugh. "What is dependent on one of nature's greatest mysteries? Is that supposed to be a hint? Come on, that's no hint at all!"

As they sat on the sofa after dinner, Sharon thought to herself, *I'm so in love with him, I know we'll get married some day.*

Chapter 23

Ray handed over the "revised and corrected" joint venture agreement between TFC International and Mitsugawa Trading, and the three doctored new-store sites.

In turn, Saji handed over a manila envelope and said, "There's thirty-five million yen in that envelope. That's a big bonus; keep it coming!"

Ray was surprised at the amount. He had only expected twenty-five million. "So why the generosity?"

"Because my client is happy and has new requests, which he needs ASAP. Specifically, he now wants the pay scales and bonus program for store managers."

"Sounds good. For fifteen million, I can have them by week's end."

"Ray, ten million, and by Thursday," Saji said, looking very serious.

Shit, this guy's not kidding—he's really starting to play hardball. I wish I hadn't blown up at Fumiko. Hell, she hasn't been back to the office. Never mind that Playbachelor hostess isn't worth a shit in the sack. Oh well, Fumiko will come around, and there's the next batch of models coming in this weekend.

★★★

When the phone rang, Ray was reviewing his various investments. He had made over $480,000 so far this year on Ozawa's tips concerning Toyoda acquisition targets.

Also, one of the potential franchisees for Hong Kong, Sir George Wang, offered a $100,000 bribe if he would include Taiwan in the deal.

"Ray, Ken Osamu here in Honolulu. Buddy, we've a whole boatload of trouble! It looks like Harold Tamaki has confessed everything, including all of our names, and I hear from a reliable inside source that the Hawaii Attorney General is considering charges against the whole lot of us!"

Ray was shocked and shouted back, "What the fuck are you talking about! I thought you said that all the money was going from Tamaki directly to the Planning Board members we bribed? How can there be any proof that any of us participated in the bribe?"

In a calmer, but agitated tone, Ken Osamu answered, "Ray, I told you. This is all based on an insider source at this time. Apparently, he made copies of all the checks he cashed."

"Have you talked to him directly?" Ray snarled.

"Not yet, but I plan to go down to the jail today and bail him out."

"Well, what a fine fucking mess this has turned out to be! You said you trusted this asshole and he was reliable."

"Fuck you Easton!" Ken Osamu said, losing his temper. "You went into this with your eyes open. You knew I hadn't previously worked directly with Tamaki."

"Well, what the fuck are we going to do now?"

"My advice is that we deny everything at this stage and say the money we sent was for a legitimate real estate investment opportunity on Diamond Head. If we can't deny we sent the money, then the next best thing is to claim it was for a legitimate deal. I can demonstrate that I've been involved in a number of real estate deals in the past year.

"When I bail Tamaki out today, I'll explain that we're going to claim he misled us and there's no evidence to the contrary. I'll see if I can negotiate something with him, along the lines of us paying for his legal defense, plus a little extra, if he doesn't implicate us. I'll call you after I've bailed him out."

"Fuck! How much more money are you talking about? My investors, sure as God made green apples, aren't going to put up another yen."

"Relax, at least until I talk to him."

Well fuck me. How am I going to tell Kenji and Ozawa that their forty grand is gone, never mind my fifty thousand? Jesus, and if charges are filed, how am I going to manage that?

For the first time in a long time, Ray felt overwhelmed and unsure of how to get out of a sticky situation. He decided he would have to consult Ozawa.

★★★

The funeral services for Fumiko were modest. Only her father stood in the reception line, and most of the mourners were either school friends or co-workers from TFC Japan. Conspicuous by his absence was Ray.

"Kenji Senmu, I know that Fumiko's gaijin love interest is responsible for her taking her life," Fumiko's father whispered to Kenji at crematorium, where only family and close friends were invited.

"I know Fumiko was convinced she was in love with this most recent gaijin lover. I'll not rest until I discover his identity and have my revenge," Fumiko's father said, looking directly at Kenji, as Fumiko's remains of ash and small bone chips were being removed.

He's serious. If the Yakuza don't get him first, this elder Samurai certainly will. Bowing deeply, Kenji said, "Fumiko was a very good employee, always sensitive to others. She had a very positive attitude about almost everything." Kenji then took his leave to allow the father to collect the urn and chant the final Buddhist prayers.

Of course Kenji said nothing about the suicide note. *No sense in putting an end to the misinformation programming of Aunt Sally Mae Japan. Besides, the Yakuza would take care of Ray. No, the suicide note would never come to light,* Kenji decided definitively.

★★★

Ray stood up to welcome Ozawa. "Ozawa San, thank you for agreeing to meet me for lunch on such short notice." They were at the I'le de France, one of their favorite spots for a quiet and private lunch.

"Well, what's the urgency?" Ozawa responded in an annoyed tone. "I had to cancel two appointments to make this lunch."

"I have some bad news, and I don't know how to handle the situation. Tom, I desperately need your understanding and your help." *Tom* was the English version of Ozawa's first name. Ray rarely used it.

"Go on," Ozawa said, narrowing his eyes.

"Well, it's the real estate deal in Hawaii. The seed money we put up was actually a bribe made to two of the Honolulu Planning Board members to get approval for the condominium project.

"Somehow the go-between we used has been found out. And after being threatened with prosecution, he has apparently agreed to reveal the identities of all the investors.

"The Attorney General is considering bringing charges against anyone involved. At least, that is what we're told by an insider who works in the Attorney General's office."

"Ray, are you telling me that the Attorney General of Hawaii has mine and Kenji's information and believes we were knowingly part of this fraud you perpetrated?" Ozawa hissed, turning beet-red.

Ray was becoming somewhat annoyed, and said, "Relax, will you! No, he doesn't have your information or Kenji's. I took your investments and sent everything down in my name."

"Well, at least you did the transfer right. But seed money as a bribe through someone you didn't even know? What were you thinking?" Ozawa asked in a more relaxed tone, as his face returned to normal color.

"Well, my contact, Ken Osamu, is someone I know and have had previous dealings with. He assured me the go-between, a Harold Tamaki, was reliable."

"How much of this is second – or even third-hand information?"

"Well, at this stage, it's all through the insider in the Attorney General's office. Ken is scheduled to make bail for Tamaki this afternoon. Oh, and he suggests that we put up a like amount of money to get Tamaki not to turn in the other investors."

"Nice try, Ray. You're even crazier than this debacle indicates if you think either Kenji or I are going to give you any more money," Ozawa said with a sneer. In fact, you had better pay us back for our investment. You've made a fortune off the tips I've given you, and it's only fair that you take the responsibility for this outrageous situation. I expect you to pay us back by tomorrow. In the meantime, I'll contact our people in Honolulu and find out exactly what's going on in the Attorney General's office."

Ray thought for a moment, *Of course, Mitsugawa has significant investments in Hawaii and probably all sorts of connections with all levels of government. Besides, the fucker is right. I've made a fortune off his tips and, after all, it's only forty thousand. Hell, I made two hundred sixty thousand off that last Canadian deal.*

"Okay, Tom, you're right. I'll take personal responsibility and pay you guys back your forty thousand. Further, if you can somehow help me make this problem go away, I'll give you another hundred thousand."

Ray then downed his glass of cognac and signaled the waiter for another.

CHAPTER 24

"Now don't cry, Pumpkin," Bill said, caressing Sarah's face and giving her a kiss on the cheek. "You're going to come spend Christmas with me."

"Daddy, I miss you so much. I don't like Mommy's new boyfriend. He's always putting you down and telling me I'm a baby when I say I miss you," Sarah said, as her lower lip quivered.

That son of a bitch, making my baby girl cry!

"Daddy, can't I come live with you? I'll be good, I promise," Sarah said, crossing her heart.

"Listen, Pumpkin," Bill said, holding on to Sarah's shoulders, kneeling and looking right into her eyes, "You're going to spend Christmas with us, and all summer," Bill added, hugging Sarah.

The announcement that Bill's flight was boarding came over the loudspeaker.

"Daddy, why do you have to leave so soon? You only came yesterday," Sarah said, as tears welled up in her eyes.

Bill felt tears welling up as well. "Pumpkin, who love a cha baby," Bill said, as he had since Sarah was two.

"Daddy does," Sarah said, sobbing as she jumped into Bill's arms and hugged him.

"Final boarding call for flight 206 for Springfield/Hartford. All passengers on board please."

★★★

"Good morning, Mr. Willis," Dave said, as he entered the expansive office. The office was more of an apartment than an office. There was a bedroom, wet bar and full bath immediately on the left off the entrance to the office. The walls were all mahogany, floor to ceiling. The cherry floors were covered by a variety of oriental carpets.

"Good morning, Dave, have a seat," Willis said, as he seated himself in a leather chair.

Willis' secretary came in with a tray of Danish and a coffee pot, cups, and cream and sugar.

"I've asked you here because it's time to make some important organizational decisions. We're almost through the strategic planning process and it's critical that we have the right people to implement it." First, let me bring you up to speed on this SEC investigation of Ray Easton and a new potential complication."

"What's the new potential complication?" Willis asked, raising his eyebrows.

"Well, it's possible that Ray has been selling confidential TFC Japan information to the Japanese mafia."

"Jesus, are you serious!" Willis said, sitting up and leaning forward, his face turning red.

"This is all unconfirmed at the moment."

Dave then filled him in on the details and history.

"So this all depends on the accuracy of Lisa's story, and Bill is convinced she's telling the truth."

Shaking his head, Willis said, "When it rains, it pours."

"Concerning the SEC investigation, they now are going to arrest Easton when he arrives for the strategic planning meeting next week."

"On what specific charges?"

"Soliciting, using and passing insider information for personal gain."

"What a chump this guy is!" Willis said, shaking his head.

"It gets better; additionally, Easton has been ripping off the U.S. military for years by using a fake ID that lists him as a First Lieutenant with a medical discharge, which gives him access to the bases and commissary.

"Further complicating matters is that, apparently, some of Easton's insider tips came from none other than our friend, Ozawa of Mitsugawa Trading.

"The SEC is still deciding what to do with this information, although the senior agent indicates their normal practice is to share it with the Japanese authorities."

"Wow, this too is serious. I guess Gene was right about this guy all along," Willis said, pausing for a moment while tapping his fingers together. "Well, I hate to say it, but this could be good news for us," Willis added. "Easton was obviously in Ozawa's back pocket and would've had to have been replaced anyhow."

"Now he won't even cost us a termination package," Dave observed.

★★★

Should we be considering sending Bill to Tokyo as CFO?" Willis asked. "That'll at least give us a bridge until we figure out what we're going to do about replacing Easton.

"I think he has moved beyond just the financial arena. I've rarely seen anyone adapt so quickly to strategic planning. Besides, in Japan, age is a critical factor in gaining respect, and as good a financial guy as he is, he's still only twenty-eight. Hell, in Japan a Section Chief under age thirty is rare."

"Okay, I hear that, but we have to do something about Japan and do it quickly. The day Easton is arrested is going to be the day he is terminated.

"Further, Japan is our fastest growing market, and given our emerging problems in the U.S., we're going to need every cent of profit we can get from International." Leaning forward, Willis said, "Sanford's comments about costs at TFC Japan are disturbing."

"Yes, but that may be good news, from a profit point of view. Perhaps we should put all the major organizational changes that need to be made on the table first."

Willis nodded. "Agreed. First, in the U.S. it looks like we need a new CEO, VP Eastern Region, VP Western Region, and Marketing Director Western Region to start with."

"How about HR and Finance?"

"I think you have a point about HR, but I believe Gene will be fine, once Rosenberg is gone. Has he given you any problems since our discussions at the end of our kickoff meeting?"

"No, he hasn't. In fact, he has gone out of his way to be helpful."

"Now what about International?" Willis asked.

"Clearly, we need a replacement for Easton, a Regional VP for Europe, and I'm afraid a replacement for Jim Meyer," Dave said, lowering his voice.

"Jim Meyer? Really, what are the specific problems with Jim?" Willis asked, raising his eyebrows.

"The only real problem is that Jim has no international experience or even a sense of international. He is a good administrator, marketer, and financial guy, but he just doesn't get international, perhaps because he doesn't travel much. Also I understand his wife has MS."

"Hmmm. Okay, let me think about this for awhile. We'll regroup day after tomorrow, say at three o'clock?"

Chapter 25

When Inoue arrived at the Mobile airport he didn't see Ashley. *Americans can be so rude; it's all part of the ridiculous assumption that they're superior. Hell, if it weren't for their incredible natural resources, they would have lost the war.*

Inoue was extremely tired from his double duty as Managing Director of Sawamura Trading and President of Aunt Sally Mae Japan.

As a result, he didn't even pick up the message telling him that J.J.'s driver would be at the airport to pick him up. The message went on to say that he was invited to dinner.

It wasn't until the next morning at 3:30 a.m. that Inoue picked up the message, when he placed a call to his office in Tokyo.

When Inoue and Ashley arrived at Aunt Sally Mae's SFC offices, the Senior Management group was waiting for them in the boardroom.

On the way over, Ashley had explained the triple disasters. First, a local bank that provided forty percent of Aunt Sally Mae's working capital line of credit had been acquired, and the line was frozen, pending the new bank's review.

Second, the business in the West was 12 percent off forecast, due to the recession in California. Finally, and most importantly, there was a major lawsuit that had emerged from TFC, challenging Aunt Sally Mae's claim that J.J.'s mother had taught the Major the "secret recipe."

178

While the lawsuit seemed trivial, it had resulted in J.J.'s mother having a heart attack and being hospitalized. J.J. was just beside himself, Ashley warned.

"Good afternoon," Inoue said cheerfully as he entered the boardroom.

"There is nothing good about it. I'm sure Ashley has told you about the lawsuit and his mother's heart attack, a direct result, I'm sure.

"This just arrived this morning from our law offices," J.J. continued, as he presented Inoue with a flyer from Sapporo. The flyer announced the pending opening of the new Sapporo store. The history of the "secret recipe" was boxed in red.

Almost shouting, J.J. said, "Perhaps you could explain how this happened."

"Jesus, relax J.J.; we talked about this when I was last here. In fact, you thought it was a great idea when I suggested it. Furthermore, it was presented by Yamamoto Senden at their presentation to us several weeks ago."

"Bullshit, what you said was that a word-of-mouth publicity campaign could be done on a rumor basis. And damn it, Ashley, you never said anything about a print campaign in your trip report," J.J. shouted.

Ashley felt she had to defend herself. "Well, nothing definitive was decided then. It was only an idea and one that we had discussed here with Inoue San before he left."

Red faced J.J. said, "Well it has caused a lawsuit and potentially my mother's life."

Trying to calm things down, Lee said, "Now J.J., I told you this morning that there is no way TFC is going to pursue this lawsuit, never mind win it, it's just a scare tactic.

"Hell, the Major has been on radio admitting that your mother helped him develop the secret recipe. In fact, maybe we should postpone this meeting until tomorrow morning when I'm sure the hospital will confirm that your dear mother is recovering nicely."

J.J. agreed reluctantly, as he got up and left with tears welling in his eyes.

After J.J. had left, Lee suggested that they continue with the meeting. Inoue brought the group up to speed on the status of Aunt Sally Mae Japan. He covered the three first stores in great detail, including pictures of the outlets and basic demographic statistics of the neighborhoods.

The group was impressed with the details Inoue presented and was positively inclined to approving the three new stores in Tokyo.

Things progressed well, until Inoue put up the financial projections for the first fiscal year.

The CFO said, "Please tell me you have added a digit by mistake."

Defensively Inoue said, "Not at all; if anything this is conservative."

"The rental expense is completely out of any reasonable estimate. What exactly is included?" the CFO demanded.

"Well, it includes the rent on the first six stores, and—"

"Hang on! I thought you said those three Tokyo stores were under contract by Sawamura Real Estate?" Lee interrupted.

"They are, but I assumed we would agree to proceed, so I included them in the estimate. And, of course, the estimate includes our headquarters office, which is located in Aoyama, a respectable business district."

"Based on Ashley's trip report," the CFO retorted, "we have only budgeted a first-year loss of one point five million, not even close to the four point three million you're projecting."

Lee then said, "Well, I think we should regroup in the morning when J.J. is available. These differences are too great to handle here. Inoue San, I would suggest you be prepared to provide details on each line item at tomorrow's meeting. Oh, and how many of these rentals are done on properties owned by Sawamura or one of its affiliates?"

"Believe me, I will be prepared. But let's be clear, I resent your implication of wrongdoing. You should have your facts straight before you make accusations, especially since you obviously haven't read and understood the joint venture agreement you signed less than three months ago.

"J.J. is obviously and understandably upset at his mother's heart attack. I can understand and accept that, but you, Lee, have no excuse for your accusations and rudeness. Remember, I accepted the role of President and CEO of Aunt Sally Mae Japan at J.J.'s request."

As Lee was about to object, Inoue raised his hand and continued. "Yes, I will be prepared tomorrow, but you had better be prepared also. Read the fucking joint venture agreement!" Inoue said as he stormed out.

Inoue was furious as he caught a cab and headed to the Hilton Hotel. Obviously, he would be spending this night on his own as well. When he arrived at the Hilton, it was 5:15 p.m., or 7:15 a.m. in Tokyo; he checked in and called his office.

Ashley called around town to the major hotels trying to find Inoue. On the third try, she called the Hilton and was told the line was busy. She tried back thirty minutes later with the same result. Finally she got through at 7:15 p.m.

"*Moshi moshi*," Inoue said when he answered the phone.

"Mush mush, yourself," Ashley said, laughing.

"I was wondering if you were going to call. What was that all about this afternoon?"

"I tried to tell you, J.J. was beside himself. And by the way, why did you say I had agreed to the Yamamoto Senden publicity proposal? I'm going to pay big time for that, especially since I took your side," Ashley added.

"Listen, you know we talked about that idea during the joint venture negotiations. Also, when Yamamoto Senden presented it, we both thought it was a good idea. Where the printed flyer came from, I honestly don't know."

"Do you want to have dinner?" Ashley asked tentatively.

"Thanks, but no thanks, I'm waiting for a call from Tokyo, and the jet lag has been brutal this trip what with the delay and all."

"Okay, I'll be by to get you tomorrow morning at eight-thirty; get a good night's sleep."

The next day was more of the same bickering over the forecast and the publicity campaign. J.J wasn't there, as his mother's condition had become critical during the night. At 2:00 p.m., J.J.'s secretary came in the boardroom to announce that J.J.'s mother had passed away.

"This meeting is over," Lee said, rising from his chair at the head of the table. "We'll be in touch shortly, but in the meantime, assume we haven't approved your forecast or the proposed three stores in Tokyo. And yes, I did go back and read the *fucking* joint venture agreement, and we have the right to approve any capital expense over fifty thousand," Lee said, as the Aunt Sally Mae team, including Ashley, walked out of the boardroom.

This is turning into a real nightmare, Inoue thought, dejectedly.

★★★

"Hello, Daddy, it's me, guess what? I'm coming to see you for Thanksgiving and Christmas! Isn't that great?" Sarah squealed.

"Hi, Pumpkin, that's great news! But are you sure Mom is going to let you go for both holidays? She's supposed to have Thanksgiving this year."

"Yes, I'm absolutely sure. She told me last night. She and The Meany are going skiing over Thanksgiving and The Meany says it's not a place for little brats," Sarah said, emphasizing *The Meany*.

"Well, that's the best news I've had all month," Bill said in an upbeat tone. "And guess where we're going over the weekend after Thanksgiving?"

"Where Daddy?" Sarah nearly shouted.

"To New Hampshire, Lake Sunapee Mountain, where I learned how to ski when I was your age!"

"Oh, Daddy, that sounds wonderful!" Sarah shouted. "Now promise me you're not going to let any business trips interfere with this great vacation."

"Scouts honor. I promise nothing will interfere with this vacation," Bill said, chuckling.

"Daddy, I just can't wait! I'll be counting the days. Love you."

★★★★

"Dave, come on in and have a seat. We need to talk specifics on the organization," Willis said, as Dave walked in.

"As you know, we've had an understanding about succession since you joined. Given the recent events, I've talked to the Board and secured their agreement.

"Effective at the strategic planning presentations, I plan to announce that I am becoming Chairman and CEO, and that you are appointed President and COO. I assume that meets with your approval?"

"Absolutely!"

"Next, you are also appointed Acting President and CEO of International; we all know that International is where our real growth potential lies, and until we sort out the various regional issues, I need you at International's tiller as well," Willis said leaning forward.

"Dave, I know this is a lot to ask, but do you accept this additional and challenging responsibility?"

"With great pleasure and eagerness!"

"Excellent!" Willis said, looking relieved. "Now, finally, Jim Meyer becomes President and CEO Domestic. I know that may come as a bit of a surprise to you, since it was not included in our succession discussions. However, I have known Jim for eight years and completely trust his judgment. It's clear that we have an enormous turnaround challenge in Domestic. We must move quickly and, therefore, we need someone who knows the business inside and out. Jim is precisely that person—Comments?"

Dave cleared his throat. "Mr. Willis, you have obviously given this decision considerable thought. I completely agree with your underlying logic concerning the need for swift change and the requirement of knowledge of the business.

"I don't know Jim well enough to have an opinion concerning his qualifications. However, I assure you I'll commit myself to working with Jim on this critical turnaround."

"Well, that's the easy part. Now what do we do with the rest of the organization?" Willis asked.

"Domestically, I'd like to explore sending the Southern Regional Vice President to replace the Eastern Regional Vice President, but this is admittedly not an immediate priority.

"However, what we do in Japan and Europe is critical and an immediate issue."

"Exactly, let me try something out on you," Willis said with a smile. "Assume Ozawa agrees that their President Joji Sakurai is retired and Kenji replaces him as President. We send Ralph Ovunc over as our representative and Chairman. We forgo the appointment of a CFO. As far as funding goes, we pay Ralph's expenses and the joint venture pays Kenji's expenses. Obviously, this is an interim solution. However, our immediate priority is to get a handle on the excessive costs that Mitsugawa is charging TFC Japan for anything and everything.

"As far as Europe is concerned, my gut tells me to give Sanford a chance. Quite frankly, his description of what he would do is spot-on. Also, in Europe his age will be less of an issue."

"I agree, we should give Bill a chance at Europe if he wants it. I also think he could handle the Vice President Strategic Planning position or the Vice President Finance International," Dave said, raising his eyebrows. "What do you think?"

"While I agree Bill could probably grow into any of those jobs, I think the most immediate priority is Europe. We really don't need to fill the Vice President Strategic Planning in the short term; I think Gene could probably help us get by in finance until Ralph finishes up in Japan. That's assuming it's within twelve to eighteen months."

Dave nodded. "Agreed, after Japan, Europe is our top priority."

"Well, the first step is to talk to Ralph and Gene," Willis concluded.

"We'll have to let them in on the Easton situation."

"Yeah, that shouldn't be a problem. They're both finance guys, so they're used to keeping secrets, at least from me," Willis said, laughing, and Dave joined in.

Chapter 26

Sawamura Trading's office was just across the street from the Imperial Palace in downtown Tokyo. The Imperial Hotel, where MacArthur had set up his headquarters during the occupation, was next door, and the prestigious Mitsuhashi department store was just down the main street. By practice, if not by law, no building surrounding the Imperial Palace could be high enough to provide a view into the Imperial Palace grounds; Sawamura Trading's building bordered on violation. The moat that surrounded the palace was visible from Inoue's office window. As Managing Director, Inoue's office was on the top floor along with the President's office.

When Inoue returned to his office, he found everything in disarray. His secretary had thirty-seven important messages for him, including three demands from Sawamura Realty's President for Inoue to call as soon as he got in.

Inoue had just returned from Alabama and was scheduled to go to the three new-store openings the following morning, starting with a 6:00 a.m. flight to Sapporo. After lunch, it was on to Nagoya and then, finally, Fukuoka the following morning. Inoue was feeling the effects of jet lag and thought he might be coming down with a cold.

The contracts for the three new Tokyo stores were on his desk, and construction had already begun. Technically, Aunt Sally Mae U.S. had approval rights over all new store designs. This had not been done for the three stores in Sapporo, Nagoya, and Fukuoka. Just another thing J.J. and Lee would rant and rave about.

As he was sorting through his messages, he heard his secretary say, "Oh yes, President Harada, Inoue Senmu is now in. Of course, I told him you were expecting his call, as soon as he arrived. Hmm, about twenty minutes ago, Shacho."

His secretary finished and came into his office. "President Harada is on the phone and he seems quite upset about something."

"Inoue kun, when I say I want you to call me as soon as you get in, I mean immediately. Is that clear?" President Harada snarled.

"Yes, Shacho, I understand. It won't happen again."

"Well, the three Tokyo leases you signed last month and have already begun to remodel are plain and simply horrible locations. How could you be so stupid!" President Harada yelled.

"What do you mean horrible? I know TFC Japan had them on the top of their desired site list. Besides, Shacho, with all due respect, what do you know about fast-food sites?" Inoue said in an annoyed tone.

"You fucking idiot!" President Harada yelled, "I've been in the real estate business for thirty years, you arrogant son of a whore.

"Whoever gave you that so-called top-site list of TFC Japan duped you, apparently rather easily."

"Shacho, are you sure of your assessment?" Inoue said sincerely.

"Absolutely! Now you've got exactly one week to get these contracts switched from us to Sawamura Trading. If not, I'll call your Shacho and tell him what a fool you are, talking the Sawamura Trading board into this ridiculous joint venture," President Harada growled as he hung up.

★★★

The Sapporo store was packed with customers. In fact, they were lined up halfway down the block. The local advertising agency, Yamamoto Senden had certainly done their job and got the word out. The store was so crowded that the local TV station came at noon to do a piece on the new American hit restaurant.

The store ran out of chicken at 1:15 p.m. and had to order more. Instead of thinning after the lunch hour, the crowd line grew to three city blocks with an average wait of ninety minutes to get served. Things were still going full steam at 4:00 p.m., when Inoue had Tanaka San change their departure to Nagoya to 10:00 p.m.

At 7:00, the NHK, the national news network, began filming. They were interviewing customers in the line that was still two blocks long.

"How long have you been standing in line?" the female reporter asked a group of college students.

"We have been here since six," they answered happily.

"Why would you be willing to wait so long for American fried chicken?" the reporter asked surprised.

"Because this chicken was invented by the woman who taught Major Tom the secret recipe!" a young male student answered, as he held up one of the flyers the advertising agency had produced. "Besides, my history professor was here for lunch and said it was excellent."

At 8:00, the news crew came into the store and began filming. Inoue was still manning a cash register and calling orders back as fast as he could. The dining area was packed with every chair taken and people waiting for others to leave.

The store in Nagoya was even busier than Sapporo had been. The Branch/Store Manager was also a TFC Japan veteran, although much older, probably in his early forties. He told Inoue that, in his seven years at TFC Japan, he had managed six different new stores and had never seen anything like this since the 1969 World's Fair in Osaka where TFC was launched in Japan.

The lines of customers were even longer and the publicity campaign had worked even better. Customers were actually talking among themselves about how the Major had learned his secret recipe from Aunt Sally Mae, as she was being called.

Even more exciting was that Keiko was true to her word and had the NHK film crew there all day. They actually picked up numerous spots of customers in line, talking about "Mama Aunt Sally Mae's" southern fried chicken secret recipe and how the Major got it slightly wrong.

Thankfully, Tanaka, the Operations Director, had learned from the Sapporo experience and had arranged for three suppliers of chicken to make periodic deliveries every two hours throughout the day, until the 11:00 p.m. closing time, which was extended to 11:30 to accommodate the remaining customers that had been standing in line for over an hour.

In fact, at 10:30, the Store Manager went out and put up a sign at the end of the then two-block-long line that warned of the pending 11:00 closing time. The sales for the day were an unbelievable 8.2 million yen ($30,400). Inoue was literally exhausted when they got to the Nagoya Prince Hotel just after midnight. He got undressed and went straight to bed.

The Fukuoka new store was also more of the same, better than Sapporo but not quite as good as Nagoya. The customer lines were still a block and a half long, and more importantly, the "Mama Aunt Sally Mae" phenomenon was even more prevalent.

★ ★ ★

The next morning Inoue was still feeling the cumulative effects of the recent pressures. On the plane ride home, he thought, *Maybe that old fuck, President Harada, was full of shit about the Tokyo stores. I'm sure he's worried that Sawamura Realty will be saddled with those twenty-year leases. I'll check things out myself, first thing tomorrow morning.*

The next morning, Inoue went directly to the closest new Aunt Sally Mae's SFC store in Tokyo. The remodelling was complete and the Store Manager was training staff for the grand opening the following day. The Manager was another former TFC Japan Store Manager, hired away at an enormous premium.

Inoue couldn't believe the location of this store. Unlike the three he had just visited in Sapporo, Nagoya, and Fukuoka, which were on main streets with plenty of commercial and residential property in the immediate vicinity, this store was at the end of a side street. The closest major road was over a hundred meters away. The next-door neighbor was a fertilizer producer who processed fish waste; the smell was terrible. And finally, the store itself was a very odd shape. Built in an L, it was only seven hundred fifty square feet and two hundred fifty of those were only good for storage.

This is absolutely hopeless. No way is this store going to make it. Hell, it probably won't be able to even pay the exorbitant rent. Whoever Saji is getting his insider information from has been found out. I know Joji Sakurai is not smart enough to continue to use the mole to mislead us. It must be Hiro's nephew Kenji, the Managing Director of TFC Japan, who's discovered the mole, whoever it is. Shit, President Harada was right!

It turned out the first new store in Tokyo was the best of the three disasters; the other two were even more removed from customer traffic and even smaller. In fact, the last store closed less than one week after it opened.

Chapter 27

"Mr. Rosenberg, Mr. Willis is on the line," Adam's secretary said.

"Jesus, what does he want? We're never going to get this fucking strategic plan done by next week," Rosenberg fumed.

"Mr. Willis, I'm glad you called. I was just about to call you to see if we could get an extension on the strategic plan. Just between us, I've got to tell you I'm worried about the amount of time this is taking. Hell, almost every day Sanford has some question or another and, Mr. Willis, honestly, I'm afraid our regional senior teams are taking their eyes off the ball."

"Adam, I want you to come up to Hartford on Friday. I'd like to see you in my office after lunch, say two p.m."

"But I'm coming in on Sunday anyway, can't it wait till then?" Rosenberg asked.

"Adam, Friday at two in my office," Willis said as he hung up.

"Mr. Rosenberg, is everything alright?" his secretary said, furrowing her forehead as she placed a cup of coffee in front of him.

Running his hand through his hair, Rosenberg said, "What bug got up his ass? You'd think he'd finally come to his senses and realize this whole strategic planning process is a waste of time. Imagine including all fast food concepts as direct competitors! Hell, we'd never be able to concentrate on such a broad competitor group. And this prick Sanford has to go! He's just a kid bean counter—what can he possibly teach us about strategic planning?

Well, when Willis finally leaves, and I take over, I'll get rid of Sanford, Liberwitz, and strategic planning!"

"I'm sure your meeting this Friday with Mr. Willis will be good news," she smiled. Picking up Rosenberg's coffee cup, she added, "Remember my intuition is almost always right." Rosenberg started feeling better, although he did wonder what the urgency was that couldn't wait until Sunday.

Is it possible that the Western Region Brand Manager has filed one of those sexual harassment complaints? Well, it's her word against mine! Besides, she wasn't that good in the sack, anyhow. No, Willis is just getting tired. The business is in the tank and he's ready to retire; that's why he's been so crabby, Rosenberg thought.

"Judy, get the Southern Region Vice President on the phone. Hell, here's another franchised store request that son-of-a-bitch has refused to approve. Who the hell does he think he is?" Rosenberg shouted.

★★★

Rubbing his forehead, Willis sat back in his chair, and putting his hands behind his head, considered the various next steps to the reorganization. He knew that bringing Jim onside with a positive attitude was a critical first step.

"Hello, Jim, Stuart here. Are you free to have dinner with me tonight at the Corner House?"

"Why of course, Mr. Willis. Is there anything I should bring, or be prepared to discuss?" Jim Meyer asked nervously.

"No, just bring yourself and relax, this'll be a good conversation," Willis said in an upbeat tone.

"What time, Sir?" Meyer asked, more relaxed.

"Say six-thirty? See you there."

★★★

Gene arrived at Willis' office at exactly 8:00, fifteen minutes before Dave was told to be there. Willis got up from behind his desk and came around to sit in one of the five burgundy leather chairs that surrounded a mahogany coffee table on three sides, with a matching leather sofa on the fourth side. He motioned Gene to sit opposite him.

"How's Jane?" Willis asked, after Gene was seated.

"She's actually doing pretty well, according to her doctor. Thanks for asking, Stuart."

"And how's your son doing?" Willis added.

"I think he should go back to Yale, but he's determined to stay home until Jane is better."

"Well, that's certainly good news about Jane. I pray it continues for you, Gene."

Willis leaned back in his chair and linked his fingers together. "Listen, Ralph and Dave Liberwitz will be here in ten minutes, and before they arrive I want to bring you up to speed on a number of things. Willis leaned forward in his chair. "Gene, you know I can't continue with the current organization. You also know your boy Adam has to go." Willis paused as he waited for a reaction.

"Yeah, I've got to agree you're right about Adam," Gene said shaking his head. "I don't know what's happened to him, but he does have to go. He's become negative about everything."

"Well, I've decided to promote Dave Liberwitz to President and COO and move Jim Meyer to President and CEO Domestic. Dave will act as President and CEO International until things are sorted out. For reasons you will hear when everyone arrives, I want Ralph to accept the appointment as Regional Vice President Japan."

"Who is going to replace Ralph if he accepts?" Gene asked, raising his eyebrows.

"Well, Ole Buddy, I hope you and your team can cover things for twelve months or so. We don't see this assignment for Ralph being long term, but it's critical. Japan is our number one market opportunity. But it's also a joint venture where we suspect Mitsugawa is inflating costs to the benefit of their *related* companies. Incidentally, we have your boy Sanford to thank for discovering this fact."

Sticking her head in the door, Willis' secretary said, "Excuse me, Mr. Willis, but Mr. Liberwitz and Mr. Ovunc are here as requested."

"Send them in."

"Ralph, long time no-see, how's everything?" Willis said as he got up and held his hand out.

"Just fine, Mr. Willis," Ralph responded, shaking Willis' hand.

After seating himself, Ralph added, "Mr. Willis, have you seen the most recent forecast for International?"

"No, not yet, but is it better than the last one?"

"Don't answer that, Ralph," Gene interrupted, raising his hand.

"Why?" Willis asked with mock surprise.

"Because what you see is after three different people have massaged it," Gene responded with an attempt at a straight face, which failed.

"Do you guys need me or should I come back later?" Dave said, with mock annoyance.

Dave cleared his throat and said, "Ralph, I thought you told Jim that after hiding four hundred thousand dollars for him and eight hundred thousand for Gene, you still had a six –hundred –thousand dollar cushion, after releasing a forecast that is two hundred eighty-six thousand better than last forecast."

For a second, Willis was fooled. "Oh no you don't, I've fallen for that one too many times." Everyone started laughing as Willis' secretary quickly came in to see what the commotion was.

Willis became serious. "Gentlemen, I've asked you here to confidentially share with you an important development in our company and to ask you to participate in the solution. I know I can count on your discretion." Willis paused for a response.

"Of course," Gene said.

"Absolutely, Mr. Willis," Ralph added, nodding.

"Okay, Ray Easton is going to be arrested by the SEC for insider trading when he arrives in Hartford. Also, there seems to be some claim by the Army concerning Easton's use of a false military ID to get access to the PX in Yokohama; apparently, Easton traded insider information for the false ID."

Dave added, "To make matters worse, Kenji called Sanford yesterday and told him Mitsugawa Hawaii had confirmed that the Attorney General of Hawaii was going to charge Easton with bribing local Planning Board officials.

"Even more disturbing is that Kenji and Ozawa invested in this real estate project. Kenji claims it was through Easton and that they had no idea that the seed money was to be used for bribing local Planning Board officials. Finally, and perhaps most importantly, there is compelling evidence that Easton has been passing confidential internal TFC Japan documents to the Yakuza."

Willis looked concerned over this new information concerning the bribes in Hawaii. *God, I hope Kenji is not implicated in any way. That's all we'd need!*

"That son-of-a-bitch!" Gene yelled, unable to restrain himself. "I knew it!" He slapped his knee. "I guess this is actually good news for us. I've been certain that asshole has been in Mitsugawa's back pocket; he sure as hell hasn't been loyal to us!"

"That brings us to the primary purpose of this meeting," Willis said, leaning forward.

"Ralph, I would like you to go to Tokyo as Ray Easton's replacement. Before you answer, I must tell you, I intend to ask Mitsugawa to "retire" their Joji Sakurai as President and replace him with Kenji, assuming Kenji is not implicated in the Hawaii scandal. In exchange, I would appoint you as our representative and Chairman. You would be paid by us and Kenji will be paid by TFC Japan. We will not insist on a CFO, as you will assume that function as well." Willis paused for effect. "Listen Ralph, if you need some time to think this over, letting me know by two p.m. on Friday will be soon enough."

"Mr. Willis, I don't need time to think about this. I've been dying to get overseas again, and Japan is not unfamiliar to me. One question if I may. I assume I continue to report to Jim?"

"Actually, Ralph, no. Jim will be taking over TFC Domestic and Dave will be taking over TFC International."

"Count me in," Ralph said with a smile.

Willis then said, "Now Ralph, our primary purpose in asking you to accept this assignment is because Sanford has discovered that costs at TFC Japan are way out of whack. He thinks, and we agree, that Mitsugawa-related companies are overcharging for everything. Getting to the bottom of this and correcting it, without destroying the relationship with Mitsugawa or alienating Kenji, is your primary objective. Also, we don't know how long that will take. But when it's finished, you have our assurance we'll find you an appropriate position."

"Well thank you for that, Mr. Willis. I assure you I'll do my best. I actually had extensive dealings with Mitsugawa Heavy Industries when I was at Shell. Can I ask what your plans are to replace me?"

"We're not exactly sure yet. Gene has assured us his team can manage the void until we make a permanent decision. There are a number of other changes that are being made that could have an impact," Willis said.

"If there are no other issues, I'd like to thank Ralph and Gene for coming this morning on such short notice. Dave, please remain," Willis said, as he stood up to shake hands with Gene and Ralph. "Ralph, we really appreciate your willingness to help us through this critical situation."

"Mr. Willis, believe me the pleasure is all mine!" Ralph said as he shook Willis' hand enthusiastically.

Chapter 28

Inoue looked out the window of his office at the bright lights and crowds milling about the streets below. It was 7:00 pm and his secretary had just left. Inoue picked up the phone and dialed Saji's private number. Very few people had Saji's private number.

I wonder who that can be? "Saji *desu.*"

"Saji kun, I need to see you right away," Inoue yelled.

Whatever the problem is; it must be serious. "What's the matter Old Friend? You sound like you've just been beaten up," Saji said in a worried tone.

"Not over the phone; meet me tonight at ten in the Orchid Bar at the Hotel Okura," Inoue hissed and then hung up.

Oh shit, this must be serious! Inoue kun doesn't lose control without a damn good reason.

★★★

The rotund Vice President of Human Resources arrived, short of breath. "You called for me, Mr. Willis?" he asked as he stuck his head in the door.

"Yes, Leslie, I did," Willis said, as he thought, *what a stupid question.* "I'm going to fire Rosenberg tomorrow at two and I need the standard release and severance package."

"Mr. Willis, when did you hear about the sexual harassment lawsuit?" the HR executive asked.

"What sexual harassment lawsuit?" Willis shouted, his face flushing.

"The one Jillian Mare filed against Adam about four or five weeks ago."

"Who is she and when were you going to tell me about this?" Willis roared.

"She's a Brand Manager in the Midwestern Region. She called me about two months ago and accused Adam of forcing her to have sex with him at a marketing conference. I didn't say anything to you about this because I discussed it with Adam and he assured me there was no truth to it. He claims she was just upset because she didn't get the promotion to the Marketing Director position that opened up. When I got the notice of the lawsuit being filed, we were right in the middle of the strategic planning conference, so I didn't bring it up. Besides I don't think she'll win; after all, it's her word against his," the Vice President of Human Resources said, seemingly unaffected by Willis' outburst.

"Jesus, Leslie, how can you be so fucking naïve? You know Rosenberg has a history of this kind of behavior. It's why he was forced out of American Labs. Gene told us that right up front."

"Mr. Willis, if you don't know about the lawsuit, why are you firing Adam, and what are we going to do about replacing him?" he said, wrinkling his eyebrows.

"I'm firing him because he's done nothing but resist the strategic planning initiative and run the U.S. business straight into the ground!" Willis shouted.

"Should I begin a search to find his replacement?" Leslie asked, as though he hadn't heard Willis shout.

"No, you should not. You'll learn details of the new organization next week at the strategic planning presentations." Willis was red-faced. *Why haven't I fired this drone!* "Now get me a release and a termination package by tomorrow morning."

"What terms do you want in the severance package? Can I assume the standard eighteen months we give corporate officers, or do you want to be more generous?"

"I plan to tell Rosenberg that if he doesn't sign the release and accept a nine month severance package that he is terminated immediately for cause. He can then sue if he likes, but I assure you he won't win, especially in light of this sexual harassment lawsuit. Now, Leslie, are there any other accusations against Adam?"

"Hmmm, let me see. There was one from a District Manager in Wisconsin a couple of years ago that claimed he had made unwanted advances at a company picnic. Then there was a complaint of the same thing from Sharon Moran, Manager of the Computing Department, International, last November, and finally, another was made anonymously about three months ago," Leslie said, finally showing some discomfort as Willis just rolled his eyes.

"All right, I've heard enough. Write me a memo detailing all of these accusations, including the dates and all details, as well as Rosenberg's response to each. Reduce the severance to six months and have the whole package here before you leave today," Willis said, as he got up and waved his hand signaling Leslie to leave.

I can't believe this turkey. Four accusations and a history at his preceding company, and Leslie doesn't think to mention it? Well, replacing Leslie will be one of Dave's first organizational moves. Maybe I'm getting too old for this job, Willis thought. He was actually looking forward to firing Rosenberg.

★★★

The Orchid Bar was a dimly lit, quiet place, where businessmen would come to discuss confidential issues. There were very few tourists and only subdued background music, mostly classical.

When Saji arrived at the Orchid Bar, Inoue was seated at a corner table with a bottle of Wild Turkey and a pitcher of cut ice. The bottle was half empty.

Inoue had a frown on his face and seemed to be staring at nothing. In fact, he didn't notice Saji when he entered the bar, even though Saji had waved.

I don't think I've ever seen him so depressed. This is a man who saved my life, more than once. Whatever his problem, I'll solve it.

"Good evening my good friend, what's so urgent?" Saji said, as he sat across from Inoue.

Without looking up, Inoue said, "I'm finished. I--no we--have been duped by your inside contact in TFC Japan," Inoue said, as he refilled his glass.

"Duped?" Saji yelled, clenching his fists. The only other three customers sitting at the bar turned and looked in his direction.

"That's not possible. My contact in TFC Japan is none other than its Chairman, Ray Easton," Saji hissed, turning almost purple as he spoke.

"Well it's all over for me, now," Inoue said softly, as he finished his tumbler of Wild Turkey and directed his gaze at Saji.

"Come on now, my friend, it's not over; we'll recover from this as we have many times before." Saji smiled, and poured himself a Wild Turkey and water. "Remember after the high school baseball regional playoff when a rival Yakuza group cornered you and me on our way to the post-game celebration? Hell, I was sweating bullets, knowing that that thug was going to kidnap me and kill you," Saji said smiling, as he refilled Inoue's tumbler.

"Shit, that stunt you pulled by falling down and faking an epileptic fit was priceless. At least it gave my bodyguard time to catch up and dispatch that thug with his sword."

"Yes, of course I remember," Inoue said with a weak smile, looking directly at Saji. "But this time it's different." Inoue then related the details of three Tokyo stores and the threat from the President of Sawamura Realty to expose him to the board of Sawamura Trading at the meeting scheduled next week.

As Saji listened, he poured his friend another Wild Turkey. *Easton, that worthless fuck! I'll actually enjoy this disappearance, even though it will be for free.*

★★★

When Bill and Dave arrived at Willis' office, he greeted them smiling. "Gentlemen, welcome! Have a seat." He motioned them over to the leather chairs. "What about those Red Sox? Carl Yastrzemski is going to take them all the way next season," Willis added, as he took his seat.

"Yes, all the way, just to lose to the Yankees, something they've managed to do every time they've faced them in a World Series since 1918," Dave said with a smile.

"Well, I can see our head strategist has faulty vision, at least in baseball," Willis retorted.

What is this meeting all about and why am I here? Bill thought to himself, as he tried to decide which baseball team to support and which key player. Unfortunately, Bill only watched hockey.

Feeling he had to contribute something, Bill said, "How about those Boston Patriots?" Everyone got a good laugh over that one. The Patriots were four and twelve last season, the fifth worst in the NFL.

Finally, getting over his laughter, Willis said, "Bill, you're probably wondering why we asked you here today."

Bill was nervous, not knowing which of Ray's disasters he would be questioned about.

As if reading his mind, Dave said, "Relax, Bill, this is good news."

Leaning forward and looking directly at Bill, Wills said, "Bill, we asked you here to present you with a couple of job offers that recognize your significant efforts on the strategic planning process, and our confidence in your potential."

"Dave, would you like to take it from here?"

Nodding, Dave said, "Bill, the two jobs are Regional Vice President Europe and Vice President Strategic Planning. Both are a letter grade A and carry the same salary and bonus. The bonus target, incidentally, is twenty percent with leverage up to forty percent based on exceeding plan. These are both very important and demanding jobs that will provide you an opportunity for personal development and further career advancement."

"I don't know what to say," Bill said, raising his open hands. "I'd thought that I might be offered the Regional Controller, CFO Japan job, but these I didn't expect. Where would the Regional Vice President Europe be located?"

"Where do you think it should be located?" Willis asked.

"Well, it should be centrally located. Paris is the best city for Europe-wide travel and is within striking of Benelux and Italy, which are likely to be key, new expansion markets."

"Makes sense to me," Willis said.

"I assume the European job will report to Jim Meyer, but who will the VP Strategic Planning report to?" Bill asked, looking confused, as he looked first at Willis and then at Dave.

Willis said, "Bill, I'm making a number of key organizational changes, which will be announced next Monday at the opening of the conference. However, the question you ask is reasonable, so in confidence I tell you the following. Jim Meyer is going to replace Adam Rosenberg, and Dave is going to replace Jim. So, in either job, you'll continue to report to Dave."

"Well, I'm honored and grateful to be offered these positions. Honestly, I'm not sure I'm the right guy for the European position. Don't get me wrong, I'm very interested in the position, but I don't have any general management experience."

Dave said, "First, we're confident you can be successful in either job we've offered. In fact, you'll have an easier time being successful in either of these jobs than you would in the CFO Japan position."

"Really? Why do you say that?" Bill said, raising his eyebrows.

"Because in Japan, seniority is largely based on experience; someone not yet thirty won't be credible in an executive position," Dave explained.

Willis interjected, "That's why we've asked Ralph to go to Japan as Regional Vice President and assume the CFO role. By the way, he'll very much need your analysis of various line-item costs in TFC Japan versus other countries."

"So what do you think?" Dave asked with a smile.

"Can I do them both?" Bill blurted, with his palms up. Everyone got a good laugh.

"Well, I'm leaning towards the European position because it gives me general management experience in an environment with enormous potential. Further, it also gives me a chance to implement some of the principles I've learned, and indeed preached, in this strategic planning position."

"You are wise beyond your years, young man," Willis said, nodding.

"Well, we want you to be sure about your choice," Dave said, leaning back in his chair. "If you are by next Monday, we'll make the announcement with the others. If not, then we'll make a separate announcement when you've decided."

"Oh, I'm sure I can give you a definitive answer before Monday. I just want to, ah, talk it over with my…my fiancée," Bill stammered, looking very embarrassed and turning red in the face.

"Congratulations!" Willis and Dave said, almost simultaneously, with surprised looks and smiles on their faces.

"Please don't say anything since I haven't even asked her yet!" Again Willis and Dave started laughing.

"Well, I guess that means we're going to have to find a new EDP Manager for International," Dave said with a smile.

Chapter 29

He looked at his watch; it was 10:18. *Where is that son-of-a-bitch?* Ray thought. *He's ten minutes late.*

It was unusually cold for November and the brisk wind made it seem even colder. Ray pulled his coat tight as he waited for Saji; he felt a cold coming on. *Why did Saji pick such an unusual place to meet?*

Ray had arrived at the designated meeting place fifteen minutes before the scheduled time, at least as he remembered it. Saji had just called an hour ago to set this sudden meeting up. *And I leave tomorrow for the States and the strategic planning meeting where I'll be the star.*

The parking lot had only two cars and the Italian restaurant was closed. Normally Nicola's was busy through midnight, at least with college students. The country-western bar next to Nicola's was also closed. Ray thought that was strange for 10:00 p.m., but didn't dwell on it.

His thoughts centered on how he would simply disappear after he milked Saji's client for all he could with the TFC Japan's insider information. *Of course, Fumiko's suicide is going to complicate things for a while until I find a replacement. Perhaps I'll just hire that hostess Sachiko as my personal secretary. In any case, I'll have to tell Saji that this is the last meeting for a while.* Ray pulled his coat tighter around himself as the wind picked up.

A BMW, cutting its lights as it coasted, stopped ten feet from where Ray was standing. *So Saji's got a new car,* Ray thought.

Hearing a car door close behind him, Ray turned to see Saji's Lieutenant, Yoji, who was carrying a long object, get out of a non-descript Toyoda white utility van. Ray hadn't noticed the car before, as it was in the shadows, and now he was confused. *Who's this guy?*

His confusion quickly dissipated as he recognized Saji, but not the younger man with him, who looked very much like Yakuza, bearing the trademarked loss of the left little finger, something that was required of all new recruits in the initiation process.

Ray decided he was indeed Yakuza, but that wasn't all that unusual; after all, Saji was head of the Osaka Yakuza. Still, he began to feel a bit uncomfortable. Despite the cold, Ray began to sweat. *Calm down, Saji is a friend…well, almost.*

"Hey Saji, just finished a job, eh, was it profitable?" Ray said with a smile, pointing at the thug. "You're going to need it, my prices are going up," Ray added, chuckling as he held out an envelope.

"No, we're just about to begin a job tonight," Saji said with a smile, "and this one is for free."

Ray had forgotten about the man behind him with the long object, which turned out to be a baseball bat, until he was hit just above his right knee, a location that caused excruciating pain, but allowed limited continued use of the leg. He buckled and fell to the ground screaming.

Pain shot through the back of his right leg like a hot knife. "What the fuck?" Ray yelled. "Why did you do that? What do you want?" Ray realized that he was in serious trouble and that he would have to think fast if he was going to save himself.

The thug standing next to Saji removed a short samurai sword and brandished it, smiling.

"Jesus, Saji, tell him to put that thing away," Ray pleaded. "Why are you doing this? I've cooperated completely and given you everything you asked for!" he cried, holding his right knee.

"Ray, you are a worthless son of a whore," Saji said, speaking softly. "You are also a liar and extremely stupid. You have given false information." Saji nodded at Yoji, who swung the bat and hit Ray's right forearm. Ray screamed as it shattered.

"Now you're going to tell me everything about your deception. If I think you're lying at all, I'm going to ask Akiba kun here to remove both of your index fingers immediately. If you continue not to cooperate, I will have Akiba kun castrate you. Do you understand what I have said?" Saji smiled as he waited for Ray's answer.

"Jesus, I'll tell you everything; just don't hurt me anymore, please," Ray said, as he began to piss himself. He didn't have any idea what Saji was referring to; after all, he had provided everything that Saji had demanded.

"Go on, tell me all the details since we started this project. Take your time and leave out no detail," Saji said, still smiling.

"When you first approached me, I was concerned how I could pull this off," Ray said, wincing, as he moved his shattered arm. "I decided to take Fumiko, a clerk in the accounting department, into my confidence and let her actually copy the various documents. She was completely reliable and managed to deliver everything on time."

"That was your first mistake, Ray," Saji said conversationally. "Go on."

"Well, last week I came home with two newly arrived wanna-be models. When I got home, I found Fumiko in a negligee sitting on the coach smoking dope. She was whining something about our two-month anniversary. I told her to leave…"

Kicking Ray's shattered arm, Saji said, "I told you not to leave anything out, didn't I."

"God, Saji, I'm telling you the truth!"

"Not all of it."

"Okay, I did yell at her and told her she meant nothing to me. That she was just a whore that was useful in my deal with you. Then I threw her out."

"Much better, Ray," Saji said, smiling. "What did she say?"

"Something about being Samurai and that I would someday regret this day."

"An extremely accurate prediction."

Fuck, what is going on here? What false information did I give? The last delivery I made was one Fumiko gave me the night before she disappeared. Although, come to think of it, I didn't actually deliver it until the following evening. Could it have been switched by her later that night to get revenge?

"Share your thoughts, Ray," Saji said impatiently.

"Well, maybe Fumiko switched the documents the night I threw her out. After all, I didn't pass them along to you until the following night."

"Your second big mistake, you fucking moron," Saji said, as he motioned to the thug next to him, who helped Ray stand and led him towards the non-descript Toyoda van that Yoji had arrived in. Yoji took the baseball bat and hit Ray in the back of the head. Ray collapsed.

★ ★ ★

The seas in Tokyo Bay were quite rough, due to the twenty-five knot winds out of the north. The yacht was a forty-footer, so it could easily handle the ten-foot seas although the passengers would clearly feel the motion.

As they exited the port, they saw no other boats except for returning fishing boats hurrying to get their catch to the Tsukiji fish market which opened at three-thirty every morning. All of the sushi shops, both large and small, would send their sushi masters to buy the best cuts of fresh fish. By four, the market was packed with buyers yelling over each other to make bids.

Yoji became seasick and went below. Saji had given the captain the coordinates that he was to follow. The captain knew them well, as this was his twentieth visit to drop off "undesirable cargo," as Saji San had explained to him fourteen years earlier.

The younger thug lit his cigarette and thought of how much fun he would have in an hour or so. He laughed as he remembered his father's insistence that he join the family rice warehousing business.

About two hours out from port, Ray came to. The pain in his head was unbelievable. He had never experienced anything like it before. While his right leg still hurt, it was nothing like the pain in his head and shattered arm.

"Ah, Ray San, I see you are back with us," Saji said laughing. "I was afraid that I would not have the pleasure of watching you suffer at the end of your life."

"What the fuck are you talking about? Saji, you said if I cooperated and told you everything you would not hurt me anymore!"

"Ah, like you, I'm a liar!" Saji said, roaring with laughter as he slapped his thigh.

"Oh my God, you're not really going to kill me! Please, I'll do anything! I can work for Sawamura and feed misinformation back into TFC Japan. I'll, I'll work for nothing!" Ray bawled uncontrollably.

This son-of-a-bitch is actually going to kill me! Fuck, I've got to do something. God, this can't be actually happening to me!

"Saji San, I'll give you one million dollars if you'll just take me to a hospital," Ray said, between sobs.

Ignoring Ray, Saji said, "Sato kun, go get Yoji kun and tell the captain to stop the yacht. We're at our, or at least *your*, final destination," Saji said, laughing, looking at Ray.

When the two thugs returned, they were struggling with an obviously heavy object. Ray had a look of sheer terror on his face when he saw the large iron anchor and heavy ankle bracelets.

"Saji, no, why are you doing this?" Ray yelled above the roar of the wind.

"Well, I guess there's no harm in telling you now. The man your stupidity has destroyed is my closest friend, a man who has saved my life on three occasions. And now, because of you, he is going to have to take his life. That is why I so enjoyed this evening, you worthless Fuck!" Saji nodded at the two thugs.

"You're, you're not going to throw me into the sea!" Ray screamed. "No, no, no," he sobbed uncontrollably.

As Sato and Yoji began to fasten the ankle bracelets, Ray began to defecate and urinate.

"Couldn't you do the polite thing and wait until you were in the water," Saji said, laughing, as he told his men to take Ray topside.

The wind had picked up to over thirty knots and it had begun to rain, almost freezing rain. Land was nowhere in sight. The yacht was pitching severely when the captain called out, "We better get moving soon. There's a small-craft warning out; gale force winds are expected within an hour, and we have a three-hour ride back."

"Well, I guess it's time to say goodbye," Saji said casually, as he motioned the other two to bring Ray to the rail.

"Any last words?" Saji yelled loud enough to be heard over the wind.

"Fuck you! I hope you go down with this fucking boat on the way back, you son-of-a-bitch," Ray screamed, as they tossed him over.

The waves quickly swallowed Ray up. Of course, he tried to hold his breath but the one-hundred-fifty-pound anchor quickly pulled him down. At about thirty feet below the surface, his eardrums broke, causing a rush of cold water into his middle ear, which disoriented him immediately. His lungs burned, as he exhaled and gasped, filling them with water. He continued sinking faster.

His last thought was of Fumiko hanging herself. He could see her in his mind's eye, as she stepped off the chair and the rope tightened around her neck. She had a smile on her face.

★★★

When Bill returned home early, Sharon was surprised. With the strategic planning conference kicking off on Monday, she assumed Bill wouldn't be home until after eight p.m., at the earliest. "What are you doing home at six? You're not feeling bad, are you?"

"Get dressed up! I'm taking you out for dinner, one you won't forget!"

"Oh yeah, where're we going, Big Shot?"

"We're going to Chuck's Steakhouse and having only the very best!"

Bill then picked Sharon up in his arms and spun her around, until they both became dizzy.

"What're we celebrating?" Sharon asked as soon as they got in the car.

"I'll tell you when we get to the restaurant and not a moment before, so don't bother asking again!"

"Well, this time the joke is on you. I already know what we're celebrating," Sharon said with a smug look.

"No you don't. You couldn't possibly know," Bill said with a trace of worry. *How could she know?*

"I do know: Carmen told me this afternoon," Sharon lied, hoping to trap Bill into telling her.

"No, she didn't."

When they got to the restaurant, the waitress that had served them on their last visit was there and remembered them. After all, Bill had left her a hundred-dollar tip, the biggest she had ever received.

"Welcome back! What're we celebrating this evening?" the waitress asked with a smile.

"Something very special."

"In that case, can I bring you another bottle of Dom Perignon and some mushrooms stuffed with lobster?"

"That sounds perfect! You've a remarkable memory. How did you remember what we ordered last time?" Bill asked.

The waitress thought for a moment, raising her eyes toward the ceiling before responding, and then said, "I always remember my best customers—especially when they order a bottle of sixty-five-dollar Dom Perignon."

After the champagne and appetizers arrived, Sharon leaned over the table. "So, when are we moving to Japan? Mr. Regional Controller, CFO TFC Japan? I told you I knew," Sharon said, pleased with herself.

"How did you guess?"

"I knew they would give that position to you. Hell, you've earned it, and besides, you're one of their brightest rising stars."

The waitress came over and, as she passed out the menus, asked, "Is the cat out of the bag?"

"Almost," Bill said with a wink.

"The specials tonight include fresh Maine lobster boiled, steamed, or stuffed with crab, prime rib of beef, and my favorite, which is rarely available, *osso bucco* with homemade fettuccini."

"Again, it all sounds great. How about we get one stuffed lobster and one *osso bucco* and share them?"

"That sounds fine with me," Sharon said with a smile, knowing Bill wanted some of each, even though she knew she would not have much of the lobster.

"So, when are we going to Tokyo? Are we going to get a house-hunting trip?"

Bill looked somber. "We're not going to Tokyo. They didn't offer me the Regional Controller, CFO TFC Japan job. They said that in Japan age is necessary to command respect and seniority is critical."

"What? That's just not fair!" Sharon virtually shouted, causing several heads at other tables to turn.

"Relax!" Bill said, blushing. Then with a big grin on his face, he added, "Instead, they offered me two choices. Either VP Strategic Planning or…" Bill paused and poured a little more champagne for both of them.

"Would you stop torturing me and tell me what the other option is!" Sharon said excitedly, almost rising out of her chair.

"If you agree, we're going to move to Paris and I'm becoming the Regional VP Europe, TFC International!" Bill said, too loudly. Again, a few heads turned at nearby tables.

"Congratulations!" the waitress said, as she brought the main courses over.

"My God, my man's a Regional VP at twenty-nine! And to think we're moving to Paris. *C'est magnifique. Je suis très content!*" Sharon said. "How can anyone be so lucky?"

The waitress arrived while they were holding hands and brought with her a German chocolate cake that had "Congratulations Regional VP Europe" on it. "Can I get you anything else? Perhaps a Grand Marnier or a cognac?"

"No thanks. I want to get him home," Sharon said with a wink.

With a knowing look, the waitress said, "I'll be right back with the check."

When the waitress returned, she said, "I hope this doesn't mean we won't see you guys anymore."

"Don't worry. We'll be back to the States often." Bill added the same hundred-dollar tip.

The waitress came back with the credit card receipt and said, "You're going to spoil me."

"You deserve it."

"I can't believe we're going to Paris—to live, no less! I'm going to start practicing my French. It should come back pretty quickly," Sharon said. "Can we live anywhere within the city? I would love to live in one of the western suburbs, maybe St. Germaine-en-Laye or Le Vesinet."

"I'll leave that up to you, as long as it's reasonably close to the airports."

CHAPTER 30

Rosenberg arrived at Willis' office twenty minutes early and walked right in. Willis was talking to the Human Resources Vice President.

"Oh, hello Adam," Leslie said.

"I told you two o'clock; you're over twenty minutes early. Return at two-fifteen," Willis said, without looking up.

Rosenberg considered protesting but decided against it. *He's just in a bad mood, trying to get ready for this disastrous strategic planning conference. Perhaps he's going to announce his retirement. Yes, that's it! That's why Leslie's in there and is so nervous. Son-of-a-bitch, I'm finally getting promoted. God, I hope so. I'll cancel this strategic planning nonsense and fire Dave Liberwitz and that kid "Bean Counter" Sanford. Then we can get back to what counts and keep our eye on the ball by expanding profitable franchises.*

Rosenberg began to prepare his acceptance speech in his own mind. *People, we have a shared vision for the future of our company. This vision is based on the principles of quality of product, quality of preparation, and quality of customer service that our founder, Major Tom, left us as his legacy. I'm honored to assume this challenge of leadership and look forward to—*

"Excuse me, Mr. Rosenberg, Mr. Willis is ready to see you," Willis' secretary said.

"Oh, okay," Rosenberg said, somewhat distracted as his chain of thought was broken.

"Good afternoon, Mr. Willis," Rosenberg said cheerfully. "I think I know why you asked me here today, and I just want to say—"

Willis raised his hand. "Adam, you've absolutely no idea why I asked you here, and that's one of your fundamental problems." Willis handed Rosenberg the release and severance offer.

Rosenberg looked the documents over briefly, and said, "You've got to be kidding! I'm your successor—the Board and you have said as much!"

"Adam, times have changed. The Domestic Group is clearly hemorrhaging. Additionally, you've refused to accept the Board's strategic planning initiative, thus continuing this discussion serves no useful purpose. The decision has been made; now either accept this offer or not." Willis leaned forward.

"But the normal severance for a Corporate Officer is eighteen months. The Board certainly doesn't expect me to accept anything less!" Adam said indignantly.

"You have exactly thirty minutes to decide if you are going to sign those documents, or not. In either case, your employment with this company is terminated right now."

"But, but you can't do that. I'm on the Board. I demand an audience with the Board! I've been here six years," Rosenberg said, his big ears turning bright red.

"Adam, the Board is obviously aware of this termination. You're wasting your time and mine as well. Either sign the documents, or not, but I've other things to address," Willis said, becoming clearly annoyed.

"God damn it! What possible basis do you have for firing me? Just because I see this strategic planning initiative of yours as the complete waste of time it is? Perhaps because the domestic numbers are a little soft? This is largely because you've slowed our franchising initiative pending this ridiculous strategic plan," Rosenberg said, raising his voice.

"Okay, Adam, so that's how you want to play this," Willis said, as he cleared his throat.

"Technically, you're being fired for multiple sexual harassment accusations. One of these is likely to result in charges. I hear that Green Bay, Wisconsin's District Attorney is considering just that. If you don't sign those documents, you'll be terminated for cause and receive absolutely no severance," Willis said calmly, as he handed over the four accusations.

"Incidentally, your numbers are horrible and your indiscriminate over-franchising is disgraceful. Now, either you can sign these documents or not; personally, I don't care. In either case, this discussion is over. Fran, have security come in please," Willis said into the intercom. Two security guards immediately appeared.

"Okay, I'll sign the fucking documents, but you haven't heard the last from me!" Rosenberg hissed.

Security escorted Rosenberg to his car and took his company keys, ID, and credit cards, then waited until he left the property before going back inside. Just to be sure, they instructed the gate guard not to allow Rosenberg back on the property—ever.

Willis reflected for a few minutes before picking up the phone. *There's no question that Jim Meyer will do a much better job than Adam; imagine that arrogant son-of-a-bitch thinking I called him in early to promote him.* He laughed out loud, which brought Fran into the office.

"Is there anything wrong?" she asked in a surprised tone of voice.

"Not at all, Fran, but thanks for worrying. Can you ask Dave to come in please?"

★★★

Inoue barely slept on his flights to Mobile. He was preoccupied with President Kato's threat to bring up the Tokyo store sites that Aunt Sally Mae Japan had entered into.

How did I get myself into this situation? I guess it was my determination to get even with that son of a whore, Joji Sakurai. Everything hinges on this trip. Bullshit, stop kidding yourself, the three Tokyo stores, which they had not approved, are destined to be failures.

As Inoue exited the baggage claim, he looked for Ashley, who had confirmed she would meet his flight.

"Over here, Inoue Senmu," Ashley said as she waved from the exit. "I'm parked just to the left of the bus stop."

"So, have you got good news?" Ashley said, after Inoue got into the front seat.

"Well, you'll not believe the news coverage in all three cities. Further, and more importantly, sales for opening day in all three cities averaged what TFC Japan does in a normal month!" Inoue said proudly.

"Come on, not one month's sales in a *day*," Ashley said with a look of disbelief.

"I'm serious. We had between four to seven chicken deliveries at each store, just on opening day."

"Wow, it sounds like things are off to a flying start!"

"How is J.J. getting along since his mother died?" Inoue asked.

"Well, it's clear he misses her. He just hasn't been himself since she had the heart attack. Inoue Senmu, don't expect much from him on this trip."

"He might cheer up when he sees the tapes," Inoue said. "By the way, I'm booked at the Hilton."

When they arrived at the head office, they were immediately told to go to the boardroom; everyone had been waiting over an hour.

Oh shit, here we go again!" Inoue thought to himself.

Ashley must have read his mind, because she said, "Let me handle the explanation as to why we're late."

When they walked in, it was clear that their audience was impatient at having been forced to wait. "Well, we're glad ya'll decided to fit us in," Lee said.

"Go to hell, Lee! Who do you think you are? I had a flat on the interstate and it took forty minutes before a truck driver stopped to help me," Ashley said aggressively.

Inoue interjected, "I think you'll agree the results I've brought you are worth the wait, and then some." Then he whispered to Ashley, before inserting the first Beta Max tape, "I'm glad I let you handle the tardiness explanation so diplomatically."

"How long is this going to take?" J.J. asked in an annoyed tone. "I'm now over an hour behind schedule," he added with a sour expression. Ashley was visibly nervous, afraid Inoue would explode.

"Well the first tape is forty minutes," Inoue said, watching Lee roll his eyes at J.J., "and I'll bet you dinner at Granny Betty's for this entire group, on me personally, that you will stay to see the entire tape. You people are about to see something you have not even imagined, or indeed will believe, in fact—"

"Why don't you just get on with it? In fact, I'll bet you a grand that we won't be impressed," Lee said with a smug smile, sure Inoue would not take this obvious no-win bet.

"You're talking personal funds?" Inoue said evenly.

Lee just nodded and J.J. smiled. "In that case, you have a bet," Inoue said with a smile, as he turned the tape on.

The tape began with the Sapporo store opening its doors to a line of about a hundred people. A few eyebrows around the room rose. Next, it shifted to an interview with a group of four house-wives standing in line who were asked what they expected. They said they thought that since "Mama Aunt Sally Mae" had taught the Major the secret recipe, they expected better chicken.

J.J's. face revealed complete shock. "Mama Aunt Sally Mae," he said out loud. At the lunch hour, the film panned a line of people that stretched for three city blocks. As the tape continued, it depicted the interviewer talking to customers at the beginning of the line. On average, they confirmed that they had been waiting more than an hour. Next up was the chicken supplier making his third delivery of the day. The audience chuckled when Inoue took over at one of the cash registers.

The film then covered a dozen or so follow-up interviews with customers who had been interviewed while waiting in line. The four housewives were included. They all agreed that "Mama Aunt Sally Mae's Southern Fried Chicken" was better. After all, every-one knew that the best food was always made by Mama.

Next up was the Nagoya store, which was even more impres-sive across all dimensions. The references to "Mama Aunt Sally Mae's Southern Fried Chicken" secret recipe, which she taught the Major, were much more prevalent. When the camera followed the line of customers four city blocks long, the audience in the boardroom spontaneously applauded.

Finally, the Fukuoka new store was covered. The number of college students was astounding. They, in particular, seemed to be aware of the whole "Mama Aunt Sally Mae" story. The film ended with Inoue handing out free dinner coupons to some fifty customers still in line at eleven-thirty, thirty minutes after closing time; the store and its suppliers had simply run out of chicken.

When the film ended, everyone applauded. J.J. said, "Lee, I guess you owe Inoue Senmu a grand."

"Yes I do. And it's the best bet I've ever lost. You're right, Inoue Senmu, I would not have believed it if I hadn't seen it," Lee said, as he reached for his checkbook. "Now, none of this was staged, right?" he said with a smile, as he handed Inoue the check.

J.J. then said, "Inoue Senmu, I hope you'll join me at Granny Betty's tomorrow for lunch. You were right. I've never seen anything like that customer reaction in all my years in this business. The "Mama Aunt Sally Mae's Southern Fried Chicken" recipe is a stroke of genius. She would be so very proud. I also owe you an apology. Ashley convinced me you did indeed talk about a publicity campaign to spread the story of my mother teaching the Major the secret recipe when you were last here," J.J. said sincerely.

"But the forecast is another matter. We just cannot afford the kind of losses you're talking about in the fourth quarter. Will the results change with the kind of success the first three stores are having?"

"Yes, my updated forecast is much improved. Costs are even higher, but will be more than offset by increased revenues. I plan on presenting it in detail first thing tomorrow morning."

The same group was all in the boardroom when Inoue arrived at 9:00 a.m. This time, however, everyone seemed to be in good moods. J.J. was actually laughing and joking with the CFO.

★★★

The TFC conference room was packed, standing at the podium, Willis cleared his throat and said, "Good morning, and welcome to our first strategic planning conference. We've a lot to cover in the next three days, and I assure you, we'll all learn from the experience and our businesses will improve as a result. Strategic planning is a powerful tool that we need to respect and use effectively."

He paused for effect before continuing, "Consistent with this, I'd like to announce some key organizational changes. Effective today, I'll assume the role of Chairman and Chief Executive Officer. Dave Liberwitz is appointed as President and Chief Operating Officer. Jim Meyer is appointed President and CEO, TFC Domestic. Dave Liberwitz is appointed Acting President and CEO, TFC International. Jim's intimate knowledge of our business will ensure that the changes necessary in the U.S. business will be effectively and thoughtfully made and implemented. Dave brings unique international experience and a proven track record as a strategist; he is also a true visionary, with a successful record of effective turnarounds. "I ask you all to join me in congratulating our new Senior Team!" Willis said enthusiastically as he began to clap. The crowd responded positively and clapped energetically.

After a few moments, Willis continued. "There are several other key appointments I'm pleased to announce. First, that Ralph Ovunc is appointed as Regional VP, Japan. Ralph is a true internationalist with an eye for financial detail. Next, I'm pleased to announce that Bill Sanford is appointed Regional VP, Europe. Bill has done a great job in his strategic planning role. I know most of you have experienced Bill's help first hand. I'm confident Ralph and Bill will be successful in their new roles."

The audience clapped again, politely this time. That is except for Sharon, who was beside herself with pride and showed it by jumping up, whistling, and applauding enthusiastically, just as she had done in college as a cheerleader. The audience then began to laugh and clap enthusiastically, led by Willis who could not help but laugh. Bill just smiled and turned three shades of red.

During the morning break, Willis said to Dave, "I wonder if Ray got tipped off about his pending arrest?"

"I doubt it, although Easton is one resourceful SOB," Dave said. "I'll have Kenji see if he can find out where Ray is," Dave added with a concerned look. *I wonder where he really is. The SEC has put a lot of time and effort into this.*

Gene grabbed Willis at break. "Stuart, I want you to know that I'm one hundred percent behind this new organization. Also, I apologize for my attitude over your strategic planning project." Clearly emotional, Gene continued, "I assure you, Stuart, I will support Dave in any way I can."

Willis looked Gene straight in the eyes. Gene's pain and worry were obvious. "Gene, how is Janice? Is the radiation working?"

Choking, Gene said, "The doctors say they don't know and won't know for three months. Stuart, I'm at my wits' end!"

Willis grabbed Gene's shoulders and, looking directly into his eyes, said, "Gene, we'll support you and your family unconditionally! Now, I want you to bring Kerry Gray up to speed on International as soon as you can, and then use him, damn it!"

Then in a stern tone Willis added, "Gene, your number one priority is Janice! I will personally kick your ass if you don't put your family first, at least until Janice is in remission! Sergeant, is that order clear!" Willis almost shouted.

Immediately, Gene straightened up and responded loudly, "Sir, yes sir!"

Chapter 31

When Inoue returned home late Monday night, he could not get the current problems surrounding Aunt Sally Mae's Southern Fried Chicken Japan off his mind. *Just two weeks ago everything looked fantastic. The whole Mama Aunt Sally Mae's Southern Fried Chicken recipe had been a divine gift, my own kamikaze. The sales at the first new stores are incredible. But the three Tokyo stores that Ray Easton, TFC Japan's Chairman, set us up for are just a disaster. And with Sawamura Realty ready to insist that Sawamura Trading take over the guarantees, well there is only one way to handle this mess.*

After he finally went to sleep, Inoue dreamt of his beloved Keiko for the first time in years. He recalled the times they had spent together on the Tamagawa River, as Inoue rowed the boat and Keiko sang love songs in her delightful, soft voice. Each week, she would write a new song expressing her love for Inoue, always very subtle and indirect. He had kept all forty-three she had composed in a special safe, where his mother's poetry was also kept. He recalled his favorite song, and in his dream, he heard Keiko singing the verses:

As the sun rises and sets,
I see your face,
when you are not there.
The breeze on my skin becomes your hand caressing me,
ever so gently,
when I close my eyes,

and you are not around.
The Sakura is like our love,
poetic beauty, nature at its finest,
fleeting as the seasons,
but as perennial as our thoughts.
May our memories live in our hearts,
now and forever.

It was her last song. She must have suspected their relationship would come to an end when she wrote it.

Inoue then dreamt he was having lunch with Joji Sakurai, asking for Keiko's hand in marriage. This time, Joji had agreed and was telling Inoue that all would be okay, and that Inoue was free to marry Keiko. Inoue was beside himself with joy. The love he felt for Keiko was indescribable.

At that moment in his dream, the phone rang. As he awoke, reality came back like an ice-cold bucket of water being thrown in his face. He suddenly changed from joy to sadness, so quickly he could not answer the phone. He simply sat there in tears. His obsession with getting even with Joji Sakurai grew stronger than ever before. *I will get that son of a whore, whatever the cost! My life and all its accomplishments will mean nothing if I do not avenge the destruction of the only love I've ever experienced,* Inoue said to himself, with the conviction of a Samurai. He immediately felt better.

★★★

Tiffany's was crowded for a Thursday evening. Bill had been looking at the various engagement rings for thirty minutes, without anyone asking if he needed any help. As he was about to leave, frustrated, an elderly woman who reminded him of his Grandma Katie came forward and said, "Good evening, young man. Can I help you with something special?" She had a knowing expression on her face and a beautiful smile.

Looking somewhat embarrassed, Bill said, "Well, I'm looking for an engagement ring, but I'm new to this, so I guess I need some guidance."

The elderly saleswoman said, "Well that's what I'm here for, and I have lots of experience. Now, do you have anything specific in mind, or would you like me to suggest a few things?"

"Well, Sharon has pretty simple tastes. I was thinking along the lines of a single diamond set in platinum. What do you think?"

"I think that would be perfect! And I have four items in particular that I would like to show you."

Thirty minutes later, Bill left with a one-carat, vvs#1, D clarity diamond set in a platinum ring. Grandma Katie had wrapped it in a beautiful silver package. The price was virtually equal to Grandma Katie's original recommendation of three months' salary, at least three months of the new Vice President's salary, including target bonus. Grandma Katie had assured him that he could exchange it if Sharon was anything less than thrilled.

***

Bill answered the phone, "Sanford here."

"Mr. Sanford, I have the travel agent, Mr. Bing Lantz, here to see you."

"Thanks, Phil, send him right up."

"Mr. Sanford, congratulations on your promotion," Bing said. "Vice President Europe—that's impressive!"

Bill turned a bit pink and said, "Come on, Bing, stop that Mr. Sanford bullshit and tell me what you've got for me."

"Well, Bill, I've got your first-class, non-stop, roundtrip tickets from Hartford to San Juan leaving this Sunday morning at ten," Bing said, smiling, as he passed over the ticket folder.

"Next, I've got your prepaid voucher for your twelve-meter yacht, the *Weak Moment*. And finally, here is a surprise, not to be opened until you're on the plane. Promise me!" Bing withdrew the envelope, holding it up to his chest, until Bill promised.

"Okay, I promise. Thanks for pulling all the details together. This really is an important trip for us." Bill leaned over and rummaged through his briefcase. "Can you keep a secret?" Bill was just dying to tell someone.

"Scouts honor," Bing said, smiling, as he raised his hand in the three-finger Boy Scout salute.

Bill then took out the silver box and blurted out, "I'm going to ask Sharon to marry me!"

"Congratulations! I suspected this trip might be more than a winter's getaway. Well now, I have my work cut out for me!"

"What do you mean?" Bill asked, perplexed.

"You'll see soon enough!" Bing said, laughing, as he got up to leave.

★★★

When he got home, Bill tried to act nonchalant, as though nothing was out of the ordinary.

"So how was your trip to New York?" Sharon asked conversationally. "Was it productive? You seemed unsure when you mentioned it day before yesterday."

For the life of him, Bill couldn't remember the excuse he had used for going to New York. "Yeah, it was fine."

"Well, did you choose one of them?" Sharon persisted.

Shit! What did I say I was going to New York for?

"Hello, Earth calling Bill," Sharon said, waving her hand.

Bill finally remembered the white lie he had told Sharon. "Sorry, I was thinking about our upcoming trip. But yeah, I think I'll give the German account to F&S." *God, that was a close call!*

"Bill, I'll give you a special *whatever* tonight if you'll tell me where we're going day after tomorrow," Sharon said with a pout on her face.

She then put her arms around Bill and kissed him slowly. Pulling back, she added, "Well, are you going to tell me or not? How am I supposed to know what to pack? I only have tomorrow to buy the appropriate wardrobe for both of us. Now tell me!"

"Okay, I'll give you enough information so you can do the shopping. But only if you promise not to ask for more details. Oh, and of course I get the special *whatever* you were bribing me with. Deal?"

Looking up at the ceiling, with her finger on her cheek, as though she were carefully considering Bill's proposition, Sharon finally said, "Hmmm, let's see. Okay on your first demand, but the second demand will depend on how satisfied I am with your answer. Deal?"

"Where we're going, the temperature will range from a low of seventy degrees to a high of eighty-five degrees," Bill said, smiling.

"You better do better than that if you expect a special *whatever*."

"Hmmm, what else can I safely tell you?" Bill said, rubbing his chin and looking very serious. "You should expect lot's of intense sun and, potentially, a lot of wind and rain. Oh, and you'll need athletic shoes, sexy lingerie, swimwear and one nice evening dress. Now don't ask for any more details!"

★★★

Saturday was spent at the Corbin's Corner Mall where Sharon dragged Bill through no less than ten stores. They spent more than fifteen hundred dollars and were exhausted when they stopped for a late lunch at four-thirty in the afternoon.

When they got home, it was eight in the evening, and by the time they finished packing and got into bed, it was eleven-thirty. Sharon set the alarm for six and said, "I'm only going to give you a down payment tonight on the special *whatever* I owe you. But you just wait until tomorrow night," Sharon said in a sexy voice, as she began to squeeze Bill's testicles and trace her tongue down his stomach.

CHAPTER 32

When Inoue arrived at the office he found out his secretary was out due to an automobile accident. She was in the hospital, and her replacement said she would be out for at least a couple of weeks.

The replacement was completely unaware of anything, and not the sharpest knife in the drawer. After an hour of trying to explain to her how he wanted the office run, he gave up and called the Human Resources Director and informed him they would be trading secretaries until his returned to work.

"*Hai,* Senmu," was the response.

At eleven-fifteen, Inoue received a call from the President of Sawamura Realty. "*Ohayo gozaimasu* President Harada, to what do I owe this honor of a direct call?" Inoue Senmu said, knowing all along why President Harada was calling.

"Don't give me that bullshit *Omae*! You know exactly why I'm calling," Harada responded hostilely.

Inoue Senmu was stunned. He had not been addressed by the degrading term *Omae*, which was normally reserved for subordinates when grave errors were made, since he became a Kacho of Sawamura Trading twenty years ago. Without thinking, Inoue Senmu hissed, "How dare you address me *Omae*! If you ever do that again, I will take it personally, you ungrateful Old Fuck!" and then he hung up, immediately regretting his action.

The HR secretary put her head in and said, "Senmu, I'm sorry for disturbing you, but Maruyama San is asking for fifteen minutes, as soon as you can spare it."

Maruyama, the CFO of Sawamura Trading, was completely loyal to Inoue Senmu, largely due to his service as Inoue's Battalion Sergeant Major during the war, and the fact that Inoue had brought him into Sawamura Trading and fostered his career. Inoue felt as though he was in need of a friend and sympathetic ear, so he told the secretary to send Maruyama in.

"Maruyama kun, *dozo, dozo,*" Inoue said, when Maruyama San stuck his head in the door. "So how is my best Sergeant Major doing?"

Bowing deeply before taking the seat that Inoue had offered, he said, "Not so good, Senmu, I'm afraid I have some bad news for you."

"Well, today's the day for it. What is your bad news?" Inoue said with a tight smile. "You tell me yours first, and then I'll tell you mine."

"Senmu, I received a call this morning from the CFO at Sawamura Realty. He says that the Aunt Sally Mae Japan store in Nihonbashi has already closed. He pointed out that they had warned you that this was not an appropriate site. Bottom line is they have found someone else to take over the lease. They need your *hanko* and…" he paused, looking down before continuing, knowing his former Battalion commander's temper.

Inoue Senmu knew something worse was coming, and said, "Go on, Maruyama kun."

"Sawamura Realty has sent us an inter-company transfer debit to cover their total loss on sub-leasing the Nihonbashi store site. They've deducted this from what they owe for last month's transactions."

"They can't do that without my permission!" Inoue interrupted. "How much was the charge?" he bellowed.

"Three hundred million yen. They said that represents the—"

"Three hundred million yen you said! How the fuck did they come up with that number?" Inoue hissed.

"Senmu please, I'm just the messenger," Maruyama said with his eyes cast down.

"Okay, you're right—continue," Inoue said in a normal tone of voice, although his face was still red. *He is right, of course. I had better make damn sure not to alienate any of my loyal friends. I know I'm going to need every last one before this mess is over!*

"They say that's what they had to pay the landowner to get him to accept the new tenant. The rent the new tenant was willing to pay over the thirty-year term of the lease, was forty percent less than what Aunt Sally Mae Japan had agreed to."

"Thirty years? Aren't our leases for twenty years?" Inoue Senmu shouted.

"Normally, yes, but when you insisted you had to have this site we had to agree to a thirty-year term; you approved this."

As Inoue Senmu was mulling the situation over, the HR secretary came in and said, "Excuse me, Senmu, but President Akiba called and asked me to have you come down to his office as soon as convenient."

★ ★ ★

Maruyama immediately got up, bowed deeply, and excused himself. The interruption by President Akiba was welcomed by the Sergeant Major.

What the fuck does that old fart want? I bet President Harada went crying to him after I hung up on him this morning. Of course, I shouldn't have done it, but he had no right to address me as Omae. *He may be three years older but he never commanded a battalion in His Majesty's Imperial Army!*

President Akiba was reluctant to get involved in disputes between his Managing Director and Senior Directors of Sawamura family companies. But since the President of Sawamura Realty had called him directly, he felt he had an obligation to confront Inoue Senmu.

When Inoue Senmu arrived at President Akiba's office, his secretary told him, "Shacho is on a phone call, would you like some green tea while you wait?"

Fifteen minutes later, President Akiba buzzed the secretary on the intercom. "*Hai*, Shacho, I understand. Senmu, President Akiba will see you in five minutes," the secretary told Inoue Senmu.

Okay, I get the message. I've been rude to a peer so the asshole is going to be rude to me. Just what I need on this delightful day. Inoue looked at his watch.

The intercom buzzed once again. "*Hai* Shacho, *wakaremashita.* You may go in now, Senmu," the secretary said politely. She bowed as Inoue Senmu passed her desk.

President Akiba waved Inoue over to a chair and continued writing. After what seemed like an hour, but was only about ten minutes, he put down his pen and said, "Inoue kun, this Aunt Sally Mae Japan project is becoming a real disaster. I've been getting calls from almost every director, complaining about one or another aspect of this joint venture you got us into."

Removing his glasses and rubbing the bridge of his nose, he added, "Now you go so far as to insult a peer and then hang up on him? Are you losing your mind?" President Akiba's face was red. "Well, what do you have to say for yourself?"

Inoue was fighting to gain control over his emotions. This was the same son-of-a-bitch that had heaped praises on him and *his* joint venture after the NHK coverage of the Sapporo, Nagoya, and Fukuoka store openings. Finally, deciding it was better to live to fight another day, Inoue said, "Shacho *gomennasai.* There is no excuse for my behavior this morning with President Harada. I will send him an apology note and some of his favorite cognac."

President Akiba nodded his approval and his color began to return to normal. Continuing, Inoue said, "I know things look very bad after TFC Japan launched their counter promotion. But surely they did so because they couldn't afford the Mama Aunt Sally Mae recipe story becoming popular. That is exactly what was happening in our satellite stores."

He continued to nod, but his level of interest was diminishing. After all, what was required of his role had been accomplished. Inoue had admitted fault and agreed to apologize. The rest were details that Inoue would handle. That was the role of the Managing Director, anyhow.

"Okay Inoue kun, but I hope you're right that this is only a short-term problem, for your sake. Time will tell. But this is your project, so you better make sure you're right. Now, I've another meeting at the American Club so I must be leaving."

★ ★ ★

It was seven in the evening when Inoue finished processing the contents of his in-box. It had included a note from Saji San's beef importation company which he used as a front for the "contracts" he executed. The note said, "Special order has been placed and executed—no charge." *Well, at least that problem is solved. No one will ever find that fucking worthless American—that stupid son of a whore. TFC Japan's Senmu will never reveal anything.*

Even though he knew things were hopeless, he was putting the final touches on the revisions he wanted Yamamoto Senden to make on the campaign that Aunt Sally Mae Japan would launch in response to the TFC Japan's two-for-one promotion. Yamamoto Senden had done a great job of coming up with a dynamite publicity campaign. It included the radio spot of the Major's radio interview where he admitted he had learned the secret recipe from the Mama Aunt Sally Mae.

This is outstanding! I can't wait to see how TFC Japan and their asshole President Joji Sakurai react to this. Hell, Yamamoto Senden said today that they're confident they'll get thirty minutes of free TV coverage within twenty-four hours of the campaign breaking.

Inoue Senmu was feeling the stress from his various problems. He decided to pack up his briefcase and head out to his favorite sushi restaurant at the Okura hotel. As he was putting his overcoat on, Maruyama appeared at his office door. Inoue noticed someone he didn't recognize behind his old Sergeant Major.

Looking perplexed Inoue said, "Maruyama kun, what's up? I was just on my way out to dinner."

Maruyama hesitated and then said, "Senmu, we have a very serious problem." The look on Maruyama's face left no doubt about it.

Inoue felt a strange calm he had not felt since readying his battalion for an attack. Without expression, he said, "Tell me about this problem."

"Inoue Senmu, let me begin by introducing you to Hoshizaka San. He is the Managing Partner at our law firm."

Consistent with Japanese business etiquette, Inoue expected the traditional, formal exchange of business cards and related small talk on a first meeting between executives. Instead, he was surprised when Hoshizaka San just bowed and said, "*Hajimemashite yoroshiku onegaii shimasu.*" Inoue responded in kind, although he didn't bow quite as low, given his status as a customer and his older age.

Hoshizaka then took a deep breath and said, "Senmu, I've received a call from our partner firm in Atlanta. They have informed me that, apparently, Aunt Sally Mae's Southern Fried Chicken is going to file charges against you and Sawamura Trading for fraud and industrial espionage.

"Further, the same source has told us that the U.S. Attorney for Mobile has formally asked the State Department for an order of extradition for, hmmm, you, Senmu, although this is only a request and is rarely granted for the charges filed."

No one said anything for what seemed like an eternity. The explosive reaction that Maruyama had warned Hoshizaka of didn't materialize. Instead, Inoue said, "So when will you be able to confirm the details of the actual charges against me?"

"Senmu, as I said, this is preliminary information; I won't have specifics for another..." looking at his watch, he said, "...four to six hours."

Inoue Senmu handed him a business card and said, "Thank you for coming this evening. Call me when you know the specifics.

"Oh, and Sergeant Major Maruyama, don't let this information get out until I get the specific details from Hoshizaka San," Inoue said, as he walked out of the office.

"Sergeant Major Maruyama? Where did that come from?" Hoshizaka asked, dumbfounded.

"Inoue Senmu was a highly decorated Battalion Commander in the 323rd Brigade during the war," Maruyama said, as he headed toward the door. "I had the honor to serve under him as Sergeant Major of the Battalion."

Inoue Senmu returned from the sushi bar at the hotel Okura at 2:15 in the morning. He was surprised to find Sergeant Major Maruyama waiting for him on his doorstep.

"Inoue Senmu *okaeri nasai*, Hoshizaka San has been trying to reach you for over two hours. He has received the details of the charges against you; Senmu, it's critical!"

"Calm down, Sergeant Major, and give me the details," Inoue Senmu said with a confidence he didn't feel. "Let's go inside and have a Wild Turkey and water as Capin Lee taught us!"

Inoue Senmu poured them both a large tumbler full of Wild Turkey and added a little water. As he handed Sergeant Major Maruyama his glass, he said, "So what are these details that have you so upset?"

Maruyama's hands were trembling and he was sobbing. With tears rolling down his face, he looked at Inoue and said, "Senmu,

Hoshizaka's sources have told him that the FBI claims to have a tape recording in their possession. One of you making specific statements that indicate you had insider information obtained from a competitor."

After taking a long drink of his Wild Turkey, Inoue said, "J.J. and Lee are much smarter than I gave them credit for. Now I know why they pressed so hard for details on how I was so sure the proposed store sites were winners. You're a smart man, J.J.!" Inoue added, lifting his glass in a toast.

"Senmu, what are we going to do about this situation?" Maruyama said in distress.

"Sergeant Major, you're going to go home and get some sleep and leave me here to think this problem though. Tomorrow afternoon, please collect whatever specific information Hoshizaka San has, and bring it to me here at three, sharp."

"But Senmu—"

"That's an order, Sergeant Major!"

As Inoue Senmu stood, Maruyama sprung to his feet and saluted, saying, "*Hai, wakarimashita!*" Inoue returned the salute and said, "Dismissed, Sergeant Major. I'll see you tomorrow afternoon."

After Maruyama left, Inoue Senmu poured himself another full tumbler of Wild Turkey and, lifting it high, said, "Here's to you J.J. and Lee. You think you've won, but wait until you see the results!" He then drained the tumbler and poured himself another one. It was three in the morning.

★★★

It was nearly noon when Inoue awoke. The bottle of Wild Turkey was almost empty. He had a horrible hang over. *This is appropriate for all that I've got to do today. Now to the business at hand. Which project is most important? The revenge against Joji Sakurai, of course!*

"*Moshi, moshi* Saji kun, Inoue *desu*. First let me say I received your note concerning the "special order," and for free—that is so unlike you," Inoue said, laughing.

"Ah, my old friend, it's so good to hear you laugh again; that's the only payment I need. While you don't know the "special order" you would have been proud at how his arrogance changed; shall we say he lost control of his bowels and bladder," Saji said with a chuckle.

"Now I have some good news and some bad news; which do you want first?" Inoue said with a chuckle.

"Come on, Inoue San, we both know I always want the good news first, and you always want the bad news first," Saji said laughing.

"Well I have another contract for you, and it's a big one which I intend to pay handsomely for."

"How big?" Saji said, trying to conceal his interest.

"The bad news is that I've been indicted for industrial espionage and fraud. The U.S. justice department is asking for extradition of me to stand trial on the espionage charge."

"What did you just say?" Saji San roared. "How the fuck did this happen?

Continuing in a controlled tone, Inoue said, "I'm not exactly sure, but I suspect that I was taped on one of my visits. But don't worry, no mention was made of your involvement and the Managing Director of TFC Japan will never disclose anything."

★★★

Maruyama San arrived at Inoue Senmu's house at 2:45 p.m. He waited on the doorstep until three; then rang the doorbell.

"Ah, Maruyama kun, you're right on time. Come in, come in," Inoue Senmu said in a friendly tone he didn't feel. But he knew he was going to need the Sergeant Major to carry out his plan.

"Sit down Sergeant Major. I was just about to eat a late lunch of soba. I ordered two *omori* servings of tempura soba. The local shop is really quite good. Please join me."

Maruyama San was confused. Inoue Senmu was acting as though nothing out of the ordinary was going on. *I know Inoue Senmu is a remarkable officer, but how can he possibly get out of this disaster?*

"Sergeant Major, I need you to do a couple of things for me this afternoon," Inoue said, as he poured Maruyama San another glass of beer. He then opened his notebook and tore out a sheet with numbers on it.

"Sergeant Major, I need you to wire from our main bank account thirty million yen to this account in Switzerland. Set it up so that it goes out at midnight tonight our time. So, is your son enjoying himself at my alma mata?" Inoue added, as he smiled and topped off his glass of beer. Inoue remembered when the Sergeant Major had come to him, asking for a recommendation for his son.

After a moment's hesitation, Maruyama San said, "Yes, Senmu, my son is very happy at Todai University; we both thank you for your support. Of course I will wire the thirty million yen tonight; however, what do you recommend I charge this transfer to?"

"Charge it to Sawamura Realty," Inoue Senmu said, smiling. "The charge to them should be made day-after-tomorrow at noon. Please don't forget the exact time. Now, let me see the details of the charges being brought against me."

As Inoue and Maruyama finished their lunch, Inoue got up and said, "Sergeant Major, before you leave, I've something for you. Wait just a minute." Inoue went to his bedroom and returned with a wooden box and a wrapped item in a scarlet, silk scarf.

"Sergeant Major, I would like to give you these," Inoue said, as he handed over the small teak wood box. When Maruyama opened the box he was shocked. It included no less than a dozen medals and citations. One actually contained the Imperial *hanko*.

"Senmu, I can't possibly accept these! They are the medals and citations from the great struggle to liberate Asia. I still remember in the Philippines, when Lt. General Kobayashi presented you with this medal of valor," Maruyama said, as he held up a chrysanthemum-shaped gold medal with the Imperial Seal. Tears began to fall as the Sergeant Major realized what this gift meant.

"Now stop that, Sergeant Major; hell, I wouldn't have won half of them if it wasn't for real heroes like you."

Inoue then removed the silk scarf from around the Samurai sword of his great grandfather. Raising it above his head, he slowly brought it down to his waist, and carefully removed the gleaming blade from its scabbard. Holding the sword horizontally, between his two extended hands, Inoue Senmu bowed deeply and proffered the sword to Maruyama San. Now there were tears in his eyes as well.

Chapter 33

Ralph had made a point of arriving at Ozawa's office before Ozawa arrived. He was sure that his most recent discovery of excess charging on cooking oil would generate over a million dollars for TFC International and endear him to Gene, Dave and Willis.

"Good morning Ozawa Hon-Bucho," Ralph Ovunc said, as Ozawa entered his corner office at Mitsugawa Trading headquarters. The office was exceptionally large by Tokyo standards. Ralph rose from an over-stuffed guest chair he had been sitting in and walked towards Ozawa offering his hand and smiling.

"I hope you don't mind, but I made myself comfortable as I was waiting for you. By the way, what time do things normally get going around here?" Ralph asked as he returned to the over-stuffed chair.

"Normally around nine, as most employees have a two-hour commute."

"Each way?" Ralph asked, genuinely surprised.

Smiling Ozawa nodded and said, "Now, what can I do for you today, Ralph?"

"Well first I want to thank you for agreeing to meet with me this morning," Ralph smiled. "I have some great cost-saving news that will increase profits by one-point-four million dollars per year!"

Ralph was animated, even more than usual. His mother had always told him it was his Turkish blood that made him so excitable and successful. He could still hear her saying, "Why do you think the Ottoman Empire lasted so long? If the Brits hadn't turned the Arabs against us in 1916, we would still be a great empire! Remember, your father sacrificed himself at Gallipoli."

I had no idea just how much I would miss Ray, Ozawa thought. *That Willis is one sharp bastard! This Turkish son of a bitch is the worst possible replacement! He keeps bringing up all these opportunities for saving money. The idiot doesn't understand that all of that saved money is coming out of one or more pockets of Mitsugawa-related companies. Hell, I just received a nasty note from the Senmu of Mitsugawa Banking that said TFC Japan has opened a line of credit with an American bank and is using it to pay Mitsugawa Bank back, our most lucrative line of credit.*

"So Ozawa Hon-Bucho, what do you think of my proposal to source cooking oil from the U.S?" Ralph was all smiles as he continued. "I'm assured it's one hundred percent soybean oil. It's also thirty-five percent less than the coconut oil we've been using, and that's a delivered price, including shipping, insurance, and duties. So assuming you've no problems I—"

"Oh, excuse me, Ovunc Kaicho, I'm so sorry to interrupt you." Then in Japanese, Ozawa's secretary continued, "Hon-Bucho, President Tanabe and Managing Director Ishizaka have requested you come to Shacho's office immediately."

"I'm sorry, Ralph, but I've been summoned to an urgent meeting by President Tanabe. Please excuse me. Perhaps we can reconvene tomorrow morning at eight-thirty?" Ozawa said, as he put his suit coat on and headed for the door. He was relieved to be out of this tedious and stressful meeting with the new Chairman of TFC Japan.

"Oh, I don't think that will be necessary, Ozawa Hon-Bucho. As CFO of TFC Japan, I think this decision is within my approval authority," Ralph said with his always-smiling face. "Besides, we only have until tomorrow U.S. time to tie into TFC Domestic's bulk selling price."

As Ozawa was beginning to protest, his secretary again interrupted. "Hon-Bucho, that was President Tanabe himself and he requests your immediate presence in his office."

Ozawa was surprised at President Tanabe's insistence. This was very unusual, as they had served together in the Great War to liberate Asia from her European and American exploiters.

When Ozawa arrived at President Tanabe's office, he saw not only his boss and Managing Director Ishizaka, but also Fukuda Sensei, the partner of the outside law firm Mitsugawa Trading used. Ozawa could not even guess what was going on, but he began to feel something major was amiss.

Ozawa stood at the door waiting to be invited in by President Tanabe. To his surprise, he was ignored as the three continued talking amongst themselves, in voices so low Ozawa could not hear what was being said. His concern increased significantly as he stood in the doorway, ignored.

Ten minutes later, which seemed like an eternity to Ozawa, a familiar face appeared next to him. It was Toyoda Motor Company's Managing Director, Harada.

"Ah, Harada Senmu, *konnichiwa, ogenki desuka?*" Ozawa said, bowing deeply to the more senior executive who was also an important customer.

Harada Senmu just grunted and gave a terse bow as he walked into President Tanabe's office.

"Harada Senmu, *Osewasama de gozaimasu,*" President Tanabe said, bowing deeply to his key customer. "Ozawa kun, wait outside until you're summoned," President Tanabe added, as he waved his hand as if to shoo a fly away.

As Ozawa sat in the President's reception area, his hands began to tremble. *What is going on? I can't believe I'm being treated this way. Harada Senmu and I played golf just a few weeks ago, and now he's treating me like a mere Section Chief.*

Ozawa had always been self-confident. His father had told him that all meaningful success was always preceded by passionate conviction. He not only believed this but had also practiced it. After all, he was solely responsible for the TFC Japan joint venture.

Forty minutes had gone by when Ozawa saw an older man with a corporate pin that identified him as part of the Foreign Ministry. The elderly man walked right by Ozawa without even glancing at him. He knocked on the door to President Tanabe's office and was admitted almost immediately.

Ozawa was pacing, wringing his hands, worrying about the conclusions the four men in the next room were reaching concerning his future. Tanabe's secretary brought him back to reality.

"Ozawa Hon-Bucho, Chairman Ralph Ovunc is on the phone, asking for a word with you."

Ozawa was taken aback at first at the title of Chairman Ovunc. Then he started to laugh, chuckles at first, followed by increasingly louder laughter. *That's right, Ralph Ovunc really is the Chairman of TFC Japan. Ray never even pretended to be a Chairman, but Joji Sakurai still doesn't pretend to be a President. The Greeks were right; life is full of tragedies. And remember, you fool, a tragedy by definition means that the victim contributed to his own demise. I never really knew what philosophy teacher Omori meant by that expression until now.* Ozawa Hon-Bucho continued to laugh.

President Tanabe's door opened and Ishizaka Senmu, Ozawa's immediate superior, waved for Ozawa San to come in. He waved in an obviously condescending manner, one the Japanese used for dogs, holding one's arm straight out and moving the hand up and down. The rude act didn't have the desired effect though. Instead of humiliating Ozawa, it angered him, and he turned around and told the secretary he would speak to Ralph.

Ten minutes later, the secretary interrupted, "Ozawa Hon-Bucho, please excuse me, but President Tanabe has requested your presence as soon as convenient."

That's more like it! Ozawa thought, as he straightened his tie, squared his shoulders, and prepared to face his bosses. *With Harada Senmu's presence, the Managing Director of Toyoda, and the representative from the Foreign Ministry, the meeting could only be about the stock tips I gave Ray on Toyoda's acquisition targets. What a fucking stupid thing to do! Hell, I already had that scoundrel eating out of my hands. And now we have this dedicated, loyal, financially competent Ralph Ovunc as a replacement. Well, that's not going to be my problem.* Ozawa's face relaxed at that thought.

"Ozawa kun, you have caused our company a great dishonor. You have disgraced yourself and this company. Most importantly, you have defrauded one of our most valuable and important partners." President Tanabe paused and bowed to Harada Senmu of Toyoda, Ishizaka Senmu. Ozawa followed suit, only bowed much deeper.

Returning his stern gaze to Ozawa, President Tanabe continued, "You have violated many laws in this country and in the United States." Raising his voice and looking menacing, he added, "What do you have to say for yourself?"

After staring at the floor while listening to President Tanabe, Ozawa looked up and said in a trembling voice, "There is no excuse for what I have done. You are correct in everything you have said, President Tanabe."

Turning his attention to Harada Senmu, Ozawa continued, "Harada Senmu, I am particularly sorry for betraying your trust. Since serving together in Malaysia, I have respected you and valued your friendship.

"President Tanabe, you have fostered my career since I joined Mitsugawa Trading, which you facilitated. I have no words to express my thanks to you and my sorrow for having disappointed you so much. Punish me as you see fit, for I deserve anything you decide." Ozawa had tears in his eyes.

After clearing his throat, President Tanabe said, "Ozawa kun, leave us for a few minutes."

President Tanabe had been visibly moved by Ozawa's contriteness. He couldn't help but recall how then 1st Lt. Ozawa had risked his life to save four of his platoon and then-Brigadier General Tanabe when a hand grenade was tossed into their midst. Without hesitation, 1st Lt. Ozawa picked up the grenade, and running from the group, tossed it away a second before it exploded. Ozawa had received serious shrapnel wounds for his efforts, but he had returned to duty within three weeks, still with bandages around his torso.

The Foreign Ministry representative was the first to speak. "President Tanabe, Deputy Minister Nakagawa has authorized me to take any action you determine is appropriate. However, you should know that the U.S. Attorney General's office has decided not to proceed against Ozawa kun and has dropped his request for extradition."

"Ah, Nakagawa kun, the best Division Executive Officer I ever had. Please give him my regards, and of course my thanks," President Tanabe said, as he looked over at Harada Senmu of Toyoda.

"Harada Senmu, what would you suggest? After all, it was your company that was directly affected by Ozawa kun's misbehavior."

"President Tanabe, before coming here today I discussed this situation with President Sasaki," Harada Senmu said. "He sends his regards. He has also asked me to tell you that we at Toyoda will abide by your decision."

"Harada Senmu, tell me what President Sasaki really said—exactly," President Tanabe asked, smiling, relieved that the decision regarding Ozawa's fate was left to him.

Having trouble keeping a straight face, Harada Senmu said, "Specifically, President Sasaki said 'Tell General Tanabe that I once owed him two favors and now he owes me one!'"

They all laughed. Ozawa heard the laughter from the reception area, but he didn't know how he should interpret it.

"Gentlemen, can I have your recommendations?" President Tanabe said looking at Harada Senmu.

"President Tanabe, Toyoda will defer to you. However, if you want my opinion, I think you might consider offering Ozawa the opportunity to retire."

"President Tanabe, respectfully, I would agree with Harada Senmu. I think Ozawa's retirement would be of value to the Foreign Ministry in its future dealings with the United States Foreign Service."

"President Tanabe, I respectfully disagree—" Ishizaka Senmu started to say, when President Tanabe interrupted by raising his hand.

"Ishizaka kun, I know how you feel. However, this decision involves not only Ozawa kun but also the reputation of our company, and that of the Toyoda company. Now, I want to thank you all for your time and good advice," Tanabe said as he stood up.

"Be sure to give my best to Deputy Minister Nakagawa and thank him for his deference to me. And Harada Senmu, please give my thanks and regards to President Sasaki."

President Tanabe's standing up was the informal sign that the meeting was over. After exchanging bows, the Foreign Ministry official and Toyoda's Managing Director Harada left.

CHAPTER 34

Bill slept most of the way to Puerto Rico—snoring so loudly, however, that Sharon had to nudge him several times as other first-class passengers were visibly disturbed. In fact, the flight attendant came by once to suggest that Sharon wake Bill up.

Bill had spent most of the previous night rehearsing when and how he was going to propose to Sharon. Of course, he also worried whether the yacht would be ready, and if it would be everything that Bing had promised. He agonized over Customs checking his baggage and finding the engagement ring. And most of all he worried if Sharon would say yes. These thoughts had prevented Bill from getting a good night's sleep. About forty-five minutes before landing, Sharon woke Bill up. To his amazement, there was a round of applause from the other six first-class passengers. Bill was simply bewildered and Sharon just blushed.

When they exited customs in Puerto Rico, they found a stretch limo waiting with a "Welcome Bill and Sharon" sign. *So this is the extra surprise Bing talked about. Nice touch,* Bill thought.

The interior of the limo was incredible. In addition to a plush sofa across the back, it had two captain chairs and a full wet bar, complete with a waitress.

"*Bienvenidos a* Puerto Rico!" the waitress said with an engaging smile. "My name is Elena, and I'm at your service today. May I suggest a pina colada made from our locally produced, special aged rum?"

"Sure," Bill said. "Incidentally, Elena, do you know how far it is to the Hyatt?"

"It is about thirty minutes from here. Do you want to go by before we go to lunch? It is now one forty-five p.m., but I don't think you can check in before three."

"Lunch? What lunch, and where?" Bill asked.

"Oh, that is a surprise!" Elena said with a twinkle in her eye. "And so is the rest of the afternoon and evening."

Sharon looked at Bill and said, "Okay, what's up? You had better let me in on this little secret of yours."

"Sweetheart, I honestly don't know!" Bill said, as he crossed his heart. The fact was he didn't know anything about the current surprise that Elena had referred to.

Forty-five minutes later, they pulled up to a small seafood restaurant in a beautiful marina. It was called Papagayos and had just four tables. It looked as though it was closed for the afternoon, as all the tables were empty.

"Sorry, Elena, but it looks closed," Bill said, trying to hide his disappointment.

"Not for you two it isn't," Elena said with an impish smile, as her nearly-black eyes sparkled.

Elena then got out of the limo and led the way down winding stone stairs and across a small wooden bridge to the restaurant. It was perched over the ocean, and there were half a dozen or so sailing yachts moored in the cove below the restaurant.

"Just wait here for a minute. I'll be right back," Elena said, as she headed towards the door of Papagayos.

Sharon was astounded at the view. The restaurant was about fifteen feet above the water, looking out over a protected cove with the Gulf of Mexico just beyond. The shoreline was full of tropical plants and enormous palm trees heavy with coconuts. Beautifully-colored birds were in an atrium that was almost invisible.

She looked lovingly at Bill and taking his hand, said, "I love you." She then kissed him and led him to the railing, which circled the deck around the restaurant.

"Okay, come on in, your table is ready," Elena said, smiling, while waving them forward. One table had been moved and put in front of a picture window, which directly faced the cove and the moored sailing yachts.

The owner served them himself and gave them samples of all the specialties. The rock lobster was Bill's favorite and the conch fritters were Sharon's.

When the desert came, Sharon excused herself to go to the powder room. As Bill was staring out at the sailing yachts, he noticed the name "Weak Moment" on the back of a beautiful twelve-meter yacht; it was navy blue with gold trim. *Jesus, so that's it. It is absolutely perfect! Even better than the pictures Bing provided. Sharon is going to flip out tomorrow morning.* Just then, a small motorboat pulled alongside Weak Moment and a middle-aged woman began to take provisions on board.

"What a gorgeous yacht that is," Sharon said when she returned. "Someday I hope we'll be able to have something like that Weak Moment," she added with a wistful expression.

"Yes, I'm sure someday we will," Bill answered, smiling. *And as you are going to discover tomorrow morning, that someday is now. At least for the next week.*

When they arrived at the Hyatt, they found that Elena had already checked them in. They had a suite on the twenty-third floor with a spectacular view. Their luggage was already in their suite.

As Sharon was unpacking her one formal dress, Elena asked Bill to join her on the balcony.

"Mr. Sanford—"

"Come on Elena, call me Bill," he interrupted. "We're practically friends now, after this afternoon's surprise."

"Okay, Bill," Elena said with a sly look. "If you think this afternoon was a surprise, wait until tonight." She then handed Bill an envelope. Opening it, Bill read:

Hi Bill,

If you want, I've arranged for you and Sharon to have dinner at one of the most exclusive and finest restaurants on the island, the Aguaviva. Now, here is where it gets interesting. If you give Elena the engagement ring you have for Sharon, she will take it to the Aguaviva, and it will turn up in a covered dessert dish—complete with violins playing Spanish love songs. Absolutely your call, old buddy, but I saw this done once at the same restaurant and it was fabulous! Either way, all the best.

Bing

Bill reread the note several times and then said, "Elena, I definitely want to do this! I've been wondering for days how I was going to propose, and this sounds like something out of a 1920s movie."

"A very wise choice, Mr., I mean, Bill. This will be a night you shall never forget!"

Bill went to his briefcase and removed the package from Tiffany's. He handed it to Elena and said, "Now don't lose this."

"I never have," Elena said, smiling, as she headed for the door. "Oh, I'll be back to get you at eight-thirty. Remember, Aguaviva is formal, so dress accordingly.

Bill was so excited he could hardly get dressed. He went to the mini bar and served himself a Johnnie Walker Black with 7-Up, before he went to put his tuxedo on. As Sharon was putting on her make-up, the phone rang.

"Hello," Bill said.

"Hello, Bill, this is your old boss, Ralph Ovunc. Bill, I just wanted you to know before it became public knowledge that Ozawa Hon-Bucho has suddenly resigned. The scuttlebutt is he was implicated in Ray Easton's insider trading scandal."

"Really? This is big. How is Kenji handling it? I mean, that's the most critical immediate issue," Bill said as he frowned.

"Well, that's one of the reasons I called you. I was hoping you would be willing to call Kenji and reassure him I'm a hundred percent behind him. He trusts you, and I've pushed him hard on the excess profits that the Mitsugawa family of companies is taking. Can I count on the Regional VP Europe?"

Bill thought for a minute and then said, "Of course you can Ralph. I'll call him in the next few days and let you know my read on the situation."

"I knew I could count on you, *Hermano*," Ralph said. "Oh, and I understand congratulations are, well, almost in order," he added, chuckling.

Sharon came out of the bathroom and said, "We're going to be late. You're not even dressed yet. Who've you been talking to?

Should I be worried?" She turned around to show off her bright red, full-length Yves St. Laurent evening dress.

Bill was stunned at her beauty. He could never remember seeing her so beautiful and radiant. "You've got to be the most beautiful woman on this island and I'm the luckiest guy in the world!" It took all his self-control not to fall on his knees, in his underwear, and ask her to marry him on the spot. Thankfully, he had already given the ring to Elena!

The Aguaviva was like stepping back into *Casablanca*. All of the wait staff was dressed formally in bright white dinner jackets. The interior was classic white stucco with exposed oak beams, obviously imported. Their waiter, Antonio, was tall, with long, well-kempt black hair and an engaging smile. Bill wondered if Antonio was aware of Sharon's dessert surprise. Something in Antonio's expression indicated he was.

"Mademoiselle, may I take the liberty of complimenting you this evening; you are just stunning." Sharon blushed, which was accentuated by her bright red dress. Continuing, Antonio said, "I understand Monsieur has already pre-ordered everything." He then placed two kir royales and two covered dishes in front of them. Removing the covers, he revealed two Caesar salads.

Sharon laughed at the presentation. "Why would Caesar salads be served in covered dishes?"

"Oh, I guess it's just part of their show," Bill said, shrugging.

When they were finished with their Caesar salads, Antonio returned with covered dishes that included an assortment of hot appetizers, all based on local seafood. There were the conch fritters that Sharon had liked so much at lunch, rock lobster stuffed with crab, fried grouper, and garlic shrimp. There were four separate sauces, one for each item of seafood—except the garlic shrimp. The wine was a 1973 Semi Chardonnay Reserve. Every item was delicious and cooked to perfection.

"So, what do you think? Was it worth the tux you had to wear?" Sharon said, smiling, as she took a sip of her wine. "Wow, this really is an exceptional wine, don't you think?"

"The food is almost as good as you are gorgeous tonight!" Bill said, as he reached over and held Sharon's hand.

Sharon just blushed and said, "You know all the right things to say to a girl."

243 — JOHN DUR

The filet mignons were so tender they could be cut with a fork. This was Sharon's favorite dish. *How did these guys know what all her favorites were?* Bill thought.

Both Bill and Sharon were amazed at the wine. Bill raised his hand to get Antonio's attention.

"Antonio, what is this wine? We both agree we haven't ever had better."

"It's a 1970 Beaulieu Vineyards, George de la Tour, Private Reserve. Senor Delgado, the owner, was so impressed with this wine that he flew to Napa Valley to negotiate an order for 200 cases."

Bill could hardly contain himself as Antonio removed the last dishes and said, "Was everything to your satisfaction so far?"

"Absolutely! The filet mignon was the best I've ever had," Sharon said with a smile, her dimples highlighting her face. She leaned towards Antonio and added "And since it's my favorite dish, I've had some of the best available, at least in the U.S."

"Well, I hope you have saved room for dessert, because we have something extraordinary for you," Antonio said with a smile, as he backed away with a bow.

"What do you think it could be?" Sharon said with a wrinkled brow.

"Beats me, but if it's consistent with what we've had so far, I can't wait!" Bill said.

"Me, too," Sharon said, as she reached out and held his hand. "Bill, I love you so much, you can't imagine."

Just then, Antonio returned with the dessert, on covered dishes of course. Behind him was a group of four musicians, two with violins, one with a bass, and one with a guitar. They were playing "Guantanamera."

After placing the desserts in front of them, Antonio nodded at Bill. Bill nodded back and Antonio removed the cover on Sharon's dish. There, in a champagne glass, was the engagement ring.

As Sharon gasped, raising her hands to her flushed cheeks, Bill left his chair and knelt next to Sharon. Taking her hand in his, he said, "Sharon, I love you more than life itself. Will you marry me?"

With tears of joy rolling down her cheeks, Sharon took Bill's head in her hands and looked in his eyes and said, "Bill, my one true love. This is the happiest moment in my life. I will marry you, and I will love you with all my heart for the rest of my life."

The musicians began playing Elvis Presley's "Love Me Tender." The guests at the surrounding tables were smiling and discreetly clapping. Bill got off his knees and Sharon rose. They embraced and kissed each other gently.

Chapter 35

It was 4:00 p.m. and Joji Sakurai was anxious to leave for his rendezvous with his favorite nightclub hostess, Noriko. Wednesday was his night with her, and since she had cancelled last Wednesday night, claiming her mother was in the hospital, he wanted to make sure he got his money's worth tonight. After all, TFC Japan was paying three hundred thousand yen each month for her apartment, and that entitled him to her company one night a week.

"Shacho, excuse me," Kenji said, as he entered his boss's office. Joji Sakurai looked up from his Playbachelor magazine.

"Ah, Kenji kun, what can I do for you?" he said, as he closed the Playbachelor and put it in the top drawer of his desk. "I hope this won't take long, though. I have an important meeting at Mitsugawa Trading's head office in less than an hour. I might even learn who my new boss will be," he lied—one of his best-developed skills, which he had honed over a lifetime.

Just how stupid does this old degenerate fart think I am? Kenji thought. *It's Wednesday, so it's his night with that over-the-hill hostess we still pay for. Besides, since he missed last Wednesday night, which the entire office knew about by the end of the day because of his ranting and raving, he must be hornier than usual.*

"Shacho, I'll be brief, then," Kenji said, as he sat down and rubbed his chin. "I'm having problems dealing with Ralph Ovunc. He digs into everything and has discovered many of our special arrangements with Mitsugawa-related companies. I need you to take an active role in managing him."

The telephone rang. "*Moshi, moshi.* Good, what time will you be there?" Obviously it was Noriko. "Okay, I'll be there in one hour, don't be late."

"Kenji kun, I have to leave now. We'll talk about the Ralph Ovunc problem tomorrow. Too bad Fumiko is gone; she was certainly talented at oral sex, perhaps just what Ralph needs to distract him," he said, laughing as he got up and put on his coat and walked out.

How did someone like that ever become the president of the company? Kenji wondered, as he walked back to his own office shaking his head.

★★★

It was 11:45 p.m. when Joji Sakurai and Noriko arrived at the small apartment in Aoyama. He was feeling no pain and was anxious to get her into bed. It was all he could think about during dinner. As Noriko was struggling to get the key in the lock, she heard a noise behind her. Thinking it was her horny lover, she ignored it. The next moment, she was on the floor, unconscious from the karate blow she had received at the base of her neck.

Joji Sakurai looked at the masked man who wore the head wrap of a Ninja. The rest of his dress was the normal dark-colored suit businessmen in Japan wore. The Ninja wrap was all black and covered his entire face, except for his eyes. Due to the alcohol, his brain had difficulty shifting from the sex he had been concentrating on since leaving his office to this disguised threat who had caused Noriko to pass out. He cocked his head and his eyes were wide open when it dawned on him he was in trouble.

As he began to open his mouth, the masked man punched him just below his breastbone with an open-handed karate punch. He felt all the air escape from his lungs, and the thug put a handkerchief, soaked in some chemical that smelled rather nice, over his nose and mouth.

The masked man lowered his body to the walkway, put on rubber gloves, and opened the door to the apartment. After dragging Noriko's body in, handcuffing her and taping her mouth, he removed his Ninja wrap and put Joji Sakurai over his shoulder and began to sing a popular drunken man's song as he walked towards the non-descript white van that was parked outside the apartment building.

The van was really quite nice inside. In fact, it looked more like a limo than a utility van, except that it had no windows. There was a fully stocked bar and small refrigerator. The floors, ceiling, and walls were all carpeted with plush pile, which made the back of the van extremely quiet.

In addition to the thug, the driver, and Saji, there was a homely middle-aged woman with a movie camera. After about twenty minutes, Saji nodded at the thug, indicating that he should wake up the evening's victim. Yoji broke a vile of smelling salts and put it under Joji's nose. He immediately began to shake his head violently. "Ah, I'm glad to see that Yoji kun here didn't hurt you too badly," he said in a friendly, soft voice with a smile so wide it showed all fifteen of his gold fillings. "Can we get you something to drink?" he continued in the same friendly tone.

Grabbing his head between his hands, Joji tried to get his bearings. He remembered the masked man's voice, but had never encountered the other one. As his mind began to clear, the recent events came back to him. Noriko falling after being struck at the base of the neck, and then the man in a Ninja's head wrap hitting him and then nothing, until now. He became furious.

"Do you have any idea who I am?" he bellowed in an arrogant tone. "I am Joji Sakurai, the President of TFC Japan." He straightened his jacket and tightened his tie. "Well?" he added, as though he was talking to a junior manager.

"Yoji kun," Saji said with a smile, as he turned toward the thug, "Did you realize you were in such noble company? President Sakurai, you must come from a long line of Samurai?"

Narrowing his eyes and puffing out his still painful chest, Joji hissed, "I demand to know who you are and where we're going! You're going to pay for this outrageous behavior! I am descended from Nobuhiro Sakurai who was the feudal Lord of Yamanashi. Do I make myself clear? Now stop this vehicle right now!"

Maintaining his smile, but with a distinct change in his eyes and tone of voice, the Yakuza head said, "So, I take it you don't want something to drink? Sattchan, I'll have a Dantori Royal with ice, please." He looked at the middle-aged women who immediately opened the refrigerator.

When she returned with a large tumbler of whiskey, he took a deliberate, long drink and, with a smile, said, "My name is Tadashi Saji. I'm the leader of the Osaka Yakuza. I grew up in Osaka and am fourth generation Yakuza." He paused and asked his assistant for a cigarette. As he lit it, he looked directly at Joji and added, "Do you know my best friend, Inoue Senmu of Sawamura Trading? We played baseball together." He inhaled deeply and blew smoke directly in his victim's face.

At first, Joji Sakurai showed no recognition. Slowly, however, his face revealed he remembered. Beads of sweat began to form on his forehead. *Oh my God! Is this for real! Inoue told me after that lunch that he would not rest until he got even. Can this be that?* he thought. *What are they going to do to me?* He began to sweat. *The Yakuza trademark is to remove the right index finger.* He looked at both his hands. Joji began to whimper and said in a pleading tone, "Oh please, Shacho, don't remove my index finger." Sobbing, he added, "I'll do anything Inoue Senmu asks to make restitution."

Looking at the middle-aged woman with the movie camera, Saji said, "Satt chan, how much more film do you have? Don't use it all before we get to the good parts."

"*Wakarimashita!*" the middle-aged woman on the back bench said. "I've about ninety minutes left so I'll be sure to use them effectively."

As the victim concentrated on this exchange, the Yakuza head interrupted his train of thought. "Relax, no one is going to cut your index finger off." The victim looked relieved, as his tormentor imperceptibly nodded at his assistant. Immediately a ball peen hammer crushed Joji Sakurai's left knee-cap. As he screamed in pain, Saji raised his glass of whiskey. "Are you sure you don't want a glass of this? It is truly very good." He then drained the tumbler and motioned for another. The victim passed out.

"How many more minutes until the harbor?" Saji asked the driver.

"About ten to fifteen, Shacho."

About five minutes later, Saji passed a cigarette to Yoji, who lit it, smiling. He then removed the victim's tie and opened his shirt. Blowing on the ember of the cigarette until it burned bright red, he slowly approached Joji's bare chest. When the ember was about a millimeter away, the victim began to moan. When it touched his skin, he screamed as he woke up to indescribable pain surging through his knee and chest.

"Oh, President Sakurai, come on now," Saji said conversationally. "You're Samurai, right? Well believe me, you'll look back on this pain in another hour and beg you were still here experiencing it," he added, chuckling. He then nodded again at Yoji who immediately grabbed Joji Sakurai's right index finger and bent it back until it snapped.

The victim shrieked in pain.

"You see, I kept my word, it's still attached," he said, laughing, as Joji passed out again.

The water in the Tokyo Bay was very calm this particular evening and there wasn't a cloud in the sky. About an hour out of port, Saji motioned to his assistant to wake up the victim. Again, he put smelling salts under his nose. Slowly, he began to stir. Then Yoji put a cigarette on his hand and the victim suddenly came fully awake, as pain shot through every part of his body.

"Oh please, please stop," he sobbed. "I'll do absolutely anything. I'll give you fifty million yen—just bring me to a hospital."

"No, no, no, the fun has just started!" Saji said, chuckling.

Once again, Joji lost consciousness.

Two hours later, when the captain of the yacht stopped the engines, Saji put the victim on an IV of a stimulant that would make sure he was awake for his final suffering.

Joji began to moan as he regained consciousness. Saji injected morphine into the IV tube. Within three minutes, the pain was gone. In fact, other than a sense of disorientation, he actually felt good.

"Oh, thank you, Shacho, I feel so much better now."

"Well, I certainly didn't want you to miss the big swimming party we have planned for you," Saji said casually. "It's such a beautiful night to drown," he added with a smile, as he removed the IV.

Joji looked confused as his pain began to slowly return. The brief respite had caused the return of the pain to be even more excruciating—exactly Saji's intention.

"Are you ready?" Saji asked the middle-aged woman with the movie camera. She nodded as she lifted the camera.

Yoji came up from below deck, struggling with an enormous anchor. "Yoji kun, we won't need that tonight, just bring that scuba-diving weight belt, and remove all but one weight," he said smiling.

The morphine had worn off and Joji began to plead, "Shacho please, please give me more of that pain reliever."

"Sachiko chan says we have five minutes left on Inoue Senmu's movie—and we certainly want to use it all!"

As Joji struggled, Yoji easily picked him up and set him on the rail of the yacht. While trying to put on the weight belt, Joji Sakurai slipped and fell into the water, screaming. Despite his useless leg and broken arm, he was able to keep his head above water for three full minutes—crying out all the time from the excruciating pain radiating from his knee and right arm. The salt water aggravated the pain of his numerous cigarette burns. Finally, he took one last breath as he began to sink slowly, still struggling. This exhausted his oxygen quickly. His lungs filled with water as he gasped and made one last attempt to regain the surface.

He failed.

Lighting another cigarette and relaxing in one of the deck chairs, staring up at the star-filled night, Saji said, "Yoji kun, bring me a glass of that Dantori Royal with lots of ice."

Hell, that SOB was no Samurai! He was just a spoiled, self-important, old fool. Still, this will make a great last movie for my friend, Inoue kun, he thought, as the yacht started its three hour journey back to port. As he sipped his whisky and took another drag on his cigarette, the yacht moved quickly and smoothly through the Pacific. *Thirty million yen for a night's work, and to boot, I've made Inoue kun's last couple of hours enjoyable.*

Chapter 36

The telephone rang at 10:00 a.m., awakening Inoue Senmu from a fitful sleep. "*Moshi moshi*, Inoue *desu*."

"Senmu, Maruyama *desu*," Inoue Senmu's CFO said in a nervous voice. "I'm afraid we have big problems. President Kumamoto has asked what the thirty-million-yen transfer to Switzerland last night was for. As you instructed, I put your stamp on the approval request. President Kumamoto is suspicious about the wire transfer and the fact that you have not been in the office the past two days. In fact, he has sent his secretary over to your house to find out what's going on."

"Thank you, Sergeant Major, your loyalty is appreciated. One more favor, try to keep a lid on things until tomorrow. Sayonara, Sergeant Major," Inoue Senmu said as he hung up.

Maruyama knew his boss and mentor would take his life this day. He would sorely miss him. Putting his head in his hands, he spent the next thirty minutes reminiscing about the years he had known Inoue Senmu.

★★★

Ten minutes later, the doorbell rang. Inoue Senmu went to the door in his *yukata* robe, trying to look sick.

"Oh Senmu, please forgive this intrusion," the male secretary said, as he bowed deeply. "President Kumamoto is very concerned about you and has asked me to check on you to see if there is anything you need."

"Please give President Kumamoto my regards and thank him for his concern. I must have some kind of a virus, but I think it's getting better. Tell him I will definitely be in tomorrow—first thing."

As Inoue was closing the door, the secretary said, "Excuse me, Senmu, but President Kumamoto asked me to ask you what the thirty-million-yen wire transfer to Switzerland last night was for."

Opening the door again, and lowering his voice, Inoue Senmu said, "Can you keep a secret?"

"Of course," the secretary said, as he entered the foyer.

"Do you recall that little vineyard in Burgundy that President Kumamoto wanted so badly last year?"

Nodding, the secretary said, "Yes, of course. President Kumamoto was so disappointed when Mitsugawa offered a superior price."

"Well, apparently Mitsugawa has had a major accident on the property, and a significant lawsuit is likely," Inoue Senmu said, as he leaned closer." I was contacted by a close friend of mine who is a business broker in Burgundy. He said he was sure he could get the property for twenty to twenty-five percent below what Mitsugawa paid. Therefore, to avoid the tracing of the buyer's identity, I wired money to a shell company I set up in Switzerland years ago."

"Oh, President Kumamoto will be delighted!" the secretary said, beaming.

"Well, remember your promise to keep this secret until tomorrow, when I'll have heard from my contact and, hopefully, be able to give President Kumamoto the good news," Inoue Senmu said, smiling.

"Not a word until tomorrow," the secretary said, as he put his index finger up to his mouth. "President Kumamoto will be so pleased. Oh, Senmu, I hope you feel better tomorrow—there seems to be something going around."

★★★

Inoue Senmu was eating his breakfast of a bowl of rice with raw eggs and seaweed strips. He also had a plate of dried fish with ginger pickles and a bowl of miso soup with tofu. *I'm going to miss my breakfasts. It has always been my favorite meal of the day. Besides, early mornings are a time for reflection and introspection.*

Taking a bite of dried fish, Inoue thought, *How did things come to this? Perhaps my determination to destroy Joji Sakurai caused me to lose focus and not pay attention to the details. And to think that worthless foreign Chairman of TFC Japan didn't even realize he was being used. That Senmu of TFC Japan is quite the young man—yes he'll have an excellent career, and to think in part because of me.* Inoue laughed out loud. The irony of Kenji being promoted because Inoue had caused the death of TFC Japan's President and Chairman just seemed ridiculous to Inoue, especially when he considered that Kenji had destroyed Aunt Sally Mae's SFC Japan and Inoue in the process.

As Inoue was finishing his second cup of green tea, the phone rang. He debated whether or not to answer it, but only for a moment.

"*Moshi, moshi,* Inoue *desu.*"

"Ah, Inoue San," Saji said in a cheerful, upbeat voice. "I just wanted to make sure you were home. I'll drop by in sixty minutes?"

"I'll be waiting for you, Saji kun," Inoue responded cheerfully.

Saji kun must have good news to sound so upbeat after what I'm sure has been a long night, Inoue thought, smiling. *So far this last day is getting off to a good start.*

***

"*Moshi moshi,* TFC Japan *desu,*" Kenji said as he answered the phone, eyebrows wrinkled; it was 9:20 p.m., long after normal business hours.

"*Moshi moshi,* Kato Senmu *onegaishimasu,*" Bill said, not recognizing Kenji's voice.

"Well, it must be our new VP Europe calling," Kenji said, chuckling. "And to what do I owe the honor of a call from a VP?" Kenji added in an exaggerated tone.

"Come on, Kenji, with profits going through the roof, can't you afford a receptionist?" Bill said, laughing. "Listen, I'm calling to catch up on things. Ralph told me about Ozawa Hon-Bucho. What a shock. Who's replacing him?"

"Yeah, amazing how quickly things can change. In the past week, not only has Ray disappeared and Ozawa been retired, but

Joji Sakurai hasn't been seen since day before yesterday," Kenji said, shifting in his chair and running his hand through his hair.

"Still no sign of Ray, huh?" Bill said. "Joji Sakurai not being seen for a couple days doesn't seem too serious. Does he have a history of such absences?"

"Not at all!" Kenji said, a little louder than he intended. "Well, other than those awarded sex trips to Bangkok for franchisees, but those were company-sponsored trips, and he was never more than a day or two late returning. Besides, he always called with some excuse."

"Hmmm, you know that's interesting," Bill said, rubbing his chin. "Kenji, I had contact from a model I met at one of Ray's parties who claimed she was being held against her will by a Saji San from Osaka, who Ray had introduced her to. She was convinced this Saji San was Yakuza."

Kenji couldn't believe what he was hearing. *Shit, is Bill going to be able to figure out my false information feed through Ray?*

"Kenji, you still there?" Bill asked.

"Yes, yes, of course. I was just thinking," Kenji said in a serious tone. "Listen, Bill, I've got an appointment that I'm late for. Can we continue this discussion later?"

"Okay, Kenji, I'll call you in the next couple of days. And listen, Ralph really is on your side. He's a great financial guy, and yes he is going to ferret out Mitsugawa's excess profit taking, but Kenji, I'd have done the same."

"We'll talk more about Ralph on your next call," Kenji said, as he hung up. *Shit! This could turn into serious trouble for me. There must be a connection between Joji Sakurai's disappearance and this Yakuza character. Damn, there must be some special relationship between the Managing Director of Sawamura Trading and this Saji San. I counted on the Yakuza taking care of Ray for his misinformation, but why Joji Sakurai?*

★★★

It was a little after 11:00 a.m. when Saji arrived. He had bags under his eyes, and it was clear he hadn't shaved for a couple of days. In his right hand he held a brown shopping bag, and in his left he carried a briefcase, something he rarely did.

"Come on in, Saji kun," Inoue said, as he opened the front door. "Boy, you smell like shit this morning! And I can tell you're not even hung over," Inoue added, laughing, while raising his eyebrows in mock surprise.

"Yes, you're right, but what a productive thirty-six hours I've had! And all because of you!" he added, breaking into laughter himself. "Now, do you think it's possible for me to use your *ofuro*," Saji said, rubbing the stubble on his chin, "before we eat and drink the goodies I brought for our last celebration?"

"Of course, in fact it's plenty hot since I had a long soak this morning."

Saji headed for the bathroom, while Inoue peeked into the shopping bag. It contained a large order of sushi from one of Inoue's favorite sushi shops in Tokyo. The assortment included plenty of Aji, Toro, and Hamachimaki; Inoue Senmu's stomach began to growl as he anticipated the delicacies. There was also a large assortment of sashimi with plenty of his favorite pickles. Finally, a bottle of Wild Turkey and Gekkan Sake. *Ah, Saji San does have good taste!*

In the bathroom, Saji got undressed and sat down on the wooden bench and began to wash himself with soap and warm water, the mandatory cleansing of oneself before entering the *ofuro*. The floor was tile, with a drain in the center. The soaking tub was five feet deep and five feet in diameter. It was round and made of hinoki, which gave off a pleasant smell. Along the sides was a circular bench, which allowed one's head to just poke out of the steaming water when seated. Saji entered slowly, as the temperature was one hundred twelve degrees Fahrenheit. He seated himself on the bench and placed a hot hand towel over his head and closed his eyes.

Thirty minutes later, Inoue Senmu came in and woke him up, handing him a large tumbler of Wild Turkey on the rocks. "Hurry up, my friend, lunch is all laid out and I can't wait much longer to eat the array of delicacies you brought."

An hour later, as Saji was eating his fourth piece of Aji, Inoue said, "So tell me all about your last thirty-six hours, and don't leave out any details."

★★★★

It was 3:30 p.m. when Inoue awoke from his nap. Saji was snoring loudly, sprawled out on the *tatami* in the living room, and the TV was on the national news station.

"Time to get up, Saji kun," Inoue Senmu said, shaking his shoulder. "It's time to see if you truly earned the thirty million yen I paid you."

Stretching, Saji opened his eyes and sat up. "What time is it?"

"It's getting close to four," Inoue Senmu said, looking at his watch, "and I'm anxious to see what I got for my millions of yen."

"Oh, I'm sure you'll want to pay me a bonus once you've seen the tape," Saji said, as he got up, rubbed his eyes and retrieved his briefcase from the kitchen-dining area. When he returned to the living room, he removed two Betamax tapes. Holding one up in his right hand, he said, "Inoue kun, this is two hours and includes almost everything. However, it has been rigged to self-destruct once it has been played through, or at midnight tonight, whichever comes first." Saji's furrowed brows and even tone underscored his seriousness. "This second one is only twenty minutes, but includes the highlights. I thought we would watch this one together, in case you had any questions."

Inoue took the two tapes and put the short version in the Betamax player. He then left and went into the kitchen and came back with two bottles. "This is a bottle of cognac from 1861, Napoleon III era. You are not to open this until the tenth anniversary of today—*wakata*?"

"*Hai, wakarimashita*," Saji said, as he bowed and held the proffered treasure above his head. Inoue Senmu returned the bow, only bowing slightly less deeply—after all, he was senior.

"We'll open and drink this second bottle now, as we watch the tape," Inoue Senmu said with a smile. "It's a 1908 cognac that the Nazis expropriated from the Martel Distillery Owner's cellar in 1940."

The tape began with Joji Sakurai acting indignant and threatening Saji with grave consequences. Inoue laughed when Joji said, "Do you know who I am? I am the President of TFC Japan." The superior look on his face reminded Inoue of that lunch thirty years ago when Joji Sakurai said, "Keiko is Samurai and you're just a Ronin! How dare you ask for her hand in marriage?" *That arrogant son-of-a-bitch! Look at him. The only thing that has changed is that he is thirty years older and thirty pounds heavier!* Inoue thought.

Seeing his friend's expression of hate and anger, Saji said, "Now watch the transformation in that worthless piece of shit!" Just as Saji spoke, the ball peen hammer stuck Joji Sakurai's knee, shattering it. As he screamed in agony, the look of disbelief on his face caused Inoue to clap enthusiastically.

As the tape continued, Inoue became increasingly happy and animated. He was particularly pleased with the scene of Joji Sakurai begging for mercy while bawling like a baby. As he poured Saji another glass of the 1908 Martel cognac, Inoue said, "This was worth every yen! You have no idea how long I've been waiting for this revenge. And you've finally given it to me." Raising his glass, Inoue bowed slightly. "*Domo arigato* Saji kun."

The tape ended with a thug hauling a large anchor up from the lower deck of the yacht.

"Well you'll have to watch the long version to see the end," Saji said with a grin, as he got to his feet. "But I assure you, it's as good an end as you could hope for."

He collected his briefcase and his coat, carefully putting the short version of the Betamax tape in his suit pocket and wrapping the 1861 bottle of cognac in a towel.

They then walked to the front door together without saying a word. Inoue spoke first. "I thank you, Saji kun, for your friendship all these years. But even more importantly I'm forever in your debt for allowing me to seek my revenge before I die."

Taking Inoue by the shoulders, and looking directly into his eyes, Saji said, "It's been a hell of a ride we've had together. I will always remember you, and the many good times we've had." Then reaching into his coat pocket, Saji removed a small medicine bottle. "Just in case," he said, looking straight at Inoue, as he handed over the bottle of pills. "Bite down on these and it's over within three seconds."

When they arrived at the front door, Saji bowed deeply and said, "*Sayonara*, Inoue Senmu." This was the first time Saji had addressed his friend using his title—a sign of great respect among friends.

Inoue bowed back, and said, "*Arigato* Saji kun." He then bowed and closed the door.

★★★

Inoue sat at his writing desk and removed ten sheets of expensive rice paper he had received from his beloved Keiko twenty-nine years ago. It had been during Oseibo of 1946. The country was still in shambles and almost all resources were scarce. Inoue had been surprised when he had opened this treasure of twenty sheets of transparent rice paper. "Where did you find this?" he had asked, holding a sheet up to the light to admire it.

"It was given to me by my great-grandmother," Keiko had said in her soft little voice. "She had received it as a wedding present in 1881 and told me to save it for my husband." Keiko had then blushed and looked down, feeling embarrassed at having been so presumptuous.

As Inoue held the precious paper in his hands, tears fell from his eyes as he recalled the many joyous times with Keiko. Among his favorite memories were the times they spent every Sunday during spring on the Tamagawa River. He would row the little boat, and Keiko would sing love songs in her delightful melodious voice. Each week, she would write a new song expressing her love for Inoue—always very subtle and indirect.

Inoue had kept all forty-three of her love songs. He took a small key out of a false drawer hidden in his desk and opened a locked, lacquered box his grandfather had given him. Inside were his treasures. He removed Keiko's songs and found his favorite—which was the last he had received from her.

With his eyes misting over, again, he read the words and recalled the day she had sung this song.

As the sun rises and sets,
I see your face,
when you are not there.
The breeze on my skin becomes
your hand caressing me,
ever so gently,
when I close my eyes,
and you are not around.
The Sakura is like our love,
poetic beauty, nature at its finest,
fleeting as the seasons,
but as perennial as our thoughts.
May our memories live in our hearts,
now and forever.

Inoue then removed a piece of rice paper, a small pointed brush, and a bottle of black ink. He began to compose his will. In it, he detailed the entire history of the industrial espionage surrounding TFC Japan. Inoue went to great lengths to implicate Aunt Sally Mae's SFC U.S.'s J.J., Lee, and Ashley, providing convincing proof that they conspired to use Ashley to seduce Inoue. He emphatically stated that his colleagues at Sawamura Trading knew nothing about his espionage activities, providing details of how he laundered money to make the payments.

Pausing, Inoue looked at his watch. It was 7:00 p.m. and he was getting hungry. *What a strange time to get an appetite,* Inoue thought.

He picked up the phone and called the Chinese noodle shop on the corner. "Inoue *desu.*"

"Ah, Inoue Senmu, good evening, what can I get you this fine night?" the restaurant owner said, immediately recognizing one of his best customers.

"Well, tonight I'm going to leave that to you, Takahashi kun. You know what I like, and what's best today—just make sure it's quick and that there's lots of it."

"So Senmu, we're hungry tonight?" Takahashi said, laughing. "Good, I've got some special things I just made for the first time today that I want you to try. My son will be there in fifteen minutes."

★★★★

Inoue went over to the *tansu* that had belonged to his great, great grandfather. This fine old piece of furniture had completely smooth, rounded edges from centuries of use. He remembered when his grandfather had given it to him when he returned from the war. "My grandfather would want you to have this for your great and noble service to the Emperor," he had said, as Inoue's father looked on in disbelief. *No, my father never forgave Grandfather for skipping a generation in giving this treasure to me. Perhaps that's why we never had much of a relationship after the war,* Inoue thought.

He opened the *tansu* and carefully removed a bottle of non-branded bourbon that he had bought at auction in the U.S. twelve years ago. It was certified to have come from an oak barrel that had aged the bourbon inside since before the Civil War.

This is a perfect time to finally drink this, Inoue Senmu thought, as he held the bottle and imagined what it must have been like being in the U.S. Civil War. He had studied the history of the Civil War and admired Robert E. Lee for his leadership and the respect he commanded from his troops. However, his favorite general was Stonewall Jackson, who he thought was a decisive strategist.

After pouring himself a large tumbler of the Civil War bourbon, he returned to his writing desk and continued his will. He made a list of bequests that took three of the precious pages of rice paper. The bequests included awards of one million yen to each of his nine nephews and nieces, except the youngest, Yuko Chan, who, at the age of three, had told him she thought he was kind. No one had ever told him that before. To her, he left a dowry of ten million yen. There were seven bequests to people in the neighborhood who were merchants and had treated him with respect—all were for two million yen and included the Chinese noodle shop owner, Takahashi. Then came the special bequests. To Saji San he left fifteen million yen. To his dear mother's younger sister, who was in her eighties and lived in the country with her eldest son, he left his beautiful family house on Lake Hakone, with the proviso it could not be sold. To his loyal secretary, he left twenty million yen. And finally to his maid, who was widowed at thirty-two and left with four children to raise, he left the income from a trust worth one hundred million yen, with any residual at her death to go to the memorial fund for veterans of His Majesty's 323rd Imperial, Southeast Asia, Brigade.

As he was reviewing his will, there was a knock at the door. It was Takahashi kun's eldest son, Nobuo.

"Inoue Senmu, please forgive me for being late," the high school student said as he bowed deeply. "My father redid the *tonkastu* three times before he was satisfied."

Inoue chuckled at his concern and said, "Nobuo kun, nothing to worry about. If I know your father it will be worth the wait. Come in. I'll be back in a second."

Inoue went back to his great, great grandfather's *tansu* and removed a small pouch of old coins. The pouch included ancient Japanese coins from the sixteenth century—three of them gold.

"Nobuo kun, are you still committed to becoming a history teacher?" Inoue asked, raising his brows.

"*Hai*, of course, Inoue Senmu," the young man said, perplexed by the question, since he had discussed becoming a history teacher a number of times with Inoue. "As you know, it has been my dream since fifth grade."

"Just checking," Inoue said with a smile, as he handed over the small pouch. "Now, don't say anything to anyone until next week, but these should help you achieve your dream."

The young man opened the pouch and emptied its contents into his hand, as Inoue slowly closed the door. He stood with his mouth wide open, and stared at Inoue in disbelief.

Inoue was pleasantly surprised when he opened the delivery box from the Chinese noodle shop. Takahashi kun had not only sent *tonkatsu* but also seaweed salad, jumbo shrimp baked in salt, pork dumplings, Chinese noodles in soy sauce, and spring rolls with hot mustard. Inoue picked at his dinner. Everything was delicious, especially the jumbo shrimp baked in salt, but Inoue found his mind preoccupied with his pending suicide.

Will I have the courage to die as a Samurai? Or will I take the pills Saji kun gave me, so I can avoid the excruciating pain? After all, I have no second to cut my head off. Maybe I did allow myself to be captured by the marines to avoid this fate, Inoue thought. He began to sweat, ever so lightly, as the reality and finality of his pending *seppuku* invaded his soul and disturbed his inner peace.

Inoue poured himself a large tumbler of Civil War bourbon, and put the Betamax tape Saji had left him into the video player. It was 9:18. The video began with Saji San welcoming an indignant Joji Sakurai into the specially-equipped van. Joji Sakurai haughtily demanded an explanation for his abduction and explained his family's importance. It was a face Inoue remembered well from the lunch that ended the only love of his life.

He couldn't help but reflect on his last meeting with Joji Sakurai that fateful day in the *tonkatsu* restaurant, when Inoue had asked Joji Sakurai for his sister's hand in marriage. He could still see Joji Sakurai's face, sneering as he had laughed out loud and said, "You? You, marry into our family? You must be insane! You are nothing but a Ronin. Your ancestors were not worthy of cleaning our ancestors' swords!" The crowded restaurant had gone silent as the other customers paused to listen to Joji Sakurai's tirade, and when he finished, several people began to laugh.

Inoue had never been more angry in his life. As he remembered the incident, his anger burned within him as his thirst for revenge overtook his thoughts. *That son-of-a-bitch looks as arrogant today as he did in that restaurant. I hope Saji San was as successful as he claimed,* Inoue thought, as he got up and poured another tumbler of the Civil War bourbon.

Inoue thoroughly enjoyed the dramatic change that took place in Joji Sakurai's demeanor after his right kneecap was shattered and his right index finger was broken. The arrogance gave way to pleading for mercy. Then the endless bribes, if only Saji would take him to the hospital.

"Suffer you bastard! Now you know what it's like to feel real pain!" Inoue said out loud.

When the tape got to the events on the yacht, Inoue sat up and leaned forward to pay close attention. As Saji administered the morphine and Joji Sakurai seemed to be relaxed, Inoue was confused. That is, until Joji Sakurai said, "Oh thank you so much! My pain is subsiding. I'll give you anything you want if you'll just take me to a hospital."

Grinning broadly, Saji removed the morphine IV and said, "Sorry, but the only reason I've given you a little relief is so that when your pain returns it will be much worse than if I'd let it continue unabated. You see, this is one of the things we've learned over the centuries," Saji added in a matter-of-fact manner, as he lit a cigarette.

A few minutes later, Joji Sakurai began to moan as the morphine began to wear off. "You see what I mean?" Saji had asked. "Oh, I almost forgot to tell you. This last experience of your life is compliments of my old and dear friend Inoue Masahiro, the Senmu of the Sawamura Trading Company. He asked me to ask you if you remembered that lunch with him twenty-nine years ago."

Confusion changed to recognition on Joji Sakurai's face. "But, but…he can't do this to me! He's only a Ronin, and I'm descended from Daimyo Samurai."

Saji kun, you're a genius! Inoue thought.

The tape ended with Joji Sakurai flailing in the Pacific, screaming without pause, as his broken knee and shattered arm shot endless waves of pain with every kick. His cigarette burns, too, caused additional pain all over his torso when exposed to the salt water. A minute later, the tape began to smoke, just as Saji had promised.

Inoue went to the *tansu* and removed his great, great grandfather's Samurai robe. It was made of silk, with beautiful embroidered mountain scenes in blue. He put it on over an all-white silk kimono into which he would plunge his sword.

Inoue then went to his family's Buddhist alter in the living room. He lit the incense and placed the mandarin oranges on the white rice cakes.

He then reread Keiko's final letter:

> *Inoue-San,*
>
> *I love you more than life itself; never forget this. It is as perennial as the Sakura. My brother has forbid me from seeing you again. As I am Samurai, I must obey so as not to disgrace my ancestors. I know you understand this and will accept it, for you love me as I love you. Forever you will remain in my heart. The memories of our time together shall be my source of strength and happiness for the rest of my life. Be strong, my warrior, and become the great man I know you are. Respectfully with enduring love and devotion,*
>
> *Keiko Sakurai*

Picking up his paintbrush, he wrote this final poem of farewell:

> *I peer deep into my soul, deeper than ever before,*
>
> *The reality that was my life imparts a force upon me,*
>
> *Leaving an imprint on my mind, as simple as the carp pond, as complex as the tumultuous sea,*
>
> *As I prepare for my last sunset, I see the faces, hear the voices, and feel the final pain,*
>
> *Of the thousands of Samurai who have gone before me,*
>
> *With the strength of their own hands, with the company of their souls,*
>
> *Ah, farewell my life, but not my love,*

I take you with me, you are my eternity

Inoue Senmu put the paintbrush down and placed his farewell poem and Keiko's final farewell letter in the black-lacquer box that contained his treasures and final will. He then picked up his grandfather's short Samurai sword.

Now we'll see if I am true Samurai or just Ronin as Joji Sakurai always claimed. I will also know if I was truly captured on Saipan or just allowed myself to be to avoid committing suicide, Inoue thought.

Inoue slowly withdrew the small Samurai sword that had been his great, great grandfather's and which he had worn during the war.

Keiko, I do this to honor you and our love together.

The blood pounded in his temples. He took a deep breath and raised the short Samurai sword above the left corner of his abdomen. Staring into the Buddhist shrine, he quickly inserted the sword and dragged it across his abdomen, slicing his intestines and bowels along the way. The pain was excruciating, but Inoue Senmu's final thought was, *I am a true Samurai.* Within five minutes he bled to death.

Chapter 37

It was a beautiful spring day; the sky was bright blue with only a wisp of white clouds. The cherry blossoms were in full bloom and the breeze caused the petals to fly like large pink snowflakes. The river Seine was flowing lazily through the center of Paris, with a string of artists working along its banks. The scent of freshly-baked French bread and ripe soft cheeses were in the air.

"What a perfect day for a wedding," Sharon said, smiling, as she squeezed Bill's hand.

"Yeah, the day is almost as perfect as you are beautiful," Bill said, smiling, squeezing Sharon's hand back in return, as the white limo came to a stop at Notre Dame.

The bridal party was small, only three bridesmaids and three groomsmen. The bridesmaids were all in pink spring dresses with white shoes. The groomsmen and Bill were also in pink tuxedos with white shirts and red bowties. Sharon had on a simple but beautiful wedding dress that had belonged to her mother. It was white lace with pink trim and a pink train that Sharon had made, with Sarah's help.

Sarah was gorgeous and was obviously pleased to have been chosen as maid of honor. Bill was proud of her and grateful for how well she and Sharon had bonded over the past six months, since Sarah came to live with them in Paris.

When the priest got to the exchange of vows, in turn, Bill and Sharon said: "Sharon, I take you as my wife; I promise to love, respect, and care for you, through all that is to come, and to remain faithful to you so long as we both shall live."

The reception was held at a small nearby bistro which Dave Liberwitz, the best man, had arranged. The small wedding party had the run of the bistro. The food was fit for Louis XIV. It included escargot, pâté de foie gras, confit de canard, cassoulet, bouef bourignon, salade St. Germaine, gumbo ecrevisse, and endless cheeses, French bread, and wines, all laid out on a buffet table. Everyone ate and drank more than they should.

Sharon, Sarah, and Dave found themselves acting as interpreters for the rest of the wedding party, which included Carmen, Ralph, Kenji, Jim, and Bill's sister, Mary. Everyone was having a great time when Dave tapped his glass to get the attention of the other guests.

"Ladies and gentlemen, may I have your attention? I would like to propose a toast, while I still can, at least coherently," Dave said smiling. "In English we have only the one word for love. But in Greek there are three: Eros, erotic love; Philia, love between friends and siblings; and Agape, selfless love. The first is easy," Ralph and Jim nodded their agreement, "but it's the second and third that build a long-term relationship. My wedding wish for you today is that you remain each other's best friends and that you always put your partner's needs and desires ahead of your own."

Bill watched Sharon and Sarah joking with each other, both laughing and enjoying the moment. As he contemplated the words in Dave's toast, he thought back to when he first knew he had fallen in love with Sharon. Her words still remained in his thoughts and made his eyes water. "You're a sensitive man and a caring father; it is these two attributes that have attracted me the most. You are in Sarah, so it's natural that I love her."